Acknowledgements

Closure was my first novel and my first love. And I'm hugely proud to see it in print under the Triskele banner. I owe a debt of gratitude to everyone who has helped transform that acorn – the image of a bewildered boy and how far I could take the idea of reincarnation – into the oak tree you see today.

Again, I owe a huge thanks to my mum and dad for introducing me to North Wales and for all the opportunities. To Adrian for being there through thick and thin – and doing his best to understand me. To my loyal bunch of writerly friends whom I rely on so much: Sheila Bugler, Amanda Hodgkinson, Jill Marsh, Liza Perrat and Kat Troth. Thank you for sharing your talent and patience with me. Also I must give thanks to various members of the Writing Asylum who've stuck with this novel through its many incarnations. And a final thanks to Jane Dixon-Smith for her stunning attention to detail and all the laughs!

Gillian E. Hamer

CLOSURE

TRISKELE BOOKS

First Edition, December 2012.

Cover design: JD Smith.

Cover photography: A D Le Monnier.

Printed in the United Kingdom by Lightning Source.

Published by G.E Hamer.

All enquiries to contact@gillianhamer.co.uk.

ISBN 978-0-9571932-2-2

"I am confident that there truly is such a thing as
living again, that the living spring from the dead,
and that the souls of the dead are in existence."
—Socrates

Chapter One

It was time.

He turned off the engine and rolled the car to a halt outside the large, white house, trusting the few people around at two am on a Thursday morning would fail to notice the same red Peugeot had already been round the block three times. He turned off the headlights, plunging the leafy, suburban street into a silvery semi-darkness.

Lowering the window half way, he paused to sniff the salty air, listening for the sound of approaching vehicles or late-night clubbers staggering back home. He looked up at the huge creamy disc of moon and smiled. A worm moon at this time of year. The moon was his constant. His light. His Grace. It energised him, made him feel stronger.

Ready.

Adrenaline pumped through his bloodstream as he imagined the feel of smooth skin, the taste of hot sweat on his tongue. He took a drag on his cigarette. He had to stick to the plan, control the urge, and remain constant to his meticulous routine. He sucked harder. The car brightened with a brief orange glow, before he stubbed the butt into the ashtray. He took no risks. He knew about DNA. He knew his stuff.

Climbing out of the car, the creak of a hinge broke the silence on Hwfa Road. He paused again as a cloud crossed the moon, his scanning eyes as keen as a wolf's. But the blackness was broken only by the sodium street lamps, shadows creeping across the ground in their world of orange luminescence.

Satisfied, he slid across the pavement and disappeared into the shrubs surrounding the semi-circular drive of the house. Clad in black, he knew he blended into the shadows as he crept around the side of the house, avoiding the crunch of the gravelled driveway.

He pulled a balaclava over his head and slipped on leather gloves. Minutes later, he studied the antiquated latch on the French windows at the rear of the building. He'd already visited the house during the day so he could find his bearings easily enough. His ally, the moonlight, reappeared, affording him more than enough light to work.

The latch gave way with a sharp crack and the French window swung open. With a slow smile, he stepped into the lounge of Apartment Four, Ty Mawr.

Edwina's eyes snapped open. A noise had woken her. Somewhere close. Lifting herself onto her elbows, she tucked her hair back and strained to listen, trying to ignore the rapid thump of her heart.

Silence.

With sudden realisation, she patted the duvet, searching for her book. She relaxed as she recognised the sound. *Goddammit.* She was always dozing off until her book hit the laminate floor. Tonight she'd read almost a whole Raymond Chandler novel. Insomnia – the curse of her life.

Edwina was finding Uni life tough. Their first year at Bangor Uni.; their first in student accommodation; their first away from home. Her best friend, Amy, had adapted to the change so much more easily. They'd been friends since primary school – had the same taste in clothes, music and men – but were very different. Amy was outgoing, carefree and flexible, while Edwina struggled to make friends, to fit in, to sleep.

With a grunt, she thumped her pillow into shape and buried her face in its cool comfort. Closing her eyes, her mind began to wander and she welcomed the familiar tug of sleep, creeping through her senses like an incoming tide. She stretched and turned onto her back, kicking the duvet to one side, and lay spread-eagled across the bed.

Something grabbed her throat, covered her mouth, forcing the taste of leather between her lips.

"Don't scream," a voice hissed next to her ear. "I have a knife."

The pressure on her throat eased, and smooth steel pressed into her cheek.

"Make a sound and I'll use it. Understand?"

Edwina swallowed and nodded, biting back the scream on her lips as she began to shake.

She couldn't see him. But she could smell him: alcohol, cigarette smoke, stale sweat … and something else. Something she couldn't define. She forced her brain to work harder, remembering from her love of crime novels, that even the tiniest detail might be important.

The hand left her mouth and she gulped air, straining to make out some feature in the blackness. Her first instinct was to yell and scream her lungs out. Was Amy home yet? Liam and Craig were on the other side of the thin partitioned wall. But she had felt that cold blade on her face. She kept her mouth shut, trying to think through her fear. Trying to keep her mind alert, to find a way out of this alive.

A tearing sound scattered her thoughts; a thick, sticky tape sealed her mouth. She sensed him moving to the bottom of her bed; the room streaked with pale moonlight as he pulled open a curtain. Light fell across the bottom half of the bed, and Edwina could see the paleness of her thighs and the edge of white panties. She lifted her knees and tugged down her t-shirt as far as it would go.

His silhouette was clear against the window, medium height

and skinny all she could determine. He gazed down at her, seeming to take in every detail. She trembled and squeezed her eyes shut, covering her breasts with her hands. He bent and smoothed the hair from her brow and ran his fingers through the long black tresses strewn against her pillow. It was a tender gesture, but it filled her with pure dread.

She heard a grunt and felt the bed dip. *No. No. No. Please, no.* She squeezed her eyes tighter. Hot tears spilled down her cheeks. She concentrated on breathing evenly and braced herself for his touch. Instead, he grabbed her hands and held them together, in front of her stomach. More ripping noises and her wrists were bound with the same sticky tape. He dragged her to her feet.

"We're going for a little ride, Edwina," he whispered. She jumped at the sound of her name. She recognised for the first time the trace of a Welsh accent. "Don't make a noise. Don't try to be clever. If you do, I'll kill you … and Amy too. Understand? Just for the fun of it."

She started again at the mention of Amy's name.

An open palm slapped her cheek. "Understand?"

She nodded, grunted through the tape.

As he pushed her along the hallway, the outdoor light crept along the corridor, and she turned to glance at him over her shoulder. She gave an involuntary yelp as she stared into a hideously-distorted face. He stared back, unblinking.

Just a mask, she realised. Why a mask? Did she know him?

"I said silence," he hissed, pressing the knife hard into her ribs.

She lurched forward, grabbing hold of the patio window for support as she felt the sharp point break her skin. A warm trickle of blood oozed down to the waistband of her panties.

"Don't piss me off. I won't warn you again."

Edwina nodded. There was no mistaking the menace in his voice.

The night air clung to her clammy skin, and gravel pierced the soles of her feet as he bundled her across the driveway, out onto the road. He stopped at a red car parked against the kerb, pulled open the rear door and pushed her inside head first. The car door slammed with an echo of finality. Edwina's eyes watered as she fought waves of nausea.

Moments later, the engine revved and the car pulled away. Edwina lay awkwardly across the back seat, paralysed for several seconds, but finally forced herself to breathe normally, concentrating on each inhalation. She prayed for him to break the speed limit or jump a set of traffic lights, but he drove steadily, attracting no attention.

That strange smell hit her again, mixing with the smoky, musty atmosphere of the car. Then it came to her. Seaweed – salty dried seaweed. She could smell it at times from the house after a storm, or if she walked on Bangor Pier at low tide when the shoreline was drying out.

Every part of her body ached and her feet burned, but she needed to try and see where he was taking her. She pushed herself upright. The t-shirt had ridden up, exposing her more than ever. Vivid red stains covered her belly and underwear. Trembling violently from fear and cold, she glanced out of the window, searching for any chance of escape, any hope of assistance. Nothing. Her eyes filled with tears again, as familiarity slipped by.

Edwina met the cold, malevolent eyes of her abductor in the rear view mirror. *Dear God*, she said in silent prayer, *let me come out of this alive.*

Chapter Two

Helen West woke with a start. Eyes wide open, she lay still. Had she been mistaken or had she heard the creak of her front door? As the only adult in the house, Helen had developed a sixth sense for night-time noises. She listened for the sound of breaking glass; the quiet tread of intruders.

Several seconds passed. A deep growl from the kitchen below filtered through the bedroom floor. Holly. The tap of claws on the stone tiles loud and persistent. Something had roused Holly from sleep. Something had upset her.

Helen threw back the duvet, found her slippers and tiptoed out onto the landing. Damp, chilly, night air crept up the stairs, and the instant she felt the drop in temperature, her heartbeat quickened, and she knew her suspicions were right. She leapt down the stairs two at a time.

The front door stood wide open.

"Hello." Her fingers groped in the darkness for an umbrella she kept at the bottom of the stairs. "Hello, who's there?"

Her heart thumped as she crept forward until she reached the open door.

"Oh my God!"

Helen bolted across the front garden and out onto the road. Her six-year-old son was walking, bare foot, the length of the centre white line. Dressed only in his striped pyjamas, fists clenched at his side, his vacant eyes stared straight ahead. The umbrella clattered onto the tarmac as she gathered his stiff body into her arms and hugged him tightly.

"Jake, sweetheart! What're you doing? Dear God, you're frozen."

His eyes remained focused on some unseen object, staring off into the distance. Helen glanced over her shoulder but the road was empty; the swaying branches of the trees the only movement in the quiet street, casting dancing shadows between every streetlamp. The distant bark of a fox was the only sound that broke the silence.

Helen shuddered and settled him on her hip.

Jake lashed out with a stinging blow to the side of her head.

Her ear buzzed with pain. Momentarily blinded, her head swam as she steadied herself against a parked car, still holding him tightly, trying to contain his flailing arms.

He kicked and punched. "Let me go, let me go, let me go!"

"Shush, Jake. It's okay, Mummy's here."

"Let me go!" Tiny fists pounded against her back. "I hate you! I hate you! Let me go!"

"Jakey, sweetie, it's a nightmare. Calm down. Please! Stop fighting. You're having another nightmare."

"I can't see. Let me go!"

"Oh Jake, please. Keep still, stop kicking."

Helen struggled to hold onto his wriggling frame as he flailed and twisted. She half carried, half dragged him into the house, and kicked the front door closed. She sat on the bottom stair and cradled him, smoothing his hair and trying unsuccessfully to press his arms and legs against her.

"Come on baby, wake up. It's a bad dream. Wake up, darling. You're home. You're safe."

"Don't hurt me. Don't hurt me!"

"No one's going to hurt you, baby. I'm here. Mummy's here. It's fine."

It broke Helen's heart to see his tiny face contorted with anger, struggling against the evil of the nightmare. Whatever demons

Jake faced in his sleep, they were definitely getting worse.

Come on, Helen! Get a grip. Jake needs you now; he needs you to be strong.

"Please, wake up. Please. Come on Jakey, we need to get you back to bed, sweetheart. Wake up for Mummy, there's a good boy."

Jake muttered under his breath – a jumble of incoherent words. Every few minutes he let out a yell and his body stiffened. Each time he cried out, Helen's heart grew heavier, until it felt like a boulder in the pit of her stomach. His breathing laboured. His mouth opened and closed as if he was drowning and gasping for air.

What if he stops breathing? What if he has a fit?

Afraid to wake him, yet even more scared to let him sleep, she caressed his shoulders.

"What are you saying, sweetie? Come on, wake up. You're scaring Mummy now. Wake up, Jake! Oh, dear God, please wake up!"

Helen was on the verge of dialling 999, when Jake woke with a piercing scream. He clung to her; his sweat-soaked little body shaking as he sobbed. She stroked his hair and kissed his face, feeling wetness against her cheek as she embraced him. Her own eyes filled as she tasted his salty tears. She felt so helpless, such a bad mother to let her baby suffer like this.

"You're safe, I'm here," she whispered, rocking him, hoping she sounded more confident than she felt. "You're fine."

Fifteen minutes passed before Jake relaxed and his breathing became less ragged. Helen carried him up the stairs, relief washing over her.

"Are you okay now?" she whispered.

He nodded, drowsily.

"Do you remember what happened, baby?"

He shook his head, thumb creeping into his mouth.

"Just another nightmare. Nothing to get scared about, okay?"

He nodded and snuggled his face into her neck. “I’m sleepy, Mummy.”

“I know, Jakey. We need to get you into bed, but let’s change your pyjamas first. Look, they’re all dirty.”

Helen helped Jake into fresh nightclothes and dabbed a cold flannel on his feverish forehead. She watched as he dragged himself back into bed, rubbing his eyes with tiny fists. Without another word, he turned on his side and fell asleep, exhausted.

A single tear, the last remnant of the earlier deluge, slid from his eye, across his cheekbone, disappearing into his mop of blond hair. Gently, she wiped away its track, kissed his sweaty brow and tucked the duvet under his chin.

Helen paused at the doorway. Her son was sucking his thumb and snoring gently. His face, illuminated by the yellow glow of the night-light, looked angelic. His untidy dark blond hair, and pale lids flickering over blue eyes – were so like his father’s.

It was so unfair.

Helen sighed. *I need a drink.* In the bathroom, she glanced at the mirror as she splashed cold water onto her face. Her sharp features and grey eyes, dark with worry, made her face look gaunt. She wrapped her dressing gown around her, and pulled her long hair into a ponytail. Quietly, she made her way downstairs to the kitchen, glancing at the clock in the hallway as she passed – 2:40 am. She yawned and rubbed her eyes, imagining another day ahead bordering on exhaustion.

Thankfully, Jake never seemed to remember anything the following day, nor suffer any after effects. The nightmares had started three months earlier, but tonight they’d taken a more chilling turn. Jake had never sleepwalked before. Never left the house. Tonight he could have been abducted – or killed, so easily knocked down by a passing car.

Vivid images filled her mind. She pushed them away. She needed that drink.

Helen poured a double shot of vodka and added cold lemonade. She took a long, refreshing sip, feeling the mix of burning alcohol and icy fizz hit the back of her throat, gripping the glass tighter to steady her trembling hand. God, she hoped this hadn't been triggered by the visit to the doctor yesterday.

A jolt of guilt added more weight to the rock in her belly.

It hadn't been an easy decision to make the doctor's appointment. Even after three years of it, she still hated the sympathetic smiles and the patronising words of comfort. Yes, she knew people wanted to be kind. Perhaps it simply hid their own inability to express their feelings; a cover for their own awkwardness. But it irritated the hell out of her. Doctors should know how to deal with such problems.

"Nightmares, you say?" Dr Dennis asked, after greeting her warmly. The doctor scanned Jake's notes. "Ah, well, this kind of thing is not unusual following, erm …" He coughed, nodding in Jake's direction.

"His father's death," she said.

"Well, erm, yes." He looked shocked by her reply and fidgeted in his seat, glancing at Jake, who was reading a comic on a sofa in the adjoining room. He dropped his voice and added. "It's a form of post-traumatic stress disorder. It can be particularly prevalent in children who lose a parent at an early age. Nightmares, panic attacks, are all common symptoms. As upsetting as I'm sure it is, Jake will grow out of this. And, unless absolutely necessary, I would prefer not to prescribe any form of medication at this stage."

"I'm not asking for drugs. And I would believe all this post-traumatic stress stuff, but Mark has been dead for over three years, doctor. So why now?"

He shook his head. "It's hard to say. Every case is different, because every one of us is different. We all handle grief in our own way. As I'm sure you understand, my dear."

He leaned over the desk, and patted her hand. Helen slid her hand away, sucked in a sharp retort and affected a strained smile.

Dr James Dennis had been her GP since childhood, and

must be near retiring age. His rotund frame and bushy white hair and beard gave him the look of an absent-minded professor. He wore wire-framed, half-moon spectacles and a permanently surprised expression.

Helen had a feeling she was about to surprise him some more.

"I'm sorry but I think that's a load of crap, doctor."

"I'm s ... sorry?" He sat upright and adjusted his spectacles.

"I don't think these nightmares are connected with Mark's death. I think it's an easy and pat excuse to blame every symptom, every problem, on it. And I won't have Mark getting the blame for this."

She felt her voice rise and her chest tighten. "You don't know this, but even though he was only three when it happened, Jake understands his daddy is dead. He knows he's gone to heaven. Yes, he misses him. But he accepts it. To him, it's okay, because in his mind he will see him again one day. If anything, he's handled the loss better than I have." She paused for breath.

"Helen –"

"I'm sorry, doctor, but I know my child. And I know that whatever's causing these nightmares, it's not Mark. And I'm sick of everyone using that as an excuse for –" Her voice trembled as she thumped the desk in time with each word, "every ... single ... thing."

Tears burned as she twisted her hands in her lap.

"I'm sorry," she muttered. "I'm sorry for wasting your time. We'd better go."

She pulled Jake's parka off the back of the chair and stood.

"Helen, sit down." Dr Dennis spoke with quiet authority.

She sat.

"I suppose you think I'm neurotic," she said. "You think I'm the cause of Jake's problems. You probably think I'm the one struggling to cope."

She gulped. *Please God, don't let me cry.*

"Helen, I don't think that at all. I think both you and Jake have handled Mark's death admirably. And I'm sorry if you think I'm using it as an excuse. I'm not. Truly, I'm not." He paused and looked over his spectacles, staring Helen in the eye. "You know, I expected a visit after Mark died. I was there at the funeral. You looked so calm. I thought it was a front – fully expecting one day you'd crack and I'd see your name on my patient list. I didn't. You're a remarkable woman."

"It's not a case of being remarkable, doctor. I had Jake to think of. He needed me."

"Yes, but you had lost your husband."

He didn't need to tell her that. Just because she hadn't broken down as everyone expected her to, didn't mean she wasn't grieving. They hadn't seen the endless hours alone in their marital bed; her body filled with a deep emptiness. Nights when she'd cried until her pillow was sodden and her eyes throbbed. Days when she could barely drag herself out of bed.

But she had Jake. It was simple – she had no choice.

Helen realised Dr Dennis was speaking and she'd missed most of what he'd said.

"...and if so, I'll gladly arrange an appointment."

"I'm sorry?"

"With the child psychiatrist. If you think it might help get to the bottom of things. I can refer you for an appointment."

Helen took a deep breath. "Do you believe in reincarnation, doctor?"

He jolted in his chair and his unkempt eyebrows rose even higher.

"I don't know that I do. Why?"

"Since before Mark's death, Jake's talked about another family. He calls them his *Ireland Mummy and Daddy*, and his *Ireland brothers and sisters*. He has vivid memories of this ... let's call it ... a ... past life. Mark believed in reincarnation, I'm not sure that I do. But these memories seem to be getting stronger. He talks more about them now than ever. I'm wondering if the nightmares may be connected."

"This is not my field. Not at all." He scribbled notes onto the pad in front of him. Glancing up, he added, "And you say this is an on-going thing. When did it start?"

"From about twenty months, pretty much as soon as he started talking," Helen said. "Mark was fascinated – totally blown away by it. Just little comments to start with – like his other mummy had long, blonde hair and he had brothers who teased him. But now he describes the house they lived in; the black and white dog he calls Chi; he has a passion for boats that's unaccountable. Lots of things. But it's becoming more and more real to him, I'm sure of that."

"Amazing." Dr Dennis looked stunned as he continued to take notes. "I definitely think I should contact Paul Owen. Dr Owen is a leading children's psychiatrist. I'm sure he would be interested in taking Jake on. And if anyone can help you and Jake, I'm positive it will be him."

Helen drained the last of the vodka from the glass as she recalled the GP's words. She leaned heavily against the kitchen unit, and stared up into the night sky. Thousands of stars glittered like tiny diamonds, lighting up the blackness. She had told Jake that Mark was one of them, looking down on them, and she held onto that belief.

Would Mark think she was doing the right thing?

She nodded, sure that he would. He'd been more open to things outside his understanding than she ever had. As she saw it, she really had little choice. Jake needed help, and this could be the answer.

Chapter Three

Gareth Parry yawned and shot a glance across the car. "You look like I feel, man. Rough as a bear's arse."

"Cheers," said Chris, scratching his dark stubble. "Nice to know you care."

Gareth blew an imaginary kiss. "Heavy night?" he asked, knowing Chris's reputation for hard drinking since his divorce. He glanced at the rear-view mirror as he pulled into the rush-hour traffic heading into Bangor.

"Not really. Card game with a few guys. Ended up bout hundred down, so not great."

"Well, I'm grateful for you getting up so early on your day off."

"We're partners, bud. It's what partners do. Besides, if there was ever trouble with any of my family, I know you'd do the same."

Gareth nodded. "Goes without saying. But still, it's appreciated."

"So, what's the story, then?" asked Chris as he drained the last dregs of coffee from a polystyrene cup, refitted the lid and balanced it between his feet. "You sounded right cut up on the phone."

"Oh, that was me mam, doing my head in. My aunt's got it into her brain her daughter, Edwina, has gone missing. I don't buy it myself. She's nineteen. You know what girls of that age are like."

Chris nodded. "So, you close to your cousin, then?"

"Yeah, brought up virtually next door to one another. She's an only child, so I suppose I was like a big brother till her family moved out of town. Me working local was the main reason the family was happy to let her move to Bangor. Now, Aunt Linda has got 'bad vibes', so me mam says. Last night she managed to get hold of one of Edwina's mates, and it turns out she's not seen her since they broke up for Easter. This friend is up at her fella's, in the Lakes somewhere, but said she thought Edwina was going home for the bank holiday. So it's all kicked off now."

"I'm guessing you've tried ringing her, emailing her?"

"Yeah, mobile's off. But then she loses one a month on average. No reply to texts or emails." Gareth shrugged. "Personally, I think she's shacked up with some fella somewhere, and not a second thought to her mam or the holidays. She'll get a kick up the arse when I catch up with her for getting everyone in such a bloody state."

Gareth indicated and swung the car into a circular drive in front of a large, white house. Both men climbed out, the slamming doors broke the gentle silence of the leafy street.

Chris paused as they followed the curve of the drive.

"Shit, that's what you call a view, huh?"

Gareth turned, taking in the rolling gardens and the sparkling blue waters of the Menai Straits, stretching out to Bangor Pier, and beyond to the pretty town of Beaumaris.

Chris whistled through his teeth. "You know I never get bored of the views round here. Never. I've been here best part of ten years, and still some days the mountains and the sea can take my breath away. I love the sea. I imagine the boats crossing the horizon, all heading for the Mersey." He shook his head, pushed his hands deep in his pockets. "Suppose you can take the Scouser out of the 'pool, but you can't take the 'pool out of the Scouser."

Gareth smiled. "You big soft git. You do talk a load of crap at times, you know."

He took time to scan the grounds; the tranquillity broken only by the distant wail of a police siren somewhere across the water on Anglesey.

"Must've been a grand house in its day," said Chris, gesturing towards the building.

"Impressive," agreed Gareth, shielding his eyes as he stared up at the leaded bay windows. "I helped her move her stuff in. I think there's about ten apartments now, at least twenty-five students living here."

"What's it mean, Welsh boy?" said Chris, nodding at a brass plaque beside the door. "Ty Mawr."

"Big House," Gareth replied with a grin.

"Figures. Never had student digs like this in my day. Back at John Moores you were lucky to find a bedsit in a squat, never mind a luxury cliff-top house with sea views. Bloody students today are spoiled to shit ..."

The side door opened and a curly-haired boy appeared. Dressed in a red t-shirt and cut-off jeans, he looked about twelve years old, but was obviously a student. He dragged a bike behind him, manoeuvring it through the gap. He paused as he saw the two men; a worried frown crossed his features.

Gareth stepped forward, reaching for his identification.

"Hello, there. I'm Detective Sergeant Parry. This is DS Coleman –"

"Parry? Are you related to Ed?"

"Yes, cousins. And you are?"

The young man blushed and his eyes shifted from Gareth to Chris and back again. "Liam." He cleared his throat and repeated louder. "Liam Cooke."

"Hi, Liam," said Chris. "Nothing to be worried about, we're just here to see if Edwina's home."

Liam shook his head; his eyes studied Gareth's face. "No. Is she okay? I said to the others I was worried about her."

"Why?"

Liam shrugged. "Just odd not seeing her around. I missed

her."

Gareth's heartbeat quickened; he rubbed his palms together, felt moisture. Something about the young guy's face, his whole demeanour, put Gareth on edge. Despite his forced nonchalance, Liam was worried. Gareth was sure of it. He'd interviewed a lot of witnesses in his time, and considered himself something of an expert on body language. And this guy's was all over the place.

"Look, is it okay if we come in and have a chat?" he said. "I'd like to have a look at Edwina's room too. See if we can figure out where she's gone."

Liam flushed an even brighter shade of crimson, but with a nod, balanced his bike against the wall and led them both into a small hallway.

"When did you last see Edwina?" asked Chris.

"Must have been last Wednesday – final day of term. Everyone was making plans to go away or head home. Ed said she was working at the book shop over the holiday, and I've got a part-time job at a DIY store, so we were going to be the only two here."

"Her friend, Amy … she's away, right?" Gareth asked as they followed Liam through a large cluttered kitchen and down a long corridor. Gareth wrinkled his nose at the dirty pots and pans piled high either side of the sink, and the half-dozen boxes of breakfast cereal lined up on the large kitchen table. The smell of burnt toast and stale fish and chip paper hung heavy in the air, masking the faint aroma of cannabis. Student life never changed.

Liam nodded. "Yeah, but then she's been away with the fairies ever since she set up with this new hush-hush bloke. We hardly ever see her nowadays. When I didn't see Ed around, I just assumed she'd decided to go home. I know she gets homesick quite a bit. It was only her job that kept her here." He paused at a door near the end of the dimly lit hallway. "This is Ed's room."

"Have you been inside since you noticed Edwina wasn't around?" Gareth asked, running his fingertips around the doorframe, then along the top ledge, before rubbing the dust on his jeans.

Liam shook his head quickly. Too quickly. He looked down at his scuffed trainers.

"Liam?" Gareth nudged.

"Well, I stuck my head in, just to see if she was sick or anything, you know. I've not messed with her stuff or anything, I wouldn't. We have rules, you know –"

Gareth raised a hand. "Hey, I appreciate you caring, man. I'd be pretty pissed if you hadn't checked up to be honest."

Chris pushed open the door. Gareth sniffed the air, his police training second nature to him. It smelled of scented candles, but still somehow had a musty, closed-up smell. One curtain was open, the other closed. Sunlight filtered through the orange material, dust motes danced in the beams, bathing the room in a tranquil warmth.

Gareth followed Chris into the room, pausing to look at the unmade bed and pile of dirty clothes on the floor beside it. He bent over and touched the crumpled pillow, tracing his fingers across the indentation. He flipped the duvet, taking a cursory glance at the mattress. Stepping back, he nudged a Raymond Chandler book with his foot. *Farewell My Lovely*. It had fallen to the floor just under the bed. He frowned as he noted the creased pages and damaged cover. He picked up the paperback, straightened the pages, and placed it back on the bedside table.

This more than any single thing set off alarm bells inside him. Edwina was fastidious about her books; she'd go berserk if she loaned them to anyone and they came back spoiled. He'd faced her fury after spilling a glass of orange juice over one of her Stephen King hardbacks …

"Well," said Chris, breaking his train of thought, "explains her mobile."

Gareth looked up to see her Nokia on its table-top charger.

"Is this her handbag?" asked Chris, bending from the gap on the far side of the bed with a small, denim bag in his hand.

Gareth swallowed. “Looks like it.”

“Hey, don’t get panicking, buddy. No sign of any disturbance is there? It’s just a typical teenager’s bedroom.”

Gareth pulled open the door of the built-in wardrobe. “Yeah, but one that seems to have all her worldly goods here. I can’t see any of her clothes are missing either. I mean, even her rucksack is here –”

“Buddy, don’t pretend you know the whole content of your cousin’s wardrobe. Women and clothes are a mystery to me. There’s no proof here anything has happened …”

“No, but there’s no proof that anything’s happened either. Chuck us her bag, Chris. Let’s have look.”

Gareth’s pulse quickened as he straightened the duvet, and tipped the contents onto the bed. House keys, purse, make-up, tampons … the usual assortment of oddments tumbled onto the bed. Her whole life was here. Why would she take off anywhere for five days without taking this with her? It didn’t make sense. Nothing made sense …

“Well, there’s zilch to learn here,” said Chris. “Let’s go and see if the kid has any more ideas.”

Liam looked even more terrified as Gareth slid into a seat across the kitchen table from him. Chris opened the side door and disappeared into the garden.

“Have you found anything?” asked Liam, gripping his coffee mug with both hands. “I mean, she is okay, isn’t she?”

“I hope so, Liam. There’s nothing in her room to say anything bad has happened. But it’s not like her to just take off, is it?”

Liam shook his head. “No. Not at all. She could be a bit wild, but she never let them down at work.”

“Have you got the number of the shop? I think I’ll give them a call, see if she’s been in.”

“No, but it’s the called The M-muse, just opposite M-morrisons. You can’t miss it.”

Gareth looked up, noted the boy’s burning cheeks. Liam studied the chipped table top, refusing to meet Gareth’s eye.

"What about friends?" said Gareth. "Do you have any numbers that might help?"

Liam shook his head again. "Sorry."

"Boyfriends?"

"I don't think she had a b-boyfriend," Liam said, colour rising again in his smooth face. "Least she never told me. We'd got pretty close, on the same course, you know. I was looking forward to spending a few days here on our own, you know …"

Chris's head appeared at the kitchen door, and Gareth frowned at him, mentally trying to work out how he'd got back into the house.

"Hey, Liam. How long's the latch on the French window been broken? Any ideas?" Chris flashed a look at Gareth.

"I d-dunno. Sorry. The landlord ain't the quickest getting repairs sorted though. Ben would know, he's like the head honcho round here, but he's gone home to Oxford. So, I dunno. Sorry."

"Well, I think you might want to get onto someone about it. It's not exactly secure as it is."

"Yeah, sure, will do. I'd not noticed, sorry."

Gareth sighed. Liam was clearly going to be no help, and was rapidly becoming more tongue-tied. He pushed back his chair, and stood. "Well, look, here's my card. I'll go and call in at The Muse, but if you think of anything … anyone … that might help us. Give me a call, okay."

"Sure, sorry I can't help, you know."

"It's okay, but I am worried. And Edwina's mam is beside herself as you can imagine. Oh, and if she turns up here any time soon, you'd better tell her I'm looking for her. Okay?"

"S-sure," Liam said as he followed them back outside, taking care to double lock the rear door.

"So, what you think?" asked Gareth, as both men walked back to the car; footsteps crunching as they crossed the gravel surface

"Not much. I've checked inside and out. Other than that

dodgy old latch, nowt out the ordinary. No tyre tracks or anything out of place I can see. Certainly no sign of a burglary or any damage. But, I dunno, there's something –"

"What?"

"I don't know, probably just me –"

Gareth's radio crackled into life, and he groped into his inside pocket to retrieve it.

"Control to DS Parry."

He pressed the receive button. "DS Parry. Go ahead."

"Are you in a position to attend a report of an IC 1 female washed up on the beach at Gallows Point? Uniformed officers are in attendance. What's your ETA?"

Gareth stopped dead. His vision blurred and swam. Chris grabbed his arm, offering unspoken support.

"Deep breaths, bud," he hissed. "I know what you're thinking, but lose that thought right now. Okay? We've no idea what we're dealing with. There's no connection here. None."

Gareth nodded. He knew Chris was right. But an ice-cold wave washed over him, filling his lungs.

Chris grabbed the radio. "Yes. ETA twenty minutes."

"Thanks, Parry. Roger that."

Before the officer turned the body over, Gareth knew. He tuned out the uniform's words, tuned out the yapping dog from the nearby witness. He tuned out the rest of the world, and concentrated on the long matted hair, the grey naked flesh, the curve of her spine. He saw the intricate Celtic design tattoo in the small of her back. And he knew. Remembered his aunt's reaction when Edwina turned up with a pierced belly button and tattoo on the same day. Remembered her cheeky grin; the sly wink. Best to get it all over in one go, she'd said.

He saw the bright green finger nails digging into the mud. And he knew.

Gareth fell to his knees as the uniform quickly pulled the

tarpaulin back over the corpse. Over Edwina. His nose was full of the stink of the mud, the stink of decay. He gagged as he felt strong hands on his shoulders, lifting him, pulling him. Taking him as far away from the nightmare as possible. Hot tears rolled down his cheeks, blurred his vision as he stumbled blindly through the swampy ground.

His cousin. Edwina. Dead.

Chapter Four

The pointed toe of Helen's patent black stiletto tapped the edge of the glass coffee table. She glanced at her watch. Dr Owen was running forty-five minutes late. It was only a minor thing, but lack of punctuality was one of her pet hates. She grabbed the white, plastic cup and sipped vending machine coffee. She grimaced. Not only was it disgusting, it was now stone cold.

As much as she'd like to blame her foul mood on the delay, she knew nerves were the real problem. Her stomach was alive with all manner of winged insects. She'd told no one of her conversation with her GP and his subsequent referral to a child psychiatrist. Somehow, just the mention of the word 'psychiatrist' made her feel like a failure – a bad parent who'd let her child down when he needed her most.

She glanced over at Jake. He was sitting on the floor, in a specially designed play area in front of the large window. He made '*brum brum*' noises as he crawled around the floor, pushing a red Porsche. Sensing her gaze, he looked up and waved. No one would know by looking at him that he had a single care in the world.

Helen looked around, massaging the stiffness in her neck. The office was painted pale grey and its abundance of chrome and glass gave it a modern, sophisticated feel. A collection of official-looking certificates – most from King's College, London

– hung next to the window. Her gaze met the immaculately made-up brown eyes of the attractive receptionist, who smiled and looked away. This annoyed Helen even more. She coughed politely. When this failed to provoke a reaction, she spoke.

"Excuse me. Have you any idea how long Dr Owen is likely to be?"

"Mrs West?"

She turned at the male voice.

"I'm Dr Owen. May I apologise for the delay. It was unavoidable and not normal practice, I assure you. Follow me please."

Helen blushed as she shook the extended hand. His grip was weak and clammy, and without reason she took an instant dislike. He was small and thin, around fifty she guessed. Neither the cut of his suit nor the pink of his shirt suited him. His hairline raced back from pointed features, and small, beady eyes were accentuated by gold-rimmed glasses.

He made no effort to introduce himself to Jake, simply turned and marched back along the corridor. Obviously, they were meant to follow.

Dr Owen waited for them at the door to his office, which bore a plaque that read, Dr Paul Owen BSc FRCP. Helen looked around as they followed him in. It contrasted starkly with the light, airy waiting area. Too much mahogany furniture crammed into a small space. The floor-to-ceiling bookcases bulged with hundreds of books. Helen was surprised. The room was hardly designed to be user friendly for a man who made his living working with children. She'd expected large open spaces, with plenty of light and colours.

Dr Owen turned to Helen. "I shall need to do a few tests on Jake before we begin. Just a few sensory tests and a behavioural questionnaire. It will only take thirty minutes or so. But I find having parents present affects the child's responses. Could you wait in reception please."

It was an order, not a question.

Helen nodded weakly. She settled Jake into the strange surroundings with a hug and a kiss, before meeting his worried gaze.

"Dr Owen has a few questions for you, sweetheart. Be a good boy. Mummy is just next door if you need me, okay?"

Jake gulped, thought about sliding a thumb into his mouth, then pulled back when he saw Helen's frown. He nodded.

Helen closed the door behind her, sneaking a final glance at Jake's wide eyes. She gave a little wave and bit back tears, and with a sigh, headed back to the reception. She risked a hot chocolate from the vending machine, more to pass time and busy herself, than out of a need for hydration. She took a sip and wrinkled her nose.

Helen glanced back at the closed door, contemplating her first impression of Dr Owen. She hoped Jake liked him more than she had. The doctor really rubbed her up the wrong way. She remembered one of Mark's favourite comments: 'He had a face you'd never tire of slapping.' The memory brought a smile as she took tiny sips of the disgusting chocolate.

Her thoughts drifted back to Mark. She tried hard not to dwell on his death. But it was impossible to spend ten years of your life in love with someone, then erase them from your heart and mind as if you'd come to the end of an interesting book.

From the instant she learned of his death, she'd known her life had changed forever. What she hadn't known back then, was just how much she relied on him. For everything. For a long time she felt helpless. She hadn't realised how utterly she would miss him. How completely she loved him. That she'd had no chance to tell him cut deeper into her heart than anything else, and she could only pray he knew.

On the day of his funeral, she'd sat on the edge of their bed staring into the mirror, listening to his favourite *Prince* album, *Purple Rain*, while trying to summon the will to apply makeup. Her hand had shaken so badly as she attempted to apply mascara, that she'd flung it across the room in frustration. She'd sat with her head in her hands, until there was a knock on the door. She really hadn't wanted to see anyone, not before she had to, but knew she couldn't hide away all day.

"Helen, dear, it's me. Can I speak to you for a moment?" Mark's mum, Eileen, inched open the door.

Helen closed her eyes, squeezed the bridge of her nose. *This could be difficult.* She'd tried to avoid Mark's parents since his death. She couldn't bear the pain of her own loss, and knew she would buckle under the weight of theirs too. Her relationship with Eileen had never been daughterly, but they had both made an effort for Mark. Helen knew Eileen had considered them too young to get married and start a family. After years of encouragement from her husband, Will, she'd eventually accepted it.

"Sure, Eileen, come in. I'm just finishing off in here."

Eileen closed the door behind her, silently picked up the discarded mascara, and sat on the opposite side of the bed. She was pale and drawn. Her eyes looked red and sore, and were smudged with mascara. The black lace blouse and jacket made her pale skin even more ghostly. Helen wanted to reach out and comfort Eileen. She shouldn't have avoided them. She knew the loss of a child was the worse pain a parent could suffer. She thought of Jake. *If anything ever …* No, she forced the thought away.

"I wanted to give you this before the funeral." Eileen's voice wavered. "Mark left it with me before his first tour in Afghanistan. He said ... he said if anything ever happened to him, he wanted you to know how he felt about you, even though he rarely told you. I don't know … men and their pride –"

Helen looked at the white envelope lying on top of the white duvet cover. Unshed tears blurred her vision. She focused on Mark's neat handwriting. Her name printed in blue against the whiteness. Eileen pushed the envelope across the bed, wiping her nose.

"Go on, my dear. Open it," she added, hoarsely.

"I'm not sure I can," Helen whispered, staring at the envelope.

"Please. It's what Mark wanted."

With a shaking hand, Helen slid her nail under the flap, not wanting to damage it, knowing it would be in her possession till the day she died. She pulled out two sheets of pale blue notepaper, covered in Mark's familiar handwriting. Her eyes flooded with tears before she'd read the first word.

Dear Smelly,

Well if you're reading this then I must already be dead! Unless Mum gave it you after you insulted her Sunday lunch just once too often!

Damn, I'm sorry babe. There I am making a joke again. But that's always been my trouble. Easier to raise a smile than show any emotion. My excuse? Well I'm a bloke, so can you forgive me? Believe me this isn't easy. But I've had this in the back of my mind to do for some time. You never know in my job, and if something happened out of the blue, I want you to know how I really feel about you, cutting out all the bullshit.

Helen, I've loved you with all my heart since I was eighteen. I can still remember the day I met you, the first time I saw you standing under that apple tree covered in white blossom at Robin's 18th birthday party. You looked ethereal – like an angel. I can see now the white summer dress you wore, the thin straps kept slipping off your shoulders. How you blushed every time you pushed them back, every time you caught me watching you. I never told you how much I ached to reach out and touch you, stroke the silky skin of your collarbone. God, I shall never forget how tanned and beautiful you looked. I never imagined in a million years I would stand a chance with you. Never. It took me another two weeks to pluck up the courage to ask you out – and then I had to get Robin to do it for me. Remember?

Yeah, at first it was lust. The physical stuff you know. The dry mouth and pounding heart, I had all that. Not that I ever told you – I was far too proud. But then, I fell in love with you. And I've loved you ever since. You are my saviour, my princess, my soul mate. I want to thank you for everything you have given me – the love, the tenderness, the passion, the trust and the support. I want to thank you for agreeing to be my wife. You are a perfect wife and a perfect mother. I was blessed to find you.

And I want to thank you mostly for giving me my little man. I've never known such complete, pure love that I have for Jake. He has made my life whole.

I'm crying as I write this as I realise how much I would miss you if you ever left me. I hope to God I never have to find out, babe. But I'm sorry for all the hurt you must be going through now. At least I've been saved the pain of losing you this way. Do one thing for me, babe – don't let Jake forget his dad. Kiss him goodnight every night from me. Tell him all about me and how much I loved him.

And I want you both to know that wherever I am right now, I'm watching over you.

I'll always love you, babe. But I want you to move on whenever you're ready. You have my blessing. No, you don't, not now, this minute, as it doesn't seem real. But when it happens you'll be ready and I will accept that. I don't want your life to end because mine has.

Be strong. I Love You. Mark x x

Helen dropped the letter into her lap. Silent tears poured down her face in a continuous stream. Without speaking, Eileen walked around the bed and took Helen in her arms. They remained like that, supporting each other and bearing the weight of each other's grief until the funeral car arrived.

A metallic buzzing brought Helen out of her reverie.

"Mrs West," called the receptionist. "Dr Owen is ready for you now."

His office seemed even darker when she returned. The doctor was filling in a form, and without looking up gestured at the seat opposite. Helen gritted her teeth, held her irritation in check and sat where directed. *This is for Jake, remember*. Eventually, he put down his pen, and looked up at her.

"Jake is with the nurse, I thought it better to speak to you alone." He spoke in a quiet, authoritative voice. Removing his spectacles, he rubbed the bridge of his nose, and then replaced them. "I've run various tests with Jake, all of which have come back normal. Outwardly, he seems a perfectly well-balanced and rational child."

"He is," interjected Helen, her chest swelling with pride and indignation.

"However," continued the doctor. "I have worked with many children with similar behavioural problems as Jake."

"My son doesn't have behavioural problems –"

"Mrs West, if he didn't, then you wouldn't be sitting there," he snapped, his annoyance at the continued interruptions evident. "Behavioural problems do not have to be out-of-control violence, bullying or any of the popular preconceptions. They can be something like insomnia, agoraphobia or real-life withdrawal. All of these mental health problems affect not just the patient but their families, teachers and friends. That's where we try to help. We try to identify the problem, understand the causes and give advice."

Although Dr Owen's words sounded sensible and sincere, Helen couldn't help thinking they sounded like a well-rehearsed script. If she opened up the first page of his glossy practice catalogue, would she find the exact same words printed there? Her cynical mind wondered how many parents had sat in that same seat, listening to the same carefully crafted words.

"Now, you say Jake's problems started at twenty months?" he

asked.

"Well, I wouldn't say problems exactly –"

"Mrs West, if you intend to obstruct my every question, I don't see us getting very far."

Their eyes met across the desk. The doctor held her gaze. Helen knew he was right; her shoulders slumped.

"I'm sorry. This isn't easy. Admitting defeat –"

"This is neither about success nor failure, Mrs West," interrupted the doctor. "In fact, this isn't about *you* at all. It's about getting to the root of Jake's problems and finding a cure for them."

Helen nodded and bit her lip, determined to ignore the patronising tone.

"Something scares him, but I've no idea what. He was much more vocal in the last dream … when he sleep walked. He screams and cries for his mummy and daddy sometimes, but I don't think he means me. He does mumble occasionally, but incoherently."

There was silence for several moments whilst the doctor continued writing. Helen shifted in her chair, crossed her legs, smoothed her skirt.

"Mrs West, I've had first-hand experience with all kinds of mental health problems in children that can also be scientifically proven as fact. From autism to anorexia, from severe conduct disorder to schizophrenia. But I have never yet come across one case of supposed child reincarnation I have been able to prove or treat with any degree of success. I believe in all cases there are rational explanations for, what are in my opinion, simply remarkable coincidences."

"That's rubbish," Helen blurted out. "How could Jake know about Ireland, and the family he describes, and the boat they owned, and the house they lived in? Are you saying he's lying or making them up?"

"Not lying, no," replied Dr Owen. "But you know as well as I do, that it's not uncommon for children to have imaginary friends, even imaginary pets. I've treated patients who have made up complete lifestyles, to escape the misery or monotony or fear in their real lives. It may be that Jake is trying to forget what happened to his father, or he may be so unhappy he chooses to live in a make-believe world, full of big, happy families."

He paused to draw breath, before continuing. "Or, this could simply be a case of something he has seen on television, in a book, on the internet or at school. Something that has sown a seed in his mind and developed from there. We can't watch our child's every movement, twenty-four hours a day. To him it would seem very real. I worked for twenty years as a consultant child and adolescent psychiatrist at King's College, London, before I opened this practice. And I can assure you I have had years of experience of this type of behaviour. This is extremely common in children grieving for a lost parent."

"Ah. I wondered when we would get round to that."

"It can't be ignored, Mrs West."

"Oh yes it can, Dr Owen," said Helen, rising to her feet. "If anyone ever actually listened to me … this all started years before Mark's death. I can see you don't want to believe what you won't admit to seeing. Well, thank you for your time, doctor, but I don't think you're the right person to treat my son."

"Mrs West. There is every chance I could try new treatments with Jake. I'd be interested in pioneering forms of cognitive behavioural therapy …"

"No, I'm sorry. I want to help my son. He is neither miserable nor scared. And I will not have him used as a guinea pig to flatter your over-inflated ego." Her voice shook as she picked up her bag from the floor. "I'm sorry to have wasted your time doctor, but I won't be bringing Jake here again."

"Mrs West!" Dr Owen pushed back chair.

Helen ignored him and left the room, slamming the door behind her.

"Honestly, Sally, I could have slapped him," Helen said. "He couldn't wait to bring up Mark's death. Just like Dr Dennis – only twice as arrogant. And Jake hated him too. He said he really scared him and only spoke to him via the nurse. I mean, he's a child psychiatrist, and he can't communicate with kids for God's sake! What a joke."

She ran her hands through her hair. "It wasn't funny," Helen added, seeing her friend's wry smile. "He's lucky I didn't smack him one. The pompous little … God, he makes my blood boil even now."

"Calm down," Sally soothed. "There's no need to get wound up again. It's over now. And you know I'm not laughing about it, but your face is a picture when you talk about this Dr Owen."

"He was *so* patronising, Sally. You just wouldn't believe it." Helen adopted an upper-class, nasal accent. "Jake may be so unhappy he chooses to live in a make- believe world. Jake may need to escape the misery or monotony." She reverted to her usual tone. "I mean, can you believe he would suggest all of this is my fault? That somehow I've made Jake's life *so* miserable?"

"What did he say when you walked out?" Sally took a sip of her latte.

"Not much. I didn't give him a chance. I had a feeling his next topic would've been child abuse. And if he'd gone there, I *would* have decked him."

Sally snorted through a mouthful of coffee; she coughed and wiped a tear from her eye. "Helen, you crack me up. You sound like a fifteen-year-old. We're not acting hard in the playground now, you know."

Helen couldn't help but smile. Even at school, she'd always had a quick temper and a sharp tongue. She leaned forward to pick up her steaming cup of coffee, nursing the drink in both hands and inhaling deeply. The smell of strong, fresh coffee always seemed to relax her, and she loved this small shop, with its comfy sofas. No one rushed you to finish your drink and move on; they were happy for you to plug in your laptop, and spend the afternoon if you so desired. She often spent a few hours here, writing an article or researching a story, without the chaos and constant interruptions of her office.

"So, what are you going to do next?" asked Sally.

"I'm not sure." Helen furrowed her brow. "It's been nearly a month since the last real bad nightmare. I pray every one will be the last."

"That's hardly pro-active is it, Helen?"

"Don't go all teacher-like on me, Sally. I don't need a lecture."

"I'm sorry, I'm not lecturing. I just think the longer you leave it, the worse it will get. And I have a suggestion."

"What?" Helen glanced up from her coffee.

"Our educational psychologist works for the local authority and several Warwickshire schools. She's does private consultations, and I can't recommend her enough. She's worked miracles with some of our most problematic students."

"What do educational psychologists actually do?" asked Helen.

"All sorts. They work with the teachers and parents of problem children, as well as the children themselves. They deal with learning difficulties and social or emotional problems. I think we should talk to her about Jake."

"Won't Jake be too young for her?"

"Not at all. They work with babies, right up to nineteen-year-olds. I worked with her the year I started at the school. It's amazing how she can turn people's lives round. Honestly, not only is she an expert in her field but she's a lovely woman as well. You'd like her."

Helen wrinkled her nose. "What if she's a sceptic, like Dr Owen?"

"Well, obviously, I can't say for sure. But from what I know of her, I doubt very

much would shock her. She's seen it all, has Dr Pat."

"Dr Pat?" asked Helen.

Sally laughed. "Oh, that's what the kids call her. Dr Pat. Her name's Patricia

Wallis. She's mid-fifties, acts like everyone's favourite batty Aunt. But I can't think of anyone I'd rather trust with my own children. It has to be worth a try, Hel."

"Anything's worth a try. I just want to help Jake."

"I know." Sally glanced at her watch and took a last sip of her latte. "Look, I have to get back to school. Leave it with me. I'll run Jake's problems past Pat, and if she's willing to take him on, I'll make an appointment. Okay?"

Helen nodded.

"Righto, I'll call you later." Sally stood and picked up her denim jacket. With her slim build and short blonde elfin haircut, she looked a good decade younger than her thirty-one years. Sally Bing had been a reliable, solid friend over the years, especially when Mark died.

"Sally!"

Sally turned at the door, one arm in and one arm still out of her coat.

"Thank you."

"Don't be daft." Sally blew a kiss, and disappeared into the mass of pedestrians thronging around the busy precinct.

"Mummy! Mummy! Help. Help me. Mummy!"

Helen woke with a start. She'd been dreaming about Mark. In her dream, they lay side by side under a blossoming apple tree, in a field of freshly mown grass. The sun's rays shone through the heavy branches and warmed her face and legs; the sky above was a deep blue. She smelled sweet apple blossoms and the heady tang of cut grass. A shadow crossed her face. Mark was shaking her, trying to wake her –

"Mummy!"

Jake was screaming.

Instantly awake, she leapt out of bed, and ran to his room.

Jake sat bolt upright in bed, eyes closed, arms held out straight in front of him – until he repeatedly swatted the air above his head as if trying to protect himself from a swarm of killer bees. His face was red and contorted. Rasping noises came from his throat as he struggled to breathe.

"Mummy! Help me. I can't see."

"Jake, I'm here. It's okay, sweetheart. I'm here." Her words went unnoticed, and she realised Jake was still fast asleep.

"Du! Galanas! Cymorth. Du!"

"What? Jake, wake up. What are you saying?" Helen grabbed Jake's arms, and held them down at his sides. Pinning his fists with her own hands, she embraced him. His body shook next to hers, and the erratic beat of his heart reached through their thin cotton nightwear. He continued talking, some of the words clear, others jumbled and unintelligible.

Helen felt Jake's rigid limbs begin to thaw, and his head drooped onto her chest. She held him tighter and stroked his hair, feeling teardrops on her bare shoulder.

"Jake, shhh, shush, come on, sweetie. It's okay. It's over." Helen soothed. She rocked him and whispered in his ear. "It's okay, little man, Mummy's here."

"I want my other mummy," Jake said, between hiccupping sobs.

Helen pulled back, looked into his eyes.

"What did you say?"

"I want my other mummy." His face was red and wet with tears.

"Don't say that, Jake," Helen whispered. Blood drained from her face and her chest tightened. She stared at his little face, couldn't remember ever seeing him so angry.

"I want my other mummy. I want my other mummy!" He pulled away from Helen and threw himself face down onto his pillow, beating his fists against the mattress as he sobbed.

Helen sat rigid on the edge of the bed. She felt numb. Yes, he'd mentioned his other mummy in passing before, but never spoken like this, never used it against her. She bit her lip, knowing she had to calm Jake; her own feelings didn't matter.

She went downstairs and fetched a cold flannel, a bottle of Calpol and a glass of orange juice. When she got back, Jake was curled in a foetal shape, sucking his thumb. Calmer now, his breathing regular. His hair and brow were sweaty, his eyes teary and bloodshot. He sat up in bed as Helen handed him the juice. He opened his mouth, accepted the spoonful of Calpol, then swallowed the juice in four large gulps.

She wiped his brow with the flannel, and brushed his hair away from his forehead with her fingers. He held up his arms in silence as Helen pulled off his sweaty pyjama top and slipped on a white cotton t-shirt. He was compliant now – all the anger dissipated with the memories of the dream.

Helen folded down the duvet and lay back on the bed, with her head on her arm. Jake snuggled up beside her, his head on her tummy. She stroked his hair.

"I couldn't see, Mummy. I couldn't breathe, then I couldn't see."

"You were shouting in your sleep. Do you remember?"

"No." He shook his head and rubbed his nose. "I know I was scared. I was trying to get help. I couldn't see. It was all black and dark. And I couldn't breathe. I think I was in the water."

"What water, Jake?"

Helen attempted to keep her voice calm. Finally, after so many months, Jake seemed to be able to recollect some of the dream. Whilst she wanted to let her son sleep in peace, she knew if she didn't find out what she could right now, it would all be forgotten by morning.

"In the sea."

"You were drowning in the sea?"

"Yes. Daddy died too."

Helen flinched as if she'd been slapped. "What?"

"Daddy was on the boat and he couldn't breathe. He died too."

"Jake, you know your Daddy died being a soldier. He didn't drown."

"Not that Daddy. I mean *Ireland Daddy*," said Jake. "He had a blue boat, but he couldn't breathe in the water and one day he didn't come home."

A chill crept across Helen, from the back of her neck, working lower down her spine. Jake had never spoken in such detail before. She had to pursue it.

"You called out for your mummy. Did you mean your *Ireland Mummy*? Was she there when you drowned?"

Jake shook his head as his eyelids began to droop. He turned onto his side and his thumb crept back into his mouth. Her heart tugged at the sight of her boy, her angel.

"Jake." She shook him gently. "Where did you drown?" He mumbled in his sleep. "What, sweetheart? Come on, tell me. Where were you?"

"The island," mumbled Jake.

Within seconds he was blowing imaginary bubbles and snoring gently.

Helen slipped from the bed, pondering what it was he'd been saying, what language he'd been speaking. She pulled the duvet over Jake, and hovered at the bottom of his bed for several minutes, watching the rise and fall of his chest. Dressed only in blue cotton shorts and vest top, she hugged herself and rubbed her goose-bumped arms.

The island, he'd said. Or had he meant Ireland?

She wasn't sure if it was cold or dread that made her shiver.

Helen sighed, pushed away her keyboard to rest her elbows on the edge of her desk, and squeezed the bridge of her nose as she stared out of the office window with unseeing eyes. She'd found it impossible to get back to sleep the night before. Jake's words would not leave her. The island, he'd said. What island? Coupled with her fear of a second nightmare, she'd spent the whole night watching her son, too scared to leave his bedside.

"Helen, have you seen Alex?" asked Jenny, her colleague in the arts and events section of the local newspaper.

Helen jumped as Jenny's voice brought her back.

She shook her head. "Nope, I don't think he's been in all day, Jen." She hid a yawn behind her hand and took a sip of Red Bull.

"Are you okay?" said Jenny, slipping off her glasses, and peering at Helen with a frown that belied her short-sightedness. "You look done in."

"I'm fine. Just a late night."

"Oh yes?" Jenny's grin widened. "Anything I should know about?"

"I was kept awake all night by the man of my dreams." Helen played along with the joke, and gave a wry smile.

"Jake, I take it? Another of those nightmares?"

Helen nodded.

"You should take him somewhere. Have you thought about visiting a medium or even a local priest? A friend of mine was convinced she was haunted by her great great grandmother …"

Helen's mobile buzzed in her top drawer; she held up a hand, gesturing to Jenny she had to take the call. 'Sally' flashed on the display.

"Hi Sal."

"Hello, how's things?"

"Not good. Jake had another bad night, and I'm shattered today, while he's gone off to school as happy as Larry. I just don't get it. And I don't know what else to do. I've even had Jen here suggest taking him to a psychic or a priest."

"Might not be a bad idea."

"Maybe."

"Anyway, I've only got a few minutes, I've got a class at twelve. Two reasons for calling, I was up most of the night myself, researching on the internet and I've come up with some amazing stories."

"Really?"

"God, yes. Unbelievable. I wondered if you were free to share a bottle of red this evening and I'll fill you in."

"You know me. My social calendar isn't exactly overflowing."

"Excellent. I'll see you around seven. And more importantly, I've just put the phone down with Dr Pat – you remember the psychologist I told you about? She's really keen to speak to you and Jake. I gave her a bit of background, and she didn't seem fazed at all. I told you she wouldn't be. She said she had a free slot, next Saturday, around eleven. I said I'd ring her right back if that's any use to you?"

"Yeah, that would be great,"

"Cool. I'll give her a buzz and set it up."

"So," said Helen later that evening, tucking her legs up onto the sofa and taking a sip of wine, "what's all this about research? Have to admit, I hadn't given it a thought. I think I spent so long convincing myself – and Mark – that it wasn't real, I've shied away from any chance to prove it might be. Even though, ironically, I've spent the past God knows how many weeks trying to convince various doctors there is a rational explanation and my child isn't disturbed."

Sally nodded as she placed her glass on the coffee table and pulled a file from her bag. "Well, you know me and research. When I get my teeth into something, I can't let it go. The more I learned about reincarnation, the more fascinated and convinced I became." Sally nodded in response to Helen's raised eyebrows. "You wait and see. Here, I've printed off a few pages. See what you think."

Helen took the print outs and quickly settled into an article on a case study created by the University of Virginia in Charlottesville in USA. Apparently, it had a whole department, with a world-class reputation, studying nothing but child reincarnation.

'The incidents start between ages two and four, when the child spontaneously narrates details of a previous life. The volume and clarity of the statements increase during the ages of five and six. By the age of eight, the child tends to talk less about their past, and by ten any remarks about a previous life generally cease. Most children with these problems develop completely normally after the age of ten. And their memories disappear completely before they reach their teens.'

Helen felt a spark of excitement. Much of this seemed to mirror Jake.

'It has also been found in a number of cases that unexpected behaviour occurs, unusual for the child, but concordant with the behaviour of deceased person. For example; phobias of guns, fear of flying or special interests or appetites.'

"Boats! Jake's inexplicable fascination with boats. I've told you, haven't I? When he sees boats on TV, or we go to the seaside, he knows all these types and shapes of boats. I tried to pass it off as 'one of those things'. But now it begins to make perfect sense. Whoever Jake's been in a previous life, he obviously worked on boats; perhaps he was a sailor or a fisherman or something."

Sally nodded. "Exactly what I thought. But have a look at this article, it's even more fascinating. If you ever needed proof ..."

Helen scanned the details of a website set up by a counsellor from the United States called Carol Sharpe. Helen made a mental note to look up her book, *Children's Past Lives: How Past Life Memories Affect Your Child.* Her own son had suffered similar problems with nightmares and strange recollections, and she too, had hit a medical brick wall. Her version of events mirrored Helen's.

Sally had printed a study where Ms Sharpe had worked with a couple whose young son had nightmares from around the age of five. He'd then gone on to build a whole past life.

Helen's eyes widened. "Have you read this? '*He knew that he'd been a fighter pilot in the Second World War, who'd been shot down by the Japanese. He knew specifications of the aircraft, and even named an aircraft carrier that research proved had seen active service near Japan during the war. He gave names and ages of his fellow crew. His parents had done extensive research, and all of his details had eventually been proved. They discovered a US Navy pilot, also called James, who was killed in 1945. The story spread over several pages, but in the end they'd traced surviving relatives, who'd supplied photographs. James recognised, and could name, the people and the aircrafts in all of them."*

Helen's hand shook as she met Sally's steady gaze. "How could anyone, after reading this, disbelieve the reality of child reincarnation?"

"I told you … I don't know, Helen. I'll be honest and say I was majorly sceptical, just like you were when Mark was alive. But what else can it be? And now, reading this …"

Helen nodded, her eyes drawn again to Ms Sharpe's words.

'When a child speaks of a past-life memory, the effects ripple far. At the centre is the child, who is directly healed and changed. The parents standing close by are rocked by the truth of the experience – a truth powerful enough to dislodge deeply entrenched beliefs. For observers removed from the actual event – even those just reading about it – reports of a child's past life memory can jostle a soul towards new understanding. Children's past life memories have the power to change lives.'

Helen's eyes filled with tears. "God, it's so hard to explain. I feel grateful someone else has voiced my fears."

Sally reached across and squeezed her hand as Helen continued.

"For the first time in weeks, months, I actually feel positive. I'm not alone. Other people have experienced what we're going through, and their children emerged unscathed. And if it can happen for them, it can happen for us, can't it?"

Helen searched Sally's blue eyes, looking for honesty in the deep pools.

"Of course it can. Of course it will. Come on, let's drink to it!"

Helen picked up her glass and snuggled down into the sofa, rolling the wine round her mouth as a wave of hope surrounded her.

Sally was right, it would get better. They were over the worst.

Chapter Five

It was time.

The car's engine roared as he floored the accelerator. The needle on the tachometer leapt into the red and dropped back as he braked hard, swerving sharply to the left, tyres squealing as they fought to grip the tarmac. A plume of black smoke exploded from the exhaust.

By the time the red Peugeot passed the speed camera, it was well within the 50mph limit.

He whooped and slammed his fists against the steering wheel. He loved driving at this time of day; loved the solitary freedom of it. Sunday morning had yet to dawn and Bangor was deserted. He felt as if he owned the roads; the adrenaline kick reminding him he was alive.

He got such a high out of beating the speed cameras. *They* thought they were so clever, hiding them behind trees and road signs, but they weren't. He knew where all of them were, and his favourite game was to see how fast he could go between each camera.

Today he'd managed 92mph, a new record, before he hit the brakes hard.

It gave him a total buzz to take on the authorities – the corrupt establishment – and win. They would never beat him. The police were all stupid. They couldn't even successfully rip off the public by making money from speed cameras. Most people had them sussed. But they weren't as smart as he was.

Off the main road, he made his way through the council estate into the centre of town, passing the boat yard on his left. A few keen out-of-town sailors were already setting up their boats for a day at sea. Bloody tourists in their 4X4s blocking up the roads. Amateurs, the lot of them, who wouldn't pass the time of day with the locals under normal circumstances. They'd take themselves out somewhere, lose their bearings or get swept out by the currents. And then wouldn't hesitate to dial 999 for the coastguard, fully expecting the same locals to risk their lives rescuing them. If it were his call, he'd let the lot of them drown.

He turned right at the traffic lights outside the station, then immediately left up the hill. He hoped she would stick to her normal routine today; he would hate to have left his warm bed, and miss his Sunday morning fry up for nothing. But his planning was meticulous and nothing would make him deviate. Planning and research - that was the key. That was why he was smarter than all of North Wales CID put together.

He tapped gloved hands against the steering wheel in time with the sound of Metallica, tweaking down the volume in case it disturbed any nearby residents, then slowed the car as he saw the sign marking the public footpath. He swung the wheel to the right, slammed the gear stick into reverse, and manoeuvred into the narrow dirt track. Turning off the engine, he took a final drag on his cigarette, and stubbed the butt in the ashtray. They'd not catch him out with DNA. He was too smart.

He settled his head back against the headrest, blew out a long stream of smoke, closed his eyes and prepared to wait.

Bethan Jones yawned as she adjusted the earpiece, and fiddled with the control on her iPod. She knew these early morning jogs were good for her, but it still needed a great deal of motivation to get her moving. She closed the front door carefully, trying not to make the letterbox rattle. It was six thirty, and Sundays were the only morning her parents got a lie in.

She zipped up her tracksuit top and lifted one leg, then the other, onto the garden wall, stretching her hamstrings and calf muscles. For a minute she jogged in place, then touched her toes to flex. She inhaled air not yet tainted by the day's pollution.

She snapped her long, blonde hair back into a ponytail. She felt good today. She took a sip of water and slipped the bottle and iPod into her belt. A fast-paced, up-hill walk to the top of Fort Hill warmed her up perfectly for her five mile jog. Hoping to run the London Marathon next year with some fellow students, her training was more regimented than usual. She was determined to get the best time.

Bethan visualised her route as she paced herself. Up through the woods, twice round the old Roman fort, back down past the BBC Studios into Temple Road, out onto Holyhead Road, past the supermarket, into town as far as the station, and then turn back and retrace her steps. If she kept her usual pace, that should take her about forty-five minutes, with ample time to shower, change and get to Morrison's for breakfast at 9:30am. A free breakfast one of the perks of working Sunday.

May was her favourite month; she loved the newly-budding trees and sweet smell of honeysuckle as she ran through Bluebell Wood. When she reached the public footpath that led into woods, Bethan stopped abruptly. Some idiot had parked between the trees, almost entirely blocking the track – probably either a drunk who'd passed out, or a courting couple from the night before. Didn't they know the laws? She grumbled to herself as she turned sideways to squeeze between the car and the dry stone wall bordering the edge of the adjacent field.

A hooded shape stepped from behind the car and grabbed her. She was off balance as she attempted to squeeze through the small space, and tumbled forwards into his arms. Before she had a chance to speak or scream, a black leather glove covered her nose and mouth. He gripped her tightly as she struggled, pushing her forwards so he could reach with the other hand to pull open the rear driver's side door. He shoved her headfirst onto the backseat of the car.

Bethan spun round as the door slammed, heart galloping, breathing ragged. She groped for the door handle. It took her several seconds to realise it was missing. The same with the window winder. She pushed herself across the backseat to the passenger side. Two holes in the fabric upholstery indicated where they too had been removed.

She screamed and beat her fists against the window. Turning sideways, she pushed against the door with all her strength. It was pointless. Frantic now, she launched herself through the gap between the front seats, getting only half way when the driver's door opened. His fist connected with her right temple, pain exploded behind her eye. She fell back onto the rear seat, dazed.

"Don't make me hurt you, sugar. Just sit still and stay quiet. If you make me angry, you'll be the one to suffer." The man spoke with quiet deliberation. She looked into the rear view mirror. The hooded top created a shadow across his thick brows, but dark eyes stared back at her. "There's no one around to hear you, even if you scream your pretty little lungs out. Just sit back and enjoy the ride."

Bethan lay curled foetal style on the back seat. Tears spilled down her face, dripping from her nose onto the shabby, stained upholstery. She wiped them away impatiently with the back of her hand. The car's interior smelled musty and had a tangy smell of the sea. Keeping her head down, she searched for some rational thought, not wanting to sit up and see those evil eyes in the mirror. His words alone told her he was a lunatic. Why was this happening to her? Who the hell was this guy?

Bethan pulled herself upright and kicked at the doors – slamming her trainers against the glass and trim as anger fired up inside. Her head throbbed where the blow had landed on her temple and her breathing was shallow, rapid. Her heart slammed against her ribs. Yes, she was terrified, but adrenaline surged.

She was determined to fight. She would not be a victim.

He turned the key, and she listened to the dull rattle of the engine, jolting and bouncing against the seat as the car drove over the rutted track. Then the movement of a left turn as he pulled out onto the road. As the engine laboured, she realised he was driving up the hill and along the coast road. In her mind she was trying to work out what route he would take. Could she attract someone's attention? Where would there be pedestrians at this time of the morning? Where would he have to stop at traffic lights or road junctions? Where the hell was he taking her?

She jumped as music blasted from speakers on either side. Some heavy metal noise she didn't recognise. It hurt her ears and stopped her thinking. Maybe she should try to build a rapport him? Anything was worth trying. Perhaps she could convince him to let her go, without hurting her. It had to be better than lying here, crying.

She sat up and slid forward, so she was in the middle of the seat, just behind his left ear. She had to shout to make herself heard.

"The music is too loud. Can't we just talk?"

She didn't want to lean any closer. Cheap aftershave mixed with cigarette smoke, and she wrinkled her nose in disgust. She found his eyes again in the mirror.

"Sure," he said, flipping the volume button on the radio. "What do you want to talk about, sugar?"

Bethan recognised a Welsh accent. And at the same time realised he wasn't heading towards the main dual-carriageway; he had turned right and they were now crossing the old Menai Bridge onto Anglesey. Her eyes scanned the familiar streets, desperately searching for someone or something to help her.

"You're local, then?" she asked.

"Am I?"

"Well, you seem to know your way around here well enough," she said, trying to sound flippant.

He smiled but didn't reply. Instead he looked through his window and slowed down. Bethan's gaze followed his. Boats were moored along the stretch of peacock blue water, and in the distance Bangor Pier shimmered through the early morning mist.

"Stunning round here isn't it?" he said. "Stupid people spend thousands of pounds going abroad every year, when we have this on our doorstep. Idiots, the lot of 'em. More money than sense." He seemed lost for a moment. "Don't try and be clever with me, it won't work, you know. I'll only tell you what I want you to know."

"Okay, so why have you done this and where are you taking me?"

"I can't tell you that. But let's say you're special."

"But I don't know you, do I? Why don't you take your hood off and face me, so we can talk properly."

She jumped as his fist slammed into the seat in front of her.

"Don't be clever with me, don't even try to be. Don't try to catch me out. I've told you – you don't want to piss me off, Bethan."

"I wasn't …" She stopped. "How do you know my name?"

He ignored her. "Typical woman, always think you're smarter than me. Don't think I don't know what you're doing. You've spoiled it now; you've made me angry. You'll make me hurt you …" He threw back the hood, and turned in his seat. "There, see. Think I was scared to show you my face? Well, I'm not scared. But you should be. You know what that means, don't you?"

Bethan shook her head. She was staring at the face of a stranger. And yet, there was something faintly familiar. The thin, pock-marked face, stained teeth and the greasy black hair, greying at the temples.

"Well, you should," he continued, his voice low and menacing. "You should try to work out what it means, the fact I don't care if you see my face. Stupid slut."

He turned his attention back to the road and accelerated. He pulled the wheel to the right as he negotiated a traffic island at top speed, throwing Bethan sideways.

"No, please, no. I wasn't doing anything, I promise. I just wanted to talk." Tears began to run down her cheeks as she steadied herself. "Please don't hurt me, please. I'll do whatever you want. If you want sex, that's fine, we can have sex. Just let me go after. I promise, I swear ... I won't tell anyone. Please!"

"Shut up!" he screamed. "Stupid slut. I said shut up!"

He spun the car off the road, wheels spraying gravel as he pulled into a secluded car park. She could hear his heavy breathing. He muttered under his breath – unintelligible words, he repeated over and over. He stopped the car and sat motionless, gripping the steering wheel for several moments. Bethan curled herself up into a ball on the back seat and wrapped her arms around her head, unable to stop the violent shakes that gripped her body.

She heard his door open, and felt a draught on her hair. She flinched as he yanked open the rear door on his side, pushing herself backwards along the seat until she was wedged against the passenger side. She kept her eyes closed and readied herself for his touch. If necessary she would kick and punch and scream until her final breath. She would not go down without fighting.

"Drink this."

She opened her eyes. He was holding a plastic bottle in front of her face.

She shook her head, closed her mouth. "No."

"Don't make me ask again. Drink it."

"No. What is it?"

He unscrewed the cap, and with a sudden movement, gripped her jaw and squeezed until her mouth pursed trout-like. He pushed the bottle between her lips, and covered her nose, forcing her to open her mouth and swallow.

She felt the sting of alcohol burn her throat. Vodka, she thought. And something with a bitter aftertaste. It smelled like petrol. He finally let go of the bottle and it fell into her lap. She spat onto the floor.

He backed out, leaving her choking and gasping for air. She heard the car door slam, and then silence. She tried to open her eyes, but her vision was blurred. She couldn't focus. The trees outside were swaying in the wind. But it wasn't windy, was it? Or was it the car swaying? She felt nauseous and it hurt to move her head.

Intense exhaustion washed over her. Perhaps this was just a nightmare; she'd awake any minute, back in her own bed, having slept through her alarm. Her thoughts grew more jumbled and confused. Her final thought clicked into place and made perfect sense.

Drugs. The bastard has drugged me.

She slipped into semi-consciousness, and slumped onto the rear seat, face down.

Chapter Six

A loud thudding woke Gareth with a start. He rubbed his eyes as his vision cleared. His head felt as if someone had crammed cotton wool through his ears, and as he ran his tongue across his teeth, his mouth tasted like old socks. He stretched and yawned, keeping his elbows bent in the confined space.

It must have been more than forty-eight hours since his head last touched a pillow and he'd grabbed more than a few uncomfortable minutes of restless sleep –

"Gareth!"

The noise started up again and with a sudden rush he remembered where he was. Why he was there.

At the same time, he recognised Chris's frown on the other side of the glass. His features distorted through the fog of condensation and blurring raindrops. But anger still clearly etched on his face.

Gareth turned the ignition key and pressed the electric window switch. A gush of damp salty air flowed into the car. He yawned again as Chris's face levelled with his own.

"Hey, matey," Gareth said with a small smile.

"Don't 'hey matey' me? What the hell are you doing here?"

Gareth looked round the A&E car park, remembered choosing this particular spot as it afforded him an uninterrupted view of the entrance to the pathology department.

And the morgue.

He fixed his most innocent expression and shrugged. “Waiting for you?”

“I kind of guessed that much. What for? Are you trying to get us both the sack, or what?” Chris stepped back and gave a furtive glance over his shoulder as Gareth pushed open the car door. “DI McRae made it abundantly clear ...” Chris paused. “Look bud, I know how hard this is for you. I do understand –”

“Do you? Really? I doubt it.”

He slammed the door shut and pulled a pack of Embassy from his pocket, noting the shake of his hands and the bloodied knuckles. A sudden memory of punching the side of his father’s shed, out of sight, out of control. Needing his father. Missing him so much. More out of his depth, more out of control than he could ever remember. His aunt’s anguished sobs mixed with his mother’s soothing murmurs coming from the kitchen.

“Yes. I do. But you stalking me isn’t going to help. You know the rules.”

“To hell with the rules and the training. I’ve done the same course. I know all the right words. I can adopt the right tone. I can recite all the proper clichés and platitudes. But that doesn’t mean ... *you know*. Not unless you’ve been here, lost someone in this way. You can’t know ...” Gareth broke off, jabbing the unlit cigarette in Chris’s direction. “You can never know.”

Chris leaned forward, squeezing Gareth’s shoulder, and took a deep breath. His voice was softer now, the anger gone. “Buddy, you’re on compassionate leave, whether you want it or not. You can’t be part of this investigation. You know that. I will find the evil bastard who did this. I promise you that if it’s the last thing I do. But you have to leave it to me –”

“I can’t.” He looked down, flicking the lighter over and over. “Shit it!”

Chris’s hand closed over his, the flame sparked with one touch. “You have to. You have no choice.”

“You don’t understand –”

"What? What don't I understand?"

Gareth looked down again, taking a long drag of his cigarette, feeling the nicotine thread its way into his veins. Calming him. Soothing him. But not healing, not taking away the pain, not easing the guilt. Not taking away the memories. Grey flesh. Green finger nails. The stink of mud. His aunt's rage. Her flailing fists.

He fingered the crescent-shaped scar on his left cheek.

"How'd you do that?"

Chris's voice bought him back from the dark edge of grief.

He cleared his throat, sniffed back tears. "My aunt … Linda." He looked up, their eyes locked. "She blames me."

"Why?"

"Because I failed her. I was supposed to look after Edwina. Her baby. She only let Edwina go to Bangor Uni. because I lived and worked here. I could look out for her. We had an arrangement." Gareth sucked in a long breath. "I'm supposed to be a copper, right? And I couldn't even protect my own cousin, for fuck's sake. So, she's right. It is my fault. She has every right to blame me. To hate me. I hate myself."

Chris stared at him. "She's taking her pain out on you, and right now you have to let her. But, it's not your fault. Not. Your. Fault. Get that right out of your head. One man did this. And I will catch him."

"And what do I do?" Gareth rubbed his nose, taking a pull on the cigarette, squinting against the smoke. "What am I supposed to do while I'm waiting? I mean, I can't eat. I can't sleep. I'm not welcome at home at the minute. I can't stay in my flat. Tell me, what am I supposed to do!"

Gareth's voice cracked and he slumped forward, dropping the cigarette and covering his face with both hands. A hand slid across his shoulder, tightened on the back of his neck as Chris supported him. Minutes passed and the tears dried up and finally stopped. Gareth straightened, rubbed his eyes, glanced around the car park, glad to see it still empty.

"Better?" Chris's voice was low.

Gareth shook his head. "No. But I'm sorry."

"It had to come. You've been robotic since Friday, bud. You need to go home and rest."

"What I need is to know what's happening –"

"Don't put me in that position –"

"I know. All the rules. But I have to know. If I promise to back off, will you at least keep me informed and up to date? I can't just walk away. I rang the station and the desk sergeant said you were at the hospital. I put two and two together … I was right. You've been at the post-mortem, haven't you?"

Chris nodded; his gaze following a departing ambulance.

"Mate. Tell me."

"I can't see how it's going to help –"

"It's not. But if it were your family, I'd do the same, you know I would. If anything happened to your Tracey –"

"Enough!" Chris growled. "Enough, okay. I'll tell you. But I swear to God if this goes any further ..."

"So, who did the PM?"

"Connolly."

"Susan Connolly?"

Chris nodded with a knowing gleam in his eye that Gareth ignored by lighting up another cigarette.

"She's bloody good." Gareth blew out a stream of smoke. "One of the best. At least that's one thing. And what did she say? What did she find? What was the cause of death? How long had the body been in the water?"

Chris held up his hand. "Hey, slow down. I'm waiting for the official report to be filed. I'll pick it up in the morning."

"But you must have her initial findings ..."

Gareth paused for a moment, thinking it unbelievable that despite his grief he could so easily slip back into professional mode. Even when it was his own cousin.

He realised Chris was silent, head tilted, studying him.

"What is it?" asked Gareth.

"Are you sure you want to know? Can you handle –"

"The initial findings?" Gareth prompted. "Had she been … been … raped?"

Chris's silence gave him his answer. Gareth bit down on already raw knuckles; the flash of pain a welcome diversion.

"How about DNA?"

Chris shook his head. "No fingerprints. No hair, skin, nothing. It seems he cleaned the body thoroughly before disposing of it."

"And he dumped her … the body … in the sea? How long had she been there?"

"Connolly thinks she'd been in the water no longer than seventy-two hours, no less than thirty-six. She also said there was no salt water in the lungs …"

"So, she was dead before he disposed of the body. At least she didn't drown."

Gareth lit another cigarette, pushing away an image that had haunted him and filled most nightmares since childhood. Drowning. He could think of nothing worse. Edwina had known, tried to help him. He was glad at least she hadn't suffered that …

"Buddy? You okay?"

"I'm okay. What else did she say? Anything else about cause of death? Or where she may have been killed?"

"Cause of death appears to be strangulation. Connolly suspects sexually motivated, part of some sadistic ritual. No sign of the murder weapon, but from the marks she believes some kind of leather strap or belt was used. A length of blue rope was used to bind the hands and feet. Erm … no alcohol in the blood and no stomach contents either."

"She'd been starved?"

Chris nodded. "Not to death. But she must have been really weak at the end. Shit, I'm sorry. So fucking sorry you have to hear this."

Gareth waved the words away. "And where? Where was she killed? Obviously not her flat. So? Was she abducted or did she go willingly?"

"There was markings on the soles of her feet, consistent with having walked, or been dragged, bare foot over tarmac or gravel. She'd been kept somewhere dirty, perhaps underground – like a cellar or something. There were tiny traces of soil, spiders' webs, brick dust and also flakes of white paint under her nails. Her knees were ingrained with dirt too, as if she'd crawled around on some kind of open ground."

"So, she'd been kept somewhere, possibly up to a week?"

"Yeah, if what young Liam says is true. I'm taking a statement off him tomorrow. I've sealed off Ty Mawr. Got SOCO going over the place at the moment. Nothing so far. Tomorrow, I start interviewing witnesses. First stop the book shop."

"Who are you working with?"

"No one. I'll take a Uniformed with me tomorrow. McRae has given me Morgan and Thomas. They're following leads at the university."

"Then let me come with you tomorrow –"

Chris groaned. "Gareth, you promised. You know I can't."

"Who would know? They'd have no idea who I was. Please."

"Sorry, bud. The answer's no. Not until I get clearance from McRae. You need to rest. I'll call you if I get anything important. You have my word. Now, go home and sleep. You look rough as hell."

Chris turned on his heel, heading towards his Volvo. He paused as the alarm beeped, turning back.

"I'll call. I promise. Go home. Okay?"

Gareth nodded, taking a final drag of the cigarette before grinding the stub into the tarmac. He raised a hand as the Volvo passed by, watching as the brake lights flashed, and the car turned out onto the main road.

Gareth ran his hand through his hair, straightened his crumpled shirt and walked towards the main building. He pushed open the entrance marked 'Pathology Department.'

Stroke of luck Chris had jumped to the wrong conclusion.

"I really can't tell you any more, DS Parry. I've told DS Coleman everything. The full report will be ready by eleven tomorrow morning. Besides, I thought he said you were on compassionate leave?"

Dr Connolly closed the file with a definitive thud. The hairs rose on the back of Gareth's neck.

"Nothing much compassionate about all this, is there? I kind of think it's more important at the moment to try to track down my cousin's killer, rather than sitting at home drowning in self-pity, or propping up a bar drinking myself into oblivion. Both of which seem like pretty tempting options right now, I must admit."

Susan Connolly spun her stool so that she faced the counter beside her, and methodically began to number small glass slides.

Gareth sighed. "Susan. I'm sorry."

She gave a curt nod, but kept her shoulders hunched and continued her work.

Gareth took a step forward, touched her back, felt her flinch beneath his hand.

"Look at me," he whispered.

She shook her head.

"Sue, come on. Look at me."

Slowly, she turned the stool until she faced him. Her chin up-turned, expression defiant. Gareth saw the sheen of unshed tears in the green eyes he remembered so well. He'd hungered for those eyes, lusted for them. He could recall in minute detail how her pupils widened when she was happy and excited. He shivered and pushed the image away.

"Gareth, I'm sorry for your loss. And despite protocol, if I knew anything else I would tell you. I don't know how I got through the PM when I heard the connection. Do you not think I've been extra thorough? Do you not think I would do anything I could to help you?"

Gareth nodded. "I know. I'm sorry. I'm a mess."

Susan lifted a hand, fingers reaching towards his shirt collar, a pained expression on her face. As she brushed the material, she sighed and pulled away.

"You're strong. You will get through this."

"Officially I'm off the case. Chris says he'll keep me informed, but I need to be doing something. Anything. I just want to be sure there's nothing he's missed or discounted. I know you. You have instincts. Anything you can tell me, anything that sprang to mind during the autopsy – even if you dismissed it as irrelevant or have no proof, even if it's only a gut instinct. Tell me. Please. I trust you. I need your help."

Susan stared into his eyes. "You never *need* anyone, Gareth. That's part of your problem. You spend so much time trying to be everything to everyone; you never let anyone get close. I can imagine how this must be torturing you. I can imagine you feel you've let your family down. And for that reason, I'll help you all I can. But right now I have a deadline and I need to work on these samples. If anything comes up, I'll let you know the minute I tell Coleman – that's the best offer I have, Gareth. Take it or leave it."

"Perhaps you know me better than anyone."

Susan clipped her dark blonde hair back into a ponytail, and pulled on a pair of plastic goggles. "If that were the case, we'd still be together."

"I told you, you're too good for me. I'd never have given you what you want. I don't do commitment. Beside, you're happy, aren't you? Dr Zhivago has put a ring on your finger, hasn't he?"

Susan hid a smile as she lit a small Bunsen burner. "It's Dr Javier, as you well know. And yes, we've set a date. Now, are you going to let me get back to my job?"

Gareth raised his hands in surrender. "Just promise to call me the minute you find anything. Please?"

"I promise. Now shoo."

Gareth reached the door and pulled it open.

"Gareth," called Susan. "I am sorry. So sorry for your loss. I understand you have to do this. Good luck."

"Thank you," he whispered.

Chapter Seven

Helen pushed the button to lower the driver's window, breathing in the scents of a country lane in springtime, where budding hedgerows bulged with blackthorn and honeysuckle. A blackbird on a low branch serenaded her as pale sunlight tickled her fingers on the steering wheel, drumming along with the tune on the radio.

She loved this time of year, loved the countryside, but each passing season, each vibrant arrival of spring brought fresh pain and deeper loneliness. It had always been a dream of hers, and Mark's, to kiss goodbye to suburbia and buy a cottage in the country; maybe a plot of land, grow their own produce, get some chickens and a horse for Jake. A standing joke they wanted to turn themselves into a modern day version of 'The Good Life.' They'd talked about moving nearer the sea, perhaps Devon or Cornwall. Once Mark left the army he was ready for a challenge, a new career, new direction. He had a passion for diving, and talked about buying a boat, maybe setting up a dive school. She'd burst with excitement at the thought of a totally different lifestyle, away from the deadlines and daily pressures of her life as a journalist.

But they'd been robbed of that chance, their future stolen …

The impatient beep of a car horn startled her from her reverie.

"Green for go, Mummy."

She met Jake's eyes in the interior mirror and blew him a kiss.

"Yup. Thank you, Jakey. Mummy is day-dreaming again."

Holly gave a gentle 'woof' from the tailgate and Helen chuckled; even her Labrador was reprimanding her driving skills.

"Are you okay about today, Jake? You understand we're going to see a friend of Sally's?"

Jake nodded but his face was screwed up into a tight frown.

"It will be okay. You trust Sally, don't you? Dr Pat is a doctor, but she's not anything like Dr Owen. She just wants to talk to you, stop the bad dreams making you sad. I am trying to help, you do understand? But if there's anything at all you don't like, we'll stop."

"And you won't leave me? Like last time. You promise?"

Helen's stomach twisted into tight knots. "Cross my heart. I won't let anyone scare you ever again."

Minutes later, she pushed the bell on the front door of an impressive Georgian manor house. Pat had been willing to meet Helen at home or her office in Stratford, but Helen insisted a trip out in the country would do them good, and they could combine Holly's daily walk. She wondered if Dr Pat's surroundings were any more inviting than Dr Owens'.

She gave Jake's hand a tug to stop him fidgeting as she heard the click of the lock. The door opened to reveal a small white-haired woman in her mid-fifties, dressed in a lilac jumper and long grey skirt. She fitted Sally's description of a slightly batty aunt perfectly, reminding Helen of Miss Marple. When Pat smiled, even the wrinkles around her eyes were full of warmth.

"Welcome! You must be Helen," she said. She had a soft Irish accent which put Helen at ease. "And you, young man," she continued, as she stooped to face Jake on his own level, "you must be the famous Jake West." She stuck out her hand, and they shook in mock solemnity. Jake giggled, and flashed a nervous glance at Helen.

"Nice to meet you, Dr Wallis," she said.

"Oh, please call me Pat. Everyone does. Now, follow me. I have tea and biscuits waiting. Or coffee if you prefer. And juice for Jake. Come along, this way." She clapped her hands briskly.

They made their way through the house, and into a conservatory at the rear. There were twin red sofas, two overstuffed chairs in the same bright colour, and two glass tables covered with books and toys. The yellow, red and orange colour scheme made perfect use of the light. The pale lemon sash curtains were closed at one side, to keep out the sun's glare.

The view from the patio was an abundance of green. A long lawn led down to a small lake surrounded by weeping willows. Beyond that, rolling acres of fields, dotted with sheep and new-born lambs. The hills on the horizon were covered in the dark green of a small forest.

Helen stood admiring the view. "You have a beautiful garden."

"Thank you, my dear. I'd love to say it's all my own work, but my husband is the keen gardener, and now he's retired he spends most of his time there. Or on a golf course when he gets under my feet." She smiled. "We can take a walk down to the lake later, if you'd like, Jake?" He nodded with enthusiasm. "Now … tea, coffee, juice? Biscuits, Jake?"

Helen admired the ease with which she settled Jake; a marked contrast from their last medical consultation. Within twenty minutes, Jake was relaxed, on his second glass of blackcurrant juice, and she'd lost count of how many Jaffa Cakes had disappeared. He giggled and played along with Dr Pat as if he'd known her all his life.

After half an hour of pleasantries, Pat leaned forward and switched on a Dictaphone.

"So then, young man, your mummy tells me you've been having some scary dreams," she began. They sat at opposite ends of the sofa. "I don't want you to be shy or scared. Just tell me everything you can remember. I want you to relax while we talk, okay?" Jake nodded. "Your mummy says you have memories of another family, another life? Can you tell me about it?"

"I don't know. It's all fuzzy."

"Okay. Let's see what we can do to help."

Pat leaned across and slid a bright pink box from behind the sofa. Lifting the lid, she pulled out a large sketch pad and a box of mixed crayons.

"How about you draw me something?" said Pat, placing the pad across Jake's knees.

"Wh … what shall I draw?" he asked, his thumbing creeping into his mouth, while his eyes searched the colourful array of crayons with interest.

"Anything. Whatever you like. Whatever you see when you think about the bad dreams."

Jake picked up a brown wax crayon and began to draw thick lines in a square pattern. Dr Pat made eye contact and smiled at Helen, as Jake selected a lime green crayon and drew a large circular shape.

"Can you tell me what you're drawing, Jake?"

Jake paused in mid-stroke; his brow furrowed in concentration.

"This is our house. And this is the sea." He began to colour the width of the pad in pale blue squiggly lines. "There's lots of blue, and lots of green too."

"So, that's your house?"

Pat pointed to the brown square.

Jake nodded.

"Who else lives there, Jake?"

"Well, sometimes I can see another family – a mummy and daddy, brothers and sisters."

"Good. That's super. What else can you tell me?"

At that moment, his eyes brightened as if a happy thought had just come to him. On the bottom right corner of the sheet, he drew a rudimentary animal shape that to Helen could've been anything from a cow to a camel.

"We have a dog!"

"Well done, Jake!"

Jake smiled; his chest puffed out in pride.

"A black and white dog. I walk him on the beach." "You live by the sea then?"

"I think so. We play on the beach and in rock pools." Jake frowned again. "I remember a blue boat."

Pat turned to a new page and selected a dark blue crayon.

"Can you draw me a picture of your boat?"

Jake repositioned the pad on his knee and drew a rough sketch of a small rowing boat in heavy navy strokes. He stuck out his tongue as he worked. Helen smiled at this trait – a sign of concentration more usually in evidence during his beloved computer games.

"It was like this. But the blue is wrong, it was a different blue."

"Like this?" Pat selected a lighter shade from the box.

"Yes!" Jake wriggled and began to shade the outline in with the brighter colour.

"Marvellous!" said Dr Pat, when he presented the finished picture a few minutes later. "And was this in Ireland? Did you sail your boat when you lived in Ireland?"

"I ... I don't know. Mummy asked if I lived on an island, I think I did. I think that it was *on* an island. But I don't know if it was *in* Ireland. But I know where Ireland is on the map because Mummy showed me!" He beamed up at the doctor with a proud, almost boastful, expression on his face.

"Well done! Now, your mummy says you got scared last time. You thought you and your daddy drowned. Was that on the island? Can you remember what happened in that dream?"

Jake shook his head. "No, it's too fuzzy. I was scared when I woke up. I couldn't breathe. But it's gone now."

"That's okay, don't worry," reassured Dr Pat. "I hope by talking about it you'll remember more details. But don't try too hard; just let the memories come, the more you try, the further away they will go. So, watch me." Jake looked up from the sketch pad. "I want you to sit up, very straight, that's it, shoulders back … and take big, deep breaths. Do it with me, then. Ready? One, two, three …"

Jake giggled as they inhaled and exhaled in time.

"Good boy! Mummy, can you join in too?" said Pat. "Ready, one, two …"

Helen joined in the breathing exercise, flashing a welcome smile at Pat. How different this whole experience, for both her and Jake. Perhaps she could relax, finally believe she'd found someone she could put her faith into. The relief was palpable, like a huge invisible weight had been untied from round her shoulders, round her throat, choking the life from her. She wanted to throw her arms round the tiny woman and hug her hard.

Pat was speaking again. "Okay, now we're all nice and relaxed. Are you relaxed, Mummy?" Helen nodded, gave a thumbs up. "And you, Jake?" Jake grinned and repeated the gesture. "Good! Right, so let us move on a little bit. Your mummy told me you spoke some kind of foreign language in your last dream. Do you remember?"

Jake frowned and shook his head. "What do you mean?"

"Funny sounding words. Not English. Like … say they speak in Spain or Germany."

"I don't know any funny sounding words."

"Okay, that's fine. You said you lived in a little house. Can you describe more of it to me?"

Helen warmed to Dr Pat even more.

"It was a little white house, with a white fence round it. Shall I draw it for you?"

"Yes please, that would be lovely. There you go," said Pat, turning to another clean sheet. The two women smiled at each other; Pat's eyes full of encouragement.Soon the white page was covered in a more detailed childish sketch of a small cottage on a green landscape surrounded by blue – which Helen figured to be either sea or sky. Pat seemed not to want to question Jake on the accuracy of his drawings; she let him carry on in his own style and pace.

Jake spoke as he used a luminous yellow marker to add detail to the building.

"The rooms were small. I shared this bedroom – here – with my brothers. And I think we had to get water from the garden. I can remember carrying buckets made of wood."

Dr Pat nodded. "So, you had a well outside?"

Jake nodded. "Yes, that's it. A well. And we used to dry fishes on a line in the garden. I don't know why, but I remember fishes over a fire. I've never thought of that before!" He looked thrilled with the revelation, glancing from Pat to Helen and back again, with a beaming smile of triumph.

"That's super, Jake! Your drawings have really helped." Dr Pat beamed at Jake. "So, was your daddy a fisherman?"

Jake shook his head. "No. I don't know what he did, but he wasn't a fishman."

"What else can you tell me about your other family?"

"I'm not sure if it's to do with my family really, but I remembered today, I hadn't told Mummy how I got the ticket to come back," said Jake in a solemn voice.

Pat and Helen exchanged worried glances. "How'd you mean, Jake?"

"I remember falling through this big hole one day. Getting a ticket from God, and then I was here with my new mummy."

"That's interesting, Jake. Did anyone tell you about that? Or perhaps you saw it in a film or a computer game."

Jake bit his bottom lip and frowned as he shook his head. "Told me? No. I think I only remembered it after the bad dream."

"What do you think was happening then, Jake?"

"I don't know."

"Was that after you and your other daddy drowned?"

"I think so."

"So, do you remember dying?"

"No." Jake's face changed in an instant. The bright expression faded, replaced by ashen, shocked terror. He turned towards Helen, blue eyes wide. "I'm not dying, am I? Am I, Mummy? Mummy?"

Helen rose, and Jake was in her arms within seconds, hiccupping loud sobs.

"Jake, Jake, sweetie, it's fine. No, you're not dying. Don't be scared. Dr Pat meant the person you see in your dreams. Not you. Don't cry. Please don't cry, baby."

Helen took a sip of coffee and replaced the cup on the saucer with a shaking hand. She took a deep breath and looked out of the window. Jake knelt next to Pat's husband, Ken, at the edge of the lake. Ken tickled the surface of the water with his fingers, and pointed out Koi carp rising among the water lilies. Jake threw back his head and laughed.

It had taken quite a time to reassure Jake, and calm his tears. Dr Pat had left her alone with her son whilst she soothed him. She'd returned with Ken, a small, wiry man with large hands, and a smiling, tanned face, who'd taken Jake on a tour of the garden and orchard beyond.

"I can only apologise, Helen," said Pat. "Jake seemed so confident. I wrongly assumed he would know what I was talking about. I didn't expect him to get so emotional. But it happens sometimes."

"That's okay, doctor, I don't blame you. It was going so well."

"Call me Pat, please. And yes, it was. But I think if we are going to probe more deeply, we need to think about hypnotism or regression. I feel there's a floodgate of memories waiting to be unleashed, something that explains the trauma he experiences during the nightmares, because that element certainly didn't come across in his drawings. They were all happy memories. But the bad ones are buried deep somewhere; we need to find the key to releasing them."

"Have you dealt with cases like this before?"

"Only once or twice, to be honest, genuine cases that is. And I do believe Jake is genuine. I had one case very early on in my career when I was still inexperienced. But to be truthful, it frightened me and I passed it onto a senior colleague."

"Why?" asked Helen.

"I was treating a young boy aged four. He believed he was the reincarnate of his own grandfather."

"No … really?" said Helen, shaking her head. "How awful."

"Yes, it was terrible for his parents. He recognised himself in an old family photograph. He pointed out his first car; he could name friends and relatives that he couldn't possibly have known. And even more chilling, he told his father that his aunt, who would have been his own sister, had committed suicide whilst pregnant with an illegitimate child."

"God, that's terrible." Helen shivered. "How did the child's father react?"

"It was extremely difficult for him. He hadn't known about this tragedy; it was a well-kept family secret, but it turned out to be true. How are you supposed to cope with the fact that your child is the reincarnate of your father? Such a stressful time for the whole family. By the age of eight all of the child's memories faded, but the father received counselling for almost a decade."

Helen nodded. "That sounds about right. I've done some research on the Net – by the age ten it's all forgotten."

"I believe that's because our souls, and our memories, are still pure as young children. When you mentioned about Jake drowning in his last nightmare, I dug out this article I read a while ago." Pat passed across a photocopy of an article by a child psychiatrist called Dr Jim Crawford.

Helen read aloud the first paragraph.

"'If a soul is reincarnated with 'unfinished business', or died a traumatic death, these matters are more likely to carry over into another life. If a person died a traumatic death, whilst still young, there was still much emotion and energy that propelled these memories forward. As I see it, a part of the person's consciousness survives its death, and is part of the new host's soul consciousness. The present incarnation is not a carbon copy of the last, but contains aspects of the original personality and experience.'"

Helen handed the article back as Pat picked up another sheet.

"Take a look at this."

As Helen took the paper, Pat said, "This was written by a mother in a situation similar to yours."

Helen felt her skin prickle. "Really?"

"Yes. This was the case study that first interested Jim Crawford. You could say it made him dedicate his career to the subject."

Helen read the article.

"'Several years ago, when my daughter was three years old, she approached me while I was reading a card sent by a family member. The picture on the front was a watercolour reproduction of a little boat on a lake.

She pointed to it and said, "I've been on a boat like that."

I said, "Really?" (knowing she had NEVER been out on ANY boat.)

She said (in a sombre voice), "Yeah. I died there."

I know my mouth must have fallen open. So, I asked her to explain what she meant. She said, "I was in the boat, hit my head and fell in the water. I kept falling and falling, but then I went to God."

She raised her arms up in the air and looked up. I was speechless and got chills all over.'"

Helen placed the paper on the coffee table.

"So, you see my dear, you're not alone," said Pat. "As scary as it is, there are lots of similar stories out there."

"This thing about getting a ticket from God …"

Pat nodded. "I've heard and read about similar stories before. But I don't want to scare Jake by talking about it. Look, I'm quite good friends with Jim Crawford. He's head of a department at the University of Virginia in the United States that specialises in this kind of child phenomenon. I'd like to have a chat with him about Jake, and get his advice before we go any further. Would that be okay?"

Helen nodded. "Anything, I'll do anything. I want the nightmares to stop. I want him to find some peace. He's had enough trauma in his life." She swallowed hard. "I just want to help my son."

Pat crossed the room and took Helen's hand.

"We will, dear. I promise you, we will.

Chapter Eight

Gareth cleared his throat. "I am really grateful you agreed to see me, Amy."

Amy looked up from the pile of shredded tissue in her lap and smiled.

"And you, Mrs Jameson," he added. "I know this isn't easy."

"It's not easy for you either, Gareth," Amy's mother replied. "How's your mam coping? How's Linda? I've picked up the phone more than once, but I couldn't … I mean, what do you say?" She broke off and sniffed. "I'm just so grateful Amy is still here. All I can think was it so easily could have been her! You think they're safe, don't you? In proper lodgings an' all, and then it hits you. You poor soul, so soon after losing your dad, too. And I can't help feeling partly to blame. Amy talked me into persuading your aunt to let Edwina go off to Uni. I gave my word –"

"Mum." Amy tugged her mother's sleeve. "I don't think Gareth needs to hear all that right now."

Mrs Jameson blushed, blew her nose, and straightened her back. "No, sorry. Of course not. I'll leave you youngsters to talk. Coffees all round, okay?"

As the door closed, Amy released a loud pent-up sigh. "I'm sorry."

Gareth smiled. "It's okay."

"No, it's not." Amy shoved the mass of tissue into the pocket of her cardigan, brushing her jeans as she stood. She crossed to the window and glanced out before propping herself on the sill. "God, she's doing my head in!"

"It's only natural. It's relief. It will pass."

"Yeah? I hope so. She's talking about not letting me go back to Uni. I mean, I've missed so much work already. She can't do that, can she? Mind you, thought of going back to Ty Mawr –" Amy stopped, her face flooding with colour. "Shit, I'm so tactless. Shit. Shit. Shit!"

She pulled another tissue from the pocket of her jeans, and rubbed her already swollen eyes.

"Come and sit down." Gareth's voice was gentle as he patted the seat beside him on the sofa. "I need to talk to you."

"I've already been interviewed, you know? Twice."

"I know. But I'm not really part of the official investigation. I'm supposed to be on compassionate leave."

Amy dropped onto the sofa and tucked her feet under her. "But you want to find whoever killed Edwina? She was murdered, wasn't she? The other detective wouldn't say. I suppose that's the way they're trained to handle it, but I don't even know where they found her …"

"Coffee!"

The arrival of Mrs Jameson with two steaming mugs saved Gareth having to break any rules. As the door closed, and they were on their own again, he jumped in before Amy could restart her own line of questioning.

"Can you tell me when you last saw Edwina?"

"Yes, a week last Wednesday. We had lectures in the morning, then walked home together. She helped me pack … and waved goodbye from the doorstep." She took a small sip of coffee to compose herself. "That's the last memory I'll ever have of her."

"What time was that?"

"About four o'clock. Danny had a tutorial after lunch."

"Your boyfriend?"

Amy nodded. "I went to meet his parents in Cumbria. It was kind of last minute, or else I'd probably have been spending the Easter holidays with Ed … and none of this would have happened."

"There's no point thinking like that, Amy." Gareth said. "Believe me. I've tried. It only brings you more grief and achieves nothing."

"But I do feel bad. I feel guilty, yeah? I've been so wrapped up in myself, so bloody full on with Danny since we got together, that I've barely given Ed a thought for weeks. She was just always there, you know? I'd see her in class, walk home together, then we'd totally go our own ways."

"What was Edwina up to, do you know? Was there a boyfriend?"

"Definitely not. Ed wasn't interested. She struggled to make friends to start with. She was always a bit shy, yeah? Whereas me, I'm always up for a party." She paused and blushed, tucking a strand of hair behind her ear. "Ed was so much more serious, real passionate about her books and her music. She adored her job at The Muse, mixed with similar-minded people there, she said."

"Anyone in particular?"

Amy wrinkled her nose, shook her head. "I don't remember anyone. She'd joined up as a volunteer too, with CADW –"

Gareth frowned. "CADW?"

"Yeah, I dunno the translation, but it's run by the Welsh Government, I think, to protect heritage sites. They own loads of places, bit like the National Trust, yeah? She disappeared most Sundays. She'd found this passion for gardening and stuff, and she'd been helping maintain some of the woodlands and grounds. Said it got her free entry to places. She'd done Ty Newydd and Beaumaris Castle –"

"Beaumaris? When?"

Amy jumped at his sharp tone. "Um, couple of weeks ago. Why?"

He shook his head. "Nothing. Carry on."

Amy's words began to blur as he remembered Gallows Point;

just a stone's throw from the town of Beaumaris.

Remembered the grey flesh, lime nail varnish, the stink of mud …

"… but she never mentioned a name."

"What?" He tuned back in. "Whose name?"

"She said there was a professor who was a regular customer at The Muse. A group of them were planning a trip to the theatre, down London, to see an Opera. He was arranging it, I think."

"But you don't have a name?"

Amy shook her head. "Sorry."

"She wasn't seeing this guy, though?"

"No, I told you."

"I spoke to Liam. Liam Cooke? I thought I picked up on a hint of a relationship there …"

He trailed off as he saw the half-smile on Amy's lips. "A crush is all. He's a sweet guy, but you've seen him, he's a child, yeah? He used to watch Ed with puppy dog eyes, but there was nothing going on there."

Gareth took a sip of coffee. "So, nothing else? No strangers hanging around? No odd behaviour?"

Amy shook her head again. "The other guy asked me the same and I've racked my brains. All I keep coming back to is that I've been the worst kind of mate. I let this happen to my best friend –"

"Amy, you didn't let it happen. No more than I let it happen. She was my cousin and I should have been there –"

Looking down, he felt Amy's hand grip his wrist and he called up the steely resolve he'd spent the past twenty-four hours constructing around his heart.

"She was so proud of you," she whispered. "Bet she never told you though?" Gareth shook his head, unable to meet the young girl's gaze. "God yeah, she was always talking about her cousin – the big-shot detective. Made you sound dead glamorous."

Amy blushed and looked away, adding, "Told everyone at school and Uni you looked like Johnny Depp. And she was right about that too."

Gareth gave a nervous laugh. He rubbed his stubbled jaw. "Yeah, sure. Captain Jack, right?"

Amy smiled. "No, your cheek bones and your hair. She was lucky to have someone like you to look up to. And she did. She respected you a lot … she really loved you."

Gareth tugged his hand away from her grip, and crossed in three steps to the window. The passing traffic blurred into a steady stream of jumbled colours. Where was this new resolve when he needed it?

Amy slid a box of tissues in front of him along the windowsill, before leaving the room and closing the door with a gentle click.

First his aunt, suffering alone. Just a few streets away – but a million miles from him. Then the show-down with Chris. And now, breaking down in front of a witness. Perhaps he should go home and hide under the duvet. Perhaps he should stop at the next pub and drink till he ended up under the table.

But when he stopped moving, when he tried to slow down, he couldn't stop the visions. The green finger nails. The intricate tattoo. The tendril of slimy seaweed curled across her ear. And then … his aunt's feral rage. Again, he fingered the crescent-shaped scar. A constant reminder of his failure.

He had to keep moving. He had to keep busy and stay strong, completely focused. He had to believe that for every step forward he took, he was a step nearer to the truth. This was one box ticked, there were plenty more to go.

Next stop. The Muse.

Gareth took the long route back onto the bypass, halting the car at the end of Audley Avenue. The downstairs curtains were still drawn at his aunt's house. His mother's car was parked in the drive. He should pay a visit, but knew his presence wasn't wanted right now. His aunt was still lashing out at everyone and anyone she could blame. He'd telephoned his mother yesterday. She said the doctor had prescribed sedatives but his aunt refused to take them.

As he pulled into the flow of traffic, his stomach cramped and he realised another day had passed without food. No wonder he was tired, struggling with his emotions. How could he keep forgetting to eat?

A large yellow 'M' sign called him as he approached the next island, and minutes later he was consuming a cheeseburger as if he'd never tasted anything so delicious in his life. The fries disappeared in seconds, and with a contented sigh he sipped vanilla milkshake, recalling outings with Edwina, shared takeaways they'd enjoyed. Why did every single memory take him back to her?

His pocket began to vibrate, and he remembered as he fished out his mobile that he'd turned it onto silent when he arrived at the Jameson's'.

Number withheld flashed.

"Hello. Parry."

"Gareth? Susan Connolly."

His heart leapt. The sound of her voice or the implication of her call? He wasn't entirely sure. "Hey, you okay?"

"Yeah, fine. Er … where are you?"

"Wrexham. Just leaving. Why?"

"Oh, been visiting family?"

"A witness. Edwina's friend, Amy."

"Anything?"

"No, unfortunately. Anyway, what's up?"

"I hoped you could pop into the Lab if you were local. No worries though, it can wait."

"What can? What have you found?"

His heart began to pulse in his temples. Something in her voice. Confusion? Fear?

"Nothing." She paused. "Well, I mean nothing additional to the PM on Edwina. I've been doing a bit of research and I think

I've come across something, but I'm not entirely sure. I could do with talking it through but I don't want to discuss it with Coleman yet, not till I am certain."

"Can you wait at the hospital? Give me an hour."

"Sure. I'll wait. Just take your time. I remember how bad your driving is."

Gareth parked the car and ran across the car park, pausing only to stamp out his cigarette, before pushing open the main door of the Pathology department. Susan jumped as he crashed through the swing doors, looking up from the computer screen.

"Come in, why don't you."

"What have you found?"

"And how nice it is to see you too, DS Parry."

Gareth ignored her attempt at humour.

"Relax, Gareth. I'm trying to help, but I could be wrong."

"About what?"

She pulled another seat beside her own. "Come look at this."

Gareth balanced on the stool and peered at the computer. Some kind of brown design, with blurred writing? A tattoo? The image was magnified but although Gareth twisted first one way, then the other, he couldn't make out what he was looking at.

"What is it?"

Susan tapped a manicured nail against the screen. "This is a blown-up image of a ligature mark on Edwina's neck. Well, throat to be exact."

"Oh."

He felt an invisible weight kick him in his gut, knocking the air out of him.

Susan continued. "Can you see this purple bruising? Here? And here?"

Gareth nodded, remaining silent, worried that if he spoke he might start to fall apart again. He took a deep breath and focused.

"Well, if you zoom out a little." Susan clicked her mouse. "You can see quite clearly that it's an imprint of some kind of buckle. It follows the contours of the ligature marks, consistent with a belt or some other kind of leather strap. But if I zoom back in again, once you know what you're looking at." She paused, more clicks. "What can you see on the buckle imprint itself?"

Gareth frowned and leaned closer towards the image. Towards the picture of his dead cousin. He pushed the thought away.

"It's not symmetrical? It's sort of crooked?"

Susan smiled. "Exactly. But if you study it, there's more to it." She picked up a pencil and followed the edge of the belt with its point. "This bottom edge here is very linear. See, perfectly straight line, like any normal belt buckle. But this top edge is totally different. Can you see?"

"I think so. The bruising is less clear."

"Yes, but not only that. I've tried to replicate the buckle. Here, look." She slid a pad across the desk, covered in a pencil sketch. "This top edge is definitely some kind of design. It has regular curves and grooves. It's very distinctive; in fact I'd go even further. I think it had either some kind of motif or a name written on the buckle."

She sat back with a smile. Obviously Gareth was supposed to see some massive kind of relevance here, congratulate her on her achievement. But at the moment he failed to see it. Unless these marks spelt out the name and address of the killer, which they clearly didn't, he wasn't sure why the excitement.

"A name? What name?"

"Well, I can't be sure. I'm still working on it. But there are definite straight edges, definite curves. I'm going to go for the first letter, the deepest cut, being a C. Or a G. But I can see from your face, you're not impressed?" Susan's nails clicked on her keyboard. "Understandable. But here, have a look at this."

The screen went black, then seconds later, another image slowly came into focus. The blurred background he now knew to be human skin, the markings that first looked to him like tattoos.

"What do you see?" asked Susan, a breathless edge to her voice.

"Um, well, I'm no expert. It's taken from a different angle, slightly lighter, but from the size and shape quite obviously similar markings –"

"You can go further than that. Exact same marks. Made by the exact same buckle. I've worked on it most of the day. Dimensions, design, all identical."

"Sorry, but it would be, wouldn't it? Isn't it just taken from above, on a different alignment?"

Reality dawned as Susan slowly shook her head. He saw the spark of recognition in her steady gaze.

He widened his eyes and exhaled. "No way."

"Way." Susan handed him a manila folder. "Name Kerry O'Grady. Age 22."

Gareth flipped open the file and scanned the report. "Why the hell hasn't this been flagged up? What's Coleman playing at?"

"Whoa, hold fire. Read the report before you kick off. I've just had all the info faxed across from Llandudno. This is a suicide victim, no suspicious circumstances, a closed case. There's absolutely no reason to connect this case with Edwina …"

"Other than the bruising." He flicked through more grainy images of a smiling Kerry O'Grady. "I can't read all this, what's the basics? How did you find it?"

"I'd done a lot of work on the ligature mark, and I was fascinated by the buckle. To me, it was the only trace of the killer we had. He'd done a fine job with DNA, so scientifically I was at a dead end. I got the idea it was relevant somehow, that this buckle stood for something. I did a search on the pathology computer of any similar post mortem bruises in the past three years. I've spent all afternoon wading through them, and when

I got to O'Grady, well it kind of leapt out of the screen at me. The measurements taken at the PM were identical, down to the last millimetre, and the design … well … the more I look at it, the more I'm convinced. It has to be, doesn't it? It's not me gone mad, or trying too hard to find something to cling to, is it?"

Gareth shook his head, met the deep emerald eyes. "You are amazing, you know that?"

Susan gave a quick laugh. "Hardly. More a geek."

"I still can't believe nothing has come up in the investigation, though."

"I've read the file. It was labelled as a clear case of cut and dry suicide. Body was washed up," she noted Gareth's raised eyebrows and nodded, "yes, washed up on West Shore at Llandudno."

Gareth ran the area through his mind. "As the crow flies, that's diagonally opposite Beaumaris, isn't it?"

"Yeah, you can see the Great Orme perfectly from there."

"And how old is the case?"

"The body was found just over a month ago. But it had been in the water about the same period of time."

"What did the PM say about the marks on her neck?"

"It was recorded as a necklace, missing or broken."

"And how come they're sure it was suicide?"

Gareth realised he was bombarding Susan with questions like an expert witness in court. But he had to know. Her instincts were right. Spot on. He could feel it.

"Simple. Discounting the lungs being full of water, she posted suicide notes to her parents, her boyfriend and sister. Apparently, no doubt it was her writing."

"Easy enough though to force someone to write a note. Easier still to post it." He paused, taking in the information. "So, no clues to where she died?"

Susan shook her head. "Nope. No DNA at all. There were marks on her body consistent with a fall, but the body had been in the water a long time and sustained quite a bit of ecological damage by the time of the PM. There was a high content of alcohol found in the blood too. Apparently, according to family she'd had a drink problem, drugs too. She'd threatened suicide on numerous occasions and was getting counselling. Her boyfriend said in his statement she was always saying she was 'going to fly'. She talked about jumping off the Menai Bridge. The inquest ruled suicide."

"Where was she from?"

"Bangor."

Another weight lurched in his stomach. "A student?"

"No, she worked in a local café. But her boyfriend was a student. She shared a flat with him near the station."

"God. So, the killer could have thought she was a student? There could be a connection with the Uni?"

"It's a big leap of faith, but anything is possible, isn't it?"

"And you are willing to state the marks are made by the same buckle?"

"Absolutely. One hundred percent."

"Then we need to talk to Coleman. You do know what it means?"

"I am trying not to dwell on it."

Gareth exhaled. "Jesus."

"I know. I can barely think it, let alone say it."

They sat in silence for several seconds, clicks and whirrs of the lab equipment the only noise that interrupted the charge of static in the atmosphere.

Gareth broke the tension, sliding his stool away from the desk.

"I need to speak to Chris. Okay?"

Susan nodded as he pushed open the door.

Gareth growled in frustration as he paced the A&E car park. He pressed redial and listened as the phone connected to Chris's voicemail for the fifth time. Come on, he screamed in silence. Come on, answer your bloody phone. Coleman was probably off his head somewhere, or up to his neck in IOUs in the back room of some grotty pub, in some grotty back street, next to the grotty bedsit he now called home.

He was still a top copper, no one could deny that. But where was he when he needed him?

He slid his phone into his pocket and paused to light a cigarette, propping himself against a crash barrier. His hands shook as he struggled against the breeze to hold the lighter steady. This was massive. Absolutely massive. He wanted to take hold of Susan and cover her in kisses, swing her off her feet. But those days were well and truly over. He inhaled long and deep, scratching his knuckles, the itching scars, as he closed his eyes and let the nicotine work on him, calm him. As much as anything had any hope of calming him at the moment.

He could hear a phone ringing in the distance, and it took several seconds to realise it was his own. He yanked it from the back pocket of his jeans, noting Chris's number flashing on the display.

"Hello!" he snapped.

"Hey, just seen you've been calling. Are you okay?"

"Yeah, yeah. I've got something to run by you. Can we meet up? Now?"

"No can do, bud. I'm in the middle of something. I'm going be working through."

He heard an edge to Chris's voice. A tightness, an emotion that he recognised.

"What's up?"

"I wasn't going to call till the morning, till we had all the details …"

"Chris, mate, you're freaking me. What's up?"

"We've got another one."

"Another what?" His head spun, and he grasped at the words like a drowning man, unable to process their meaning.

"Another body. Same M.O. Identical rope, identical knots."

"No. Where?"

"Washed up on Caernarfon Bar. You know the sandbanks, far end of the Menai Straights? I'm in the police station in Caernarfon; the body is on its way to Ysbyty Gwynedd."

The voice sounded distant. His head swam. He knew Chris was still talking but the words were a jumbled mess. Another one.

Another one.

Shit.

"Do you realise what this means?" said Chris.

"I realised about twenty minutes ago," whispered Gareth.

"What are you talking about? Listen mate, we've got a serial killer on our hands!"

Gareth swallowed. "I know. Because Edwina wasn't the first."

Chris paused. "What? No, actually, save it. I'm on my way to the station. Meet me there. McRae wants you back on the team, soon as. I told him you'd be in. You up for it?"

"Yeah, course." He blew out a stream of smoke. "Christ …"

Chapter Nine

"Right then, listen up guys and gals. Can we get a bit of order in here?"

Gareth glanced up from his computer screen; the list of names and addresses of sexual offenders in the area had long since begun to blur. DI Ian McRae stood in front of the rectangular arrangement of desks, turning his head one way, then the other, until he had the attention of every person in the hurriedly assembled investigation room.

Around him, chairs scraped and mumbles stilled. Gareth refused to look up. He hadn't yet mastered the art of coping with his colleagues' reactions. Either the pitying, watchful gaze of the women or the nervous, accusatory glances from the men. He wasn't sure which was worse. Probably the unspoken insinuations he shouldn't be there, wasn't up to the job.

Chris had brushed off his fears with a wave of his hand. "You're paranoid, bud, over sensitive. No one's said a bad word to me, people are just concerned. You're liked, accept it."

But still nagging uncertainty ate away at his confidence. Why? As far as he was concerned, he had all the right reasons for being back on the case. He'd earned his place. Or rather Susan Connolly had earned it for him. So, was it a lingering fear he might crack again or break down in front of another witness? No, it wouldn't happen; he'd made a decision. The only way he would rid himself of this pit of boiling anger in his stomach would be to do his job well and find the son of a bitch.

"Right then, I don't think I need to tell you guys that what we're dealing with here is possibly the biggest investigation this force has ever faced. Certainly, the biggest most of you will ever have worked on. But you are in *my* team, and I have faith in every last one of you." McRae slid his coat from his shoulders, adjusted his cufflinks and flicked an invisible speck from the arm of his silk shirt.

He continued in his softly spoken Scottish accent. "Coleman ... let's take a look at what we know so far. Care to summarise the basics, please?"

McRae took a seat as Chris scraped back his chair and walked to the glass screen in the front of the room. There couldn't be two more contrasting characters in the whole of the police force. McRae, quiet and studious, immaculately dressed, and who had never, in all Gareth's time under his leadership, raised his voice once. He didn't need to. He only had the best on his team. It was a privilege to get there, everyone knew that, and even harder to stay. One bad result, one false move or example of poor judgment and you were out the door. He ran his department as efficiently as he ran his life.

Chris tucked his shirt into his trousers and tightened his tie as he turned to address the room. Gareth saw the beads of sweat on his top lip, the damp patch on the back of his crumpled shirt, and knew this was the part of the job Chris hated most.With his pen, Chris pointed at the row of three photographs along the top of the screen.

"Kerry O'Grady, age twenty two. Edwina Parry, age nineteen. Bethan Jones, age twenty."

Gareth's neck burned as numerous eyes flashed in his direction. He kept his gaze fixed forward, staring at the board as Chris began to write dates.

"These are the dates each body was found, and these are the last known sightings. We have Parry here, and the tenacious Dr Connolly, to thank for bringing O'Grady into the equation.

Good work, I'm sure you all agree." Gareth's cheeks blazed, more rustling behind him. "So, for the time being – subject to an ongoing file search by DC Whitlock – we are assuming these are all the victims to date. For future ease, we have named O'Grady as Victim One, Parry as Two, Jones as Three. I shall use these abbreviations from now on."

This was normal procedure, done to distance the real person behind the statistic from the often grueling details of the investigation. But Gareth was glad he wouldn't have the painful jolt to contend with every time Edwina's name was mentioned. Glad he could disconnect his cousin from 'Vic 2'.

Chris cleared his throat, and continued. "All three girls lived in Bangor at the time of their disappearance. Victims two and three were both students at Bangor Uni. Victim one wasn't, but she stayed with her boyfriend in student accommodation. This obviously gives us strong links to the Uni. We need to find out everything about each girl. Shared classes, shared tutors, shared outside interests? While we've not yet ruled out these may be random attacks, we need to be sure of any links between the victims, however tenuous. Nothing must be overlooked, no matter how irrelevant it may seem. Okay?"

Chris looked round as mumbled acknowledgements filled the room.

"Right, cause of death. You each have a copy of the initial post-mortem reports. There are similarities between each victim's murders, but there are differences too. Alcohol present in Victim One, drugs in Victim Three – possibly Rohypnol but we're waiting on the toxicology report."

Chris paused and held up a glossy photograph of the buckle imprint Gareth had seen in Connolly's office.

He continued, "This guy has done a mighty fine job of removing any trace of DNA so far. For me there are only two constants, the rope he used to tie up the victims and this belt and buckle. The rope is undergoing further tests; once we know more I shall want to know everything about it, down to every outlet where it can be bought and all details of recent sales. For now, I want to focus in on these ligature marks. This is a real 'Hallelujah' moment because it's our first direct link to the killer. Almost like his signature mark. Cause of death in both Vic two and three was strangulation, and although drowning was the cause with Vic one, there were signs of attempted strangulation with the same belt. So, he's keeping it. Why? Some kind of trophy? Or some other relevance? We have got to know. We need to find the belt. I know it goes without saying, but find the belt, find the killer."

Gareth flicked through the photographs of the post-mortem, pausing as Edwina's blank stare gazed back at him. He swallowed, turned the page, and studied the magnified markings on the neck of the final victim, Bethan Jones. Susan Connolly had been right; the marks were there, just as she'd predicted they would be, and so far as he could see it was all they had to go on.

McRae stood, a copy of the PM report in his hand, and joined Chris at the front of the room. He held the file aloft.

"Study this report in detail, all of you. It's not pleasant reading for sure, but you need to be completely conversant with all the facts. I agree with Coleman. To me, this ligature mark is the key. And the other thing that strikes me as vital is where he keeps the victims, some up to a fortnight. I want a search run on calls reporting any kind of odd behaviour or strangers hanging around, anything even slightly out of the ordinary needs to be looked into. I want every squat and derelict property searched, starting within a ten-mile radius. He could be keeping them on his own property, of course, but that's risky, plus there's a chance he's keeping them outside. Again, when you read the PM report, another consistent is ingrained dirt on the hands and knees, and two of the victims had flecks of white paint under their nails. I understand the samples have gone off to be analysed but it will take some time, so again, make a mental note and keep focused.

"Finally in summary, two points I want you to focus on. Who

and why? I know we have the possibility hanging over our heads that this is a random serial killer, sexually motivated, and it may prove to be. I pray it's not. They're the hardest kind of murderer to catch because there are no constants, no trends to follow or motives to fathom. But let's discount that for a second. If this guy does have a reason, then he is following a pattern, and we need to learn what that reason, that pattern, is. We need to get inside his brain, and get one step ahead of him. We need to find a link, from there we might find a motive, and from there it should be a small step to our guy. I want anyone and everyone who knew any of the girls to be questioned, and any who knew more than one of the victims, I want brought in for further interviews. Understood?"

More murmurs, polite coughs.

Gareth nodded.

"I've made a list here of who I'd like to partner up, and who I'd like to target which areas. If you have any strong objections, you know where my office is, but I trust my decision will be final." He looked around the room; the silence remained unbroken. "Anything else to add, DS Coleman?"

Chris paused, gripped the back of a chair, and licked his top lip.

"No, sir. Except … I know we are a good team. Shit, no, we are the best. But it goes without saying that this investigation is major, for more reason than one." Gareth returned Chris's glance with a terse nod. "I want to get this wrapped up as soon as possible. I want to get this sick bastard behind bars where he belongs. And I want to be able to release the bodies of the victims so they can at least be buried with dignity and rest in peace. This is personal, for all of us. Read the report and let's get cracking."

"Listen to the man, guys and gals, he speak the truth," said McRae as he slung his jacket over his shoulder. "Let's debrief 08:00 tomorrow. Best of luck out there." He paused alongside Gareth's desk. "A word, just now, Parry. My office."

Gareth flashed a look at Chris, who responded with a shrug. Gareth stood and followed McRae to his office.

McRae hung his coat neatly on the back of the door, before sliding into the leather chair behind his desk.

"How are you?" he asked, leaning forward so his elbows rested on the polished surface.

Gareth took a seat, cleared his throat. "Fine, sir."

McRae raised his eyebrows. "Really?"

Gareth felt his cheeks colour. "Well, you know. Considering."

McRae nodded. "If I'm totally honest my concerns at the moment are how you will cope. My usual instincts would be to follow normal procedure, where a close family member is concerned, and keep you a mile away from the investigation. But it's fair to say this is in no way normal. And there's nothing in the rules to say you can't work on the team when a distant relation is concerned – if you think you're up to it. We need every resource we have, and some. And we need our best detectives on the job. I count you among them, Parry."

"Thank you, sir."

"Coleman assures me it's the right thing, the only thing, to do. He knows you better than I do – and I trust him. Please don't let us down or prove his judgement wrong."

"I won't, sir. You have my word."

Gareth said a silent prayer. God, give him strength to keep his word. His knuckles began to itch, and he pushed his hands beneath his thighs to stop himself scratching the burning skin.

"How are your family? Your aunt?"

"Not good at the moment, sir. I hope she improves with time."

McRae nodded, propping his chin on his hands. Gareth squirmed under the scrutiny of his gaze. "I'm sure it will be a blessing once the body can be released for burial. I'll do all I can to speed up the process."

"Thank you, sir. It may help."

McRae studied him from under thick eyebrows. "Right, I think I've come to a decision. I think you're up to it …"

"What's that, sir?"

"We've called a press conference downstairs this afternoon. We have to put something official out as there's so much bollocks being printed just now it's unbelievable. Two objectives. I want you to make a direct appeal to the perp. Speak to him one to one, man to man, tell him you're on the case. You are on *his* case. Try to spook him a little, without provoking him. Secondly, at the same time I think your story will evoke sympathy from anyone who may be hiding him, covering for him, or maybe just has suspicions. I want you to face this guy across the power of the media. Do you think you're up to the job?"

Did he? Was he? A sickly sensation rose inside him, tugging at his guts. But it made sense. Who better to hit a nerve with a member of the public who may be unaware of the full details of the investigation? True, it was a chance they'd open the floodgates to an assortment of nutters and freaks, but there was always going to be that element and that risk.

Most importantly, it could be the first glimpse of the tiny needle in the giant haystack they faced. Anything he could do to assist that search would be his duty.

McRae leaned forward, his face level with Gareth's. "Parry? Can I count on you?"

Gareth pulled himself up straight, fixed his eyes forward and nodded.

"Without a shadow of a doubt. Bring it on, sir."

Chapter Ten

"... someone knows who this person is. Even if you aren't aware of it right now.

Someone, somewhere knows a detail that could be vital. However small and insignificant you think it is, please come forward. We need your help to find the key. One small lead to start the chain of events that will lead us to this murderer's door. Please help us. Please help me. I wouldn't wish on anyone the guilt I carry with me every day.

I will not rest until I can close my eyes at night without seeing the image of my cousin lying on a mortuary slab. I will not rest until I have some kind of closure, some revenge for the evil that brought such a premature end to Edwina's life. I cannot carry on with my own life until I see justice done and this man is behind bars.

If you are listening, you know who you are. I am coming for you. I work with the best detectives in the country. You can only run for so long; there is no way you will hide forever.

I urge you for the sake of all the victims' families to do the right thing now, it will be in your interests long term. Give yourself up and stand up to your punishment like a man.

That's all I have to say. Thank you."

With a growl, he lobbed a threadbare cushion at the screen and the close-up face of the young detective with the solemn expression and red-rimmed eyes. He drowned out the voice notifying the public of the relevant web address or telephone number they could call, in the strictest of confidence. He turned away from the faces of the young women that alternated across the screen.

Throwing his head back, he let out a roar of laughter, jumped from the seat and flicked off the power.

"You can't run. Oh, no. Nowhere to hide. Stand up! Stand up, y'hear, take yo' punishment like a man." He spoke between snorts of laughter. "Who do you think you are, eh? Like a man!"

He leaned against the doorframe as laughter stole his breath away. "Oh, you big man. You clever man," he gasped between pants. "Coming for me, are you? Are you, really? Oh, sweet Jesus, yo' killing me."

He grabbed hold of his side, bending double, waves of laughter erupting from him, until he choked back the noise, rubbing his watery eyes as he straightened.

"Well, let me tell you, big man. I got a surprise for you. I might save you the trouble."

In four strides, he crossed the saloon, balancing against the hull as the boat rocked on the ebb tide. He slid open a cupboard door, giving it a shove with his foot as the wooden panel stuck in the runner. Reaching inside, he pulled out a metal crate, bending to lift the lid which opened with a loud squeak. He removed a coil of blue rope and a pair of black leather gloves. Finally, with a gentle, almost reverential movement, he picked up a worn leather belt and threaded it through the loops on his jeans, patting the gleaming buckle as he secured it round his waist.

"Yeah, big man detective fucker. I do so love a challenge."

He straightened, fingering the belt. His gaze stretched across the expanse of blue, across the choppy water to rest on Bangor Pier in the far distance.

It was time.

* * *

Carly Clarke cursed under her breath, staggering as the toe of her trainer stubbed a tree root on the slippery path. Grabbing an overhead branch, she pulled herself upright, sniffing away tears. The steep, wooded path down to the beach had been perilous enough in daylight. Now, with the air thick with mizzling rain, and the after-effects of too much alcohol, the return journey was almost suicidal. But she had little choice. She cursed Marcus – and men in general – as she pushed forward through the dripping branches.

It had seemed like a lovely idea. A sunset barbecue on the beach at the old Bath House. An opportunity to chill out with friends, smoke a few joints, and put the world to rights. In hindsight, perhaps it was naive, but she'd been horrified when the evening turned into a drunken orgy.

At one point she'd tried complaining to her flat mate.

"Kate, I don't like this. It's getting out of hand. The guys are all stoned."

"So?" Kate shrugged and rolled her eyes before popping open another can of cider. "Just chill. You Americans are so po-faced."

"It's not that. It's Marcus. He's coming on to me real strong."

Kate laughed. "Well, I'm not surprised, Carl. You've been leading him on for the past month. The poor guy is desperate. Relax a little."

Relax my ass, she thought. If she had any intention of losing her virginity it wouldn't be to a drunken English sleazeball. Kate may put out to all and sundry, but she did not.

Carly cringed as she recalled Marcus's wandering hands. She could still taste the bitter tang of beer as he'd forced his tongue into her mouth.

He'd had his hand inside her bra and was struggling to unzip her jeans, when she finally managed to push him away. Breathing heavily, he'd lunged at her again, grabbing her hair. She pushed him away, halting him with a solid kick between his legs.

Marcus rolled away, hunched motionless, while Carly rubbed

her toes. At first, she thought he'd calmed down, seen reason. She waited awhile, hovering at the edge of the grassy bank, in case he wanted to talk. But when the pain began to subside, he leapt to his feet, his eyes dazed and filled with fury. Shouting her name and a barrage of insults, he lurched towards her. She hadn't waited to see what would happen. Before she had the chance to find out, she was on her feet and running. And she hadn't stopped.

As she reached a bend in the pathway at the top of the steep incline, she paused, hands on hips, to catch her breath. Her head throbbed from the exertion of the climb, not helped by the thickness of alcohol. She wished she'd said no to the third vodka. Or was it her fourth? Suddenly woozy, she fought back a wave of nausea. Bending to clutch her knees, she took several deep gulps of air and waited for the moment to pass.

When she turned and looked back down to the beach below, the dancing orange glow of firelight was still visible, flickering through the trees. She could hear the squeal and occasional shouts from those partying or getting it on. Someone had a portable stereo, and the strains of Muse drifted across the water like a scene from a poignant movie. She sniffed back a sudden rush of tears.

How could such a beautiful idea turn out so badly?

After the crowds and buzz of New York, this place was like a different planet. A complete and utter culture shock. It had taken her a long time to adjust, but now she had, she loved it, and didn't want her time here to end. North Wales was so beautiful. She adored being on the coast, with the mountains only a few miles away. She spent countless afternoons walking along deserted beaches or climbing rugged mountain tracks.

With a sigh, Carly turned her back on the view, and pushed open the rusted gate that led from woods, through a field and eventually out onto the road. As the gate squeaked in protest, she heard a sound behind her – the snap of a branch, like a gunshot in the darkness. She stopped and listened, holding her breath. Nothing but the faint hoot of a distant owl. She pulled her sweatshirt around her. The evening was turning colder now as the breeze carried the rain, moving in from the Irish Sea like a fine, grey delicate veil.

She hurried along, breathing deeply as the path started to climb again. This open field was another of her favourite places. The same wealthy Victorians who constructed the Bath House built this so-called folly – a ring of standing stones encircling a slate burial tomb. Carly didn't care if it was a hundred, or a thousand years old, it was mysterious, calm.

Halfway up the field, she heard the creak of the gate opening, and the dull thud as the old-fashioned chain weight pushed it back against its post. She stopped in her tracks and turned. She hadn't imagined it this time; someone was definitely following her.

"Marcus?" She squinted into the gloom. "Marcus, is that you?"

Silence.

She strained her eyes and ears, but could hear nothing except the faint rush of the incoming tide far below, and the thud of her pulse in her ears.

"Marcus, if it is you, quit goofing around. Go back to the party and leave me alone."

Silence.

She set off again, quickening her pace. This was ridiculous. She'd walked the length and breadth of Manhattan on her own, numerous times, and never once felt nervous. And yet here she was, not a few hundred yards away from friends and civilization, and acting like a scared halfwit.

Jeez, I need to get a grip.

She shook out her long black hair in a gesture of confidence and defiance, and marched across the field.

Her anxiety was fuelled by the disappearance of two female students over the past few months. She'd seen it on the television news and the University buzzed with speculation. She didn't know either of the girls, but she'd heard various tales of how they both disappeared without trace. All female students had been warned to be on guard, and always go out after dark in pairs.

The empty warning echoed in her ears, maybe her actions had been foolhardy. It was too late now. She had to keep moving. Within half an hour, she could be curled up in her warm bed, with the events of the evening nothing more than a regrettable memory.

Was it her imagination, or could she hear heavy breaths closing in behind her? She took long strides, starting to jog as she made out the gate leading onto the road. The welcoming glow of the orange streetlights, misty in the fine drizzle, egged her on. The headlights from a passing car lit the road for a few brief seconds. A warm yellow light illuminated the windows of houses strung along the road.

Only a few more yards and she would be safe.

Her feet slid and skidded on the wet grass but she held her balance. She worked on keeping her breathing regular, telling herself she was being paranoid. But she kept running, totally focused, never once looking back, although the noise had stopped and she couldn't sense anyone behind her now. Her run in with Marcus had made her jittery. She reached the gate, and let out a sigh as she swung it open and stepped onto the pavement.

A hand grabbed her hair, pulling her backwards. A rush of hot air hit her left cheek.

"Make a sound and I'll slit your throat. You get me?"

Cold steel pushed against her neck. She gulped and nodded. The voice wasn't Marcus's. She twisted and turned, trying to see his face, hoping to recognise him, praying it was all some huge joke, but her attacker held her in a vice-like grip, and, within seconds her head swam and her ears rang from lack of oxygen. They shuffled forward, joined together in a parody of a romantic dance, out onto the road. His gloved hand covered her mouth now. The knife below her ear.

He stopped at a car, releasing his grip on Carly's mouth as she heard the jangle of car keys. She sucked in deep gulps of air, looking around desperately, wanting to scream, but paralysed, too scared to utter a single word. There was nothing, no one. Not a sign of life.

The faint echo of music in the distance reached her ears. How she wished she were still down on the beach. Safer there than here. Why did she leave alone? How could she have been so stupid? She swallowed down the urge to scream, sure he would carry out his threat if she did. Her head jerked back sharply as his hand grabbed her round the neck. A rush of adrenaline pumped through her system. She struggled and kicked, her feet finding their target, but having no impact on his grip.

"Bitch!" he hissed.

He grabbed her chin, his fingers hard and cruel, and pressed a wet cloth over her nose and mouth.

Blackness.

Chapter Eleven

Dear Mrs West

My name is Jim Crawford from the University of Virginia. I just spoke to Pat Wallis, whom I believe you recently visited. I think she mentioned me to you.

I specialize in the phenomenon of child reincarnation. I believe strongly that this is a very real occurrence for a great number of children. Pat emailed me a taped recording of her interview, and a copy of the notes taken during her consultation with yourself, and your son, Jake.

I have studied the notes at length, and found very many similarities between Jake's condition and others I've researched over the years.

I would be very keen to communicate with Jake and yourself, as I believe I may be able to assist - particularly in relation to the problem of increasingly distressing nightmares. We've recently pioneered a successful regression therapy to help with such cases, and I'd like to see if they could help Jake and open up his past life memories for further investigation.

If you would like to contact me, or have any questions, all my details are at the foot of this email. Please do not hesitate to get in touch.

I look forward to hearing from you.

Kind regards

Jim Crawford.

Helen felt a surge of emotion as she clicked on reply and began typing. At last, after so many years …

Dear Dr Crawford,

Thanks so much for your prompt message. It is refreshing to finally find people with a genuine interest and concern for Jake. My experiences in seeking medical help, prior to visiting Dr Wallis, were disastrous.

I would be willing to investigate whatever form of therapy you feel would be appropriate for getting to the bottom of Jake's problems. I will need more information, but as long as you can reassure me that regression is a safe option, I would be more than willing to give it a try.

Please let me know if you require anything further, and what the next steps are.

Best wishes
Helen West.

Helen pushed her chair away from the desk and rubbed her eyes. It had been a long week and she was glad to get the last working day over. Friday evenings were her 'me time'. Jake was tucked up in bed. She'd enjoyed a long soak in the bath and was on her third glass of Chardonnay.

She opened a box of truffles and took a sip of wine. She was looking forward to settling down to watch an old episode of Inspector Morse – one of her and Mark's favourite programmes. She lit a couple of aromatic candles and stretched out on the sofa. She turned onto her side, burying her face into the cushion. The background music, relaxing vanilla fragrance, and effects of the alcohol, began to take over.

Her head nodded and her eyes closed.

It was the same dream as before. She was walking with Mark, in a field of freshly mown grass. In front of them an orchard, made up of rows of apple trees, their branches bending under the weight of white blossom. They were laughing and chasing each other between the trees. Mark caught her round the waist and spun her high into the air. Sunlight warmed her face. Happiness warmed her heart.

Their eyes locked, their lips met, and she relaxed. His lips moved from her mouth, to her neck, and then his warm breath tickled her ear. She loved the gentleness of his voice; still after so many years it made her knees weaken.

"Jake needs you, babe. I'm here for you. Never forget that. Jake needs you."

"What!"

Helen woke with a scream on her lips. It was only a dream. Just a bloody dream. She hugged the pillow to her chest as a pain that was almost physical engulfed her. All over again, she had to accept Mark wasn't there. Mark was dead. She would never touch him, or hear him, or smell him ever again. She gripped her knees to her chest, and rocked slowly, as tears rolled down her cheeks.

Suddenly, she recalled Mark's words from the dream. Something about Jake? Had he said Jake needed her? She turned down the volume on the TV and tilted her head towards the ceiling.

Nothing.

She adjusted the volume again, and wiped her eyes. Enough with the self-pity. Night time was always the hardest, and although alcohol did help her relax, it made her maudlin at times. She sighed, took another sip of wine, and tried to concentrate on Morse. A car chase scene. Lewis at the wheel, famous Oxford architecture flying past.

With a sigh, she sat up. It was no good, she had to go and check on Jake. She may have imagined Mark's words of warning in the dream, but she was too hyped up to concentrate. She switched off the TV and blew out the candles, pausing to give Holly a gentle shove with her foot. The dog roused herself with a grumble and sloped off to her basket in the kitchen.

Helen pulled herself up the stairs, gripping the banister for support. The alcohol made her feel light-headed, and the dream had upset her more than she wanted to admit. She pushed open the door to Jake's room. Her hand went to her mouth. He sat bolt upright in bed, eyes wide open, staring at some invisible sight at the end of his bed. His face was distorted in terror, but he was silent and still as a statue, transfixed by whatever was unfolding in his mind's eye.

Helen fought off the urge to panic. Dr Pat said she thought it better to try to wake him from the normal nightmares, but Helen sensed this was something different. Something worse. This was more sinister, more unnerving; she'd never witnessed this silent, cold contemplation before. The expression of horror on his little face sent shivers right through her. It looked as if he'd seen a ghost.

"Jake?" Helen approached the bed. "Jake, sweetie. Are you okay?"

"Rwyf eisiau cysgy."

"Jake?"

"Fy enw ydi Jacob. Rmyf yw un a'r ddeg."

"What, sweetie?"

Helen lowered herself onto the edge of the bed. Jake remained motionless; eyes wide open and fixed straight ahead. His whole body was rigid, his spine straight. Helen's hands shook as she leaned across the bed. She took Jake's right hand in hers, startled as he yanked it away.

"Mi Foddodd. Mi Foddodd!"

Helen hadn't a clue what language he was speaking, but she could tell he'd repeated the previous words. This time with more emotion. This time angry.

"Sweetheart, it's Mummy. Can you hear me?"

"Maen ddrwg."

"Jake, can you hear me? I don't understand you, sweetie. What are you saying?"

"Maen ddrwg!"

"Yes, I can hear you, Jake. But I don't understand. Speak properly, Jake. You're having another bad dream." She took his hand again. This time he didn't resist. Helen crawled across the bed and gathered Jake into her arms. She kissed the top of his head.

"What can you see, baby?"

Silence.

"Jake, what can you see in your dream?"

Silence.

She pulled him into her lap. His body was still rigid, but his eyes were closed, lips moving, forming words that didn't come.

"Come on, look at me, Jake. Wake up, honey."

Helen smoothed his hair and cradled him in her arms. Her instinct told her she had to try and calm him. She decided to try one of Dr Pat's exercises.

"Jake, can you hear me? I'm going to start counting from one, and as soon as you hear me, I want you to join in, okay? Concentrate on my voice, try to forget the dream. And start counting with me. Ready?"

Jake continued to mouth silent words.

"One, two, three, four, five, six, seven, eight .... " Helen paused, there was still no reaction. "Listen to my voice baby, I'm sure you can hear me if you try. Come on. Nine, ten, eleven, twelve ..."

"Mae'r Merched Wedi Marw!" Jake's scream startled Helen. His eyes shot open. *"Mae'r Merched Wedi Marw!"*

Helen gripped Jake as he screamed – a chilling, piercing note that froze Helen's soul. He began to hyperventilate; his body shook as if he were having convulsions.

Helen kept her grip tightly.

"Rhiowch gymorth imi! Blesio chynertha!"

Jake screamed again. This time, his arms flailed wildly as he seemed to fight off an invisible assailant. Helen gathered his arms and pinned them to his sides.

"Jake, stop it! Stop fighting. Stop it now!"

He continued to gasp for breath, but his arms relaxed. His body convulsed.

"Jake, you have to breathe! Breathe slowly. It's okay, sweetie. Just try to take normal breaths. Slow down, nice and slow; there, it's okay, baby."

Helen's voice caught in her throat. It scared her beyond measure. She pulled him against her chest and rested her chin on his head. He started to pull long drawn out breaths, and with each lungful his breathing slowed. As she rocked him, his body started to relax. She heard hiccups, realised Jake was crying, soft sobs that shook his body.

"It's okay, baby. Just a dream. Mummy's here. It's fine."

"No!"

"Yes, Jakey, it's okay. It's not real," she said, fighting to keep the tremor out of her voice. "It's just another bad dream. Dry your eyes, baby. It's all over now."

"No, Mummy!" He pulled away from Helen and scrambled to the top of the bed. He curled his body into a ball, hugging his pillow. "Mummy, I'm scared."

"It's just a dream, baby. You know, you talked to Dr Pat about it. There's nothing to be scared of. It's not real."

"It is. It is real."

"Jake, please, calm down. Let's curl up and go to sleep, and it will all be fine again in the morning."

"No!"

"What's the matter, Jake?"

"Don't turn out the light. Don't make it go dark!"

"Okay, we can leave the nightlight on. Don't be scared." "I am scared, Mummy."

"Why?"

"Because I saw them! The girls! The girls are all dead!"

A chill engulfed Helen's body. She wrapped her arms around herself as if they might protect her, but from what, she had no idea.

Jake cowered against the wall, in the furthest corner of his bed, gripping his pillow with both hands, holding it in front of him like a shield. Silent tears poured down his face. One hand released the pillow, and his thumb crept into his mouth. It was clear the dream was still vivid to him.

"What do you mean, sweetie?" Helen struggled to keep her voice calm and steady. "What girls are dead?"

"I don't know. But I saw them. I saw them!"

"Okay, baby, it's okay. What you saw isn't real."

"It is. It is real. They're dead. I saw them!"

"You were having a dream. You know, like before, when you saw the island and the blue boat. Like we told Dr Pat. Remember?"

Jake shook his head, stubbornly.

"Yes, Jake. Dr Pat explained it to you. It's a memory of another life that you see when you're sleeping."

Jake sucked on his thumb, and started to rock back and forth.

"I know it's real and scary now, sweetheart. But it's only a nightmare; nothing can hurt you. You're awake now."

"No! Mummy no! This isn't a dream."

"Yes, it is Jake …"

"No!" Jake knelt and raised himself to his full height and shouted, "This is real!"

"Okay, okay, calm down, sweetie. Do you want to tell me about it?"

He shook his head. "No, I can't. It's bad."

"I know, but maybe it might help to talk about it."

"No, he's bad and he will know."

"Who?"

"The bad man."

"Who is he?"

"I don't know."

"Who were the girls?"

"I don't know."

"Where were they?"

"In a black room, there were no windows. I saw them crying. I heard them scream. They were scared, Mummy, scared of the nasty man."

"And was this with your other family, you know, your Ireland mummy and daddy?"

Jake's brow furrowed. "I think so. But … I'm not sure."

"Were you alone?"

"No, someone was there, someone showed me. We saw the girls and we saw the bad man. Then we ran away from him. It was dark and scary. Oh, Mummy!" Jake let out a gasp. "Please don't let the nasty man come and get me too!"

"Shush Jakey. Shhh … Come on, let's cuddle. I promise you, I swear on my life the bad man isn't here." Helen pulled down the duvet, crawled into bed, and held out her arms. After a few seconds, Jake shuffled forwards on his knees into her embrace. She pulled the cover over them and hugged Jake tightly.

"See, baby," she whispered into his hair. "It's all safe here. We have Holly downstairs on guard. If any bad men come, she'll bark and let us know. It's safe for you to sleep now. I promise. Okay?"

Jake nodded, and Helen watched as he snuggled his face into the pillow. He looked pale; she could see the exhaustion in his eyes. Within a few minutes he was sleeping, but he still whimpered occasionally, and it was a while before his breathing smoothed.

Helen's head spun. What on earth had happened tonight? She tried to follow it through, trying to recall the strange words Jake had used. If only she'd had a tape recorder handy. She'd been so determined to quieten him, she'd forgotten to ask him about it. Her brain buzzed with questions. Who were the girls? Who was the 'bad man'? Where had these latest memories come from?

But the traumatic experience had also drained the last of her own resources, and against her will, she too drifted to sleep.

* * *

Helen's fingers trembled as she pushed the keys on her mobile phone. She felt bad calling on a Saturday, but she had to talk to someone. The waiting had been agony, but if her calculations were correct it was about nine am now in the US state of Virginia.

The transatlantic beep of the ring tone made her pulse quicken.

"Hello. Jim Crawford."

"Dr Crawford? This is Helen West speaking. We exchanged emails recently about my son, Jake ...."

"Mrs West. Hi there! It's nice to hear from you."

"You too, Dr Crawford. And before I go any further, I want to apologise for calling you on a Saturday."

"Hey, no worries. I have private classes later today, so it's just a routine working day for me."

"Well, I feel very forward contacting you on a weekend, but I had to talk to someone."

"Why? What's happened, Mrs West?"

"Helen, please."

"Then please call me Jim. So what's on your mind?"

"Jake had another nightmare last night. But it was totally different from any he's had previously."

"How?"

"Well for a start there was much less physical movement – no screaming and very little of the usual thrashing around. Secondly, when he spoke he used a foreign language ..."

"Ah, you mentioned this in the notes I got from Pat Wallis."

"Yes, there has been the odd word or two before. But this time he spoke, well shouted, everything in this language. I've never heard anything like it. I've tried to liken it to something I've heard, and the nearest I can come up with is Gaelic. Honestly, it's like something out of a Tolkien novel. I really struggle to describe it."

"You didn't think to write it down, or tape any of it, I take it?"

"No, I'm sorry. Dr Pat suggested keeping a tape recorder handy, but I hadn't had chance to organise it. And it wasn't the time for taking notes."

Jim Crawford tutted. "No, I'm sure shorthand was the last thing on your mind. It may have helped, but it's no big deal. So, was this what upset you?"

"No, no, not at all. The worrying thing is that whatever Jake saw in his dream last night, he's convinced it's real. He's not sure it's connected with the past life memories that he's had before. It certainly scared him much more."

Helen relayed the after effects of the nightmare to Dr Crawford. He asked a few questions, and Helen explained the circumstances and recounted Jake's words as accurately as possible.

"So, what do you think, Dr… erm … Jim?" she asked.

"I don't know. I really don't know."

Helen imagined him tapping his pen against the desktop and shaking his head as he mused. She liked his strong American twang and wondered what he looked like.

"I'm going to take a look at some case studies," he continued after a pause. "We have several thousand on file at the University. Off the top of my head, nothing you've told me rings any bells. But, that's not to say there's not something out there."

"Is there anything I can do?" asked Helen. "Anything that can stop the nightmares? It's hard to see your son going through this night after night."

"I won't patronise you by telling you not to worry. He's your only son, you're gonna worry, right? Hang in there, okay. I'm afraid to say that right now there's little that can be done. But, if we can get to the bottom of what's causing the increase in the nightmares, and try to get to find out about these deaths he says he saw – then hopefully we can look to try to stop them. My initial thoughts are that these deaths are something traumatic that occurred in his previous life, but I can't be sure. They don't usually manifest themselves so strongly."

"I see."

"There's lots to do. It won't be easy, but I think it can be done. At the very least, I promise you I'll give it my best shot."

"Thank you." Helen couldn't manage another word.

"Hey, I promised Pat Wallis I'd look out for you. And she'll kick my butt if I let you down!" He laughed.

"I can't thank you enough, Jim."

"Don't thank me at all yet, Helen. Thank me when we've cured Jake, okay?"

"Okay."

"I'm not trying to get rid of you or anything, but you're gonna be getting one hell of a phone bill, so we should make a move. Are you on MSN or Skype? It's probably cheaper for non-urgent conversations."

"Yes, I have both. I'll email you the details."

"Sure, but hey, promise me, if you have any concerns or need to talk, you just pick up the phone, okay. Don't worry about the time difference. Honestly, it's not a problem."

"Thank you."

"I said don't thank me yet …"

"I know, but thank you anyway. I don't want to cause you any hassle by calling in the middle of the night or something though …"

"It's no hassle. I'm a light sleeper. You learn to be in my line of work. I've spent much of my life on call twenty-four hours."

"How does your wife cope?"

"If I ever marry, I'll be sure to ask her."

"Oh, I see. I'm sorry. I assumed …." Helen stammered and her cheeks burned, suddenly glad of the expanse of Atlantic Ocean between them.

As if sensing her embarrassment, he moved on. "Right, well I have to be at University for ten. But I promise I'll email you within the next few days, when I've had a chance to do some research and talk to a couple of my colleagues who may be able to help."

"Okay, yes that's fine. Thanks again. I really do appreciate your help."

"Sure, no worries, and if you need to talk to anyone closer, I know Pat Wallis won't mind you calling her either."

"No, it's fine. I feel much calmer now."

"Good, we'll speak later then, okay? It's been nice to talk to you, Helen. You have a nice day, now."

"You too. Bye Jim. Thank you."

Chapter Twelve

"You sure about this, buddy? Last chance to walk away."

Gareth paused, one hand on the shop door. "I was going to walk away, Chris, I'd have done it that day at the mortuary. That was the hardest thing I've ever had to do in my life. Believe me, this is a walk in the park."

Chris took a final drag on his cigarette before flicking it into the gutter with a nod. "Had it figured you were there to see Connolly that day. Not me."

"You put on a good act then …"

"So did you." Chris met Gareth's eye; his face, first stern, slipped into a sly smile. "So, the rumours are true then?"

"What rumours would they be?"

"Come on, you know. The one about you showing the gorgeous doc your hidden talents."

Gareth pushed the heavy door with his shoulder as Chris followed him up the steps. "No idea what you're getting at, mate. Besides, I'm sure you've heard the other rumour – that a gentleman never reveals his secrets."

Gareth's skin prickled at the sudden drop in temperature. Dusty windows and high bookshelves blocked the bright afternoon sunshine. He sniffed. The Muse had the musty, antiquated smell he always associated with bookshops, old or new. He wasn't a bookworm; too many memories of hours of tedious revision and failed examinations. He was too busy, too active, too in demand, to bother with fiction. Books could wait until he could no longer live the life he wanted and was forced to find solace in a virtual one. The last time he'd set foot in one of the high street chains was to buy the latest, must-have crime thriller for Edwina last Christmas. He pushed the thought away, concentrated on keeping the dam intact.

What sounded like a wind chime tinkled and with a swish of curtain, a stooped grey-haired woman with crimson lipstick that bled into a network of tiny lines around her mouth, appeared from a back room and propped herself against a wooden counter.

"Good morning. Can I help you, gentlemen? Anything in particular you're looking for?"

Her eyes were bright, but suspicious; her gaze followed Chris as he moved sideways between the bulging piles of paperbacks and haphazard rows of hardback atlases and travel books, biographies and various study guides. Gareth could easily see why Edwina had loved the place; organised chaos had been very much her thing.

He cleared his throat. "Good morning, ma'am." He reached into his inside pocket and flashed his identification. "Detective Sergeant Parry and DS Coleman, North Wales CID. Could you tell me if you're the proprietor here? We would be grateful if you could spare us a few minutes to answer a couple of questions regarding an ongoing investigation. We won't take up too much of your time."

She scowled for a moment. Deep furrows lined leathery skin as she took her time to read the details of his badge, white eyebrows creasing into a frown. And when she spoke her voice took on a superior tone. "I am co-owner here, yes. Has there been an accident? Is Glyn okay?"

"Glyn?" Coleman's voice came over his left shoulder.

"My son. Co-owner here."

"We're not here about your son, Mrs … er …"

"Rogers. Eirian Rogers. Oh, thank the good Lord." She swooned slightly, touching the back of her hand against her forehead. There was something old-fashioned and melodramatic in almost every movement and word. "I'll just have a seat if you don't mind." She lifted herself onto a stool behind the desk. What Gareth had taken for a wind chime was an assortment of thin, gold bangles which adorned both arms. They seemed oddly out of place with the rest of her attire, and clinked together as she adjusted herself on the stool.

"I'm sorry to be a drama queen," she added. "I live on my nerves, you see, and with Glyn involved in such a dangerous job, well, I suppose I always jump to the wrong conclusion." She patted her chest, more tinkling, fingered a large silver cross pendant and fanned her face with a catalogue. "Dear me, dear me. Give me a few moments. I'll be fine."

"I'm sorry to have upset you, Mrs Rogers, it wasn't our intention," said Gareth, flashing a warning look at Chris.

One thing Chris lacked, in Gareth's opinion, was tact with witnesses. Chris nodded, shoved his hands in his trouser pockets and turned to examine a display of books on the paranormal, one of his obsessions. The disparaging glance said it all. Chris had clearly made his mind up that this was a waste of time and energy, and Gareth was welcome to beat his head against a brick wall if he so wished.

"You mentioned your son is co-owner here? Hardly a dangerous job in the scheme of things?"

He smiled and gave what he hoped was a boyish wink.

"Oh, no, one hardly puts one's life on the line at The Muse," she said, allowing herself a smile. "Glyn works on the RNLI Lifeboat, out of Beaumaris. We live in Menai Bridge, you see. He divides his time between here and there. He adores it. I think he lives out all his childhood fantasies, rather like James Bond, you know, high speed chases across the wide open sea. Whereas I'm left here with the weight of the world on my shoulders." She paused for breath, took out a handkerchief and dabbed her nose, accompanied by more bangle chimes. “Mind, I should be used to it. The waiting at home, I mean, with both my boys off at sea most of the time. Thirty odd years, Glyn’s father was on the same lifeboat. God rest his soul. Captain for the last ten. Gave his life to the RNLI, he did. And after all the lives he saved, you’d think the Lord would’ve thought he’d earned a decent rest and retirement. But then, cancer shows no mercy, no preference for race nor creed. But there you are …”

Gareth heard a loud cough from behind him, and could almost sense Chris loitering near the door, one hand on the handle. He refused to turn in his direction. Ignoring his partner’s impatience, he slid a hand inside his jacket pocket, removing the photo of Edwina. He flipped the photo over, held it up in front of Mrs Rogers’ face, concentrating on the whiteness on the reverse.

“Do you know the girl in this photograph?”

Mrs Rogers leaned forward, squinted for a second, then nodded. “Yes, her name is Edwina. She used to work evenings in the shop, two or three days a week, sometimes more during the holidays. But she doesn’t work here anymore, I’m afraid. Are you looking for her?”

“Erm … no. I’m aware she worked here. I wondered what you could tell us about her. Or perhaps fill us in on the reasons she left –”

Gareth paused as he registered the slow shaking of her head.

“I’m afraid I can’t help. Glyn does the hiring and the firing. And Edwina covered evenings when I wasn’t here. I have dancing lessons on a Monday; Bingo on a Tuesday, you see, so I rarely ever saw her. Polite enough girl, from what I recall. Loved her books, very studious, I’d say. Oh, and the brightest smile. Could light up a room that smile, and the customers loved her. Never had a word of complaint. Real shame she’s gone.”

Gareth felt something tighten inside his chest. “Have you no idea why she left?”

She shook her head again. “No. I came in one day and there

was a new girl here. Glyn was training her up. I can't recall … wait, I think he said she'd let him down over the Easter holiday, not shown up for work. I think I made some remark how unlike her it was. I'm sorry, I really don't know. I can call Glyn if you'd like me to ask for you …"

"No." Gareth raised a hand. "We'll catch up with him in due course, I've no doubt."

"So, is she in trouble then, the young girl? I can only speak as I find, mind, but she didn't strike me as the wild type at all. I hope it's nothing serious …"

"I'm afraid it is serious. Edwina is dead, ma'am. But I'm sure you understand this is part of an ongoing investigation. We can't reveal further details at the moment."

"Dead?" The woman rubbed her ear as if she'd misheard; her bangles clinked.

Gareth took a moment to observe her reaction. The shock seemed genuine, but would someone who clearly kept her finger very much on the pulse be unaware of Edwina's death? He found that hard to believe.

"You didn't know?" he asked.

She shook her head. "Was it an overdose?"

"Suicide? Why?" said Gareth, swallowing a spark of indignation on Edwina's behalf.

"No reason, none at all. I just thought … you know …"

Gareth shook his head. From the corner of his eye, he saw Chris shrug in response.

Mrs Rogers stared from him to Chris and back again, clearly hoping to read something in the detective's solemn expression. Her cheeks flushed a pale pink and she resumed the fanning motion. "Students, you know? Drugs and the like –"

"Edwina didn't do drugs," said Gareth.

"Oh no, I'm sure she didn't. I wouldn't want to be casting aspersions. But these students, some of them are a bad lot, you know. And the most innocent ones can get tangled in the web …"

"Edwina didn't do drugs," he repeated, slightly louder. Something in his words or his expression made the woman shut her mouth with a snap.

"No."

"And it wasn't suicide, ma'am," added Chris. "It was murder."

Gareth watched her eyes widen, flash to Chris. "No!"

"Yes," said Gareth. "I'm afraid so." He leaned forward. "Anyway, thank you for your help. This is my card; my direct number is here at the bottom. If you think of anything, anything at all, please give myself or DS Coleman a call. Okay?" She fingered the card and nodded as he continued. "We will need to speak to your son, Mrs Rogers, just to help us build up a better picture of Edwina's life, perhaps her final few days. I'm interested to find out when he last spoke to her or saw her. Do you know where he is at the moment, or what time he's due back?"

"He's not due in today. He has some training course, over at Beaumaris. I'm sure he'll be there all day."

"That's fine. Thank you for your time, Mrs Rogers."

Gareth backed away from the counter. As Chris pulled the door open, he heard his name.

"Detective Parry? I say, I'm right aren't I? I've just remembered her last name. Parry. Were you related?"

He nodded. "She was my cousin."

"Sure you don't want a chip?"

Chris pushed the polystyrene cone under Gareth's nose. He recoiled and shook his head, turning to blow out a stream of cigarette smoke, watching it catch on the breeze as it snaked out over the ocean.

"Nothing tastes as good as chips by the sea," said Chris with a swallow. "Takes me back to family outings as a kid. We only made it as far as New Brighton most Bank Holidays, but as long as I could sit on the concrete steps, watching the ships going up and down the Mersey, with a portion of cod and chips in my greasy paws, I was as happy as Larry."

"Yeah? Always liked your food then?" said Gareth with a wry smile.

Chris's face clouded into a frown as he sucked in his ample gut. "I'm just big boned, bud. I'm sick of telling you. Pure muscle, it is. Take a feel." He flexed a bicep and held out his arm.

"I believe you. Finish your chips."

Gareth stared out across the choppy waters of the Menai Straits. Listening to the squeals of children on passing canoes. Even being this close to the ocean brought on the trickle of fear in the pit of his stomach, the damp palms and quickened breaths. An image flashed into his mind, building his panic. What if a child fell off a canoe? Sinking down into the inky water. Him duty bound to leap to the rescue. How could he? How?

An accident on a dinghy was the original source, eight years old on a scout trip. The boat overturned, trapping him by his life jacket, ripping the cord, dragging him under as the dinghy capsized; feeling the rush of water into his lungs, feeling the air squeezed out in one gigantic gulp, tasting acrid salt on his tongue, filling his head and his chest until he was sure he would explode like an over inflated balloon.

He shook his head, pushed the images away, and concentrated on the scenery. From Beaumaris pier, it had to be one of the most idyllic views in the whole of Wales. If not the whole of Britain. Snowdonia stretched out before him like a giant oil painting. A vision of greens, blues and greys, as if one of the great artists had created the most magnificent canvas with remarkable detail. And to his right, jutting out into the water, was Bangor Pier and the town beyond. The unmistakable architecture of the university rose against the skyline. All roads leading him back to Edwina.

"Hey, I think we have action stations." Chris stood and threw the chip paper in the bin. "Looks like the lifeboat coming in now. Let's go and catch up with Mr Rogers."

"Dead? Oh my God. Dead?"

Glyn Rogers staggered against the desk in the compact communications office. His face turned a waxy shade of grey and he took short gasps while holding his chest in a manner reminiscent of his mother.

"I can't believe it. I'm sorry. I don't know what to say." He looked at each detective in turn, eyes brimming with tears. "I've not seen her for weeks. She left all of a sudden, let me down with no notice. But I never thought, I mean, how could I? I assumed she'd gone home, or met a man, or … I don't know really what I thought, other than how out of character it was." He paused, revealing a set of small pearly-white teeth as he grimaced. "God, I left a couple of snotty messages on her voicemail. I rang and rang, and in the end I lost my temper a bit. Of course, I didn't know. How could I know? I'm sorry."

Chris flashed a look at Gareth, and he knew exactly what it meant. It may have been the guy's mother who admitted to a problem with nerves, but he was definitely affected by the news more than they would usually expect in an employee, employer relationship. There had to be a reason. But Gareth was professional enough to know that reason didn't mean Glyn was guilty either.

Chris cleared his throat. "Of course, there's no way you'd know. Don't worry about it."

"She was such a lovely girl, we got on really well. She loved books as much as I did. I suppose when she left, I felt hurt … you know, personally hurt. Edwina was a good friend to me, a good listener." He looked up, eyes bright. "I suppose I'm trying to explain why it's such a shock. I expect you're thinking my reaction is a bit over the top, but I was genuinely fond of Edwina. I tried to contact her. I even went round her house over the Easter weekend, thinking she might be ill or something, but no one was home. She wasn't … I mean, she wasn't there, was she? At home, I mean. Dead? While I was downstairs hammering on the door?"

Chris shook his head. Gareth's mind raced. How did he know her bedroom was upstairs? Or was he being paranoid and that was a natural assumption anyone would make?

"No, she wasn't found at home," said Chris. "But I'm afraid we can't go into detail at this point. This is a murder investigation which has reached quite a sensitive stage. We're doing our best to keep some details out of the media, helps eliminate the freaks, you know?"

"Of course. But murder? Oh, God. Of course, I understand."

"So, can you remember when you last saw Edwina?"

"It would have been the Tuesday before Easter. She worked the evening shift as normal. We closed up together at 9pm. I dropped her off at Ty Mawr ..." He trailed off with a loud sniff. "She waved from the doorstep, big wide smile. We'd been talking about the trip to London. She was so excited. I'll never forget her smile –"

"And after the day she failed to turn up for work, and the visit to her digs, you've not bothered to try to contact her or ask anyone about her?"

"No. I didn't know her friends or family. I wouldn't know who else to contact."

"What about her pay? Her P45?"

"I didn't think. Well, she left without notice, didn't she ..."

Chris gave a grunt, changed tactics. "I have to admit I'm a bit shocked that you had no idea about her death."

Glyn scowled. "Why? How would I? What are you inferring, detective?"

Chris slid off the edge of the desk. "Inferring? Me? Nothing, sir. It's just DS Parry here made a public appeal on TV last week, and the local newspapers have been awash with stories, although unconfirmed, about missing female students. Did you never tie any of this up with Edwina's disappearance?"

"No, detective. Remiss of me, no doubt. But I'm sorry I did not."

"And your mother tells me you've already trained up a

replacement?"

Glyn's frown deepened. "My mother? You've spoken to my mother already?" His tone had lost the nasal whine; there was a steely edge creeping in. His dazzling white smile was even more forced.

Chris affected a surprised tone. "Oh, didn't we mention? Sorry, yes, we called at The Muse. Your mother told us where to find you."

"I hope you haven't upset her. She has a delicate disposition."

"No, we left her in full working order. She couldn't assist us I'm afraid."

"Well, no, she wouldn't. She hardly knew Edwina. I take charge of the staffing."

"That's what she said."

"I'm sorry. I'm protective of my mother, she's somewhat highly strung, nervous you know. She's a trained actress, classical. I think the reality of real life is sometimes a shock to her, and I do my best to protect her. Understand?"

It explained his mother's dramatic responses and odd appearance. Clearly, in her mind she was still on the stage at The Old Vic.

"Perfectly," replied Chris. "Trust us, she's fine. We are just looking for any help we can, exploring every avenue. Edwina's death was traumatic, we're keen to catch the person responsible before he has chance to do it again."

"I can't think of anything to help you. I'm sorry. Really."

"What about friends, associates? Did she mention anything that may have been worrying her? Did you notice any sudden change in her demeanour?"

Glyn scowled, ran a hand through his damp mop of curly brown hair. "Nothing. I mean, I'll think on it, I promise you. But nothing springs to mind. If she was worried about anything, I'm sure she would have told me. And friends … well, her housemates and fellow students, of course."

"Boyfriend?"

"I … no … not that I'm aware of." Glyn stammered, dropped his gaze. "She never seemed interested in boys, passed them off as immature …"

"What about men?"

Glyn looked up. "What do you mean?"

"Well, some young women are attracted to the older man, aren't they? Someone mentioned Edwina had a group of friends she'd met at *The Muse*, and that there may have been a professor included?"

Glyn's eyes widened. "Oh, yes. I see. Professor Randall. Art and History. I have his number in my phone. He'd got quite close to Edwina recently. I'm sure he'd be willing to speak to you." The smile lingered as he scrolled through the contacts on his mobile and scribbled the number on a pad. "There you go. I'm sure it won't take you long to rule him out of your enquiries once you've spoken to him."

"Thank you, sir." Chris folded the paper. "And if you think of anything at all, here's my number. Would you call me, please?"

Glyn stood, accepting the card. "Of course. And good luck, detective. I hope you catch this evil man."

Gareth glanced back several times as they crossed the green in front of the lifeboat station, and each time Glyn was still leaning against the window frame, following their progress. On the last occasion, Gareth noted he had his mobile to his ear.

"He's making a phone call. Coincidence?" he said as slid into the passenger seat of Chris's Volvo.

"Dunno. Something weird about him. Can't put my finger on it. The shock was genuine though, I'd swear on that."

Gareth nodded. "Yeah. He's uneasy though. Hiding something, perhaps something Edwina knew. And why did he have a kind of triumphant air about him when we questioned him about the professor?"

Chris shrugged as he clicked his seat belt buckle into place. "Dunno. But while we're this close to the uni, I say we drop in unannounced and pay a visit to Professor Randall."

Gareth nodded as he took one last glance at the blurred figure of Glyn Rogers, still motionless in the window.

Chapter Thirteen

He gave the storage compartment one final kick for good measure. Nothing. The God-awful persistent praying, in the God-awful Yankee whine, had finished hours ago – replaced by thick, rattling breaths and bouts of coughing, accompanied by occasional weak sobbing. Now, there was only silence. Bending, he took hold of the thin end of the belt that hung out of the lid. He yanked it once. Twice. Three times. Holding the strap with care, like a fisherman handling a catch, tensing his fingers against the leather, waiting for any sign of life. The familiar tug of a catch on the hook. There was none.

He jumped up the steps in the bridge and cut the engine. Here would do. Quite a perfect spot. As close as he could get to Puffin Island and Penmon lighthouse without getting caught in the vicious currents. With luck, and a strong tide, the body would be washed up in a few days. Red Wharf perhaps or Benllech. He liked to add a little variety to his work. Keep the cops on their toes, and give other local plods a taste of the action. A nice, grisly body must make a change from petty drug busts or speeding fines. And also confuse the idiot detectives of North Wales CID just that little bit more. But no, he was forgetting himself. What had that cocky Detective Sergeant Parry said? *I work with the best detectives in the country. I am coming for you.*

He covered his mouth to conceal his grin. Idiot. Fucking idiot. He really had no clue what he was up against. Okay, it was only a coincidence that Edwina had a big-shot detective cousin. It hadn't been part of his plan and it had him pissed for a while. But it was karma, right? All the more of a challenge, not to mention an opportunity for him to hone his skills before the next one. The important one.

Hadn't his mother always said he was an exhibitionist as a boy? Especially in front of his sister. How he loved to hear applause and laughter when he knew he was centre stage. His heart hammered as he thought of his sister. He pushed the thought away. Yes, he liked to show off even now. So, it was only natural that a big part of him got a massive kick out of gloating in front of Detective Parry. He had so much planned; he was itching to make a start.

But he had more pressing issues at hand. Another minor inconvenience to get out of the way before he moved onto the next stage of his plan.

He pressed the button to release the anchor, listening to the rattle of the chain, the gentle splash as it entered the water. Grabbing his binoculars from the hook on the door, he scanned the horizon, turning on the deck a full three hundred and sixty degrees. Last thing he needed was some nosey fisherman turning up at just the wrong moment, or as had nearly happened with Edwina, some mad-headed jet-skier arriving out of nowhere.

Nothing to be seen but mile after mile of choppy blue water, dark blue today under a thundery looking sky.

With a nod, he bent his head and jumped down two sets of steps, back into the bowels of the small boat. He took a key from his pocket and unfastened the heavy padlock on the storage bench, before lifting the lid with a grunt. He stood back, his heart pounding as he gazed down at the young woman. Her hands gripped a silver cross, fingers laced across her chest as if in prayer. She looked at peace. That was good. He was pleased her God had come good for her in the end.

He reached forward and undid the buckle on the leather belt. With care, he slid it from around the grey skin. Touching the leather to his lips, he placed it into the next drawer along and covered it with a soft cloth. Her neck was bruised in places, with a trickle of dried blood under her chin. Bending, he gripped the body under the knees and across her back. She was lighter than she looked, and it took little effort to lift her from the box, and secure her ankles and wrists with a length of rope. He tied a small Hessian sack to the ropes around her feet and grabbed beneath her arms, manhandling her up onto deck. He gave another quick look around as he steadied himself against the doorway. Satisfied at the seclusion, he dragged the girl across the deck and hefted her over the side rail.

The corpse balanced for a moment, as if gravity was unable to make a decision. Then with a slow-motion kind of grace, the head fell back, exposing the blackened skin on her neck, and she slid silently into the water. He watched as her hair spread out across the inky water as the weights pulled her upright, and dragged her down, slowly lower, until finally she disappeared into the blackness.

No drama today. No unexpected disasters. He remembered the young Scouse girl. How her eyes opened as she'd hit the icy water, dragging in a loud rasping breath as she woke with a start. How had he let that happen? He'd never make that mistake again. He hadn't panicked, he'd remembered his training. He caught hold of her thrashing body with the boat hook, pulled her back to the side of the boat. As she reached out to grab his hand, eyes wide with relief, he'd swung his lump hammer hard against the side of her head. She'd crashed backwards, in seconds the water was a pool of red, rather like a scene he remembered from Jaws.

Yes, he'd coped, but he didn't like surprises.

With a triumphant last glance out into the ocean, he stepped down into the bridge, started up the engine and headed back to shore, whistling a jaunty tune as he gripped the wheel. He felt good. Everything was working exactly to plan. And now the little Yankie bitch was out of the way, it was time to move on.

Time to make the final preparations for the next one. The big one. It was time. At last. He threw back his head and laughed; the noise carrying across the water on the strengthening breeze. Today, he felt invincible. Nothing could go wrong. Nothing could hurt him.

If DS Parry was coming to get him, time was running out – that cop really needed to get a move on.

Chapter Fourteen

Helen lifted her face to the warm shafts of sunshine and watched Jake. He sat on his haunches on a blanket in the centre of the lawn, patiently observing as Pat's husband separated seeds into individual pots. Then with a little plastic trowel, Jake filled each pot with compost, tongue poking out, brow furrowed in concentration.

Her heart tugged as she realised all the things Mark missed out on. Jake too …

"Take a seat, Helen," said Pat. "I'll make a start on lunch in a moment, but I want to have a chat with you first in private."

"Oh?" Helen's breath caught in her throat. "How did Jake get on today? You mentioned these were different tests ..."

"Yes, behavioural tests and a language experiment. Don't worry, he did fine on all counts. Jake is above average for his age on all the intelligence tests." Pat smiled. "You have nothing to worry about on that score."

Helen exhaled as she took the seat beside Pat on the sofa. "Good … that's good to know."

"Jim Crawford decided we need a base set of results to start from, so we can say all the boxes are ticked. Jim's putting a lot of time and effort into this, and he wants to make sure he hasn't missed anything. We also wanted to test Jake's linguistic skills. On a conscious level, he has no knowledge of any foreign languages. More than ever it proves he's genuine. He just couldn't make that up. He doesn't have the capacity to do so. But that said we're still no closer to discovering the source of the language."

"I see. Last time I spoke to Jim he mentioned I should try to record the next nightmare. If there is one, that is. I pray there won't be, of course. But I do have a voice recorder on my phone, so it wouldn't be a problem. I just hope I keep calm enough to think about it at the time."

Pat nodded and folded her hands in her lap. "I know how hard it must be to see your child suffer, living on the edge of your nerves, waiting for the next time. God didn't see fit to bless me with a child of my own, but I see the bond between you and Jake. I understand how you would rather bear pain yourself than see your child in distress. And believe me, we will never do anything to cause Jake anymore upset. But both Jim and I believe the language may prove to be important." She paused. "Has Jim spoken to you about a similar case an old colleague of his was involved with?"

Helen shook her head.

"Well, there are a lot of similarities with Jake. The boy had also lost a parent at a young age –"

Helen sat up straight, startled by Pat's words. It was the first time Pat had connected Jake's nightmares with Mark. And after all they'd discussed. All the prejudice she'd faced from other doctors, surely now Pat wasn't coming around to the same line of thought. She looked up, meeting Pat's pale blue eyes, struggling with the sharp retort on the tip of her tongue.

"Don't worry," said Pat, her voice gentle. "I'm not going down that well-trodden route, my dear. But you know, if you need to talk about Mark, or anything else, I am here for you. I see the pain in your eyes at the mere mention of his name. As a friend, you can talk to me about anything, you know."

Helen bowed her head, concentrating on the pattern of her skirt until the colours began to blur.

"Thank you." She sniffed and ran a finger under both eyes. "Most of the time I think I'm okay. It's been over three years, I should be coping. But all this with Jake is making me very raw. It brings emotions back to the surface I've struggled hard to keep buried. It's a difficult time."

"How did Mark die?"

Helen gulped. "In Afghanistan. On a tour of duty. It's been a tough balance between trying to give Jake a normal life, one not tinged with tragedy, and trying to keep Mark's memory alive. He asked me never to let Jake forget his Daddy …" Helen broke off, coughed, then continued. "From the day I heard he'd been killed, I knew everything had changed. Since then it feels like it's been a constant battle against that change."

Helen realised how cathartic it felt to actually admit what a tough battle the last three years had been.

She sniffed, rubbed her eyes. "I swear to God it's only Jake who has kept me going. Kept me sane. It's like there's still a little bit of Mark here."

"It's clear to me you have a wonderful little boy who is testament to that." Pat said. "The sudden loss of a loved one at any age is a tough thing to cope with. But the loss of a partner at such a young age and in such sudden, violent circumstances makes it doubly traumatic. Have you told Jim Crawford about this?"

Helen shook her head.

"I think you should. I think you have a lot of pent-up guilt as well, Helen."

"I don't –"

"So, you've never once questioned whether these nightmares are your fault? Or your lack of parenting skills?"

Helen's silence answered Pat's question.

Pat reached out and squeezed Helen's hand. "See? I'm not judging or blaming you, my dear. It's only natural as a parent to doubt ourselves when our children are suffering. This is no different. But as a professional, I can assure you that nothing you've done, or anything to do with Mark's death, has resulted in Jake's problems."

"Then why have all the other doctors implied it?"

"Because they are either inexperienced, incompetent ... or stupid."

"Pat!" Helen blew her nose and smiled. "Say it like it is why don't you?"

"Well, some of them deserve it. Anyway, there, that's better. A smile." Pat gave Helen's hand a final squeeze, and settled back into the sofa. "I only mentioned the parent in this other case as it's one of many similarities. This four-year-old American boy was the reincarnation of a German World War II fighter pilot. He'd never been out of his own small mid-West village, but he could name towns in Germany, as well as the details of German planes and warships, even down to the correct spelling. Also he was documented to suffer regular nightmares, and at these times of trauma he spoke the German language perfectly. And yet at all other times he had no knowledge or memories of the language at all."

Helen raised her eyebrows. "Very like Jake.But how did they know it was German?"

"The father was a schoolteacher. He got a language expert to translate. No doubt it was perfect German. Jim Crawford spoke to his ex-colleague who worked on the case, and he says they used techniques on the child to force the subconscious mind to work harder, to speak more fluently, and to unearth many more memories. Apparently, as he unearthed more memories, the nightmares began to die off and eventually stopped. Obviously this is our goal with Jake. That's what I wanted to talk to you about, my dear."

"What are the techniques?"

"Hypnosis."

"But we spoke early on about this, I'm sure you said you weren't qualified –"

"I'm not. But Jim Crawford is."

Helen frowned, searching her mind for a way that Dr Crawford could carry out hypnosis on Jake from across the

Atlantic Ocean. "But how …"

"Jim arrived in Birmingham last night."

"What?"

"He's actually another of our lunch guests, he'll be here in about an hour. I was hoping it would give you, and Jake, a chance to get to know him. No pressure, of course. If you don't feel Jake is ready then neither of us will be offended if you choose not to stay."

"But … but he's travelled all this way, just to meet Jake?"

Pat nodded. "Yes. He's fascinated by this case, Helen. He's put hours of work into it already. He made the excuse of having holiday entitlement he needs to use up, but I know Jake is the real reason for his visit."

Helen paused, her mind buzzing. Another doctor, after she'd promised Jake no more. But this was Jim. And he was coming all the way across the globe to treat her son. How could she say no? Why would she say no?

"I know it's yet another stranger Jake has to meet," said Pat as perceptive as ever. "I understand how you feel. But if I could offer you only one piece of advice in the whole world, my dear, it would be that you're in safe hands, the best hands, with Jim Crawford. Don't hold back from him and trust him implicitly with Jake. Let him help you both. He will get to the bottom of this. He will find peace for both of you. I promise. Trust him. Okay?"

Helen bit her bottom lip, the sincerity in Pat's words touching a nerve.

"Okay. I trust you. At the very least Jake can meet him."

Helen's fears were unfounded. By mid-afternoon Jake was interacting with Jim Crawford as if they'd been friends for life. There was no doubt the doctor knew his stuff, Jake was putty in his hands. As Helen watched from the conservatory window, Jake was busy impressing Jim with his recently learned knowledge of plant names.

"They're getting on rather well, aren't they, my dear?" said Pat at her side. "As I was sure they would. Jim is an expert in his field, yes. But he's a thoroughly nice man too, don't you think?"

Helen nodded. Jim was younger than she'd expected. No more than forty and clearly fit. He'd mentioned a passion for badminton, and it showed. He had an easy-going style she warmed to. A sense of humour and a confidence in the way he carried himself. No airs and graces, so unlike her past experiences of psychiatrists prior to Pat.

"He's asking if you would be happy for him to go ahead with the first hypnotherapy session?"

"Today?"

"The sooner the better, Helen. I think we should go for it while Jake is so relaxed. He trusts Jim, it's clear to see. What do you think?"

Helen relaxed her hands, realising she was gripping the chair upholstery like a drowning man clinging to driftwood. Perhaps Pat was right. It was time to let go. Time to let the professionals get on and do their job. She had to trust someone. And in Pat and Jim she was certain she'd chosen the right people.

"Let's do it."

"Okay then, Jake. You know what we're going to do today? You're sure you understand everything I've told you and your mom?" asked Jim.

Jake nodded, flashing a look across the oval dining table at Dr Pat.

"No questions?"

"No. Except ..."

Jake screwed up his face, and Helen could tell he was struggling to hold back tears. He tugged at the bottom of his blue Bart Simpson t-shirt.

"What?"

"I will wake up again, won't I?"

"Oh, baby ..." Helen stood and took a step towards Jake, but Jim held up a hand.

"Yes, Jake. Absolutely. Definitely. Positively. You have to trust me on that before we can go any further. You do trust me, don't you?"

Jake nodded.

"Say it, Jake."

"I trust you."

"Good. Thank you. There is nothing, absolutely nothing to be scared of. Your mom is here. Dr Pat is here. And so am I. Just relax and listen to my voice. It will all be fine. I promise."

Jim glanced at Helen and gave the thumbs up. She sat back down; her hands gripping the arms of the chair.

"Okay Jake, I want you to make yourself comfortable. Put your hands on the table in front of you, like this." Jim positioned his hands, palms down, and Jake copied. "That's cool. And then I want you to listen carefully to my words. Ignore everything else, and just listen to my voice, okay?"

"Okay." Jake wriggled on the chair.

"Right, I am going to start counting from zero up to twenty. I want you to join me as I count, just like we practiced, okay?"

Jake gave a quick nod.

"By the time I get to ten, you'll start to feel sleepy. Try to keep counting as long as you can, then I'll ask you some questions and the memories will come through much clearer, much easier for you to talk about. And then, when we've finished, I'll start counting from twenty back down, and you'll wake up as soon as I reach zero. Understand?"

"Yes. I'm ready." Jake smiled at Helen. "Goodbye, Mummy."

Helen clutched her chest, bit back the gasp that threatened to escape, and said in her brightest voice. "Don't say that, Jakey. Please. You're not going anywhere."

"Oh, but I am. I'm going back, back to my other mummy and daddy. But I'll be home soon, I promise. I love you, Mummy."

"I love you too, sweetheart." Helen swallowed hard. She wanted to hold him and hug him, breathe in his scent – but Jim asked for minimal physical contact.

Jim paused and gave Helen a smile of encouragement. He motioned to Pat to activate the Dictaphone beside her. Pat nodded, pressed record, and picked up her pen and notepad. Helen's heart was thumping like a drum. She kissed the first two fingers of her left hand and then crossed them; a habit dating back to her schooldays.

"Okay Jake, concentrate on my voice and let's begin. One .. two .. three .. four .. five …" Jim's voice was calm but resonant, and he kept a regular rhythm as he counted.

Jake's voice started strongly, but began to quaver after eight.

"Are you feeling sleepy now, Jake?" asked Jim.

Jake nodded and mumbled.

"Seventeen .. eighteen .. nineteen, and twenty ... You are totally relaxed now. Can you hear me, Jake?"

"Yes." Jake's eyes were closed. His hands still flat on the table.

Helen jumped. His voice sounded different. Older, more developed. And with a definite vernacular edge that didn't belong to Jake.

"Do you feel okay, Jake?"

"Fine."

"Right, well I want to take you back in time. Imagine the years flying past you until we arrive at your past life. The life you see in your dreams. Is that okay?"

"Yes."

"Good. We won't keep referring to it as your past life from now on; we'll talk as if it were happening now. It will be easier for you. So, can you tell me your name?"

"Yes, sir. It's Jacob. Jacob Lloyd."

Jim and Helen exchanged glances. She let out a long rush of air. It felt as if she'd been holding her breath for ever. *At last*, she thought, *progress*.

Jim continued. "And how old are you, Jacob?"

"Eleven."

"Can you tell me about your family?"

"Yes, sir. My dad, Joe. My mam, Mary. I have two brothers, James and John. And a baby sister, Sarah."

"And where do you live?"

"On the island at Clanwyn."

"Clanwyn? Can you spell that for me, Jacob?"

"Spell? You mean write? No, I don't write too well, sir."

"Okay, that's fine. So whereabouts is your island? I don't know the name."

"It's on the Straits, at the Menai."

Jim looked across at Helen, his eyes questioning. Helen shrugged and shook her head, although the name sounded familiar.

"What country is that, Jacob?"

"Wales of course. On Anglesey."

Helen gripped her pen tighter. The accent – that explained it. It was Welsh. Not the strong Welsh accent she heard on TV, but a weaker, diluted version with a trace of Liverpudlian.

"Okay, sure. Sorry I'm from the U.S ..."

"U.S.?"

"Yes, you know, America."

"Am-er-ica?" Jake pronounced the word awkwardly.

"You've haven't heard of America? Okay that's cool. No worries." Jim smiled. "Let's move on. Do you know what year it is?"

"No."

"Do you know what year you were born?"

"No."

"Right, then can you think carefully of any information that might give me a date? Like, can you remember a special event or anniversary? Maybe something your mom or dad told you about?"

"No, sir, I don't know."

"Please, Jacob. This is really important. Please try harder."

"Okay … well I remember a party for Yuletide. I remember we went to the mainland. But I don't remember a year."

"Do you go to school, Jacob?"

"No. My mam teaches us at home, when we're not out fishing with our dad. Oh, I just remembered …"

"What?" Jim leaned forward, elbows on the table.

"Last year, Mam was teaching us history about the Kings and Queens of England. She said the King had just died, and there was a big funeral and lots of sad people in the cities."

Jim looked at Helen. His eyes were bright with excitement. Pat continued to scribble notes furiously on her pad, flicking pages over in rapid succession.

"Can you remember which King? It's important, Jacob. You're doing really, really well. Just try to remember what your mom told you."

"I'm trying. Yes, I remember one of my friends has the same name and we joked that he was King now, because the old King had died."

Jake smiled.

Helen corrected herself. Jacob, not Jake. It was Jacob smiling at a memory from his childhood.

"And …" urged Jim.

"George. It was King George the fourth, sir. He died last year."

Helen watched as Pat jotted down the details. It was a date. It was a start. Jim took a deep breath, checked his notes, and returned to the questions.

"That's great, Jacob. Well done."

Jake smiled. He looked relaxed and perfectly at ease. Helen straightened her back and uncrossed her legs. She was so tense, her body ached. She rolled her head a few times to ease the stiffness in her neck.

"So," continued Jim, "you mentioned visiting the mainland. Where do you go?"

"Few places. Bangor sometimes. Mostly Caernarfon."

Finally, somewhere she had heard of.

"How do you get there?"

"We have two boats. An old cable boat that our dad built from driftwood. And a shrimp boat Dad gave us for our own. Me and our John painted it special like."

"What colour is your boat?"

"Blue, sir. A lovely bright blue."

The blue boat, thought Helen. *Jake's famous blue boat.*

"And you sail across to the mainland?"

"Yes, mostly. If Dad's away, Mam takes us on the Vole ferry, but not very often. I don't like going off the island much, though. I love the island."

The island. For so long she thought Jake had been talking about Ireland, when he'd meant this boy's beloved island. She found herself wondering what this eleven-year-old child looked like. Did he resemble Jake? Was that how reincarnation worked? She doubted she would ever know. The history of the British monarchy wasn't one of her strongest points, but she had a feeling that George IV put this somewhere in the early 1800s, so any photographic evidence seemed highly unlikely.

Jim continued with the questioning, and Helen forced herself to concentrate. She didn't want to miss a precious word of the conversation.

"So, you said your father often went away? Is he a fisherman?"

Jake shook his head.

"But you mentioned a shrimp boat?"

"We fish for our own food like, from the boat or the shore. We fish most days, and smoke it in a hut in the garden. Pollack, mackerel, bass and flatfish. Mam makes nets too, and we catch crabs and lobsters in wooden pots. My brothers and I are better fishermen than our dad for sure. We went out in the shrimp boat one day, and came back with it full to the brim of fish! And we collected mussels and cockles, which Mam sells in the summer to buy clothes for us and the baby."

Jake's face lit up. He smiled, and puffed his chest out, clearly proud.

"What age are your brothers, Jacob? Are you the eldest?"

Jake shook his head. "No. James is the oldest. He's a year older than me. Then our John's eight. Then we had a sister Emily, but she died when she was four. Of the fever. Our Grandma died the same day of it too. And John was ill, but he got better. But he has the limp. And then our Sarah was born last year."

"I see. So, where ..."

"I miss my family. I miss my brothers so much." He stopped abruptly. Big, fat teardrops squeezed under Jake's lids and plopped onto the veneer surface of the table. "I miss my mam and dad. And our Chi. I loved my dog, Chi."

"Okay, Jacob, I know this is hard. I know they miss you too."

Jake gulped and swallowed. Helen was about to stand, Pat held up her hand and shook her head.

"He's fine," she whispered. "It's normal for them to experience emotion. Don't worry."

Helen nodded and took a deep breath.

"It's alright, Jacob," Jim continued. "You're doing so well. Let's talk about your father, okay?"

"Yes, sir."

"Where does he work if he's not a fisherman by trade?"

"He worked the pilot boats, sir. He was a Captain."

"The pilot boats?" Jim looked at Helen again. She shrugged. "Can you tell me what that was?"

"Yes, sir, they're Liverpool Master Pilots for the Trinity House. There are three pilot boat workers, working shifts. They help the big ships to come up over the Caernarfon bar safely, and then navigate them through the Straits and out the other end at Lavan Sands. The currents are right treacherous around the Swellies, many a ship lost on the rocks there. Once they're out onto Lavan Sands, or out past Beaumaris, the pilot boats turn back and the big ships carry on to Liverpool."

"That's really interesting, Jacob. So your father has an important job. You must have been proud?"

"Yes, it was a very busy shipping route, he always said. Lots of dangerous rocks all around the islands. We used to climb up to the top of this beacon, a lookout it were, built on the rocks to warn the ships. Ever so tall, Twr Bach. We used to wave at our dad out in the pilot boat. Watching him guide the big sailing boats or the cargo boats full of slate. We were right proud of him."

"I bet you were, Jacob. Rightly so. Can you tell me anything about your house?"

"Yes, there's a row of four cottages, all painted white. They's only small. Me and my brothers share a room. Pilot boat cottages they called. Ours is at one end, and two other families live in the others. And the end one gets used as a storeroom and shelter for the animals. We keep sheep, pigs and chickens."

"You have busy lives. What did you want to do when you were older? A farmer, or a fisherman ..."

"No, I was going to work for the Trinity House, like my dad before he died. I wanted to be a pilot boat captain too."

"Your father died? Can you tell me? If it upsets you too much to talk about, then we can move on."

"Yes, we drowned."

"We?"

"Yes, I drowned at the same time as my father. I died too."

"No!" Helen yelled.

She began to shake, frozen to the spot. She wanted to speak, needed to stop this. But she couldn't move, couldn't breathe. She had to wake Jake, shake the life back into him. This had gone too far. She couldn't lose Jake, not Jake. Not after Mark. No, she couldn't bear it.

Jim was at her side, warm hand on her wrist, warm breath in her ear.

"Helen, look at me, it's okay. I know what you're thinking. But it's okay. Trust me."

Helen found she couldn't breathe. She forced herself to inhale, focusing on Pat's worried face alongside her.

"Breathe steadily, my dear," said Pat. "Hold my hands. You're having a panic attack."

She resisted Pat's hold, twisting to study Jake. His face was still calm, a trace of a smile on his lips. His eyes remained closed, fingers splayed on the table.

Helen licked her lips. "God, I'm so sorry. But did you hear what he said? He's dead, Jim."

"But of course he is, Helen," whispered Jim. "Try to think rationally. You're confusing Jacob with Jake. I know this is hard to get your head round, it's hard even for me – but it's not Jake talking." He flashed a look at Jake. "This is Jacob. And of course he's dead. We know he died as a child; he's reincarnated as a child. What we don't know are the circumstances of his death."

Jim took hold of Helen's left hand. Their eyes met. She glanced from him to Jake and back again. The thought of losing Jake made her feel sick.

"I want to carry on, Helen."

"No!"

"Yes. We have to. We're so close now."

Jim's voice was low and pleading. Helen flashed a look at Pat.

"It has to be your decision, my dear. But I give you my word, Jake is totally safe."

Helen swallowed. "It's so hard, hearing your own child talk about dying. Especially having lost my husband, it brings all the terrible memories flooding back. I just don't know if I can cope with this."

"You can, Helen. You are. Just keep it in your head this isn't Jake talking. Stay focused on the information that's coming through. We're going to learn so much, it has to be worth it. Just a little while longer. Another fifteen minutes, and I promise I'll finish the session."

Helen closed her eyes in silent prayer. "Okay. Okay. Carry on.

Before I change my mind."

"Thank you. I appreciate it." Jim gave her hand a squeeze and returned to his seat opposite Jake. "Jacob? Are you there? Can you hear me?"

"Yes."

"Good. Are you able to tell us what happened when you and your father died? If you find it too difficult, then you have permission to stop."

"I'll try, sir. Some of the memories are faded. But I'll do my best."

"That's all I ask, Jacob. Tell me everything you can."

"It was an August evening, ever such a hot day it had been, right at the end of the summer. Blue skies and lovely sunny. Me, our James and Dad had gone fishing just off Puffin Island. The mackerel shoals were in, we had a right decent catch. We planned to stop off at Beaumaris on the way home to see if we could sell any."

Jacob paused as if putting his memories in order.

"But a storm blew in before we got in sight of shore. It just came up from nowhere. The sky turned grey all round us and lit up with sea-lightning. The thunder scared me, echoed right across the water, it did. The rain came as hail, so hard it hurt. The wind howled and the waves twice as high as the boat. We pushed against the tide to make for the nearest shore, any shore, but it was tough going."

"So did your boat capsize in the storm?"

"Well, no, sir, not straightaway. We managed to get round Puffin Island and into the lee. And then we saw a big ship, one of the new steam-driven ships she was, in trouble and sinking out on Lavan Sands. Dad said it looked as if she'd been holed on the rocks off Penmon and had drifted out into the bay. Dad was a good sailor – the best. He managed to get our shrimper out into the Straits, struggling against the storm. I'll never forget the noise, seemed to fill the night. Screams like I'd never heard, barely seemed human to me. We pulled folk out the water, and threw the bodies back if they were already dead. We filled our boat, rescued about twelve, and put ashore at Penmon. We left James with them till help came. Mostly women and children they were, and awful terrified."

"What a wonderful story, Jacob. So what happened?"

"We went out a second time. The weather was worsening, but Dad wanted to rescue some of the others still in the sea. He'd seen women and kiddies, he said, and couldn't just leave them to drown. The ship had nearly disappeared by this time. We could barely see it, the rain so heavy and the waves high as chimneys. I remember we'd pulled another five or six people aboard, when a big wave hit us and overturned our boat."

"That's awful. Do you remember the name of the ship by any chance?"

"No, I don't think we ever knew it. Dad didn't mention a name, and it was too dark to see anything."

"Do you remember your Dad saying anything about the ship at all?"

"Only that it was a steam ship and looked to have a few hundred passengers onboard. He said it had probably sailed from Liverpool."

"So what happened when your boat overturned?"

"I don't remember much. It was very cold, icy cold, and pitch black. I managed to pull myself onto some of the wreckage. I saw my Dad. He floated past me face down. I could see he was dead. I tried to hold onto him, but I was weak and the current strong. I screamed and screamed, but no one came. I don't know how long I was out there, but I slipped off the timber. I got so cold and wet, and was so tired. I think I just went to sleep in the water and never woke up. I don't remember dying, but I must have."

Jake stopped talking, and no one dared break the silence.

"That's very sad, Jacob." Jim's voice cracked.

"Yes, sir. I find it hard to think about," said Jacob.

"Thank you for telling us. Thank you for talking to us. I'm going to bring Jake back now. We may talk to you again soon.

Twenty … nineteen … "

Helen watched as Jim calmly counted backwards, and brought Jake out of his trance. On zero, Jake opened his eyes and looked round, blinking owl-like. His gaze met Helen's and he smiled broadly, tiny white teeth showing.

"Hello, Mummy. I'm back!"

Chapter Fifteen

Well, least I got my answer, thought Gareth as he and Chris seated themselves in front of Professor Randall's desk in his small office in the School of History, Welsh History and Archaeology. Gareth could tell from Chris's forced posture that he wasn't happy. Not happy at all. If Glyn Rogers had been honest with them, this whole interview could have been carried out via telephone, saving them valuable time.

Professor Randall was at least eighty, bent almost double in an electric wheelchair, with what looked like advanced arthritis. And behind the inch-thick tinted lenses, his eyes failed to follow their progress as his secretary showed them to their seats. He may have possessed every academic qualification under the sun, and been blessed with immense intelligence, but he was clearly not the person they sought.

"Aaah, yes, yes, poor sweet Edwina, I remember her well." He spoke quietly, but with confidence, after Chris made the initial introductions. "I heard what happened. Well, not the details, you understand. I wouldn't want the details. But the university is ablaze with speculation and rumours. Not to mention fear. My colleagues tell me we're leaking foreign students by the plethora. Terrible, terrible thing. I hope you catch the bugger, and quick mind."

"Thank you, professor," replied Chris; his voice more

controlled now, his frustration less obvious. "We have officers working in conjunction with the heads of department to make sure all students are as safe as possible."

Gareth cleared his throat. "We won't take up too much of your time. We are led to believe you knew Edwina through a reading group at a bookshop called The Muse?"

The professor turned to Gareth, head tilted like a blackbird listening for underground worms. Gareth shifted in his seat, unable to see the man's eyes behind the darkened lenses, but feeling the burning sensation of his stare.

"Your name is Parry?" Randall asked finally.

"Yes. My cousin, sir."

"I'm sorry. My sincere condolences."

"Thank you."

"And they expect you … allow you … to work on the case?"

"My choice, sir. And a lack of resources. This is a major investigation as you can imagine."

Again, a pause, while the professor seemed to consider his response. Gareth felt awkward, like a child in a headmaster's office. Sat on the naughty chair. For all the loss of his physical abilities, it was clear the professor was still mentally a match for any man.

"I see. You have my utmost respect and admiration, young man."

Gareth raised his chin. "I'm doing it for my family, sir. I'm doing it to give us all closure."

"I liked your cousin very much. Edwina interested me. One of eclectic tastes and personality. Quite a diverse individual for such a young age. But she had one of the brightest minds around at the moment. She loved books with a passion, and she was coming round to appreciate my taste in opera too. We hoped to make a trip down to London later in the year. I shall miss her company very much."

"Is there anything you can think of that Edwina may have told you in the past that may assist us in our investigation, sir?"

asked Chris.

"No, alas. I've given this much thought since I heard of her death. It was such a shock to me. When I heard, I spent an evening piecing together all the snippets of conversation we'd had in the hope that some clue may have presented itself. It didn't. If it had I assure you I would have contacted the police before now."

"When did you become aware of Edwina's death?" asked Gareth. "I only ask as when we questioned the owners of The Muse, they hadn't connected Edwina with the missing girls, whereas you seem in full possession of the facts."

"Who? The Rogers fellow and his affected mother superior?"

Gareth bit back a laugh at the clear disdain in his tone. "Yes, sir."

"Well, it's hardly surprising, I'm not sure any of that family live in the real world. If she's not off at her amateur dramatics or ballroom dancing, she's holding court at the bookshop like some Queen of an Edwardian Royal castle. And he's not much better. Complete Mummy's Boy. I've not got time for these folk who carry on their lives like a three part operetta. I mean, we all have tragedy to cope with in our lives, don't we?" He paused, flexed his twisted fingers with a grimace. "Still, to answer your question and give them due, the Head of Department told the staff the news, asked us to keep the name quiet until the police made it public. It's believable they wouldn't have known. They do live in their own world. I'm sure you picked that up?"

Gareth nodded. "They seemed a little reclusive. They weren't able to offer any suggestions either. I'm grateful you've taken time to consider my cousin, Professor. I'll leave a card here on your desk. If you think of anything that may assist us further, could I ask you to telephone the number at the bottom?"

"Of course. Of course. Your cousin was never anything but happy and obliging to me. A good student. We were close, but of course I doubt she would have discussed boyfriends or the like with an old codger like me. But she seemed grounded. I'm sure you already know that. She would have gone on to make your family very proud, I'm sure of it. I've often thought that God always takes the best people early. Perhaps he wants their company. I suppose that explains why I'm still lingering."

With a smile, he held out a hand which Gareth shook across the desk; surprised at the strength in the old man's grip.

"Good luck, gentlemen. With your permission I shall take it on myself to keep my nose to the ground, my ears open, and any other cliché that seems appropriate. It's amazing what one picks up when people assume if you are registered partially sighted you must also be deaf and retarded. Rest assured I shall contact you if I hear anything."

They both took turns to thank the professor for his help, before the same blonde secretary arrived to escort them down the labyrinth of shadowy corridors, their footsteps echoing across the stone tiles. Once the outer door swung shut, Chris turned towards Gareth, anger etched on his face, both fists clenched.

"I suppose he thinks he's smart sending us on a wild goose chase, Mr Glyn-bloody-Rogers," he snarled. "I've a good mind to show him what I think of his idea of a joke, and let him enjoy a night of hospitality in the cells."

"Hey, calm down, mate. The old guy was sharp as a button. He may yet nose around and find something out. Fate may have played a hand here." Gareth paused to breathe in the salty breeze blowing across the car park. He lifted his face to the warmth of the May sunshine, savouring the heat of the afternoon after the chill of the musty building. "Besides, I rather think Mr Rogers was more interested in finding a straw to cling to, to distract us from questioning him further. And I'm more keen to find out the reason why."

Chris nodded, fumbling in his pocket for a packet of cigarettes, offering one to Gareth as they stood beside his car. "You may be right. He's definitely still on the back burner. One to keep an eye on, I think."

"Yeah," agreed Gareth.

Gazing up at the stone building, he admired the intricate architecture framed by a cloudless blue sky. He had a good feeling about Professor Randall. Had high hopes he could prove to be an interesting ally. But through the glimpse of elation, still the niggling doubt about Glyn Rogers wormed its way into his conscious. As he climbed into the car, he thought again of his last sighting of the man, one hand propped against the window frame, the other cupped to his ear as he spoke into this mobile. Was he imagining he'd read fear on his face? Or was it genuine shock? Perhaps calling his mother to ensure she'd been left unscarred by a visit from CID. Or was there another reason? What did he know that he didn't want to tell the police?

Yes, on the back burner. But definitely still on the heat.

* * *

Gareth lifted the carrier bags from the boot and slammed it down with his elbow. He keyed in the security code and dragged his weary legs up the three flights of stairs of his apartment block, stifling a yawn. The bag handles cut into his palms. It was the first shopping he'd done in a month, other than his almost daily visit to the corner-shop-cum-off-licence. He'd forgotten how to cook, almost forgotten how to eat; the enjoyment of a full English breakfast or a Sunday roast a dulled memory. He'd lived on the occasional takeaway or a boil-in-the-bag curry for weeks.

He slid the key into the lock and pushed the door open with his foot. The smell of last night's chicken madras takeaway assaulted his nostrils as he made his way to the kitchen. His bedroom door was ajar, his bed still unmade, duvet on the floor, pillows twisted against the wall. It was major clean-up time. Strip beds, wash duvets, vacuum, polish, scrub. The works. He grimaced as he thought of the work needed to bring the bathroom up to his usual standard. Maybe that would have to wait till tomorrow.

His mobile began to ring and he shrugged of his jacket. Number withheld.

"Parry."

"DI McRae here."

"Sir."

Gareth was at once alert.

"I've just come off the phone to the Commissioner. He's given the okay to release Edwina's body for burial. I wanted to let you know as soon as possible. I thought it may be some comfort for your aunt."

Gareth dropped onto the breakfast stool, half in, half out of his jacket.

"Oh, right. Thank you, sir."

"I thought it would be welcome news. If I can do anything to assist you further, please let me know."

"Of course, sir. Yes, thank you."

"Are you okay, Parry?"

Gareth shook his head, last thing he needed was McRae worrying about him. "Of course, sir. It's just a bit of a shock. I knew there would come a time, but I suppose the thought of telling my aunt, and facing her reaction, isn't one I'm looking forward to."

"Would you rather I made the call?"

He paused. *Would he? Yes. Should he?* "No, sir. It's something I need to do. There are things I need to sort out. Family stuff. Thank you, anyway."

"Okay. How did you get on today with the investigation?"

"Drawn a blank, I'm afraid. No one knows anything out of the ordinary. I'm leaning more towards this being a random serial killer. There seems little to link the girls, none seem to have any known vices or shared enemies. The more we discover, the less we learn, if you know what I mean. This is going to be a hard one to solve unless he makes a mistake pretty soon."

"They always do, Parry. In my experience, they always do."

Gareth's stomach growled as he selected his aunt's number on his mobile. Propped on the edge of his bed, he wiped his palms on the mattress, trying to calm the bats that seemed to have taken up residence in his stomach. The phone rang. Once. Twice.

"Hello."

"Aunt Linda. It's Gareth."

Silence.

"It's Gareth."

"What do you want?" Her tone was icy. A stranger's voice.

"I've just had a call. We can go ahead and arrange the funeral. Soon as convenient."

He'd wanted to say her name. Had every intention of saying *Edwina*. But the word dried up as it reached the edge of his tongue.

He heard an intake of breath; a sudden choked rush of air.

"Do you want me to call Mam, or come over, sort out arrangements?"

Silence.

"Auntie? Come on. We have to talk." He rubbed a hand through his hair, his throat hot and tight. "I don't know why you're doing this. Believe me, I feel bad enough. That's why I'm back on the case, trying to do my best to catch the person who is really responsible. This is hard enough for me –"

"This isn't about you." The stranger's voice again, controlled and soulless. "This is about me. And my daughter. All I need is the death certificate. I've spoken to the funeral agent, everything else is in place. Of course, I'll tell your mam to contact you with the date and time in due course."

"Auntie!"

The line went dead, a steady buzz in his ear.

He threw the mobile against the wall with as much force as he could muster. He collapsed back onto the bed, pulling the duvet over his head, giving himself time and space to organise his feelings.

This wasn't fair. What the hell did she think she was achieving by punishing him? He punched the pillow, thumping the material into shape, glad he hadn't wasted a drive to Wrexham, concerned his frustration may have spilled over into an argument or violence. And what would there be to gain? Yet more reason to hate him.

He threw back the duvet, headed into the kitchen and reached for a tumbler from the cupboard. Sod the cleaning. Sod everyone. He needed a drink. He poured a treble into the glass and made his way into the lounge. As he passed, he noticed the red light flashing on the answer phone. He pushed the vertical blind to one side as he pressed play, looking out onto the street below, dusk creeping shadows between the buildings. The lights of the off licence tinting the far side of the street in a golden glow.

"One new message. Thursday 9:10pm."

"Detective Inspector Parry?"

A pause. A crackle of distortion. A voice clearly disguised. Gareth dropped to his knees, one ear near the speaker, heart hammering, alcohol forgotten.

"Hello, Detective. You don't know me. But let's say I knew your cousin, Edwina Parry, late in life. I saw you on TV. Quite a performance. Congratulations. However, I don't like being threatened. That said, I'm always up for a challenge. You have twenty four hours to carry out your threat, twenty four hours to catch me, you and your fellow men. It's time. The next victim is already in my sight. Friday evening. Let's see who reaches the finishing line first. Happy hunting."

Chapter Sixteen

"The tape recording is real cool. Did Pat get all the names down?"

Jim rewound the Dictaphone as Helen ticked off Pat's meticulous notes.

"Yes, I think so. Your guess is as good as mine about the spelling." Helen shuffled through the pages. "But it's a start. There's so much to do."

"Yeah, the whole thing sure is amazing. I don't recall having heard anything like it before. Not in any research studies I've read. We got an awesome amount of information."

"And when he described the drowning …" Helen broke off and rubbed her arms, unable to find the words to continue.

"I know." Jim met her eyes with a gentle smile.

"So, let's get cracking. Where do you think we should start?" asked Helen. "It was good of Pat and Ken to take Jake out for a couple of hours. We'd best take advantage. As much as he loves his new found hobby of gardening, I'm not sure how long the local nursery will keep him occupied."

Jim laughed. "He's a bright spark, for sure. How about dates, places, shipwreck … in that order?"

"Fine. Hopefully some of it should be quite straightforward."

Helen pulled her chair closer to Pat's desk, picking up the spicy tang of aftershave as Jim settled into the chair beside her and pulled his laptop towards him. It was the first time in ages she'd felt relaxed with another man. The first time since Mark's death she'd felt safe and secure. It was a good feeling. Even though her mind was filled with worries, questions and fears about Jake, she had every confidence in Jim. He and Pat were a formidable team.

Jim Googled 'Great Britain Monarchy – King George IV.'

"Blimey!" Helen's eyes scanned the 2,357,000 results it retrieved within seconds.

Jim clicked on the Encyclopedia Britannia link, and waited for the site to load. "Sorry I can't help you out much. History of the British monarchy has never been one of my strong points."

"Least you have an excuse. What's mine? Other than I detested history at school."

"Are you feeling okay now, Helen?"

She turned to face him; a worried frown creased his tanned forehead. She could see concern in his eyes.

"Absolutely. I'm sorry I got upset earlier."

"Hey, it's cool. Completely understandable. I'm just glad you trusted me. I'd have totally understood if you'd kicked my butt all the way out your life."

"No, not at all. I just found it tough, separating the two lives. I think I've got my head around it now. Then again, maybe those couple of glasses of Chablis over lunch helped too. Pat is a wonderful host."

"Pat is wonderful. Period. One of the best." Jim paused, squinting at the screen. "Ah, at last. British Monarchs. Let's see. Erm, George VI, George V. Nope. Oh, yeah, here's the beauty. Let's see what it has to say on him."

Helen's eyes skimmed across the screen; following Jim's finger, she began to read aloud. "Okay, born 1762. Made Prince of Wales. Blah … blah. His father George III died in 1820 and he took the throne. Fine. But when did he die? Ah, here we are … 'in later years the King became a total recluse and died at Windsor Castle on … 26th June 1830.'"

"We're talking almost two hundred years ago," Jim said.

"Is that a long time scale for a case of reincarnation then?" asked Helen.

"Kinda. It does vary. But there are a lot more in the fifty to a hundred-year old vicinity. I have a hunch the memories fade over time. Even those belonging to the reincarnated souls."

"Makes sense, I suppose. Now, Jacob said his mother told them the King had died the previous year. So that would make his death sometime in August 1831. Am I right?"

"Yup. One hundred and eighty years ago. And he spoke as if it happened yesterday." Jim shook his head.

"Okay, so we have a date," urged Helen, eager now for more. "Let's try finding out where this island is. Jake has talked about it for so long; I'm itching to see what it looks like. I almost feel as if I know the place."

"That will be interesting, you know, to see if Jake recognises the island."

"You think he will?" asked Helen.

"I took a boy all the way from his hometown in Nirvana, back to his reincarnate home of New York, and as soon as we arrived he recognised the Hudson River and South Street Seaport."

"It's not dangerous, is it? I mean, it would be so exciting to take Jake back there, to see if he knew the island but there's no chance it would be counter-productive, is there?"

Jim shook his head. "No, never in my experience. I can't imagine he would be anything other than thrilled. Come on, let's see if we can find it."

Jim hit a few keys and pulled up a map of North Wales.

Helen leaned in close and scanned the coastline.

"Right," said Helen, referring to the notes. "He said they visited Bangor. Which is here." She stabbed a finger at the monitor. "And he also mentioned Caernarfon, which is here. And this must be the Menai Straits. Bangor is at one end, and Caernarfon is at the other. So, that's not helped much."

"Look!" Jim pointed to a small island, on the eastern tip of Anglesey. "He mentioned Puffin Island and Penmon, didn't he?"

He scanned the notes. "Yup, they went fishing around the other side of Puffin Island, he said. So the shipwreck must have been in this area. He said they took the survivors ashore at Penmon. Look, there's a lighthouse symbol here."

"So, the island can't be a million miles away, can it? It must be in this area."

They scanned the map. Helen recognised a few name places. Beaumaris, Menai Bridge, Red Wharf Bay. Now she heard the name, she recognised pictures of the stunning Thomas Telford suspension bridge, built across the Menai Straits. A well-known landmark, but she hadn't connected it. She'd never been onto the Isle of Anglesey. So far, she couldn't find an island that sounded anything like the Welsh name Jacob had mentioned.

"What was the name again?" asked Jim.

"Well, looking at these complicated names on here, I'm less sure than ever on the spelling or the pronunciation. But it sounded something like Clanwyn."

"I can't see any other islands at all around this end of the island. Let's work our way around the coastline."

"Okay." Helen nodded. "I wish I knew the area, I might be a bit more help."

"Is it far from here? Hey, I'm sorry my UK geography is almost as bad as my knowledge of the monarchy."

"Maybe two hundred or so miles. About a three hour drive. So by American standards, I guess it's not too far."

"Hey, look!" Jim tapped a fingernail against the screen. He seemed suddenly distracted, yet alert. "Didn't Jacob mention something about a ferry at Vole? There is a little place here, called Foel. Do you think that's the Welsh spelling? Perhaps their F's are V's and vice versa."

"Where?"

"See there, where it says Sea Zoo. Right on the banks of the Straits."

"Yes. I think you may be right!" Helen clapped her hands in excitement. "We must be getting closer. He definitely said they got a ferry crossing from Vole, well Foel. So that means it must be within walking distance of the island, surely?"

"You'd think so. Unless they had horses, but he didn't mention horses, only farm animals. They sure couldn't have hopped on a bus."

Helen scanned the coastline. A small village called Newborough. Suddenly she saw a name; it seemed to jump out from the map.

"Jim, look. Here. Llanddwyn. The way the Welsh pronounce 'Ll' sounds like 'Cl.' Thinking about Llangollen and Llandudno. And we missed it because we've been following the roads, and there are no roads here, they stop at Newborough. It must be the place. I'm sure of it."

Jim nodded. "Well, it's directly opposite Caernarfon, so that fits. And Jacob said his father was one of these pilot boat captains that guided the larger ships up and down the Straits. So that would be a perfect spot, wouldn't it?"

"Yes, and for a lighthouse or beacon. And I don't know what it is, probably a sandbank or something, but here is Caernarfon Bar. He mentioned navigating the boats safely over it."

"I think we've cracked it, Helen." Jim beamed at her. "It's just so great when these things come together. It's like a jigsaw puzzle, when all the pieces start to click into place. Anyway, let's Google Llanddwyn and see what we find."

Another screen opened and Helen inched her chair closer.

"Well, there's quite a lot on here, let me print these few pages." Jim rolled his neck. "Reading this makes it sound a charismatic place; lots of history and folklore. But you're right, there's no road access, and it's a long walk from the nearest village. And the island isn't actually an island; it's connected to the mainland of Anglesey by a strip of beach, which remains uncovered at all times apart from exceptional high tides."

Helen plucked a sheet off the printer. "Hey, the pilot boat cottages get a mention. They must still exist."

Helen read aloud from the Maritime History webpage. "The

Menai Straits are an important shipping route, as the export of slate from Bangor, Caernarfon and Felinhelli increased. During this time, cottages were built on Llanddwyn to house the pilots who guided ships into the Straits. Two of these cottages have been restored, with one housing an exhibition about local wildlife." Helen thumped the air. "Yes!"

Jim smiled as the printer whirred into life again. "I think I've found a picture of the cottages. I want to show it to Jake, see if he recognises it."

Helen took a sip of coffee as they waited for the picture to emerge. "Well, it's a small white cottage. That's what Jake said after the last nightmare. I think it's spot on."

"It certainly looks promising," agreed Jim. "And there's lots of history about the island too. It sounds a fascinating place. Listen to this … The name Llanddwyn – excuse the pronunciation – means 'The Church of St. Dwynwen. She is the Welsh patron saint of lovers, making her the Welsh equivalent of St. Valentine. Her feast day, 25 January, is often celebrated with cards and flowers, just as is 14 February for St. Valentine.' It goes on to say that she lived in the 5th century AD and tells her life story and why she was canonised. She actually died on the island. The spot is marked by a huge stone that's split into two, by heavenly intervention according to myth, so that St Dwynwen could see the sunrise one more time before she died. It's supposed to have magical healing powers now …"

"Patron saint of lovers. How romantic. And magical and religious significance." Helen mused. "It certainly looks beautiful. Stunning scenery." She leaned over Jim's shoulder, to look at the latest pictures to appear on the screen. "What are those ruins? And the crosses, what are they? Is that a Celtic cross?"

"I'm not sure," replied Jim. "I'm trying to find out more information. It seems a close kept secret. Oh hang on, there's a few lines here … 'The island became so popular with pilgrims during Tudor times that the offerings made funded the building of the church (the ruins you can see today) on the site of

Dwynwen's original chapel. Besides the church ruins, there are also two crosses on the island, one is of a Celtic design and bears the date of Dwynwen's death, 25 January 465, whilst the other dates from 1890.' That's the only reference I can find."

"Obviously a very uncommercialised place and they want to keep it that way. There's a lighthouse on it too, isn't there?"

"Yes, I've found a few mentions of an old beacon, possibly what Jacob described, and a new lighthouse built in … where was it … 1845, called Twr Mawr."

"I like the accent!" Helen teased, as Jim struggled to pronounce the difficult names. "I'm really hyped up. I'd love to go and see the island. It would feel like a homecoming for Jake, I'm sure. I think we've done miracles. I can't thank you enough."

"Both you and Pat have done as much work as me. It's a team effort. And let's not forget Jake is part of the team. None of this would be possible without him."

"So we know when, we know where, now we just need to find out why."

"The shipwreck?"

"Yeah." Helen nodded, draining her cup. "Let's go for the full house. Let's see if we can find out when and where Jacob and his father passed away."

"Any suggestions?"

"I have actually. Something I used at work once for researching an article, it lists all the shipwrecks around the British Isles."

Jim moved aside and Helen took the seat in front of his computer and typed Lloyds Register of Shipping into the search engine. A blue page opened with the heading 'The Website of the Mariner's Mailing List – Welcome to the Lloyds Register of Shipping'.

"There we go," said Helen. "I didn't think it would be too hard to find. I used it years ago when researching an article about the top ten diving sites around the U.K. It's a really old institution that's been going for hundreds of years. Listen … Lloyds Register of Shipping is a British publication that describes, classifies and registers vessels according to certain criteria. It also lists all known shipwrecks around the British Isles, dating back to its inception in 1764."

"Jeez, well that answers my first question," said Jim.

"What's that?"

"Well, to an American 1831 seems a zillion years ago. I was going to ask if this register would date back that far. And it evidently does – and some!"

Helen laughed. "This seems to be the only way to access – via the calendar years. So let's work our way back to 1831, and see what we find. Fingers crossed there weren't too many shipwrecks that year to search through."

She scrolled down a list of ships that had met their end in 1831 and together she and Jim worked their way through the list of about twenty, one by one.

After a few minutes, Jim spoke, "Well, most of these are either around the Scottish coast or in the English Channel. From what I can see, there are only five that went down off the coast of Wales. We must be getting closer. Have to admit I'm getting really excited. Does that make me sound sad?"

"Just a little." Helen smiled up at him. "But then, if you're sad then I'm sad too."

The next section opened.

"Right," said Helen. "Let's see if this one fits. 'The Rothsay Castle.' Well the picture isn't great, but it looks like a steamer, rather than a sailing ship. Not that I'm an expert …but … Oh God, Jim …"

He leaned over her shoulder. "I think we've hit the jackpot, Helen."

"The Rothsay Castle wrecked on August 15th 1831 on the sandbanks at Lavan Sands near Penmon Point, Anglesey." Helen read in a hushed voice. "One hundred and seven people lost their lives. The Rothsay Castle was one of the first steam-driven ships. She was not originally designed as a sea-going vessel. She had only one lifeboat, and at the time of the disaster she was known to be unseaworthy. The Rothsay Castle was a disaster waiting to happen."

Helen turned to Jim. She could feel his proximity, smelling his aftershave again; his warm breath tickled her right ear.

"How sad," she whispered. "What a tragic loss of lives."

Jim scanned the next page. "Listen to this ... On leaving the Mersey estuary, the paddle steamer encountered a strong NNW wind and rough sea. One of the passengers went to see the captain, Captain Atkinson, to ask him to return to port, but he found Atkinson drunk and unwilling to consider turning back. By 10pm the ship had still only reached the Great Orme and had two feet of water in the stokehold. The pumps were found not to work, there was not even a bucket available for bailing, and the single lifeboat had a hole in the bottom and had no oars. At around 1am on August 18, the Rothsay Castle ran aground on Dutchman's Bank and after a while broke up, the captain and two mates being swept to their death when the funnel collapsed. Bodies were washed up over a wide area of Anglesey and the mainland. An inquest was held at Beaumaris and the jury concluded: had the Rothsay Castle been a seaworthy vessel and properly manned, this awful calamity might have been averted. They therefore cannot disguise their indignation at the conduct of those who could place such a vessel on this station ... As a result of this disaster, a lifeboat station was established at Penmon on the SE tip of Anglesey in 1832 and a lighthouse built there in 1837."

Jim and Helen sat in silence for several minutes, both lost in their own thoughts.

"I want to see what else I can find," said Helen. "See if we can find anything that mentions Jacob, or maybe his father, Joe."

"Yeah, I agree. We owe it to Jacob, I think."

"I'm going to trawl through some of the Liverpool newspapers and publications that were around in 1831. It may take me a while."

Helen cleared her throat and blew her nose, missing the sound of the study door opening as Jim returned.

"Helen, what's wrong?"

"I found this ..." She handed Jim a piece of paper. He read aloud.

"'Loss of the Steamer – Rothsay Castle, Passengers and Crew.'"

He looked down at Helen as she wiped her eyes, cleared her throat and read aloud.

"'Information received Telegraph Office, Liverpool. August 18th 1831. We have received the following melancholy announcement from Liverpool: - The intelligence of the total loss of the steamer Rothsay Castle, from hence to Beaumaris. She struck on the Dutchman's Bank, off Puffin Island, at 12 o'clock on Wednesday night, in a heavy gale of wind, at about N.N.W. Upwards of one hundred and twenty persons must have been on board, including the crew, and many female passengers. Our first accounts state that nine passengers only, and three of the crew, were saved; but subsequent communications suggest as many as twenty. We may still hope that more may have been saved. The vessel, it is said, became a perfect wreck about one hour and a half after she struck. Owing to the very heavy sea, the signal-man at the island has been, during the day, unable to reach the main land to obtain further intelligence. The above is the only authentic account hitherto received in Liverpool. – Barnard L. Watson. Superintendent of Telegraph.'"

Jim dropped into a chair. He rubbed his hand over his face.

"It gets worse." Helen handed him a final piece of paper.

"The principal and melancholy fact, however, is undoubtedly that the subjoined are the names (from the agent to Lloyd's) of those whose bodies which have so far been recovered dead. A total of twenty five counted so far and bought to Beaumaris." Jim paused, took a deep breath. "Those eighteen named so far: Mrs Wilson, Manchester; Mrs Hammond, Leeds; Rev. S. M'Carthy; Mr. Paine, Manchester; Jones, the steward, and his wife; Jones,

Fireman; and Hughes and son, and Evans, sailors belonging to the crew; Mr. James Nuttall, Liverpool; Miss Ginny Broadhurst, Liverpool; Mrs Valerie Owen and daughter; pilot boat Captain Joe Lloyd and son Jacob; Mr Marsden, London; Mrs Owen, London." Jim paused, gulped. "A further seven bodies recovered have so far remained unnamed ..."

Helen's eyes burned with tears. Hearing the roll call of names made it feel so real. Not a story anymore. Not a nightmare. But real life and real people.

"He's there, Jim," Helen managed to whisper. She touched the piece of paper gently. "Jacob's right there."

"I know." Jim leaned forward as if to comfort Helen.

"He's real and that proves it. His name there, on that telegram, proves this is all real, doesn't it?"

"It does, yes." Jim nodded.

"Poor, poor Jacob. He died as he described. I want to prove he lived as he described. I want to go to Llanddwyn. I want to see what Jacob saw, feel what he felt, live as he lived. I want to touch the place and breathe in the sea. I want his life to feel as real as his death to me."

"Whatever you want."

"It's such a relief. Such a huge relief. It proves I'm not mad and Jake's not mad. But it's so sad, Jim. I didn't expect to feel like this. It's like I've lost another loved one. I can't describe it. I don't know what I expected, but I didn't expect to feel so … so … raw."

Her voice faded and she sobbed quietly.

Chapter Seventeen

It was a full moon.

A blue moon, so he'd heard on the radio. A rare event, something special. It seemed quite fitting.

He leaned back against the door, pulling himself into the shadows of the alleyway, wishing he was on his boat. He loved night time at sea. Alone on the water, a clear sky and a huge moon, lighting the surface like a giant silver mirror. The swell soothing and calming him, many nights rocking him to dream-filled sleep.

"Hey, darlin', got a light?"

A fat blonde blocked the light from the pub doorway opposite.

He pushed himself back further into the gloom.

"Hey, you deaf? Asked if you gotta light. Damn lighters bust."

"No," he whispered, cursing the loud-mouthed tart, dressed up in some kind of bulging uniform. Black hold-ups, curling down her thighs, losing a battle with rolls of cellulite.

"What?"

"No. Just fuck off."

"I beg your pardon?" She leaned in closer, massive tits straining buttons.

"You will do. Fuck off. Do one. Lose yourself, understand, you fat slag?" His eyes flashed, fists clenched. The colour drained from the podgy face, pale beneath the make- up. "Understand?"

She gulped and nodded as she stepped backwards onto the pavement, tripped as she hurried away on the high heels.

Whore. Dressed like one, acted like one. A harlot, his mother would call her. And she'd know. Worse kind of harlot herself. But if there was one thing he hated more than a normal whore, it was a fat whore. A wave of repulsion sent chills through him despite the humidity of the evening.

He thought of Grace. Tall, graceful, lithe. A goddess.

There could never be another woman like Grace. Ever.

More loud music spilled out of the pub as a drunk toppled down the steps, unlit cigarette between his lips, squinting out into the darkness.

"Hey, fella, you gotta light down there?"

Shit. He had to move. He was attracting too much attention.

He stepped out of the alley, into the glare of the pavement; keeping his head down, he headed towards the restaurant.

His feet stopped dead. There she was. Smiling and waving, blowing a kiss to another girl. Grace. He shook his head. No, not Grace. Stupid bastard. He watched as the petite blonde turned, disappeared down the steps towards Church Street. Just as he'd hoped.

He forced his feet to move as his heart hammered. He had to get moving. He slipped back into the shadows, reversing his footsteps, then turned and broke into a run.

It was time.

"Night, honey!" Nia Morton shouted across the street to her friend Lauren, arm-in-arm with her boyfriend, Carl. Nia waved and blew a kiss, dodging out of the way as a squealing hen party raced past, pushing the bride-to-be in a wheelchair. All dressed in sexy nurses' outfits, a cacophony of cat calls and whistles followed them along the main road.

The pedestrian precinct in Bangor town centre heaved with

partying students, drinkers and clubbers. The recent hot weather had encouraged more people than usual on a Friday night to hit the town. Outdoor tables were jam packed, every available seat taken, and some sitting on pavements and walls. The noise was deafening, not helped by a police siren echoing in the distance.

"Are you sure you don't want to come with us?" called Lauren, raising her voice above the din. "It's only just gone midnight, you know. We're going over to Bullitt."

"No, I'm fine thanks, babe. I need an early night, my folks are visiting tomorrow, and I have to get the flat cleaned. It's a tip."

"Okay, no worries. You're getting a cab, right?"

"Yeah, yeah, just round the corner, usual place. I'll be fine."

"Okay, I'll call you tomorrow. Night."

"Night, babe. Night, Carl."

As Nia watched her friends walk away, she pondered on what had been a superb night. Having turned twenty the previous Monday, tonight was her second birthday party in a week. A fantastic Chinese meal at Lychee Garden, followed by cocktails at one of the trendiest bars in town. She was so lucky to have such great friends.

She groaned as she thought of the work facing her back at her flat, visualising the stacks of dirty dishes and the overflowing laundry basket. Tomorrow her parents were coming up from London to spend the weekend, and she wanted to make a good impression. Most of her family couldn't understand her decision to swap the bright lights of her home in Chelsea for the remote, rugged beauty of North Wales. Only her father, who also studied at Bangor, understood and encouraged her love of the area.

Nia paused to concentrate on the steps that led down to Church Street. She knew she wasn't drunk, but fair to say she felt tipsy. She had to focus on each step, and every one was a major hindrance in these shoes. Negotiated successfully, she stepped onto the pavement, deciding to cut through the alley behind the shops and out onto the main road. There were always taxis at an unofficial rank on the corner of Church Street.

She checked her appearance in a shop window as she passed under a street light. Her slight figure, large bust and bobbed blonde hair made her a success with men. She swam or used the gym three or four times a week, and liked to keep her natural tan topped up on the sunbed. She knew she could be vain, her friends certainly teased her enough, but she liked to take care of herself and look after her appearance. And in her opinion there was nothing wrong in that.

Her black stilettos clicked on the cobbled surface; the noise echoing around the passage. It was eerily quiet; a direct contrast to the noise of the bustling main street. She wrinkled her nose against the smell of pee and hurried her pace. The yellow street lamp at the far end of the narrow space beckoned her. The proverbial light at the end of the tunnel.

She wiped her forehead with the back of a hand. It was a humid, sticky, evening for late May. Although lightly dressed in a white blouse and black leggings, she could feel perspiration trickle down her neck, making the hairs stand on end.

Nia jumped at a movement behind her. A loud clanging noise resonated in the confines of the alley as a metal dustbin lid clattered to the floor. It rolled in an ever-decreasing circle, before finally spinning to a halt with a crash.

She stopped and turned, peering into the darkness. She couldn't see a thing.

"Hello!" she called.

No reply.

Shaking her head, she continued along the alley. There was no way anyone could have followed her, she would definitely have heard the footsteps. Perhaps there were rats in the bins. The thought of scurrying rodents made her quicken her pace. She gripped her handbag tighter.

Something shot out in front of her, almost making her stumble. She squealed, as a ginger cat brushed against her ankles, before disappearing into a pile of black bin bags. She clutched her throat, chest rising and falling as she breathed deeply. She didn't want to hang around in this alleyway a second longer than necessary, but she had to steady herself. She wished she hadn't drunk the last cocktail, too much Tia Maria clearly. She'd not considered stray cats rummaging in the refuse.

With a confident shake of her head, she focused on the end of the alleyway. In the distance, she could see the outlines of cars parked under the yellow street lamps. Only a few more yards, and she would be out of this smelly, creepy hellhole.

Nia emerged into the relative brightness of a small road that led down past the church and onto the bypass. Several cars were parked in front of the church gates. A red Peugeot was the only car in the lay-by with a taxi sign on its roof. She checked the identification plate on the rear bumper, before approaching the driver's window. It was one of the tips on the leaflets that had been circulated – always make sure you're getting into a genuine cab. She could see the registration number, and Bangor Council authentication details. She relaxed slightly. With any luck she'd be home in twenty minutes.

Nia rapped on the front window. A shadowy figure sat in the driver's seat but made no effort to acknowledge her. She knocked again.

"Excuse me. Hey, wake up!" she shouted. "Any chance of a ride to Fford Penrhos, just across from the hospital?"

Silence.

For a moment, Nia planned alternative options, deciding she'd have to find another way home. She raised her hand to give it one more try, when the window slid open a fraction. A plume of smoke leaked through the gap. Nia could see the orange, glowing tip of a cigarette in the darkness.

"Sure. Climb aboard," replied a male voice.

She opened the door, and slid onto the back seat, pulling the door shut behind her with the armrest.

"Fford Penrhos, please. Just off Fford Caergybi, left at the island by the hospital. Number twenty-four, please."

Nia tutted at the guy's lack of conversation skills. Her words elicited no more than a muted grunt, but as he started the engine and manoeuvred out of the parking spot, she could only assume he'd heard her request.

Under the fusty, heavy odour of cigarette smoke, the scent of sand or seaweed lingered in the grubby upholstery. She picked her white handbag up off the seat, trying to make herself as small as possible, so her body touched the minimum amount of car seat. She took her phone from her bag and flicked it open to check for messages. Just one from Nick, her ex, full of the usual sarcastic comments. She pressed delete.

Nia glanced up from her mobile. *Tesco's?* She spun round in her seat. The lights of the twenty-four hour petrol station lit up the night sky.

"Excuse me, I said Fford Penrhos. It's back the other way. You should have done a right at the last island, pal. Do you not know where it is?"

No reply. Nia inched forward in her seat, breathing in a mix of sweat and cigarette smoke to add to the heady perfume of the car.

"Hey, pal. I think you're going the wrong way ..."

"Hey, I'm not your pal. Sit down and shut up, bitch."

"What?"

"I said sit down, and shut the hell up."

"What's going on?"

"Don't make me ask you again, sugar. Sit back down and stop yelling."

"But I don't understand. What's happening? Where are you taking me?"

They were on the dual-carriageway, heading out of town. Nia didn't drive, so she had no idea which direction they were heading and everything looked so different in the dark.

She looked into the rear-view mirror, could make out heavy hooded lids over expressionless eyes. She could see his black, greasy hair above the headrest. Every time a passing car illuminated the front seats, she saw the side of a sallow, thin-faced man she didn't recognise. It all seemed unreal, as if events were unravelling in slow motion. Her brain seemed unwilling to take on the severity of the situation. She felt calm, when in fact she knew she should feel terrified.

"Look, I don't know what you're playing it, but this is beyond a joke. Take me back into town this minute!"

"Oooh, hark at her. Take me back into town at once, *driver*." He mimicked Nia's upper class southern accent.

"I mean it. Take me back or else …"

"Or else what? Who do you think you're talking to, you posh bitch?"

Before she had chance to react, a hand shot between the seats and yanked her handbag off her lap. He opened his window, and in one fluid movement threw the bag out. It hit the rear door before bouncing off into the central reservation.

Nia cried out. Tightness gripped her throat, and she felt a thread of panic building inside her chest.

"There goes your only chance of escape," he hissed. "Did you really think I was stupid enough to leave you with a mobile after you've been flashing it about? Don't mess with me, sugar."

"I don't understand why you're doing this. If you just take me home, we can forget about it. I promise I won't tell a soul."

The driver snorted. "If I had a quid for every time I've heard that line. If I wanted to take you home, I wouldn't have gone to the trouble of kidnapping you, would I? Dumb cow," he muttered under his breath as he swung the wheel to the left, negotiating an island at speed.

The force of the turn threw Nia against the door. She had an idea. She glanced across his shoulder at the odometer. They were travelling over 80mph. She wondered what the odds of surviving jumping from a moving car at that speed were. No, she'd wait until the next island or traffic lights, and then jump out and run like hell.

She ran her hand over the interior door panel, so she had her bearings when the time came. Puzzled, she used both hands to search for the door handle. All she found were two jagged holes in the fabric. With a moan, she slammed her fists against the glass.

"Oh, I've removed the window and door handles too. But then I think you've just found that out, haven't you?"

Nia's skin crawled as he chuckled at his own wit. "Very clever. But you've made a *huge* mistake kidnapping me."

"Really?"

"Too right. You'll live to regret this 'til the day you die."

"Really?" His voice dripped sarcasm. "Care to tell me why?"

Nia opened her mouth to speak.

"No, actually, let me guess. I'm going to regret it because you are Nia Morton. The only daughter of the Right Honourable Charlie Morton, MP for Hammersmith South. Right?"

Nia felt the blood drain from her face.

"Right?"

"Yes," she whispered. "How do you know?"

"I know everything, sugar. Everything."

Nia recognised the tall arches of the Britannia Bridge and knew they were crossing onto Anglesey. He turned a sharp left as they reached the other side. Nia pressed her face against the window, struggling to make out her surroundings without the aid of streetlights.

She pushed against the door, banged her fists on the glass.

"Help!" she yelled. "Help me."

"Shut up! You're wasting your breath, you silly cow."

"Someone might hear. Someone might see. You won't get away with this."

She pulled off a stiletto and smashed the pointed heel against the door window. The glass splintered with a crackling noise.

"What the f …"

The driver yanked the car off the road. Nia bounced up and down as the wheels spun over the grass verge.

"What the hell are you doing?" he roared.

"Help! Someone! Help me!"

Nia smashed the shoe against the glass again and again. The jagged fracture widened; a maze of hairline cracks appeared. She beat against it with her fists; the warm trickle of blood running down her wrists. She hammered furiously, but the toughened glass wouldn't give. Blood spattered the window, but she kept smashing her fists against it, smearing bright red gore all over the glass.

In her fierce determination, it took her several seconds to realise the car had stopped moving.

A hand grabbed her collar. She jumped and squealed as the driver yanked her backwards. A fist connected with the side of her head. She howled in pain and grabbed at the wrist that was now pulling her hair, tearing at the skin, trying to ease the pressure on her scalp, trying to stop the searing pain.

She turned her head and sunk her teeth into the bony arm.

"Shit! You bitch."

A resounding crack echoed through the silence, as he swung his free fist and drove it into her nose. Pain hit her with the speed and force of an express train and she fell backwards on the seat, tasting her own blood, mixed with her attacker's, on her tongue. She cradled her face, touching her nose gingerly to see if it was broken.

The outline of her attacker crouched beside the door. She could hear heavy, ragged breathing and smell alcohol on his breath; the stench made her feel sick.

His face, pale grey and distorted through her tears, hovered inches above hers.

"Have you had enough yet?" he hissed. "Or do you want some more?"

She spat blood onto the car floor.

"Fuck you," she whispered.

"Mind your language, young lady. Whatever would your Right Honourable father say if he heard you cussing like a commoner?"

"Go to hell."

"Fine."

He slipped a hand into his jacket pocket and withdrew a hypodermic syringe. He held it up, tapped it, and pulled off the cap.

"No!" Nia pushed herself backwards along the rear seat. "Don't. Please. I'll stay quiet."

"Good choice." He slammed the door and climbed back into the driving seat. "Just be a good girl and speak when you're spoken to."

The car bounced down the kerb, back onto the road. He accelerated away and Nia threw herself forward, one arm either side of the headrest. She clawed his face with her long fingernails, covering his eyes with her hands, obscuring his vision.

"Get off! Get off me you dumb bitch!"

He braked hard, causing the car to swerve to the right. A horn blared, as headlights on full beam bore down on them. He pulled the steering wheel to the left, using one hand to steer and his other to yank Nia's hands away from his eyes. The car swayed as a white van sped past, missing them – by what seemed to Nia – inches.

"Will you get off? You mad bitch! I'm going to kill you for this!"

"I don't care. I'd rather die now, than later at your hands."

The car smashed into the kerb with a loud thud, jolting Nia out of the seat. Her head connected with the roof, sending waves of dizziness surging through her, but still she clung to him. She imagined the impact would have buckled the front wheel or shredded a tyre. The car rocked from side to side. He gripped the steering wheel as trees and hedges flashed past the windows, uncomfortably near. Branches scraped against the glass. The high-pitched squeal added to the eeriness, like a terrified child's scream inside Nia's muddled head.

Nia continued to gouge at his face with her nails. Blood and spittle formed at the corners of her mouth. She scratched at his cheeks, sinking her nails deep into the flesh, praying she scarred him and drew blood. She wanted to disfigure. Maim. She felt no guilt. Even if she died tonight, she needed to leave some proof behind, something to draw suspicion. Squeezing forward into the gap between the seats, Nia clamped her teeth onto his left ear lobe, biting down as hard as she could.

He screamed in pain as the car zigzagged across the double white line in the centre of the road.

Finally, he used her own form of defence, and clamped his teeth into her right wrist. She screamed in agony and pulled her hand away, releasing his ear as the momentum threw her back onto the seat. He used the opportunity to straighten up and make sure they were on the right side of the road. Another horn sounded angrily as the car behind overtook them.

The headlights shone into the rear of the Peugeot as it passed. Nia waved her arms above her head and beat on the rear window. The horn honked again as it sped past. Presumably, the driver thinking it was another drunk on the road. It was too much to hope that he'd taken the registration number and would be public spirited enough to take it to the police.

"You mad bitch. You stupid mad bitch." He struggled to control the car as it rumbled along, one wrecked tyre. "I should kill you for that."

Nia watched as he traced his fingertips across his injured cheek, a jagged crimson gash visible even in the gloom.

"You think I'm gonna sit back and let you murder me. I'd rather die trying to escape. I won't make this easy for you. I'll hurt you as much as you hurt me."

She panted. Adrenalin made her heart pound, but nerves constricted her chest, making it tight and difficult to breathe. She rubbed her injured arm and fingered the bite mark.

His laugh chilled her.

"I like your spunk, sugar. You're a feisty little bitch, aren't you? I almost admire you for it."

"So, let me go."

"I said almost."

"Fine. Whatever. Stop the car, let me walk. Trust me to forget this ever happened."

"I can't."

"You can. Please, let me go."

"I can't. I've waited too long for this. All the planning, all the research, all the trial runs. I've too much to lose. I can't back out now. I don't want to."

"How'd you mean? All the trial runs."

He remained silent, drove steadily now, well within the speed limit. Nia knew that driving on a flat tyre might attract attention, but he wouldn't risk changing it. Although he might be confident the safety glass would hold, she knew he wouldn't risk stopping the car. He'd carry on to their final destination, wherever that may be.

She could see nothing at all outside the rear window. No streetlamps, no houses, no lights. Nothing.

"What do you mean?" she asked again. "Do you mean the other girls? They were planned?"

"Oh God, yes, sugar. They were meticulously planned. Research and planning are the keys."

"Why?"

"Because I had to make sure I got it perfect."

"Perfect for what?"

Her eyes met his in the rear view mirror.

"For you, of course."

Chapter Eighteen

"I can't believe it. I mean, there could be some young girl out there at this very minute going through hell." Gareth looked from Chris to DI McRae. He clenched and unclenched his fists. "What an idiot! Why didn't I check?"

Gareth felt a hand on his shoulder. In his despair, he hadn't seen McRae leave his seat. "Probably because you weren't expecting to get a call from a serial killer on your home telephone?" McRae sighed. "I totally understand your frustration. Believe me. But I don't think it's productive. You need to get a grip on yourself just now, channel the anger and put things into perspective if you're going to be any help to us here today. Understand?"

The words were gentle, almost lyrical with the softness of his Scottish accent.

But the warning was clear.

Gareth pulled himself upright, cleared his throat. "I'm sorry, sir. I think it's shock."

"I'm sure it is, Parry. But we need to put all our efforts into checking this phone call is genuine, and, if it is, trying to find the girl. We can't have anything make us lose focus or go off the rails. Are we clear?"

Gareth nodded, his face ablaze. Lose focus? No way could he tell his superior of the sleepless night he'd spent scouring the streets of Bangor. Driving from nightclub to nightclub. From expensive restaurants to back-street takeaways. The numerous bars he'd sat outside, engine running, until he feared he'd either get a good kicking from the bouncers or reported to the police for kerb-crawling. But he'd had to do something. After he put in the call to DI McRae, interrupting him at the theatre, how could he take his boss's advice to sit tight, wait for another call and let the constabulary do their job. Desperate for company and support, he'd left numerous messages for Chris, but heard nothing until 7am when he finally called back, his voice thick and slurred. Judging from the state of his dress and growth of his beard, he'd had little more sleep than Gareth the previous night – but for totally different reasons.

"Now, let's take another listen to the tape," said McRae, sliding back into the seat behind his vast desk. "Coleman, can you do the honours?"

"Hello, Detective. You don't know me …"

Gareth stiffened as the nasal voice filled the office, echoing off walls and glass. He'd replayed it so many times on a constant loop he could recite the words verbatim. First he'd listened in disbelief, a sneer on his lips, not understanding the words, convinced it was some kind of wind up; a practical joke by one of the many wankers at the station. But then the reality dawned. No one would do this, could be so cruel. Or so accurate.

"Quite a performance. Congratulations. However, I don't like being threatened. That said, I'm always up for a challenge ..."

He turned away, seeking solace in the blueness of the sky outside the window, watching a few clouds caught in the sea breeze, rushing across his postcard view.

He heard Chris's voice.

"… and no trace of any discernible accent. The lab has the original at the moment, obviously undergoing further tests. But to the naked ear, there are no indications of any background noises."

"So, yet again he gives us nothing." said McRae, fingers laced in front of him on his desk, brow furrowed in concentration.

Coleman shook his head. "Nada. All the lab can say is this

call was made on a mobile phone. Not much help, sir. And also, I wonder how he got Parry's number?"

"Edwina's mobile phone?" suggested McRae.

"No, sir. That was in her room."

"A phonebook or notepad then. Did you check they were in her handbag?"

Gareth shook his head. "Best of my knowledge, she stored everything in her phone. People don't do diaries anymore, do they?"

"Any other suggestions?" asked McRae, looking from one to another. When both remained silent, he added. "So, we need to keep that in mind, too. Eyes and ears open, Parry. This guy may specialise in stalking. Who knows if he doesn't have you in mind as a future victim."

Gareth looked up, his expression steady. "I'd welcome it, sir. I'd like to meet this guy face to face, I assure you –"

"I've no doubt," broke in McRae. "But I don't need anyone to play Rambo right now. Understood?"

"Yes, sir." Gareth replied, exhaling a long breath. "But it all feels very much one sided. I mean, how the hell does he expect us to play the game if we don't know the rules? What is he trying to achieve?"

"He's a nutter, bud," said Chris. "Not sure it's possible to reason with a psychopath –"

"On the contrary, detective," interrupted McRae, "I think we have to try. We have to get inside his head. If I picked up anything from that recording it's that this guy is struggling to maintain the calm, collected persona he hides behind. I think he's royally pissed off. He's rattled enough to contact Parry. It's a huge risk, however he's managed it. Why? It surely can't be part of his plan. So, what has pushed him to overstep his boundaries?"

"He likes a challenge?" said Chris. "He said so himself."

"Why not then contact us before the first murder? Or Edwina's. Why now? Why so late in the game?" McRae shook his head. "There's a reason. I'm sure of it."

Gareth cleared his throat. "Sir, I assumed it was the television appeal. Doesn't he say as much?"

McRae nodded slowly. "He does. But that means nothing. He's hardly going to tell us the real reason, is he? Sure you goaded him. That was our intent, no? To flush him out. It worked. But there's more to it than this guy being a show off, there has to be."

"Perhaps we've got too close for comfort?" suggested Chris. "Someone on the team has made a discovery, and he knows about it. Perhaps we all know but haven't put the pieces together yet?"

McRae nodded. "Good thinking, Coleman. We've rattled him. Forced his hand. I think rather than setting a challenge, goading us to take him on, I think he's trying to do the opposite. Slow us down, keep us at bay." He paused, drummed his fingers on the veneer surface. "I'm going to call a team briefing this afternoon at 3pm. I want everyone's reports on my desk by lunchtime, so I've a couple of hours to go through all the interviews, put everything in order, and hope in doing so, I find some link to this guy. We're close. I can smell it."

Gareth thought back to Glyn Rogers. The unnatural dislike he felt for the man, and his overreaction to the news of Edwina's death. The hurriedly made phone call as they'd left, knowing he was in sight of the policemen. What was that?

Gareth looked up, hearing his name. "Sorry, sir?"

"I asked if you'd spoken to your aunt."

Gareth nodded, lowered his eyes. "Not good, sir."

"I'm sorry. Do you think you should visit her?"

Gareth shook his head. "I want to be here, sir. I'm more use here at the moment. Besides, I can't go anywhere. I keep expecting a call to come in reporting a missing girl."

"Still nothing?" McRae directed the question across the room at Chris.

Chris shook his head. "No, sir. We've doubled patrols around Bangor, but no reports as yet."

"Mmm. Interesting," mused McRae. "Why? Is he bluffing? Or has he failed?"

"Or maybe she lives alone. No one knows she's missing yet. I think that's the more likely option, don't you, sir?" Gareth wiped his palms along his thighs, the skin sticky with sweat. "I can't see him failing or bluffing. He's not the type. Something tells me this abduction is important. Perhaps that's why he's decided he wants more attention. Perhaps he doesn't think he's getting the credit he deserves."

McRae nodded. "Good. I like the thinking, Parry. Stay with that line of thought. And answer this question. How do we accept his challenge?"

"Sir?"

"He set down a challenge to you personally, Parry. I think it only fair you acknowledge acceptance."

"How?"

"It worked last time. A press conference. I like the thought of him sitting somewhere, eagerly watching every news bulletin, waiting for his reply. I think we should give it to him. I think we should play the game." He paused, eyes bright, pale skin flushed. "We can beat him. We can do this."

"You want me to speak to him again?" asked Gareth, swallowing down a lump of nausea at the thought. He'd hated the pressing crowds, the popping flashlights, the ignorant journalists shouting questions and jostling for position. Front page fodder. And behind it all, the thought he may be communicating with his worst enemy.

McRae nodded. "I think so. It worked last time."

"But we have no proof he has made another kidnap attempt yet, sir," added Chris.

"I think we all know it's only a matter of time. Once we hear, then I want us to be ready to move quick. Make a flash statement, have Parry act as official spokesman, but have some hidden message in there that only our guy will understand. Let him know we accept his challenge, and that we're right on his tail."

"Even if we're not …"

"Yes, Parry. Even if we're not." McRae stood, carefully removing his jacket from the back of his chair. "Coleman, round up the troops, tell them I want them all in the investigation room this afternoon. No excuses. And I also want a full transcript of all calls received after Parry's last press conference, both local and national numbers. Can you organise that for me, too? Sorry to pile on the pressure, Coleman, this station is like the Marie Celeste today."

Coleman nodded as the DCI headed for the door. "Of course, sir."

"Oh, and Coleman." McRae paused, turning to face them.

"Sir?"

"Get a shower, man. I can smell whiskey from here. If you don't have toiletries, there's a bag in my bottom drawer. Do not turn up at the debrief in that state."

The door closed.

"Yes, sir," Chris hissed, before dropping into a chair. "Fuck."

"You do look like shite, mate," said Gareth.

"So do you."

"I have an excuse."

"So do I …"

Gareth raised his eyebrows. "What? Been up all night talking to ghosts again?" he asked, with a playful smirk. It was a standing joke that Chris watched weird satellite shows about ghost hunting and the occult in the early hours to feed another of his fixations – all things paranormal.

"Mind your fucking business."

Gareth recoiled, the smile slipped from his lips. "Chris, mate. I hate to see you in this state. I'm only trying to help."

"Right …"

"Yeah, right."

"Then leave me alone to do my job and keep off my back. Don't you think I've enough shite off McRae? That is unless you have issues with the way I do my job too. Is that it?"

Chris's eyes flashed and his round face shone red, broken only by the blackness of his beard and shadows like deep purple thumbprints beneath both eyes.

Gareth stood, hands raised in surrender, and backed out of the room in silence.

Gareth slid the mug of cold, congealing coffee to one side and pushed back his chair. Glancing round, he realised he was alone in the canteen, breakfast over an hour ago. Chairs and tables neatly arranged and polished, ready for the lunchtime invasion.

He shook his right hand to stimulate the blood flow, and stared down at the notes; at least half a dozen sheets filled with his tiny writing, everything he'd discovered about each of the victims condensed into his own form of shorthand, easy to cross reference.

He lifted another sheet of paper, this one more sparsely covered. The heading was 'Connections' – and after an hour's work, the page was virtually blank. He'd hoped to draw some comparisons. Even something as tenuous as hair colour or similarities in routine. But there was nothing, at least that he could see, that connected any of these girls. He dropped his pen, picked up his mug, and marched to the coffee machine at the front of the room.

But there had to be, didn't there. That was a given as far as he was concerned. There had to be.

He'd turned the table to face the window, where heavy grey clouds now spoiled the expanse of blue. He'd thought of going back to the investigation room, to Chris, forcing him to talk. But he knew now wasn't the right time. He could forgive him for snapping. McRae's observation, however sugared, was enough to offend anyone. He wasn't one to blow things out of proportion, but it was up to Chris to make the first move. If not an apology, then at least an acknowledgement. There'd be a time for talking, and he would need to be there for his partner when that time came.

He slipped into his chair and rolled his neck, scanning through the notes he'd made, determined to find something. He hated to think of a morning's work wasted. There had to be a chance sparkle of diamond among the piles of carbon. That was how investigations worked in his experience. The hard part was recognising the gem, not passing over it in a haze of malaise while sifting through the slag.

Hobbies: Kerry O'Grady – none. Heavy drinker, heavy clubber, drug user. Bethan Jones – sport. Marathon runner and keen swimmer, co-leader of the Uni's Duke of Edinburgh Award Scheme. Edwina Parry – books and music. Reading group and debate society.

Achievements: Kerry O'Grady – none. Bethan Jones – Recently awarded CADW Young Entrepreneur Award for her services to the tourism industry. Edwina Parry – Finished top ten of first year young achievers and recent winner of the debate society.

Families: Kerry O'Grady – estranged from own family in Liverpool. Bethan Jones – lived with parents in Bangor, one sister age fourteen.

Gareth flicked through the cross reference files compiled by the vigilant DC Whitlock. Sandra was a wizard with stats. She'd not managed to find a single person with a link between the three girls, neither students or tutors, nor family members. She'd also found no links of any meeting between the victims either inside the university or in the outside world. Nothing to say the girls had ever come into contact with each other.

It was ridiculous. Totally. That they could draw a blank at every crossing.

He jumped as his mobile beeped and vibrated on the table. Would he forever now have this aversion to telephones? Expecting every call to have ominous consequences. Idiot. He scrolled down to SMS. His heart picked up speed as he saw his aunt's number, and quickly opened the new message.

St Martins in the Field. Wednesday @ 10am.
Wrexham Crematorium @ 11am.
Family flowers only. Donations to St Theresa's Hospice.

He scrolled down, expecting more. Nothing. This could be the announcement in the local newspaper. Not a personal word from his aunt at all. And who'd made the decision about flowers? Edwina loved flowers, had a passion for gardening. She would have loved lots of flowers, however sombre the occasion. He didn't have any issue with the donations made to the hospice that had been so supportive during his father's illness, but it wasn't fair that people were denied the chance to show how much they cared for his cousin.

His finger trembled over the redial button. How dare his family treat him like this? Like nothing more than a casual outsider, not a thought to his feelings. However much Aunt Linda blamed him, however she needed to cope with her grief, enough was enough. She hadn't been there that day at Gallows Point. She hadn't had to see the grey flesh, smell the stink of the mud …

"Hey." A hand on his shoulder made him jump. For a second it was Edwina's voice. Ever the peacemaker. But then it was gone, and he turned to look up at Susan Connolly.

"Hey." He let out a long pent-up breath. "Take a pew. You okay?"

"I could ask you the same," she said as she shrugged off her coat.

He handed her the phone. She frowned as she read the text.

"Who sent it?" she asked, handing it back.

"My aunt."

"Oh."

"Exactly."

"It can't be easy for her, Gareth. She's lost her only daughter –"

"And I've lost a cousin and a father in the past few years. It's not easy for me, but I don't take it out on her. She's making me feel like the fucking murderer –"

"Language ..."

"Sorry. But I've had it with her. I was about to phone her. Have it out –"

"Then I arrived at the right time. Calm down." Susan rested a hand across his fist. "Take deep breaths. Let it go."

Gareth took her advice, taking his time to breathe slowly, focusing again on the scudding clouds outside the window. Aware that Susan had gone to fetch herself a hot drink, he allowed himself to count to fifty and back again. He guessed he was learning the art of maturity, years ago he'd have already rung his aunt – and be sorely regretting it by now.

He heard a scrape of chair as Susan returned, blowing on a mug of tea.

"Better?" she asked.

"Not much to be honest."

"Look, I've been thinking. I'll put the offer out there. But if you're not keen, I won't be in the least offended."

"What?"

"I mean, I don't know if you're with anyone right now. But the offer's there as a friend ..."

Gareth touched her wrist. "Susan, you're babbling. What?"

"Sorry. If you want support next week, I'll go with you to the funeral. It depends if you want company. I know you, you probably –"

"Susan, shush." He smiled at her raised eyebrows. "Thank you. That would be great. I really appreciate the offer. But what about Dr Zhivago, won't he have something to say?"

"Of course not," Susan replied, extracting her arm from his fingers. "But I see no real need to tell him. Do you?"

Their eyes met and Gareth nodded, noting the pinkness of her cheeks as she sipped her tea.

"If that's what you want." He changed the subject, sensing

Susan's discomfort, recalling the nervous trait as she smoothed her hair back behind her ears. "Anyway, that's not what you're here for, is it? How'd you find me?"

"I was looking. Coleman said I'd find you here."

So, Chris had been to the canteen and left without making his presence known.

"What finds you here on a weekend?" he asked.

Susan wrinkled her nose. "On duty. Had a call to rush through a PM at the crack of dawn. Then I got talking to Surinder in the Lab. He's working on the tape you sent across, and to be honest I got sucked in. You know what I'm like, especially when I have involvement in the case."

Susan pulled a thin file out of her bag. "I wanted to ask your advice on this. Neither Sunny nor I are convinced enough to go official just yet. I've left him beavering away at the Lab. But I wanted to bounce the idea off someone –"

Gareth pulled his chair closer to Susan. "Go on."

"Take a look at these graphs. These are two of the routine tests we run. I won't bore you with the technical jargon, but basically it involves slowing the sound waves right down and then monitoring the audio."

Susan held the papers aloft; both showed squiggly lines on what looked to him like a graph he'd last seen in his Math's GCSE.

"God, it takes me back to school. Enough to bring me out in a cold sweat."

Susan smiled as she laid the sheets side by side on the table. "This one," she said, tapping the left page with a manicured nail, "is the test run on the voice recording. And this is the background noise analysis test. Now, you may be a simpleton when it comes to physics, but what can you tell me about both recordings here."

Gareth stared at the sheets of paper, first one, then the other, taking his time to study the blue and red lines. "Well, I dunno. Except that the results look similar."

"Exactly! You can clearly see the noise undulations. Here the pitch of the voice follows these curves. See? And here, the background noise frequencies have definite peaks and troughs too. When you put the two results together, they're almost identical."

"Erm, great." Gareth paused. "What does it mean?"

"To make it as simple as possible it means that something, some movement or change in atmosphere, caused this variance in the sound. But critically, it changed both the voice and the surroundings."

Gareth shook his head. "Sorry but you need to go even simpler."

"Okay, this is the theory Sunny and I have come up with." Susan pushed back the chair and stood, both palms resting on the table. "Imagine I'm on a cross channel ferry and I'm shouting across to you on the other side of the deck. Okay?" Gareth nodded, suppressing a smile. "Yeah, okay, nutty scientist, I know, but go with it. Now, imagine we hit some rough seas." Susan began to dip her knees, then straighten, as she spoke. "Notice how my voice rises and falls. Imagine a rough tide, high waves. Well, the same effect would occur on any background noise. As the boat rose and fell on the swell, any surrounding noise recorded on the deck, would follow the same undulating sequence. Make sense?"

Gareth nodded. "Yes, I think so. But what is the background noise then?"

"That's what Sunny is working on now. We think it's road noise."

"Traffic?"

"Yes."

"On a boat?"

"That's where it gets complicated." Susan sat down again with a sigh. "But not impossible. What about a boat alongside a road, or a pier or jetty? But it would have to be a busy road for the level of traffic noise. It's quite a distance to the source, I'd say, which is why nothing could be heard to the naked ear. But it's constant. More like a dual-carriageway than a country lane ..."

"Or a bridge," Gareth muttered.

"What's that?"

"I said ... or a bridge. What about if the boat was anchored beneath a bridge? Like the Menai or Britannia, would that have the same effect on the recordings?"

"Not *beneath* the bridge. The sound would have to travel along the surface of the water. But certainly somewhere close by would make sense. And yeah, those bridges across to Anglesey are always busy with the Irish ferry traffic, aren't they?"

Gareth slumped back into the chair; his gaze fixed on the pages. "Jesus, Sue. He's on a boat. Perhaps keeping the victims on a boat?"

"I can't say. But it's all that Surinder or myself could come up with. And it does make sense. The bodies have all been washed up at sea, haven't they? So much easier to dispose of a body from a boat." She paused, twisting the ring around the third finger of her left hand, deep in thought. "I know this is out of my remit and I should leave it to you detective types, but as a Bangor lass, I'd hazard a guess he's local if we're right about the bridges. The Swellies between the bridges are notorious for strong currents and riptides. If he can navigate a boat along that stretch of the Menai Straits, he's no novice; in fact, he's an expert with local knowledge. Only those who grew up round these waters and know the tides well are usually willing to risk it."

"Like a member of a RNLI crew, per chance?" Gareth muttered under his breath.

"Sorry?"

"Nothing, ignore me." He stretched his back and shook his head. "Jesus, Sue," he repeated, turning to study the flashing emeralds, "you are fucking amazing. Do you know that?"

"Just a geek, I told you. I can't be one hundred percent sure I'm right."

"Give me the odds?"

"I'd say I'm eighty percent certain."

"That's good enough for me. Come on, we need to go tell McRae."

Chapter Nineteen

Jim pulled the Volvo into a parking space next to the remote café. Helen climbed out and winced as her back clicked into place. She grimaced; she always got stiff and grumpy after long car journeys. Jake, on the other hand, had been chatty and positively buzzing from the moment he climbed in the car. Helen opened the rear door, and he jumped out, racing in circles around the car park until Jim took his hand to show him his digital camera.

Helen surveyed the landscape. The vista was breathtaking. She turned in a three hundred and sixty degree rotation to take in the whole view. Mountains and valleys, trees and fields – not to mention a few hundred sheep – spread out in every direction. One or two hazy white clouds hovered in an azure sky. Shielding her eyes, she took in the horizon where the mountain tops were covered in a carpet of purple heather. Late May sunshine drew her head upwards and warmed her face.

It had not been a hard decision to bring the journey to Wales forward. Another nightmare, more trauma accompanied by the intelligible language, had persuaded Pat and Jim that things were snowballing. Getting to the bottom of Jake's distress as soon as possible was vital.

Jim stood beside her, turning in each direction to take shots of the whole valley and the mountains beyond. "I never knew there were so many variants of green."

Helen smiled. "I know. Every field, every tree, every hedgerow seems to be a slightly different shade. It's a good job I'm wearing sunglasses. It's almost too much green for my eyes to cope with."

Jim chuckled. "So where exactly are we?"

"The last town we went through, when we crossed the river Dee, was Llangollen. This mountain range is known as the Horseshoe Pass. For obvious reasons," she added, gesturing to the steep, looping road they'd travelled.

"Well, it sure is stunning. And I can't believe there are so few people around. If this were over in the US it would be crammed with tourist buses and day trippers."

"I think it does get busy, it's a popular spot. I thought it would make an ideal half way stop off and a nice spot for lunch. It's a little out of our way, but Dad suggested the detour was worth it. And I have to say I agree."

"So do I. Most definitely. And you've done a first rate job with directions so far."

Helen laughed. "Thank my dad. He knows this area like the back of his hand. He and Mum are always up here. I came a few times as a child, but I've not been here for years. He gave me lots of tips and places to stop off. If we took in all of them, we'd never reach our destination."

"We're in no desperate hurry. I don't want to stress Jake. The longer he sees this as nothing more than a vacation the better."

"He seems fine again today, doesn't he?" She ruffled Jake's hair as he bounded over. "Come on, little guy, give the camera back to Jim before you break it, and let's go get some lunch."

"Yeee-aa-hh!" Jake yelled, as he ran full speed in the direction of the café.

"Typical man," said Helen, as they followed. "Always thinking of his stomach."

A few hours later, Helen told Jake to take a look out the rear door window. Jake pressed his nose to the glass, and cupped his hands round his eyes.

"See, Jake," said Helen. "We're going over a bridge. This is the Britannia Bridge according to the map. We're leaving mainland Wales, crossing onto Anglesey, over the Menai Straits. How pretty is that? Look."

Helen gestured to their right. Jim slowed the car as she pointed out a small church on an island in the middle of Straits. Swirling currents of water as dark green as a dense pine forest, surrounded the island, and Helen could just make out a cross on its highest point.

"I can't see any mention of that on my map," Helen commented, as she scanned the book on her lap. "But it looks beautiful, I love old churches. Maybe we could try and find it one day, if we get time?"

"Sure," replied Jim. "Now, first turn off after the bridge, you said. Yep, there we go. Bowmareese, Menai Bridge, Amluch. Gee, these names are unpronounceable. Have the Welsh never heard of vowels?"

Helen chucked and so did Jake.

"It's Am-lock," Jake said. "Am-lock and Bo-maris. You make it sound all funny."

Helen and Jim shot a quick glance across the car.

Jim indicated right, and turned out on the main road. A little while later he pulled the car into a lay-by. A signpost announced it was a local beauty spot and viewpoint.

"There, that looks like the old Menai Bridge we read about," said Helen, as she helped Jake climb onto the wall for a better view. "That's the Britannia on our right, which we came over, and the Menai to the left. And there's the little Church Island – look." She pointed. "Hey, it's not totally cut off, you can see from here, there's a causeway across to it. It's really, really beautiful here. That old suspension bridge is a wonderful backdrop."

Jim's camera clicked away. He turned and asked casually, "Hey, Jake. You recognise any of this, buddy?"

Jake shook his head. "No. I don't think so. I don't remember the bridges."

"No, forget the bridges. They weren't around a long time ago. I mean the Menai Straits. The water or the mountains. Any of it seem familiar to you?"

Jake shook his head again.

"No." He jumped down from the wall, turning his back on Jim. "I'm thirsty, Mummy. Can I have some juice? And I'm sleepy, too."

Jake climbed back in the car, slamming the door behind him, and lay down across the back seat.

Helen checked Jim's face, and he gave a reassuring smile.

"He's very subdued now, isn't he?" said Helen, her voice low. "He was buzzing earlier. It's almost like he doesn't want to talk about it now we're here."

Jim nodded and scratched his chin. "I've seen this reaction before, it's not unusual. They start to get scared by the feelings being back at a place provokes. So they try to ignore them, I guess, hoping, they'll go away. Don't worry. I'm sure he'll start to open up, the more settled and safe he feels. Come on, let's get to the hotel and he can have a sleep."

"What about him recognising the place names? That's pretty odd."

"Not really. You remember we talked about Xenoglossy? That's a perfect example. Obviously there's a lot of Jacob stored in Jake's subconscious. It's always there; it just pops up now and then. He didn't even realise what he'd said. It's fascinating stuff admittedly, but nothing to worry about."

Helen turned to hand Jake a bottle of juice as she climbed back into the car. He was curled on the rear seat, thumb in mouth, snoring gently. His eyelids flicked and his nose twitched. His lips opened and closed as if in silent conversation.

"I wonder what he's dreaming about?" Helen whispered.

"Who knows. As long as he's peaceful."

They drove through the small town of Menai Bridge, nestling at the base of the massive Thomas Telford construction. The main street was lined with craft shops, art galleries and estate agents. The view across to the mountain range of Snowdonia, on mainland Wales, was stunning. Jim stopped the car numerous times to take pictures. It had to be one of the most picturesque places Helen had ever visited.

The road between Menai Bridge and Beaumaris followed the cliff edge. It was narrow and winding, situated on the edge of a sheer drop. Helen closed her eyes and felt her heart miss a beat as Jim slowed the car right down, engaged second gear, and crawled his way along. The trees obscured the view, until suddenly they emerged into the blinding sunlight bouncing off a vivid aquamarine sea.

The colourful town of Beaumaris lay in front of them, skirted by a small harbour lined with row upon row of boats, all gently bobbing on their moorings.

"Look at the castle," she exclaimed. "I read about it. Apparently it's one of the most sophisticatedly built medieval castles, with double concentric walls. I remember seeing aerial pictures of it. Built by King Edward the First in 1295. But it was never actually finished. It's impressive, isn't it?"

"Awesome," replied Jim. "We'll take a walk around the town later, and I can get some photos. Now, where's the hotel. What was it called?"

"The Bulkeley. It's on the seafront, opposite the pier, it says. So I'm guessing we need to take a right any time soon."

"Here we go." Jim negotiated the car into a narrow street that led onto a lawned area in front of the promenade. "And there it is – The Bulkeley Hotel. Looks nearly as old as the castle."

"It looks lovely," said Helen. "I can't remember all the details but there was a lot of history attached to it."

Helen turned and looked out of her window as Jim manoeuvred the car into a space in the hotel car park.

"So, that's where it happened then?"

"Sorry?" asked Jim, glancing over his shoulder as he reversed.

"The Rothsay Castle. On the map, Lavan Sands lie directly off Beaumaris. Out there. Right in front of us. That's where Jacob died."

"Shush. Little ears." Jim put his forefinger to his lips.

"God, I forgot." Helen turned to glance at Jake, who was still snoring. "Carried away by the moment. It feels kind of sad, being here. I wonder if the wreck of The Rothsay was ever recovered."

"I don't know. I did try and find out. But there was very little information. And no mention on the Lloyds Register either."

They both sat and gazed out to sea for a few minutes, enjoying the silence and taking in the charm of the area, the splendour of the mountains across the expanse of water. Sailing boats passed back and forth, their multi-coloured sails flapping in the breeze. Seagulls swooped low across the water, following a fishing boat returning with its catch.

"It's a beautiful place. It's hard to believe it has any connection with such a tragedy."

"I know." Jim seemed lost in thought. "But remember the research. Back in the early nineteenth century, this was a real busy shipping route. Because of slate exports, it was virtually the Route 66 of the day. Every website made the point. I'd think there are lots of wrecks out there."

Helen nodded. She knew Jim was right. It was just hard to take in. And hard to explain she was feeling an emotion not far removed from grief. It sounded absurd to be grieving for a little boy and his father, who'd been dead for one hundred and eighty years. But that was exactly how it felt. She sensed Jim felt it too.

She pushed open her door. "Come on. We'll get checked in and relax this evening. Tomorrow we get to take Jake to Llanddwyn."

* * *

The road that led from Newborough down to Llanddwyn beach was a single-track with few passing places. Luckily for them, this particular Sunday morning was quiet. They rounded a bend and came to a metal barrier in the road, with a red and green traffic-light system in place.

"What's this?" asked Jim, pulling alongside the machine. "Oh, there's a fee to drive through the forestry commission area it says. Two pounds."

Helen reached for her purse."There you go. It must be quite a special place to charge people to go down to the beach."

Jim leaned through the open window and slid the coin into the slot. Both barriers retracted and he drove through.

Within seconds, they were submerged in a dense forest. The temperature dropped as thick branches blocked out the sunlight. Helen shivered and rubbed her bare arms. It was such a contrast from the baking sun. The atmosphere in the forest was eerie. She turned to look at Jake.

"You okay, Jakey?"

"Why's it gone dark?" he asked, his thumb creeping into his mouth.

"Just the trees, sweetie, blocking out the sunlight. We're driving through this wood to get down to the beach. The sun will be out again when we get there. Are you looking forward to paddling in the sea?"

"Yeah!" His bad mood disappeared as quickly as it arrived. "Can I build sandcastles too?"

"Sure thing," answered Jim. "But only if I can help."

Helen lowered the window and sniffed the warm air. The smell of pine was overpowering, but she could also detect a slight salty tang in the air.

The road ended at a junction; the track to the right was blocked by another barrier. To the left there was a large car park, almost full. Jim manoeuvred the car into a remaining space, and pulled on the handbrake.

"There we go," he said. "Who's for an ice cream?"

"Me!" Jake's hand shot into the air.

Helen watched them run across to the ice-cream van parked under trees in the far corner of the car park.

The sun was as strong as ever now. With trees behind them, and sand dunes to the front, this was a perfect suntrap. One or two elderly couples had set up picnic tables next to their cars, presumably finding the walk down to the beach too much trouble.

Helen opened the boot and removed towels, bags and Jake's toys. By the time Jake and Jim returned with melting ice creams, she was organised and ready to go. Jake already had a splodge of strawberry pink ice cream down the front of his white t-shirt.

They followed the track through the sand dunes, the sand burning Helen's feet. Her bare shoulders and legs prickled in the heat. She called to Jake not to run too far ahead.

"I'm getting nervous, Jim," she whispered, popping the last of the cornet into her mouth.

"Me too."

"I wonder how he'll react?"

"I have no idea. I don't think he recognises the place so far. But then I don't imagine this car park was around back then."

With no warning, the narrow track between the dunes opened up onto a long expanse of golden sand and sparkling sapphire ocean. The continuing forest of fir trees to their right added to the drama of the setting; growing right down to the edge of the sand, and following the curvature of the beach as far as the eye could see.

"Oh, wow." Helen stopped in her tracks. "This is stunning. Absolutely stunning."

"It sure is," Jim agreed. "I keep thinking we can't beat what we've already seen, but this little country keeps proving me wrong."

"Look at those mountains across the water. The light reflecting off the sky and sea makes them look blue. I've never seen anything like it. It could be Australia or South Africa or somewhere exotic. I mean, if you showed someone a photograph of this, how many would guess North Wales?"

"Helen, look. That must be Llanddwyn." Jim pointed off into the distance.

Helen shielded her eyes and followed Jim's gesture. At the furthest point of the right hand curve of the beach, Helen could make out an island jutting out into the sea. The bright sunlight glittered and glinted off the surface of the water, creating an iridescent haze. Against the shimmering horizon she could clearly see a white lighthouse jutting up into the sky, recognising it from the pictures they'd seen on the internet.

"Yes, it is. It looks miles away though!"

"It looks a fair walk. We'll just have to take our time."

"Are there cars parked there?" Helen said, pointing to a clump of trees further along the beach.

"It sure looks like it. I wonder how you get to that car park? It would cut the walk by at least half. Hey, there's a lifeguard over there in that Land Rover. I'll go and have a word."

Helen walked down to the edge of the sea, gripping Jake's hand. She shivered as the cool water lapped over her burning feet, enjoying the delicious relief. Jake paddled in the water up to his knees. He looked up at her and beamed.

"Why couldn't we bring Holly? She'd love it."

"She would." Helen nodded. "But she's just as happy being spoiled rotten at Grandma's."

"Can she come next time?" asked Jake, jigging up and down on the spot as tiny waves washed over his feet.

"We'll see. We may not come here again ..."

"Oh, yes we will." Jake nodded. "I like it here, Mummy. Can we stay?"

"What do you mean?"

"Can we stay here forever and ever? This feels like home."

Before Helen had a chance to answer, Jim approached.

"Well, how weird is this. Apparently that car park is reserved for the residents of Newborough village only."

"What?"

"That's what the lifeguard said. It's the old road down to Llanddwyn Island apparently. And that road we passed in the woods, the one with the barrier across, that's it. But you need a key for the barrier, and you only get a key if you live in the village."

"How bizarre. I've never heard of anything like that before. Wonder why?"

"No idea. But there's little point moaning. Let's walk a little way and see how far we get, okay?"

"Sure. I don't have a problem with walking anyway. It's just the heat today that's going to be a killer."

Helen waited for Jake to scamper off in front of them, before recounting his words to Jim.

"So something has obviously triggered a recognition, even if he's not consciously aware of it. Let's just watch him, see if he picks up anything the closer he gets to the island."

Helen nodded, and strained her eyes. The glare of the sunlight on the water made it difficult to make out anything more than a hazy outline of the island.

Jim picked up a handful of pebbles and impressed Jake by skimming them across the water, each bounced six or seven times. Jake attempted the same, and stuck out his bottom lip when they disappeared on the first bounce with a resounding plop. Helen hid her smile. Jake had always been competitive and known to throw a massive temper tantrum if things didn't go his way.

Jim paused and stood, hands on hips, staring out to sea. He sipped bottled water as Helen and Jake took a break in the shade.

"You know I can honestly say I have never seen an ocean so crystal clear. It's almost aquamarine. It seems to be beckoning me to take a dip – and I'm afraid in this heat I can't hold back a moment longer!"

With that, Jim pulled his t-shirt over his head and waded

into the calm water. There was no surf at all, just a gentle sway of the tide against the shingle. When he reached waist high, he dived under the surface and swam under water. Minutes later, he broke the surface with a huge splash.

"Hey, I can see fish down here! Come see, Jake!"

After drying off a short time later, and another half hour of walking, the island appeared. There were very few visitors this far along the beach, most choosing to set up their temporary camps nearer to the car park.

They crossed the thin stretch of sand that joined the island to the mainland. A further expanse of beach, on the other side of the island, had caused the pressure of the tide to form a triangular bridge of sorts, along the narrow strip. The sand was a different texture here – white and powdery, and almost impossible to walk through.

Helen looked up and wiped sweat from her brow. A pathway led from the beach, up a steep incline. All she could make out from this angle was thick yellow gorse bushes intermingling with patches of lavender heather. The colour was so bright it hurt her eyes.

"Jake," she called, "come put your trainers on before you climb up there."

Jake stood perfectly still in the middle of the track. He stared up at the path in front of him, his mouth open. As if in slow motion, he turned to face Helen.

He spoke, pronouncing each word slowly, as if not sure of their validity.

"Mummy. I've been here before."

Chapter Twenty

"Keep moving! Stop wasting time."

Hands shoved her hard in the middle of her back. Nia stumbled forward over what felt like a tree root and staggered to her knees, yelling as she twisted her ankle. Her hands, secured with sticky tape behind her back, were no help. With nothing to break her fall, she fell heavily, winding herself.

"Don't," she pleaded as she struggled to her knees. "I'm going as fast as I can. I'd move a lot faster if you untied my hands and took this bloody blindfold off. And I've lost my shoes."

"Stop whinging. You're doing my head in. I threw your shoes away. If you'd kept them on your feet and not used them for smashing windows, you'd still be wearing them, mind."

He grabbed under one arm and dragged her to her feet. She cried out as he manhandled her.

"Get off me! Stop it. Where are you taking me anyway?"

"Just shut up, and keep walking."

"Not till you tell me where we're going."

"I said shut up. Don't make me tell you again, sugar. You're getting on my nerves now."

"You said …Ow … you bastard!"

Nia broke off as his palm connected with her right cheek with a resounding slap. The hood he'd pulled over her head when he'd dragged her out of the car did little to lessen the impact. Her eyes watered and her jaw hummed.

"I asked you to be quiet. Now, I don't want another scrap, mind. But if you keep up your whining, I'm going to lose my rag. And you're in no position to put up much of a fight right now. So don't make me hurt you."

Nia nodded and sniffed.

"Good girl. You're learning quick. Now just keep walking."

They'd been walking for about ten minutes since parking the car. They'd driven down miles of pitch black lanes, through acres of thick forest. At one point he got out to open and close a gate; she'd seen an ancient, peeling, 'PRIVATE PROPERTY' sign reflected in the car's headlights. She heard the hoot of an owl, could smell the heady scent of pine trees, and feel a woodland floor beneath her feet. But she had no idea where she was.

A few minutes later, Nia sensed a change in the atmosphere. Fresh air and a cooling sea breeze seeped through the hood. She could smell the acrid scent of seaweed, and in the distance hear the gentle rush of waves against sand. Another shove sent her skidding down a grass verge. She lost her balance and landed on her backside. She pushed herself up as a hand grabbed her arm.

Stepping forward, she felt cool sand under her feet. She tilted her head from one side to another, listening for any sounds that might help her place her surroundings. She knew she must be somewhere on the west side of Anglesey, but the arduous journey had pushed any real sense of direction to the back of her mind.

"You trying to work out where you are?" His voice close behind her.

"No."

"Yes, you are. Well, don't bother. Because no one's ever going to find you out here, sugar."

"Why are you doing this to me?"

"I'll tell you when the time's right. There's things we have to do first. Just keep walking."

"You won't break me, you know."

"We'll see."

"I mean it. I'd rather die than surrender my dignity to you."

"I know."

"So what's the point? Why don't you let me go?"

"Why don't you just shut your mouth and walk!"

Nia closed her mouth. After another ten minutes or so, time already beginning to lose its meaning, she felt the pull of her calf muscles as they began a gradual climb. The sand beneath her feet turned back into grass. She grimaced as tiny pebbles cut into the soles of her feet.

Finally, they reached the top of the incline. The wind started to whip around them, gusting from her left. The path dropped downwards, Nia had to concentrate on putting one foot safely in front of the other. She could hear the ocean below, rolling against rocks and swirling through chasms. She kept walking, the blindness disorientating her – increasingly worried of losing her footing and plunging onto the imagined rocks below.

But his presence, close behind her, was a good enough reason to keep moving forward.

Although terrified, she was determined not to let him see it. If she could remain calm and act unthreatened, she felt he was far more likely to let his guard down, make a mistake and supply her with a means of escape.

"Keep going straight. It's …" he yelled, raising his voice above the noise of the ocean far below.

"What?" she called, losing half of his words in the wind.

"I said keep going straight. The track is narrow here and near the cliff edge. I don't want you killing yourself at this point, causing me all this inconvenience for nothing."

Nia heard the click of a lock turning. He bundled her into a cool, damp room. The creak of a second door, wood scraping on a rough surface followed by a dull thud, then he took hold of her arm again and led her down a flight of stone steps. She wrinkled her nose as a damp, musty smell mixed with rotting seaweed filtered through the coarse material. She jerked as he pulled her back, pausing again, before pushing her through yet another door, and down another flight of narrow winding steps.

At the bottom, he released her. She winced as he tore the sticky tape from her wrists. He untied the cord from around her neck, and pulled off the hood. He pushed her forward down four or five stone steps, into a dark, dank room that stank of sewers.

"Welcome to your new abode."

It was the first time she'd seen him smile. The uneven brown teeth did nothing to inject any humour into the facial expression. "It's not exactly The Ritz, mind, but you'll find everything you need in here. I've left food for your breakfast. Don't eat it all at once."

"This is hideous …"

The concrete floor and peeling plaster walls were its best features. A single unlit light bulb hung from a frayed cable in the centre of the room. A black framed narrow bed, covered with a grey, wool blanket stood in the middle of the room. The only light came from the open doorway behind her. The shadows extended across the floor from every side, leaving only a narrow rectangular strip of white light in the centre of the circular room. She squinted against the gloom. A tray on the floor next to the bed was covered by a filthy blue tea-towel. Whatever food was on there would already be infested with god knows what.

She turned to voice her objections, but faced only the inside of a thick wooden door as it slammed shut.

"Hey!" she yelled, hammering her fists against the timber. "Hey!"

Silence.

"You bastard! Don't you walk away from me!"

Silence.

She punched the door for several minutes until her hands throbbed, and she realised the pointlessness of her actions.

She trudged down the steps, rubbing her tingling wrists. There was nothing to do but wait it out. He had his reasons for bringing her here and there was no point wasting energy trying to provoke a reaction before he was ready. He'd gone and he wouldn't come back until he chose, no matter how much she screamed and shouted. She needed to conserve her strength, and keep on her guard for the first opportunity to escape.

The darkness was total. Complete and utter blackness. They'd descended at least two flights of stairs, so she knew she must be underground. The room had the feel of a dungeon. It was chilly and dank, the walls damp to her touch. She picked her way carefully over to the bed.

Nia climbed onto the mattress, slipped off her blood-soaked top, still sticky against her skin, and wrapped herself in the blanket.

She recoiled and gagged as a thought engulfed her brain. The other girls. The other missing students. He'd bragged he was responsible, and nothing he'd said or done made her doubt his words for a moment.

She curled into a ball and let the tears come.

* * *

Nia woke from an uncomfortable sleep. She sat up stiffly and massaged her aching neck. The room was still as black as a mine shaft and smelled as bad as she remembered. Having slept in fits and starts, she felt groggy and confused, and had no idea of the time. She stood and stretched. Moving forward in the general direction of the door, she took tiny steps until her toes touched concrete. She climbed the steps slowly, using her hand against the wall to steady herself.

"Hello! Hey! Are you in there? I need to use the bathroom. Is anybody there?"

Nia put her ear to the gap in the frame and listened. She felt sure she could hear movement on the other side. She banged against the wood with clenched fists, harder and harder, until it vibrated in its frame and her hands started throbbing again.

"Hey, I can hear you! I know you're there. Will you please let me use the bathroom?"

After a further few minutes, she heard a key turn in a lock and a metallic grating as a rusty bolt slid into place. The door creaked as it opened. He stood in the doorway.

"Here." He handed her a round vessel. Nia's eyes reacted to the sudden light and she squinted, rubbing her eyes as she focused on an old fashioned white porcelain chamber pot, decorated with blue roses.

Nia looked down at it with distaste, not even wanting to touch it.

"You're having a laugh, right?"

"Nope, let's say we have no toilet facilities on site. It's that or nothing. Your choice."

"I'd rather nothing, than that."

"Fine." He opened his hand; as the chamber pot hit the floor with an echoing smash, porcelain exploded into a million pieces.

"You idiot!"

"Me?" he smirked. "I offered. You're the one who didn't want a pot to piss in."

He chortled at his own joke.

Nia ignored him. "So, what do I do now?"

"Not my problem."

"Yes, it is your problem," she hissed.

"No, it's yours. That smart mouth of yours just keeps getting you into trouble, don't it? Like father, like daughter."

"What?"

"Nothing."

"You said something about my father."

"Forget it."

"No. What do you know about my father? What's he got to do with this?"

"I said forget it!" he snarled.

"And I said no!" Nia replied, with equal venom. "What has my father got to do with this?"

Her abductor turned and began to climb the steps. Before she realised what she was doing, Nia sprang towards him, flinching as shards of broken pottery pierced the soles of her feet, and grabbed the back of his fleece jacket.

"Tell me!"

His fist connected with her face. The force shot her down the steps and slammed her face-first into the iron-framed bed. In her ears, the impact sounded like a shot from a firing pistol. Fireworks exploded in her skull. She grabbed her nose; blood began to pour down her chin. The thin grey light from the open doorway illuminated large crimson droplets dripping steadily onto the grey mattress, turning purple as they soaked into the fabric.

"You just can't leave it, can you?"

He paced the floor muttering to himself. With her pulse resounding through her ears, Nia struggled to hear. "Typical woman. You just keep pushing and pushing 'til you provoke a reaction. Why won't you listen, mind? Why don't you be a good girl and do as you're told? You trying to get me in trouble, that it?"

He spun round and grabbed the sheet that Nia had wrapped tightly round her body, yanking her onto her feet.

"Why do you make me hurt you?" he screamed into her face. His eyes blazed and spittle flew from his lips. Specks of moisture sprayed over her face and she twisted her body away from his grasp.

Nia cowered and her eyes filled with tears. The pain was immense; she could feel her eyes already swelling. She knew her nose was broken, and she had an idea her jaw was dislocated too.

"Why?" he repeated, shaking her roughly. "Look at the state of you. Just look at what you made me do. I'll get the blame. But it's not me, no. This is all your fault, right?"

Nia nodded.

"Say it! Say it's not my fault!"

"I'm s … sorry. A-all my fault."

She wiped her nose on the sheet, sparks of pain exploded behind her eyeballs.

"Now you're patronising me." Nia noticed that his voice had lost the hysterical edge. In an instant he was in control again. "I can't stand being patronised, mind."

"I'm not. I promise." Nia spoke thickly, through clotting blood.

"Yes, you are. But I think you're like your father, and you just don't know when you're doing it."

"Why do you keep mentioning my father?"

"Why do you keep asking stupid questions? Have you not learned your lesson by now?"

Nia bowed her head and stayed silent.

"Right, get yourself cleaned up. I'll be back in five minutes. I have something I need you to do."

"But I need the toilet. How can I get cleaned up? I need soap and water." Nia held the sheet under her nose, catching the still seeping blood.

"Like I said, not my problem."

With that, the door slammed shut. Tears rolled down her face. Now what was she supposed to do? Nia grimaced as she urinated in the furthest corner of the room. The smell was worse over here. A bitter, acrid smell. And she realised she wasn't the first to use this area as a toilet. She gagged and held her breath, finishing as quickly as possible then followed the curve of the wall, on her hands and knees, until she came to the food tray. She grabbed the tea towel, and felt about on the tray. Her fingers closed around a plastic bottle. She unscrewed the cap, sniffed, then tasted. Water. She took two mouthfuls, swilled the blood out her mouth, and spat it onto the floor. Once her mouth was clear of blood, she gulped down four or five mouthfuls of the delicious cold water – feeling it cool her throat and slide into her empty stomach – before she forced herself to stop.

The door creaked open, and he re-entered the room, leaving

a three inch gap, so that dusty white light filtered into the room and lit the bottom section of the bed.

Nia sat on the mattress, head against the wall, knees pulled up tight. Before the pain, it didn't seem real, somehow. But now, as her eyes started to swell shut, it was dreadfully, undeniably real. She was stuck here with this madman; this mans who hurt her, who could … kill her. But why? The not-knowing was more terrifying than anything.

He approached the bed. She cowered against the wall. He threw a piece of paper onto the bed. It was a plain A4 sheet of white paper with computer printing on one side.

"Read it. Aloud."

Nia picked up the paper and turned it towards the grainy light.

"Hello Daddy. I am safe and unharmed. The man holding me is demanding a ransom for my release. He wants one million pounds in used bank notes. If you involve the police, he will kill me. He says watch the news. The police will be no help. I shall ring you again at midnight tonight with further instructions. In brackets, it says B. E. G."

He laughed. "Yeah, thought I'd allow you a little artistic licence there. Just make it sound realistic, mind. Beg for your life. Because it will really come down to that. If Daddy doesn't pay up, I'll kill you. Simple as."

"My father doesn't have that kind of money in ready cash …"

"Your father has that, and a whole lot more, in ill-gotten gains. A lot that he keeps from the ears of his precious daughter."

"What do you mean?"

"I don't have time for this. You know what to say, right?"

"Yes, I can read this script. But you have a bigger problem. I don't have a clue what his number is. I have it on my phone, but you threw it out."

He reached into his jacket pocket. Her mobile phone landed with a thud on the blanket beside her. Nia's eyes widened. He'd obviously grabbed her mobile before throwing her handbag out the car window.

"Do it. Try anything and no second chances."

He slid a long, stainless steel knife from behind his back. The light from the doorway glinted off the blade. A good eight or nine inches long. The size of the blade there to give a warning. It worked.

Nia nodded.

"Do it," he repeated, flicking the mobile forward with the tip of the knife.

Nia switched the power on, and scrolled through the contacts until she reached D. After a few seconds, she heard a dial tone.

The static-sounding voice answered on the first ring.

"Nia? Nia? Angel? Is that you?"

Nia stared at her abductor; he nodded once.

"Hello, Daddy. I am safe and unharmed. The man holding me is demanding a ransom for my release. He wants one million pounds in used bank notes. If you involve the police, he says he will kill me. He says watch the news. The police will be no help. I shall ring you again at midnight tonight with further instructions. Please Daddy, this is real. This is horrid. Help me. Help me! I'm in a cellar …"

He grabbed the phone off her and disconnected the call, putting his face close to hers. She gulped back a sob of terror.

"Don't fuck with me, sugar," he hissed. His body smelled rank; she could smell fish on his breath. He pressed the silver blade against Nia's throat; the sharp edge biting into her skin.

"But other than your smart mouth nearly causing you to get your throat cut – that was very well delivered. Right, have a nice day, I'll be back later."

"You're not leaving me here?"

He turned, headed towards the stairs. "Yup, 'fraid so."

In an instant, Nia was on her feet, seeing the sliver of light in the doorway as her last chance of escape. She leapt on his back, pushing him off balance, and leap-frogged over him in one fluid move as the knife clattered to the floor. Her heart pounded as she reached the top step. Hearing a grunt behind her, she lunged for the door. Her fingers brushed the handle as his hand grabbed her hair and yanked her backwards.

She screamed, hitting the floor with a sickening thump. In a second his weight was on her pelvis, pushing down as she struggled upright.

"Bad move, sugar. Bad, bad move."

She shook her head, reaching for his face, trying to claw him. He grabbed both wrists and pinned them behind her head. Fish breath engulfed her.

"See, the more you fight, the more ways I can imagine punishing you. And you've just fucked up your last chance. I think it's time you got a taster."

"No," she whispered. "I'm sorry. No, don't hurt me."

"Just close your eyes and enjoy it, sugar. And thank your Daddy if you need someone to blame."

Nia turned her head one way, then the other as she felt his hot breath on her neck. She could hear him panting as he burrowed his face into her hair. His right hand grabbed her breast, while his left tugged at the waist band of her trousers, pulling them lower, twisting the material into her flesh. She screamed and kicked her feet helplessly against the floor.

"I'm s-sorry. Don't do this. You will regret it one day. Please don't …"

She broke off as he pulled back from her, eyes half-closed like someone savouring the bouquet of a fine wine. The fractional pause was enough for Nia to roll onto her side. Frowning, he looked down at her, and she stared back with what she hoped was her most pitiful gaze.

"Please. I beg you. Don't …"

With a growl, he jumped up and without another word disappeared, slamming the door behind him.

* * *

He paused, one hand resting on the door, taking deep gulps of dusty air. Shit. This wasn't supposed to happen. Fuck.

What the hell was he doing?

Letting himself get close to her. Allowing her to get under his skin. Letting her get in the way of the plan. Listening to her whining.

Just do it. Kill her. Get the money. Move on.

What was his fucking problem?

He'd never felt anything before, with any of the other bitches. True, the sex hadn't been part of the original plan, and he'd suffered for going so far. But they'd been asking for it. Harlots, the lot of 'em. Fucking harlots. And once he'd started, he couldn't stop. Wasn't his fault. He was a man. His chance to prove himself as a man. Prove he was better than women, stronger than women. Show his mother what he was capable of. Prove her wrong. Prove himself.

He'd considered letting the first one go, course he had. He wasn't a fucking psycho, after all. Except he couldn't. The risk was too high. They'd run to the police, no matter what lies they told. That's what woman did. Lied to you. He couldn't risk it.

So, why now?

He'd spent so long imagining what she would feel like. How it would feel to terrorise her, give her what she wanted and then squeeze every drop of life-blood from her.

So, what happened?

He remembered her blue eyes. Reminding him of Grace. Eyes wide, pleading, begging. He'd buried his hair into her neck, wanting to taste her, bite and hurt her. He sniffed her hair, shampoo that smelled of apples. Delicate blonde hair, as fine as silk. Just like Grace.

He'd wanted to hurt her. Punish her. Use her. Rape her while he imagined her bastard father rutting away on his beloved sister, pinned against a gravestone. Nothing more than a whore for him. Now his daughter would be his whore, his very own harlot. But God, how he'd make her suffer. And make sure Charlie got to hear all the details, see all the evidence.

But then, with little more than the smell of an orchard of apple blossom, he was eleven again. Grace was in his arms, the velvet skin cooling beneath his fingers. She was speaking to him.

Please, don't. Please, help. Help me.

He'd had to get the hell out there.

Nia. Grace. Nia.

He moaned aloud. "Oh, Grace."

Oh, shit.

Chapter Twenty One

Gareth kicked away from the pull of sleep, like a swimmer performing a complicated poolside somersault. He needed to wake up, desperate to put distance between himself and the dream.

Edwina in the water, below him, dragged under by vicious currents that spun her in a widening vortex. This time she was joined by another girl. Both of them spinning so fast, their faces were blurred. Gareth knew this was the latest victim. The one he was supposed to save. He crawled forward on his belly along the rickety wooden jetty, arm outstretched, leaning out as far as he dared over the water. Heart pounding, his fingertips touched Edwina's – once, twice – then with a piercing scream she spun away from him and disappeared under the water. Forever.

He sat upright with a jolt, kicking away the tangled duvet. His nerves continued to hum for several seconds as his heart rate slowed. He swallowed and blinked, looking around his room, glad to see the first purple streaks of dawn illuminating the window. At least he wouldn't have to go back to sleep. He could get up, start the day, sluice away the remnants of the nightmare with a long, hot shower.

As he did first thing every morning, and last thing every night now, he made his way into the lounge to check the answer phone. Zero messages flashed on the display. With a sigh of relief, he stooped to light his first cigarette of the day, sliding aside the blind and pushing open the window to let out the smoke, let in the fresh morning air.

The city spires spread out below him, the churches and colleges rising out of the early morning mist like the lost city of Atlantis. He'd fallen in love with Bangor the first day he transferred there. The mix of old and new, established and modern, excited him. The constant buzz of a university town, with its eclectic blend of students all living in harmony. Now, he doubted he would ever feel the same affection towards the town, tarnished by the kind of evil he'd only ever seen in films. There were times when it still didn't seem real that he could be so involved. He couldn't accept Edwina was dead.

Most of the early hours of the morning had passed with him reliving the previous day's team meeting. That too seemed unreal. At the time, he hadn't cared, adrenaline pumping, but now he had a deep fear that he may well have done irrevocable damage to his career; at the very least in terms of his place on McRae's team.

Gareth had been shocked by McRae's half-hearted, cynical reception of Connolly's findings on the voice analysis tests. In front of a packed investigation room, he'd locked horns with McRae. And lost.

"Sir, these tests are pretty conclusive. That and the fact all the bodies have been dumped in and around the Menai Straits, make it almost certain he's on a boat somewhere near one of the bridges. He could have the latest victim there as we speak. We have to send in a search party –"

"DS Parry, firstly, please do not tell me my job. Secondly, what victim?"

"Sir, you said yourself that it's surely only a matter of time. We could have the opportunity to prevent another death here."

McRae nodded. "True. But at the moment we have no missing person, and we have no suspect, and we have no scene of crime. Short of examining my crystal balls, I don't see how."

A torrent of chuckles and coughs flowed across the room.

"But the background noise, sir. The road noise. If the forensic techs are right it points to the bridges. Surely that's the area to start the search. It seems logical to me."

"Then I regret we don't share the same logic. There is more than one busy road that runs along the coast, more than one bridge. Heck, there's a whole stretch of dual-carriageway between Bangor and Rhyl courtesy of the A55. Would you have me search every ocean going vessel along that coastline?"

Gareth shook his head. More muted laughter.

McRae raised his eyebrows. "No? Good. Parry, I'm not doubting Dr Connolly's word, or her expertise, although she admits she's not one hundred percent sure –"

"Eighty percent," Gareth interjected.

McRae sighed. "As I said, she's not yet one hundred percent sure. It is an interesting theory, I concur. But, and it's a big but, we have no missing person report at the moment, just some empty threat."

Gareth blew a stream of smoke out of the window and watched it snake up into the sky. He'd backed off at this point, sensing McRae's frustration, not wanting to push too hard and end up in charge of menial desk duties. He didn't understand why there was such a lack of urgency. They'd had forewarning of the next kidnap. Why wasn't the team doing house to house enquiries? Why at the very least hadn't McRae ordered a team to search any boats in the Straits?

He inhaled the final drag of his cigarette and stubbed out the remainder in the ashtray. He made a decision as he headed towards the shower. He'd pop into town for a newspaper, and call into The Muse on his way back. After all, McRae hadn't specifically ordered him not to question Rogers again. It wouldn't hurt to find out if he had an alibi for Friday night, now would it?

The unmistakable smell of draw hit him as he pushed open the shop door. His heart flipped as he imagined arresting Rogers for possession or even dealing. Recently reclassified as a Class B drug, he'd be well within his rights to do so. His finger twitched against his warrant card. It would make his day to see that man spend a night in a cell.

The shop was empty, but he could hear the distinctive sound of The Archers theme tune from the back room. He gave a sharp cough as he approached the counter, and after several seconds of scurried noise, a tall, athletic girl with frizzy blonde hair that cascaded down her shoulders, appeared from the other side of the curtained doorway. Gareth's gut twisted. At least six foot tall, an Amazonian goddess, dressed in layers of white and gold. She was like something out of his wildest dreams. Had this meeting taken place a few months earlier, his Lothario instincts would have leapt to prominence. Even now, he knew if there was the tiniest hint of encouragement, he'd be hard pushed to turn this beauty down.

"Morning, can I help you?"

Gareth's dream of angels was smashed into pieces by the broad West Country accent.

"Erm, hi yes. I was hoping to have a word with Mr Rogers."

"Ah, he's not in today. Sorry. Anything I can help you with?"

"Alas, not. Is Mrs Rogers around?"

"No, she's at church on a Sunday morning. Dare say she'll be down later, though. Can I tell her who called?"

There was a hint of suspicion in the sapphire eyes, and he hoped she'd missed the smirk he attempted to cover. The rounded vowels and earthy accent just didn't fit this vision of statuesque beauty. It was like she'd been cast in the worst role possible by a deaf movie director.

Gareth reached into his pocket, flashed his identification. Her stare morphed from mistrust to intrigue in a matter of nano-seconds. "Oooh, the po-lice huh?"

He nodded. "And your name is?"

"Vanessa. Vanessa Hughes."

He bit back a smile at the pronunciation of her surname.

Oooze. "And you've worked here how long?"

"Just a few weeks. I took over from one of the girls who got abducted." Her hand shot to her mouth and her eyes widened. "Oh, I bet that's why you's here, isn't it? You're investigating them kidnappings, yeah?" She leaned forward and Gareth had to force himself to look away from the rounded cleavage straining against the flimsy top. "Is it true she was murdered? So I heard had her throat cut from ear to ear, then dumped out at sea. It's just too terrible to think about, ain't it?"

He nodded, swallowed, knowing there was no way he could tell her that 'the girl' was a member of his family.

"Have you had any luck yet finding the bloke?" she asked, leaning her elbows on the counter. "A lot of my friends are thinking of quitting, you know. None of us dare go out alone now. Some think I'm mad to be here on my own, but we have security cameras, and you can't let these nutters dominate your life, can you?"

"No, you can't. Are you enjoying your time here?"

She wrinkled her nose in the cutest fashion. "It's okay. A little bit dull, you know. I'm about to finish a drama post-graduate course, so I'm used to things with a little more life, yeah."

"And how do you get on with your employers?" asked Gareth, seeing no reason to miss an opportunity to get more background on Rogers.

"Ah, the old lady, she's fine. She's a doll. Not the full ticket, like. But we're on the same wavelength, her and I. Some would say I'm a fantasist too. We'd both have been happier on a 1920s Broadway stage, though, know what I mean?"

Gareth smiled and nodded. He knew exactly what she meant. There was something infectious and endearing about this girl's honesty.

"It's that son of hers I can't be doing with," said Vanessa and hugged her arms. "He gives me the right creeps, he does. Staring eyes that undress you, yeah. And the worst case of bad breath I've ever known. Ugh, and his teeth." She shivered. "I can't stand being in the same room as him. He's the type of guy to give you nightmares and no mistake."

Gareth pushed out his chest; secretly glad Glyn Rogers had such a violent effect on the girl. From the moment he saw her statuesque beauty, he couldn't help worry for her safety. But it sounded like she'd got her head screwed on right, whatever her artistic sensibilities.

He slid a card from his pocket. "This is my number, if you hear anything at all you think might assist me – here or at Uni – will you give me a call?"

"Sure thing." Gold painted nails flashed as she took the card. "Do you want me to tell the bosses you called?"

"No. I'll call again. Keep them on their toes. But you have my number. Use it if you need me. And Vanessa," she turned, one hand on the curtain, Juliet leaving stage right, "you do know there's a smoking ban now in Wales. I wouldn't want your employers to catch you breaking the law. Understand?"

He held her gaze a second longer, then stepped out of the fusty coolness into the sunlight, hoping she got his meaning.

Gareth's thoughts were captivated by Vanessa Hughes as he drove out of town, deciding to pay another call to the Lifeboat Station at Beaumaris. Hopefully as Rogers wasn't at the shop, he'd be there. It was a beautiful morning; the sunlight reflected off the turquoise water of the Menai Straits as Gareth took the A55 across the Britannia Bridge. He found himself slowing his speed, scouring the water far below. Looking for what? A struggling young woman on the deck of one of the many small boats that bobbed on the gentle current. Like he could be that lucky.

With a sigh, he pressed the accelerator, flashing a look at the grill of the impatient black BMW right behind him. Some people took no interest in the beauty of their surroundings. The tyres bumped over the uneven road surface as he crossed onto Anglesey. He slacked off again; his thoughts suddenly off on a tangent. He indicated left, off the bridge, ignoring the blast of horn at his late signal, and drove under the dual-carriageway, back up the slip road and once again found himself crossing the bridge – this time heading back to the mainland.

Yes, there it was again. A most definite noise. As the front, then rear tyres crossed the expansion joints there was a loud, methodical double thump.

Chunk-ker-chunk.

Every twenty feet or so. It was a pain in the ass for a driver, but a very distinctive noise.

When he got back onto Bangor side, he pulled off the A55, spun round the island and pulled into a lay-by, grabbing his mobile from the dashboard.

He drummed his fingers against the steering wheel as he waited for connection.

"Hello."

"Sue? It's Gareth."

"Oh … hi."

"Where are you?"

"It's Sunday morning. I'm at home, knee deep in housework. Why?"

"Damn. I hoped you were at the hospital. I wanted to run an idea past you."

"We seem to have a mutual appreciation society going on recently. What is it?"

"It's probably easier to show you, than try to explain. Oh, that's a thought. Hang on two minutes. And then listen really carefully, okay?"

"Er … sure."

Gareth floored the accelerator, flying down the slip road back along the lead onto the bridge. As he reached the first bump he slowed the car down to 50mph.

"Right, listen now. Tell me what you hear."

He held the phone in his left hand, out over the passenger seat. When he reached the other side, he pulled off the dual carriageway again, idling at the kerb.

"What could you hear?" he asked.

"Traffic noise or tyre noise. And some bumping."

"Exactly."

"Am I right?"

"Kind of."

Gareth took a few minutes to detail his discoveries; he could hear from Susan's enthusiasm that she thought he'd made a breakthrough.

"I am right, aren't I?" he asked. "If you could pick up the same rhythmical road noise at the same distance apart, or even identify if certain bridges had different joints and spacings, that would be categorical proof the road noise on the tape was a bridge?"

"Yes, spot on. In fact I'd go further. It would mean running tests on both bridges, any bridges in the area in fact, but I'm pretty sure we could identify the exact bridge from the recording. The only complication is there would be more than one vehicle crossing at any one time. So, I'd have to pin-point one vehicle, try to find a distinctive noise, and trace its progress across. It's going to be quite a bit of work, but this is a biggie, Gareth. Well done you. I'm going to give Surinder a call right now."

"Cool. Let me know what he says. I've got everything crossed we can nail this between us."

"We'll make a forensic scientist of you yet, Detective Parry. I'll call you later." There was a pause. "Are you all sorted for Wednesday?"

He'd been trying not to think about Wednesday. "I'm not sure what *all sorted* constitutes. But yeah, as I'll ever be. I ordered flowers yesterday. Sod the rules about donations." He paused. "I want it over. But I'm glad you'll be there, Sue."

"No worries. Right, I'm itching to call Sunny. Speak soon."

He saw Rogers standing on the concrete slipway, staring out to sea, hands sunk into his pockets, deep in thought. He was alongside before the other man noticed his presence.

"Detective. Good morning. What brings you out here? Again."

Gareth feigned a nonchalant smile. "Just passing, you know."

"From where to where?" Glyn asked with a frown. "Beaumaris isn't on a direct route to anywhere really."

"Oh, just routine enquiries, you know."

"And how is your investigation progressing? Any leads as yet?"

Gareth shrugged. "It's early days. We have lots of information to follow up."

"And how exactly can I help you? I'm sure I told you all I knew a few days ago."

"There have been developments." Gareth paused, noting the tense line of the other mans' jaw, the muscle flexing in his cheek. "I wondered if you could tell me where you were last Friday evening?"

Rogers' eyes widened. He remained silent for several seconds before he gave a bright smile. "Why would I need to tell you that, detective? Am I a suspect?"

Gareth shook his head. "Not at all. We are simply trying to eliminate people from our enquiries."

The white smile was fixed, forced. "Has there been another abduction?"

"I'm afraid I'm not at liberty to say, sir."

"Then I believe I'm not at liberty to answer your question, either."

Gareth bit back an angry retort. He'd get nowhere antagonising Rogers further. "As you wish. I can of course ask you to accompany me back to the station and we can do this formally. But quite honestly, sir, if you don't have anything to hide, I can't see why it's such a big deal."

"It may be a big deal to me, detective. I may have reasons I don't want to discuss my movements on Friday evening that have nothing to do with your investigation. I know I'm telling you the truth. It's your choice whether you want to believe me. I hope you do. If you do not, then I suggest you arrest me, and allow me to contact my lawyer."

"Sir, I make the rules. Not you."

"Then I regret we've reached something of an impasse, detective."

Gareth clenched his fists inside his pockets. "Your choice. But I have to say I find your tone unnecessary and offensive. There's a possibility we have a serial killer on our hands. We have numerous victims. My job is to prevent the next."

Rogers turned his gaze to the wavelets splashing at his feet, rubbing the toe of his boot in a tendril of slimy seaweed. Eventually, he let out a long sigh.

"DS Parry, I'm sorry. I am defensive by nature, and although we could carry on this pointless verbal tango all morning, I see no point. I was with a friend on Friday evening." He looked up, licked his lips. "All night, in fact. It would be awkward and probably troublesome to get this corroborated, but if it becomes one hundred percent necessary to produce an alibi, then I am able to do so. But it will be under duress, understand? And you will have to face the consequences if it turns out not to be mandatory."

Gareth nodded, weighing up the options. Rogers clearly had secrets that he would not easily spill, and with the tight controls of the law, Gareth knew he was on dodgy territory to push for more at the moment. And he had a feeling Rogers knew it too.

"Okay. For the moment that will suffice. Can I ask you one more question, and I'd appreciate a direct answer."

Rogers gave a curt nod.

"Last time we spoke, you made a phone call as my partner and I left. Who were you calling?"

"My mother. I was worried how your visit may have affected her. She was fine, I'm glad to say."

A buzzing noise emanated from the building at the top of

the slipway. Rogers looked up and began to reverse towards the door.

"That's a call out. I have to go. Detective, believe it or not we are on the same side. I liked Edwina. Like you, everything I do is in the name of family honour."

With that, he turned and pulled open a blue door, disappearing into the gloom. The rhythmic hooter continued to echo as Gareth made his way back to his car. There was something about the man. Something he couldn't put his finger on that made every hackle on his neck rise. And there was this overriding sensation that he was missing something important, relevant.

He shook his head as he slid behind the wheel of his car, glancing at his mobile.

Shit, six missed calls. Chris's mobile. He pressed redial. It answered on the first ring.

"Shit, buddy, where are you?"

"Just picking up some bits of shopping. Why?"

"It's all kicking off here like you would not believe."

Gareth's heart began to pound. "Why?"

"We've got another body."

"Shit. Already?"

"Not the latest threat, still nothing on that. A new one. Been in the water about a week."

"Oh, my God." Gareth felt the burn of nausea in his throat.

"Yeah. McRae wants everyone in the office by lunchtime."

"I'm on my way."

He threw the phone down on to the passenger seat, pausing for a moment to open the window and take gulps of sea air. *Vic number four*. His gaze fixed on the red inshore lifeboat, spray flying as it sped across the water, disappearing behind the jut of headland with Glyn Rogers onboard.

There was unfinished business here, but it would have to wait.

Chapter Twenty Two

Helen attempted to keep her voice calm.

"What's that, sweetheart?"

"This path ... I already climbed it. I know this place. I lived here with my island mummy and daddy. That's why we came, isn't it?" Jake thumped the air. "Yes! Our house should be further on. Come on. Hurry!"

He started to run up the uneven track, slipping on the loose stones.

"Wait, Jake! Wait for us."

Jake reluctantly slowed his pace. Helen reached the crest of the small hill and the island lay spread before her. She gasped. There was so much to take in. A lighthouse jutted out into the sea at the furthest point. Another smaller lighthouse or lookout tower stood to its left. There were ruins, two or three broken walls and a jumble of stones, in a dip straight in front of them. And between them were two huge crosses, one a crucifix and one a Celtic cross.

They made their way over to a brown display board. Helen gripped Jake's hand. He tugged impatiently to drag them away.

"Hang on a minute, Jake. We want to read this."

"The island," Jim read, *"known by locals as Lovers Island, is named after Dwynwen, the patron saint of Welsh-born lovers and one of twenty four beautiful daughters of Brychan, a prince*

of 5th century Wales. Following her death on the island in AD465 her chapel became a popular place of pilgrimage for lovers, who sought to discover their destiny by watching the movement of an eel in the island's freshwater spring. The saint and her pilgrims are commemorated by crosses on the island and there are the remains of a 16th century Tudor church built on the site of her original chapel.

In spring, the island is carpeted in bluebells and spring squills. Soay and Jacob's sheep graze an enclosure and cormorants fish from the rocks offshore.

In the 1800s it was not so peaceful. Pilots were based here to guide ships over Caernarfon bar and to man a lifeboat station – cannons were used to summon help from Newborough. Two of the pilot's cottages have been furnished as they would have been in the 1850s, with one housing an exhibition on local wildlife.

Shipwrecks were frequent here; a forty foot column, Twr Bach, was built in 1819, to warn sailors of the rocks around the island. This was later replaced with a lighthouse, Twr Mawr, built in 1845 in the style of local windmills, which is still standing, although no longer in use.

Please follow the pathways carefully. And please enjoy your visit to Llanddwyn – the magical Lover's Island.'"

It was a beautiful story, but Helen struggled to take in all the information. Jacob had mentioned a tower, *Twr Bach*, and now they had proof it existed. Everything checked out so far, exactly as he'd described it.

"Mummy!" Jake tugged her arm harder. "Come and see the island. Come and see our house."

Helen and Jim exchanged glances.

Jim smiled. "Okay, Jakey. You take us then. We'll follow you. But don't go too far ahead, we don't want to lose you."

Jake bounded off again. He paused on the path and looked with interest at the tumbled down ruins.

"I don't remember this. I think there was a little house where we kept sheep in the winter."

"It's probably deteriorated a lot since 1831," whispered Jim to Helen. "He wouldn't have seen it so overgrown with the walls collapsed, so he doesn't recognise it. They obviously used the old chapel as a barn. So, that checks out too. Jeez, I have goosebumps."

"Me too." Helen nodded and swallowed the lump in her throat.

Jake was on the move again. He paused in front of the Celtic cross.

"But I do remember this. And that big cross over there. I remember we made fires round here with Daddy. We lit them to pass messages to the other side of the water. He used to tell us scary stories about the crosses. He said they were giant crosses, on giants' graves!"

He turned and grinned, bobbing up and down on the spot.

"I can't see any cottages, Jake. Where are they?" asked Jim.

"Over the hill by the beach. We used to keep our boats there."

"Okay, let's have a look. Can you take us?"

"Yeah! Come on. I love it here. I love it so much. Come on, Mummy!"

"I'm coming, Jakey."

Jim spoke, keeping his voice low as they continued along the trail.

"This is going really well, Helen. The more he sees, the more he remembers. And it's great to see him so happy. And I have to say this place feels totally special. Such peace, such tranquility. It makes you feel as if you never want to leave. I can't explain it, but I've never been anywhere like it before."

"No, me neither." She waved her arm across the scenery, the historical remains. "I'm lost for words. I mean, look at the four mile stretch of sand. It's just stunning ... too much for my eyes to cope with."

Jim turned and took several photographs.

"Jake!" Helen shouted. "Jim, where's he gone? He was here a second ago."

"Okay, calm down. Let's just get a move on, he can't have gone far. Jake!"

Together they ran over the next incline and down a gravel track. A small beach and a natural inlet that made a perfect harbour lay in front of them. Two large yachts were anchored, their occupants enjoying a picnic on the beach.

"There he is," said Jim. "And there are the cottages."

"What a place. Such tiny cottages. Oh, and look at those boats, Jim. They're gorgeous. Must've cost a small fortune."

"Well, I guess it's easier to reach this beach by boat than on foot. It's an exclusive hideaway. It's beautiful, especially on a day like today. Come on, let's go see Jacob's home. See how Jake reacts."

Helen got her first glimpse of Jake's island home. The Lloyd family home, she reminded herself. A row of three small stone-built cottages stood opposite the path down to the shore. Painted white, with black slate roofs, the cottages had obviously been recently renovated. The doors stood open to two of them and signs indicated that they were available for public access. A huge anchor, and what she assumed was the cannon used for distress calls, had been relocated to the small garden in front of the houses.

Jake leaned against the low garden wall, gazing up at the end cottage. His expression had changed from excitement to contemplation, and Helen could tell his mood had darkened again.

She knelt beside him, put her arm round his shoulder. "So is this your house, Jake?"

He nodded, his bottom lip jutting out, frowning.

"Do you want to show us around?"

"No."

"I thought you wanted to show us your house?"

He shook his head.

"Hey, what's up, little guy?" Jim knelt on Jake's other side.

Jake shrugged. He looked down and scuffed the grass with his trainers.

"You sad, Jake? Is that why you don't want to go inside?"

"Yes," he whispered.

"I understand," said Jim gently. "Being here has made you miss your family. Or maybe you're worried they're in there and won't recognise you. Is that it?"

"I know they're not here. It's not that. I miss Chi. She used to run to the beach, down there." He pointed. "I watched her from my window, up there."

"So that was your bedroom? Where you slept with your brothers?"

"Yeah."

"Will you show me your bedroom?"

Jim stood and held out a hand.

After a pause, Jake grasped it. "Okay."

Helen and Jim ducked their heads as they made their way into the small cottage. The front door opened up into a small sitting room with tiny windows. The furniture was basic and shabby. A black slate fireplace dominated the room. A door on the left led through to a white-painted kitchen and small scullery.

Jake paused in the doorway, twisting his head as he took in the surroundings.

"It's different." He sounded subdued, disappointed.

"Well, they've refurbished it. That means they rebuilt the house recently, so it will be a lot different than it was when you were here. So don't worry if some of it doesn't look the same."

"Okay."

Jake wandered between the two small rooms. Occasionally he pointed out something he remembered, or something that had changed.

"The stairs are through here," he said, pulling back a curtain opposite the scullery door.

Helen and Jim raised their eyebrows as they followed him up the narrow wooden staircase.

The bedrooms were cramped; Jim had to crouch because of low, oak beams. Again the furniture was sparse. A wooden wash-basin stand stood in the corner next to the small window, with a matching blue and white porcelain jug and bowl on top.

Jake reached out, touched the pitted mirror. "This is where we washed. I remember that. Looking out the window while Mummy scrubbed us with hot water and yellow soap. It was horrible and smelly." He wrinkled his nose at the memory.

Helen glanced out the window. From the corner of her eye, she saw a man in a green wax jacket leaving the cottage next door. He carried a heavy box in his arms, and marched off in the direction of the lighthouse. He had a look of officialdom about him, maybe a park ranger or local warden. Helen made a mental note to ask his advice if they met later. He might have some idea of how to go about tracing records of inhabitants of the cottages over the years.

Jake was showing Jim where the beds had been.

"I shared a bed, I remember. And there was a little cot behind the door. And across in the other room, is where Mummy and Daddy slept."

He stood with his back to them, staring out of the window, deep in thought. As Helen watched, his shoulders slumped.

"I want to go now," he muttered.

"Okay, let's have a look round the back of the house where the garden is …"

"No, want to go now. Please … let's go."

Helen could tell Jake was on the verge of tears. She took his hand. "Okay, sweetie. We can go if you want."

"I feel funny. I feel a bit sicky."

"Let's get you back outside. We can have a drink and a rest."

They trooped single file back out into the glare of the sunshine.

"Are you feeling okay now?" Jim asked Jake as they sat down

on the springy grass against the side wall.

"Yes. I didn't like it in there. It was like people were still there. I can hear them talking and laughing. And it's not real, isn't it? I mean they can't be here now, can they?"

"No," said Jim. "But their presence can sometime remain. It's nothing to worry about. You've done brilliantly."

They sat in the shade at the side of the house for a while, drinking orange squash and eating biscuits, before walking to the edge of the island and following the path around the two old lighthouses.

Once he'd left the house, Jake's mood improved and he was soon chattering away again, making the occasional comment about beaches where he played, and rock pools he'd fished in. But as they passed the largest of the lighthouses, Jake fell back into its shadow; his head tilted, eyes narrowed, as he looked up at the white tower.

Jim paused alongside; his hand on Jake's shoulder.

Jake shook his head. "I don't remember this. It's not right."

"No, the lighthouse wasn't here back then."

"But it's not right."

"Your memories confuse the present and the past that's all. Nothing to worry about, Jake."

Jake trembled. "I don't like it."

Helen reached out for Jake's hand. "We can leave now, Jake. Come on."

Jake ignored Helen's hand, gazing up at the black door. He walked forward, climbed the steps and laid his palm flat against the metal door. He stood, feet apart, for several seconds; his body trembled as he appeared to be concentrating, listening.

"Hey baby, come on, let's go," Helen called again.

Jake spoke with his back to them; his hand still pressed flat on the rusty surface. "Bad ..."

"What's that buddy?" asked Jim.

Jake turned, jumped down the steps with a backward glance. "Don't like it. No, don't like it." he whispered. "Want to go.

Now."

Jim shrugged as Helen took Jake's hand, and allowed him to drag her away from the tower.

"I think he's tired," she whispered. "Can we head back to the car now?"

Jim nodded and scooped Jake up onto his shoulders. "Come on, buddy. I'll carry you for a while, and you can pretend you're the King of the Island!"

Jake smiled, but the frown remained. Helen trembled and rubbed her arms. She could only imagine what was going on inside his head.

They passed one or two tourists on their way back to the car park. By the time they reached the car, they were all exhausted. Jim ended up carrying Jake most of the way. As soon as they reached the car, Jim started the engine and switched on the air conditioning. Jake curled up on the back seat and within minutes had fallen sound asleep.

"What a place," said Helen, laying her head back against the cooling leather upholstery. "And poor Jake. What a mixture of emotions he went through. I can't imagine how he must've been feeling. I was all over the place emotionally. God only knows how he felt. But I'm so glad he recognised the island; it made it all feel worthwhile."

Jim nodded and spoke in a hushed tone. "Everything checked out. But I still feel there's something we're missing. There has to be a reason behind the traumatic nightmares, it can't just be down to the past-life memories. I'm sure of it. I'm convinced there's more to it."

"How do you mean?" Helen turned to face him, adjusting the fan to blow icy air onto her face.

"Just, the more I know, the less I understand why the nightmares affect Jake so badly. He doesn't have a problem with talking about his past-life. Once his memory is evoked, he's fine. Yes, he got sad going back to the family home. That's only natural. He misses his family. But he didn't get scared, or worried or upset. Certainly not terrified. He was excited and ready to go back. In fact, he never wants to leave. If that's the case, why would dreams about the island turn into such horrendous nightmares? It doesn't make sense."

"I see what you mean. You think there's something more causing the nightmares?"

"Yes, some other trauma that Jacob, via Jake, is trying to get through to us. Maybe the Welsh translations from my colleague will help. Hopefully I'll have the results when we get back to the hotel."

"Why didn't he talk about it during the regression?"

"I don't know." Jim rubbed his sweaty brow, and ran his hand across his brush-cut hair – a trait Helen had noted as a sign of concentration. "I don't know," he repeated. "But I intend to find out."

Chapter Twenty Three

"Wake up!"

His voice intruded on her dream. The creak of the door and the sudden glare of light woke Nia from her semi-slumber. She sat up and rubbed her eyes, flinching at the spasm of pain. Her hands stung almost as much as her face throbbed; the tiny cuts on her palms were now scabbing over from where she'd smashed the car window.

He threw a plastic carton of pre-packed sandwiches, a chocolate bar, and two bottles of Evian water onto the mattress.

"Food time."

"I'm not hungry."

"Eat."

Not having the energy to argue with him, she sat up and moved along the bed, making sure the stained sheet was wrapped around her and hooked under her bra straps. She'd had to remove her top; the feel of drying, congealed blood and the bitter smell made her nauseous. She opened the water, took grateful sips, and peeled the paper off the chocolate bar, biting into it carefully, trying to ignore the flare of pain. She closed her eyes, relishing the taste, hoping it would help keep her energy levels up.

"Right," he said, as she swallowed the last piece. "It's almost midnight and we have work to do."

"What?" Her voice croaked as she swallowed the last of the

water.

"Another call to Daddy."

He threw her phone onto the bed, followed by another sheet of paper.

"I can't."

"Do we have to go through this again? Don't push me, sugar. You know the consequences."

"I just don't understand …"

He slid the long kitchen knife from his inside pocket. Nia closed her mouth with a snap.

"Good girl. Make the call."

Nia picked up the phone and scrolled through the directory. It answered on the first ring; she heard her father's laboured breathing. Her throat tightened and the words blurred through her tears.

"Daddy, don't speak. This is being timed, so it will not be long enough to trace. Please listen carefully. Deliver the money at 6am to the chapel on Church Island, across Belgian Promenade at Menai Bridge. Inside there is a cupboard, it will be unlocked. Put the money in two sports bags, and leave it inside the cupboard. Go alone. You will be watched. Your phones are tapped. If you contact anyone, I will be dead before 7am. This is real. I'm scared Daddy. He's hurting me! Help. Help me!"

He grabbed the phone, pressed end, and slipped it into his jacket pocket. He patted her on the head.

"Well done. Good job."

Nia rubbed her eyes and sniffed. "You didn't give him a chance to respond. What if he doesn't have the money? What if he can't get it by tomorrow morning? You won't really kill me, will you?"

Nia looked up. For a moment their eyes met, and Nia felt a connection. A tug of emotion. She put all her faith into her woman's intuition and decided to pursue it.

"Please don't kill me. I don't deserve it. I don't know if he will pay this ransom. I don't know if he loves me enough."

"Sugar, don't play little girl lost. It really doesn't fit. I prefer it when you're playing the feisty bitch role, it suits you better. Besides, it's not an issue. Your father has more than enough money, and we both know he'll pay up."

"So, what if he doesn't know the area? What if he doesn't know Church Island or how to get there?"

He snorted and turned away.

"What's the matter?" she asked.

"Let's just say I have information that your father knows all about Church Island."

Nia felt anger rise in her belly, like a fiery dragon rousing from its slumber.

"You seem to know a hell of a lot about my father. Allegedly."

"Yes, I do, don't I? Allegedly."

"Well, you shouldn't believe everything you see or hear in the media. My father is a good man, a top MP, and does loads of charity work."

Nia was sick of being the victim. What had she or her father ever done to this evil pervert that gave him the right to take her freedom and treat her this way?

She saw his pale face contort into a hideous, ugly expression; the knife gripped in his right hand with such force the knuckles had turned white.

"A good man. A charity man. A brilliant father," he hissed, his voice shaking. "You know nothing, absolutely nothing, about that evil bastard. A brilliant father. God, if only you knew."

Nia stared at him; terror nudged by curiosity, and strangely, pity. His wild eyes reminded her of a wounded animal, scared, tortured and trapped.

Instead of backing away from the upturned knife, she knelt forward, resting her left breast on the tip of the blade.

"So tell me. Or kill me," she whispered, her eyes not leaving his bloodshot gaze. "I mean it."

"There's no point, G –"

"Yes, there is. I need to know. I feel we have a connection and don't I have a right to know the truth? You obviously have all this built-up hatred for my father and I'm the one suffering for it. It's not fair. Whatever did I do to you?"

"You lived."

His voice was so quiet; she almost missed the words.

"What?"

"You're alive. You're alive. You're alive!"

He jerked the knife away from her flesh so suddenly she flinched. He no longer seemed able to see her. He sprung up and started pacing. Back and forth. Back and forth. He gripped his hair and muttered under his breath.

It came again to her. A tortured soul.

"Talk to me. You must hate my father very much to kill all those other innocent girls."

"I didn't kill them," he yelled. "I just left them and they died. That wasn't my fault. Why was it my fault? They should have escaped. I couldn't be here twenty-four hours a day. I won't go down for that, mind. I won't!"

The pacing continued.

"Forget the others. Tell me why you hate my father. I have the right to know …"

"Right? The right?" he screamed into her face, spittle flying. "You have no rights. You do as I tell you. Why keep pushing me? I can't kill you, not yet. No, not yet. Don't make me hurt you."

He leant against the door and slid down onto his haunches, taking long breaths as he raked his fingers through his hair.

* * *

He pulled a pack of cigarettes from his pocket. His hand trembled as he lit it and gulped the nicotine into his lungs. He coughed and spat. Fuck. He had to calm himself. Keep it real. If he fucked this up now, well … it weren't worth thinking about. Probably end up dead himself. Not like he could tell anyone, confess he was losing it.

Twice he'd had to stop himself calling her Grace. So many things about her reminded him. And the way she'd pushed herself onto the blade, not a trace of fear in her eyes. That took guts. That was the kind of thing Grace would have done.

Why did this keep happening? Why was he letting her get to him? Of all the sluts in the world he should hate this one most. He should be punishing her until she couldn't stand, couldn't move, couldn't breathe. Instead, he was being weak. Being the coward his mother called him for. Letting another woman take control. But God, how Nia Morton reminded him of his beautiful sister. So much it hurt. So much they could have been twins. If only …

But Grace was innocent. Okay, this harlot might have the eyes and the hair. She might smell of apple blossom, she might feel like cool delicate silk under his fingertips, but he had to control this urge that brought Grace's face into his mind every time got near her.

He gripped his hair and tugged, harder. He wanted to feel pain, needing to remind himself why he was doing this.

For Grace.

* * *

"Tell me." Nia urged. "I want to understand."

He looked up, took a long drag on his cigarette. "Where to begin …"

"At the beginning … you know my father. How?"

He sighed, a deep rattling sigh, shook his head.

"Look, you can still get the money," Nia urged. "I just need to know why you hate my father so much. If he's not the man I think he is, then I think I have the right to know."

"You've got an older brother?"

"Yes. Richard."

"I had a sister, an older sister. Her name was Grace."

Nia waited.

"Did you know your name is a Welsh name?" he asked.

She nodded.

"Did your father choose it?"

"I think so. My mother said it was one of his favourite names."

"Makes sense."

"I know he studied at Bangor. Did you know him then?"

He nodded. "Everyone loved Charlie Morton. A brilliant student, a talented rugby player and all round good guy. The men wanted to be him. The women wanted to be with him. He could have had any girl he wanted, you know?"

Nia nodded. Even approaching sixty, her father still had an eye for the ladies. His wit and charisma always a big hit. Unfortunately, he'd never managed to stay faithful, but he was always discreet. Nia had no idea why her mother still stayed by his side, she certainly wouldn't have. But the more she learned about the workings of Westminster, the more she realised his behaviour was the norm.

"But unfortunately," he added. "He decided he wanted my big sister, Grace."

Nia grimaced and hugged her knees to her chest as skin crawled on the back of her neck.

"Grace was beautiful. Think of that model ... Claudia Schiffer ... and you're not far off, but she was as beautiful inside as she was out, was Grace. She was perfect. Total perfection."

He gazed into the shadows, his mind elsewhere. Somewhere in the early seventies, Nia guessed.

"She was a small town Welsh girl, you know? She worked in Penrhyn Castle as a tourist guide. She'd been spotted by a modelling agency, mind. Had one photo shoot down in London, and was right ecstatic about her new future. And then she met the famous Charlie Morton."

"I'm beginning to think I can guess the rest ..."

"Oh, no. You'd never guess." He paused, his eyes flashing anger as he shook his head. "Try and imagine the worst thing you can think of. And then double it. No, in fact treble it."

"Tell me."

"You sure you want to know?"

"No. But I need to."

"Well, the inevitable happened. Your father seduced my sister. I was only ten years old at the time, mind, she was eighteen. But I could see it happening before my eyes. She was blown away, never met anyone like him. I don't think she was ever more than a brief flirtation and a fetching piece of eye candy for old Charlie. But Grace fell deeply and passionately in love, became obsessed by him. I learned later she lost her virginity to him, one summer evening. Her skirt hitched up astride a gravestone in the cemetery on Church Island. Romantic fella, your father, huh?"

"And then he dumped her ...?"

"Obviously. He ditched her quite unceremoniously and moved on. Even flaunted the next one in front of her. Broke off all contact and refused to even speak to her. For no reason. She'd done nothing wrong, mind. Just got bored and moved on. But she couldn't, move on that is, she was devastated."

"I'm sorry. If it's any consolation, I'm sure your sister isn't the only woman my father has treated badly over the years ..."

"And then she got sick," he continued. "Coupla months later, she got taken to hospital. I was too young to really know what was going on, but seemed she started haemorrhaging. She hadn't been eating, hadn't been looking after herself at all."

He took a final drag on his cigarette and ground the stub into the floor.

"She lost the five-month old son she didn't even know she was carrying."

"My God …"

"She was an innocent, you see. I won't say she didn't know the basics, but she wasn't worldly-wise at all. My parents were both religious; my father was a lay preacher. Grace shamed the family. We were ostracised by the people of our own Chapel, our own village even. My parents were devastated, they didn't cope with stress well. My father had a mild stroke, had to give up the job he loved. Six months later, Mother had a complete nervous breakdown. She became a stranger to me. Hated me because I wasn't Grace."

He paused for breath.

"I'm sorry … what happened to Grace?"

"One night, after they'd sectioned my mother, took her into hospital, I found Grace lying on our parents' bed. She was beside herself, weeping and praying. I thought it was because Mother was sick. They'd always been close, always so alike. Like a pair of golden angels." He paused. "But then Grace told me it was guilt. Said I was too young to rightly understand, but she blamed herself for all their troubles. All the arguments, all the anger. She'd hurt them, she'd shamed them, and finally made them ill. I was a kid but I tried to comfort her, as best as an adolescent boy could. But she was inconsolable. She said she couldn't live with the shame, couldn't live with herself. I said I needed her, who was going to be there for me? But she just shook her head and closed her eyes. She said 'I love you, sugar. I love you.' I thought she'd gone to sleep. I was just glad she'd stopped crying. She looked so peaceful."

He broke off, wiped his nose with the back of his hand.

"Then I saw the empty paracetamol bottle my mother kept next to the bed for when her arthritis pained her. It was empty."

"No!"

He nodded slowly, hands clenched in his lap.

"Can you believe I'd sat cradling her in my arms? I held her for over an hour. I didn't even realise her body had gone cold. And how is a lad who hasn't even reached his teens yet supposed to cope with that? Huh? Who writes those kind of self-help books? Which smart-arse social workers are going to heal those kind of wounds?

I'd let my beloved sister die right in front of me, in my arms for God's sake."

"It wasn't your fault ..."

"Of course it wasn't. But that's not the point, see. I could have saved her, I should have saved her. I was the only one there and I just let her die. And can you imagine how Mam reacted? How much she blamed me?"

"But you didn't know, you were only a child."

"Yeah, that's what the smart-arse social workers said. Pretty much word for word. Funny thing was they thought I was self-harming, trying to hide the bruises my mother inflicted on me. But do you think all the clever words made the pain and guilt any easier to bear? Because I can tell you for a fact it didn't."

"No, I wouldn't imagine for one minute that it would. But it is true. You weren't responsible."

"No, I know that. I know that now. It's taken me twenty odd years though."

"My father ..."

"He took everything from me, ruined my childhood, my life. And now it's payback time."

"And the other girls ..."

He turned, the smile was evil, the eyes dead. "You know what they say ... practice makes perfect."

Nia swallowed.

"This is your father's fault. All of it. He took what was mine, now I want what is his."

"So, you are going to kill me then, whether you get the money or not?"

He met her gaze but remained silent.

"You are, aren't you?"

"That's the plan. Yes."

Chapter Twenty Four

"Right, guys and gals. Firstly, thank you all for abandoning your weekend plans at short notice. I think it's fair to say, overtime will be the norm for all of us until this case is solved." McRae cleared his throat, shrugged off his jacket, and folded it across the back of his chair. "I've just come from hospital. Dr Connolly was good enough to carry out an emergency post-mortem on Victim 4."

Gareth saw a flicker of emotion in McRae's face; the corpse had left a lasting impression. Gareth knew exactly what his boss had seen, could still see. Floaters were one of the worse corpses, if there were any such thing as a good corpse. The bloating and disfiguration could make identification impossible in some cases.

McRae turned to the white board, taking hold of a marker pen. "Basic facts and figures, can you all make notes just now, until we get hard copy of the PM report. White Female. Age, eighteen to twenty-four. Blue eyes. Height, five foot, six inches. Weight, nine stone, that's fifty-eight kilos in new money. Dark blonde, shoulder-length hair. No tattoos, birth marks or piercings.

"There's good news and bad news. Bad news – still no positive ID, although Dr Connolly pointed out some fairly recent large scale dental work, so we're hoping that might help. But this body has been in the water up to a week. So, why no missing person report filed? What does that tell us? Where's her family? Friends?

Is she a loner? Not local? She's the right age for a student, so I've left Whitlock at Bangor Uni, going through attendance records for the past month.

"And now the good news, though I'm struggling to call it that. It's definitely the same guy. One hundred percent same MO. Same rope used, although cleverly this time he tied a hessian bag full of sand, pierced at two corners, to her feet. The result being that the body was weighted, and taken straight to the bottom, but as the sea washed through the bag, flushing out the sand, the body gradually came to the surface, finally getting washed up in the estuary at City Dulas. Why? This is a new method. Is he just trying it out? Or is there a reason he didn't want the body found straight away? I don't believe this guy leaves anything to chance. He's too careful. So, why the delay? What's he been up to in the past week?"

Gareth cleared his throat. "Leaving messages on my answer phone, sir?"

McRae nodded. "Yes. My first thought. It must be linked to Friday night's abduction. He needed that to go off smoothly. He wanted that out of the way before this body appeared. Why?"

"But we still don't know there was an abduction on Friday night," said Chris. "We don't know if his plan worked."

"No, not yet, agreed. But his actions, along with the phone call, tell me this one is important. He doesn't want anything to cock it up. His plan is meticulous."

"Sir, on this latest victim, are there markings to the neck?" asked Gareth.

McRae nodded, pulled out a chair and sat. "Yes. Exactly the same."

"And cause of death?"

"Connolly thinks strangulation, but pending further tests. Definitely not drowning, no sign of water in the lungs. She's running alcohol and narcotic tests as we speak and again there was evidence of prolonged sexual abuse."

Gareth swallowed, pushed away the memory of smooth grey

flesh, slimy seaweed across the diamond stud …

"I'm going to release this to the media straight away. Parry, I want to go ahead with another press conference with you as police spokesman. I want to communicate with this guy again. It provoked a reaction last time. Let's try and force him into an error. I'd like to get organised for the local evening news slot. Our hands are tied until we get a positive identification, and getting the details out there is probably our only chance. If anyone was going to report her missing, it would have happened by now –"

Gareth turned at a sudden noise. The door flew open and DC Sandra Whitlock rushed into the room, brandishing a sheet of paper.

"I've got an ID, sir. Not confirmed yet, but Lewis is taking a witness to the morgue as we speak."

McRae thumped the desk with a clenched fist. "Brilliant work. What's the story?"

"More a matter of good luck, sir. A student, name of Kate Summerton, saw the police car and came looking for us. She'd been away on a study course, got home last night, realised her flat mate was missing, and was on her way to report it. Apparently, they'd had some sort of row and hadn't spoken for a few days prior to her going away, so she'd not known there was a problem or raised the alarm. She's agreed to identify the body. Lewis will ring us as soon as it's confirmed."

"And family?" asked Gareth.

Whitlock shook her head. "She's American. On a foreign exchange scheme. Nothing reported. I checked and the Uni hadn't received any calls from worried parents, so perhaps they weren't all that close. I don't know. But it explains why we weren't aware of her."

"Do we have a name?" asked McRae, returning to his position at the front of the room, pen in hand.

"Carleen Clarke. Known as Carly. Age twenty-one."

McRae wrote the girl's name in the empty space alongside the sub-heading of Victim 4, followed by a question mark.

The trill of a phone filled the room.

Whitlock dug her mobile from her handbag. "Hello?"

She nodded once. McRae used his fist to erase the question mark.

* * *

"… having spoken to her parents, we can confirm the latest victim was a twenty-one year old female student, Carleen Clarke. Also known as Carly. If anyone knows Carleen we ask you to contact the crime team. Your call will be handled in the strictest confidence.

We are focusing our enquiries in and around the university, and we continue to urge any female students, staff members, or members of the public to take extra care, not to go out after dark alone, and generally raise levels of awareness. Please remember to report any suspicious circumstances immediately.

The investigation has reached a critical level and we are in the process of following up several important leads. To reiterate what I said last time, this is a matter of when, not if, this man is caught. He should be under no illusion that the net is closing around him. He's making mistakes, leaving behind valuable evidence. I am confident we shall be making arrest within days rather than weeks.

Thank you. Any questions?"

Gareth sat up straight, away from the microphone, stretching his back and flinching as two flash bulbs popped in the front row. God only knows why they needed to take photographs, he was hardly a celebrity.

With a sigh, he picked out a man in a worn leather jacket and nodded in his direction.

"Arnold Hardy. Daily Post. When you say an arrest is

imminent, how confident are you? Can we give anything to our readers to help them sleep easy in their beds?"

Gareth forced a smile he had a feeling came out as more of a sneer. He hated these old hacks, this one in particular. And Hardy hated the police in equal measure. Gareth cringed having to read McRae's prepared script. There was no point in lying, in his experience it always came back to haunt you. Where was McRae when it came to answering awkward questions?

"Arnold, you know I can't go into details, the investigation is at a critical stage. We have lots of evidence from each of the murders that have helped us build up a clear profile of the killer. We've interviewed several important witnesses, and at this very moment, the team is collating all of this information."

Arnold looked up from his notes. "So, you have no prime suspect then?"

Gareth cleared his throat. "For obvious reasons, I can't divulge that at this time."

"Only … our readers might say, might they not, Detective, that North Wales CID are getting nowhere fast with this investigation. This is the fourth victim, am I right?"

Gareth met the journalist's wide stare with an icy one of his own. "That is correct, yes."

"So, if you are so close to an arrest, isn't it possible you could have moved quicker? Tightened your so-called net sooner. And saved this young girls' life?"

Arnold nodded to the screen behind Gareth where a large photo of Carly was on display.

Gareth felt the familiar burning itch in his knuckles. The room was hot and claustrophobic. Beads of perspiration clung to his back and crept under the tight collar of his shirt. His stomach crawled with apprehension; a nest of ants on the move through his gut.

"This case has been a difficult and complex one. I think CID would be the first to admit. But we have made some massive breakthroughs, and believe me we are all working flat out to bring this enquiry to a close. No one has more reason to see this over than I have. As you know, this is personal. And there is nothing to be gained by undermining the police officers who on a daily basis handle situations I hope none of you in this room ever have to face."

He pushed back his chair. "No further questions. Thank you."

Gareth forced himself to stride out of the room, looking like calmness and confidence personified, waiting until he found the solitude of the corridor to grimace and slam his palm into the nearest door frame.

"Parry?" DC Cerys Evans appeared at his side, nodding towards the press room. "You finished in there? There's a call for you, old guy says it's urgent."

"Who? I ain't in the mood …"

"Some Professor. Randall, is it?" Cerys was halfway down the corridor. "On line two."

Gareth's bad mood was instantly replaced by a spark of hope. He hurried to his desk, snatching up the phone.

"Professor, you there? Sorry to have kept you."

"Quite remarkable, at this moment I'm watching your face on the evening news, wonders of modern science, what?"

"Indeed. My colleague says you needed to speak to me?"

"Well, yes. I have a snippet of news that may or may not assist you, but I felt duty bound to pass it on."

"Yes …"

"I've been doing a spot of sleuthing, asking the odd question here and there, and think I've dug up some dirt on the young Rogers fellow –"

"Glyn … what?" Gareth could hear the breathless edge to his voice, forced himself to relax his grip on the telephone.

"Well, it seems he has somewhat unsavoury habits. I mean, I like to think I'm a man of the world, even if I don't partake in any of the more distasteful aspects of society. But still, some things give you rather a nasty taste in your mouth; rather make you wish the discovery have been left undiscovered, if you know what I mean. Especially when you're on first name terms with the fellows involved –"

"Professor, I apologise, but you're not making a lot of sense."

"Ah, no, perhaps not. It's just … I'm not sure how one discusses such things nowadays, things were different in my day …"

"What things, Professor?" Gareth forced back the rising wave of frustration, attempting to keep his voice light.

"Things of a sexual nature."

Gareth paused. "So, what is it, Professor?"

"Rent boys, so I heard. And before you ask, I gave my word I would not name the source. But what chills my blood is that Rogers and his associates prey on young, broke students who need cash badly enough to get involved with this sordid business."

"Are you certain?"

"Absolutely. I don't know all of the … details. But the student who told me had been approached by Rogers himself after a late-night poker game at The Muse, where it appears this gang grooms its victims."

* * *

"Another pint in there when you're ready, Barry."

Gareth pushed his glass away and propped his chin in his hands. What a day. What a fucking awful day. Another victim, straight out of the blue, while they'd spent all weekend waiting for an abduction that never happened. Next, the press conference. What a fucking disaster. How he'd not ended up flattening Arnold Hardy, he had no idea. He knew it was the nature of the beast. These old hacks worried away at any sign of failure like a scab on an unhealed wound. It was protocol to smile and turn the other cheek, to answer them with the required degree of patronising civility. Usually he could handle it, but today he'd failed big style. Perhaps because the old bastard got uncomfortably near the truth.

And then the telephone call from Professor Randall. Where to go with that one? Was it enough to pull Rogers in? Probably not. Not in terms of questioning him about the murders. He'd have the Independent Police Complaints Commission on his back before first light. Besides, the last conversation had led to a brick wall. But still Gareth couldn't quell the feeling he was missing something; that Rogers was telling him something, by telling him nothing at all.

Fuck them. Fuck it all.

He raised a thumb as a full pint appeared under his nose, and took a long quenching pull on the smooth bitter. When he left the station, after the phone call, he'd been hyped, angry and in need of strangers' company. Safety in number perhaps. The thought of going home, seeing a 'new message' symbol flash on his answer phone, was more than he could cope with at the moment. The dulled oblivion of alcohol seemed a welcome retreat. His local, The Freemason's Arms, was his place of choice. Busy enough with the regulars to offer the security he craved, but quiet enough that no one would disturb him and he could wallow in his own thoughts.

"Can you rustle up a chaser, Barry? I'll take a vodka and coke, cheers."

"Rough day?" asked the landlord as he returned with the drink.

"Like you wouldn't believe, mate."

Barry nodded to the small TV above the bar. "Seen the news, aye. It's a rum do."

"You're not wrong. It's a fucking nightmare. And tonight, I want to drink until I forget it for a few hours." Gareth downed the remainder of the pint and slid it towards to the far side of the bar. "Another when you're ready. And a packet of salted nuts. Bring it over, I'll be in the corner, thanks mate."

He slid from the stool and headed for his usual seat in a small alcove window. His throne, he called it. A place he could people watch, both inside and outside the pub, without being observed. His thinking space.

As he slid into his seat, he heard the text alert on his phone, and pulled it from his trouser pocket. His heart quickened. Paranoia to think the killer had his mobile number too. One new message. Sue Connolly.

'Too busy to call, working on PM. Call from Sunny, you were right. It's Britannia Bridge on the recording. 100%. I'll have both reports ready to collect 10am. See you in morning.'

Gareth punched the air. Yes. Brilliant. Two fingers to you, Detective Chief Inspector McRae. Perhaps now he would think about searching the Straits. Gareth couldn't wait to get hold of the report and put it under McRae's nose, hovering while he read the results.

He clicked on reply. "Cheers, Sue. I'm having a bevy. I'll have one for you. I'll be at your office 10am. Night xx'

He thought about the kisses for a second, before hitting the send button. If the girl didn't know how he felt by now she was an idiot. And she was far from that.

Barry arrived with his pint and he took another mouthful of beer. Laying his head back against the flock wallpaper, he undid his tie and slid it from round his neck, unfastening the two top buttons on his shirt. He sighed, and looked out of the window, noting a couple of middle-aged women, the-mutton-dressed-as-lamb variety, flirting with two young men under the canopy of the smoking area. Beyond, a flash of blue signified the deep waters off Bangor Pier. The sun had dropped behind the rise of land on the opposite bank, casting purple shadows across the sky. The heat and humidity finally beginning to cool as the sun gave up its grip on the day.

It was quiet in the bar tonight, a sign of the times. Many of the local pubs had started to shut on a Sunday evening. Unless you had a regular trade of students, which the Freemason's thankfully didn't, not all that many people could afford a third night of weekend drinking, especially with work looming the following morning.

Gareth took a sip of vodka and coke, and pushed a handful of nuts into his mouth. What a weekend.

He shared one view with McRae – they were near. He agreed with McRae's thinking that the answer phone message was a diversion. It wasn't designed to boast. That was what the killer wanted them to think. It was designed to throw them off track, slow them down. And if so, who or what were they close to?

And also, the other worry that played on his mind. How had the guy got hold of his home number? Who had he given it to? How could it have been traced when he was ex-directory? It wasn't Edwina. He was sure of that. He wasn't even certain Edwina had his flat number. She always used her mobile to text if she needed him. He couldn't remember a time she'd called his home. No, not her, for definite.

A braying laugh caught his attention. One of the tarty-looking women had her head thrown back, wrinkled cleavage on display, laughing like a donkey in pain. He shook his head, sipped his vodka. If that was her idea of flirtation, he pitied the poor guy she'd fixed in her sights. He watched as the woman reached out, crimson-painted talons, and tugged the young guy's t-shirt, pulling him closer so she could whisper in his ear. He returned the gesture; his hand on her arse. She pulled away, feigned shock, eyes wide and that laugh again. Mouth wide open, a set of donkey-sized teeth, to match the braying, on display. He grimaced and looked away. Sometimes people watching gave him the creeps.

He reached for his pint. A memory lurched at him, swirling out of the gloom of his thoughts, hitting him in the guts with the force of a boxer's upper cut. His hand went to his mouth, holding in a cry. How had he missed that? Oh, God. How?

He drained the last of his bitter, picked up his tie, and hurried for the door.

Chapter Twenty Five

The following morning, Helen and Jake ate breakfast at their usual table in the restaurant. She glanced at her watch, almost nine-fifteen. Jim had agreed to meet them for breakfast at nine.

She could've done with a lie in herself. Yawning behind her hand, Helen leaned across the table and chopped the top off Jake's boiled egg. In the early hours she'd woken, mind full of Mark, and realised, with a sudden rush of guilt, that she hadn't thought of him in days. Yes, she knew she could justify it – with the nightmares, the regression and the trip to North Wales, she'd barely a second to herself to think. She could dress it up however she liked, but the truth was that since Jim had arrived, she'd barely given Mark a second thought.

"Morning, morning, morning." Jim's cheerful voice came across the room as he approached. "And how are my two most favourite people on this beautiful morning? Getting stuck into those eggs, hey Jake?"

Jake looked up and beamed.

"Morning, Helen. How are you?"

"Fine. You?"

"Slept like a Lord. Jake have a good night?"

"Yes, he went out like a light. I thought you were having a lie in."

"No, I've had an early start, been out since eight," he said, pouring coffee from the pot. "I've been doing a little research."

"Oh?"

"Yeah, I noticed a tourist information bureau opposite the castle. So I've just been to see if they could tell me where to go for information on the Trinity House Pilot Boats and also the land registry for Llanddwyn. They were pretty helpful. Apparently the guy who runs the tourist information in Newborough village is also a local historian, genealogist and ex-mayor, as well as being on the Llanddwyn preservation society board. So, he seems an obvious first choice. The lady in the office gave him a call, and he's happy to see us after lunch."

"Well done. You don't mess around, do you?" Helen was impressed.

"Nope. When I get my teeth into something I am real tenacious and see it through to the end."

"Did you get the translation?"

"No. Not yet. He did say it might take a couple of days. I should learn not to be so darn impatient when someone's doing me a favour."

"So, we have a morning free then?"

"Well you two do. I have some work to do. I want to write up a report about yesterday. But you're welcome to take the car."

"We'll stay local. Meet you in reception about 2pm then."

The door to the public library creaked as Jim pushed it open. The sign for the tourist information bureau assured them they were still heading the right way.

"Good morning. I'm Ivor Williams. You must be Dr Crawford?"

A man in his mid-fifties, with a ruddy complexion and rotund build, appeared from behind the library main desk. He spoke in a deep, booming voice, with a strong Welsh accent. A grey-haired, waspish-faced woman also sat behind the counter, eyeing their arrival with interest.

"Hello. Thanks for agreeing to see us at short notice, Mr Williams," said Jim.

The two men shook hands.

"Oh, please call me Ivor, let's drop the formalities."

"Of course, thank you. Then please call me Jim. And this is Helen West and her son, Jake. I think your colleague from Beaumaris explained that we have an interest in history on Llanddwyn. And she tells me you're the person we need to speak to."

"Well, I won't presume to know everything, but I've loved the island all my life and spent a good deal of time there. It's a special place, aye."

"It is indeed. We all felt that and said the same."

"So you've been already then, have you?"

"Yesterday. It was spectacular scenery. Hard to believe it was in the UK."

"Wales." A shadow of a frown crossed Ivor's face.

"Er, yes of course, Wales," Jim said.

"I don't suppose you have anywhere so beautiful in your country, have you?"

"Not at all." Jim winked at Helen.

"No, I would doubt it very much. Come into my office, and we'll see if we can find anything of interest to you in our records."

Helen, Jake and Jim followed him into a small glass-enclosed office, and sat on the proffered chairs.

"Now, what period were you interested in?" asked Ivor. "Mid-nineteenth century, was it?"

"A little earlier, 1831 to be precise."

"Very precise." He looked up and searched their faces as he slipped on a pair of reading spectacles. He looked at Jake for the first time. "You're a quiet little fellow, aren't you?"

Jake nodded. "Yes, thank you."

"He's fine," said Helen, ruffling Jake's hair. "He's exhausted himself over the past couple of days."

Ivor leaned over the desk. "So what do you think of our island then, Jake?"

Jake smiled. A gentle, thoughtful smile that made him look older and wiser than his years. "I love it. I've always loved it. I wish I still lived there."

"Lived there?" Ivor frowned. "No one has lived on the island for over fifty years. I think you might be getting confused."

"No, he isn't, it's fine," interrupted Jim. "That's why we want to research the history of the island. I'm a child psychiatrist and Jake is my patient. But obviously, I'm sure you understand client-patient confidentiality."

Helen smiled at Jim's subtle method of preventing any further difficult questions.

"Oh, yes of course. I'm only too glad to help. I'm also a local historian and genealogist, I'm not sure if you knew?" Jim nodded. "Oh, you do? Well, if you need to know anything, any time, then please ask. We're known to be accommodating around here. We had a Hollywood film crew around a few years ago. They made a feature film on the island, you know? Demi Moore stared in it. Quite a local event. I was still Mayor at the time, so I got to meet all the big stars."

"Sounds super," said Jim. "But what we'd really like to see is the tenancy agreements for 1831 please. I'm assuming land registry details would be a waste of time. I mean, I'm guessing that Trinity House built and rented out the cottages. So no one other than the company has ever owned the land."

"Oh, okay, let's see." Ivor looked affronted that the opportunity to discuss his involvement with the Hollywood glitterati had been diplomatically deflected. "Yes, you're correct. Trinity House owned the land until the council bought it from them in the 1980s. Prior to that the cottages had been boarded up for best part of fifty years. Crying shame, but there you are."

He pulled open several drawers on a grey filing cabinet, and eventually pulled out a folder, marked 1830-1840.

"Righto, there's a list of all the tenancy agreements issued in that decade. Obviously the original paperwork has long gone, but the specifics are down there."

"Thank you," said Jim, as he took the file. "If we wanted to trace relatives of a family that we believe lived on Llanddwyn, would you be the person to help us?"

"Oh yes, I'd be delighted. It won't take me more than forty eight hours. And if any relatives have survived, and are local, with my influence I'm sure I could set up a meeting." He pushed his chest out, and smoothed his tie.

"That would be great. If our search through the archives proves positive, then I'll give you the family history. Thanks again, Ivor."

"That's fine, no worries at all. I'll leave you alone for a while. I'll be next door, so call if you need me."

Jim flicked through the thick, yellow pages. He came to 1831.

"Yes, it's here, Helen. Not that I think either of us had any doubt that it wouldn't be. Mr J. Lloyd and family. It gives the payment details, and length of lease. It's amazing to see it all down in black and white." He paused. "And here, from September 1831, the name changes to Mrs M. Lloyd (wdw) and the rent reduces significantly. Obviously Trinity House were subsidising her rent. That was nice of them."

"So, yet another box ticked."

"Yes, it would seem so. Everything Jacob told us has checked out perfectly. Here we have proof that they lived there, and proof that Joe died when Jacob said he did. I'm going to pass these details on to Ivor and ask him to contact us if he does trace a living relative, somewhere on Anglesey. Not that they would remember Joe or Jacob but there might be some family tales of heroism that have been passed down from generation to generation."

* * *

Later that evening, Helen stood in the shower. Hot water sprayed down onto her upturned face, breathing in the citrus scent of her shower gel as the water beat against her aching neck, stinging the patches of sunburn across her upper arms.

"Mummy!"

Helen strained her ears. She switched off the tap and stood perfectly still.

"Mummy!"

This time she was out of the shower cubicle in seconds. She wrapped herself in a white towel and dashed into the bedroom, leaving a trail of water across the tiles. Rivulets cascaded down her body from her dripping hair.

Jake sat upright in bed, pointing with his right hand. For a moment, Helen's heart leapt into her throat. Deja-vu. She thought back to one of his early nightmares, when he'd stared unblinking at some invisible entity in the corner of his bedroom.

But Helen could see that Jake wasn't asleep. And this time, he was pointing at something concrete. The television. He still sat, arm outstretched and finger pointing. Helen noticed him tremble slightly.

"Mummy, mummy, that girl on the TV. I know her. I've seen her before. She's the girl in the dream!"

Helen swallowed. "What girl, Jake?"

She followed Jake's gaze and glanced at the screen; it appeared to be the leading story on the local Welsh news programme. She picked up the remote from the bedside cabinet and turned up the volume.

"...with any other information or if anyone knows of the movements of Carleen Clarke over the past few weeks. Police are appealing for anyone with information to please call North Wales CID on 01407 763333 and ask for the officer in charge of the investigation, Detective Chief Inspector McRae. You can visit our website for further information. And now onto other news ..."

Helen turned off the TV and sat on the bottom of the bed.

"What do you mean, Jake?"

"I've seen that girl. I've seen her in my dream. She died and the bad man laughed."

Jake closed his eyes. Helen felt the blood drain from her face. She didn't understand what was happening. What was Jake trying to say?

She moved next to him, turning his body towards her, she gripped his arms.

"Jake, sweetie. This is important. Very important. You must tell me exactly what you mean. Exactly what you've seen. Take your time."

Helen managed to control her voice. She was shaking so badly inside, yet to her ears she sounded rational and calm.

"When I saw that girl's face, I knew it was a girl I saw in the bad dream. I saw her screaming for help. Then she went quiet. But Mummy, there's another girl. She's still alive. Still shouting. I heard voices, scary voices."

Helen's pulse pounded in her temples, but she kept her face calm. "Okay, Jake. That's good. Perhaps if you talk about it, you might remember more of the dream."

Jake shook his head. "I don't think there is more. Not yet. But there will be."

"What do you mean?"

"The dreams I've had before, the really scary ones. I think that's when the bad man hurts the girls. I hate it, Mummy. I hate it!"

Helen stroked his hair. "Why haven't you told me about any of this before?"

"I … I don't know. I didn't know until I saw her face. And then I remembered all the bad stuff. I usually forget it when I wake up. But now I can see all the scary stuff. I'm so scared! I hate it"

He threw himself down face first on the bed and buried his head in the pillow. He began to cry softly but it wasn't the wild, piercing sobs that accompanied the nightmares.

Helen felt her own eyes well up with tears. "Jake, sweetheart. Come on. Don't cry. You're being so brave."

He spoke through the pillow, his voice muffled and barely audible. "If I can see it, then why can't I stop it? Why is this bad man hurting the girls?"

"I don't know, sweetie. But I promise you, it isn't your fault."

Helen stroked the back of Jake's head, running her fingers through his hair. His sobs dried up into an occasional muted hiccup. She dried herself off, pulled on her pyjamas, and fetched a bottle of orange juice from the mini-bar. After a few minutes of gentle encouragement, Jake sat up and sipped the juice. His face still wet with tears, his sweaty hair clinging to his forehead.

"You mustn't upset yourself, Jakey. I know this is hard to understand … even I don't know why you see these things. But just because you can't … well, *control* it … that doesn't mean it's your fault. It's not your fault, sweetie. You don't make this bad man do bad things. But you might be able to help stop him. Do you want to talk to Jim? Mmm? He might be able to help …"

"No! Please don't leave me, Mummy. Don't leave me alone."

"Okay, that's fine. Let's cuddle up and try to get to sleep, okay?"

Jake nodded. He yawned widely. Helen crossed to the bathroom, ran a facecloth under the cold tap and wiped him down, before turning down the duvet, and covering him with a light cotton sheet.

She kissed his forehead as she slipped into bed beside him. "Go to sleep now, baby."

Helen lay awake. It was impossible to sleep. She lay alert, on edge, waiting for the nightmare to start; struggling to control the spinning vortex of thoughts flying around her brain. And she was afraid. She couldn't just lie there doing nothing. If what Jake believed was true, every second wasted could be another nail in a young girl's coffin. She had to talk to someone. And the most obvious someone was Jim.

She listened to the steady rise and fall of Jake's breathing. Restless to begin with, he'd been sleeping peacefully now for almost an hour, with no sign of any irregularity to his sleep pattern. Besides, she'd only be next door. If she left the door ajar, she would hear any disturbance.

She extracted herself carefully from his arms. The clock read 11:15 pm. Not too late. The yellow glow from the bathroom illuminated Jake's sleeping face. He hated the dark, and with the absence of his beloved night-light insisted that the bathroom light be left on, the door half open. Helen stood for a moment gazing down at him. He looked so peaceful, the hint of a smile playing on his lips. Who would ever believe his inner turmoil? Why was this happening to them?

She shook her head. As far-fetched as the whole thing might sound in the cold light of day, right here, right now, she believed Jake one hundred percent. And something told her this could be the first thread to unravelling the mystery behind the traumatic nightmares.

Helen tiptoed across the room, wrapping a satin dressing gown over her pyjamas. She glanced back, Jake hadn't moved a muscle. He continued to snore gently, curled into a foetal shape. She pulled open the door, and slipped into the corridor. Reaching Jim's door, she knocked three times.

Within seconds, Jim opened the door wearing boxers and a t-shirt, a look of surprise and concern in his raised eyebrows. Helen shook her head and put a finger to her lips; she gestured for him to reverse back into the room, closing the door half way.

"What's the matter?" he whispered. "Is it Jake?"

"No … well, yes. But not how you mean. Not a nightmare."

"What, then?"

"Jake saw a picture of a young girl from some university around here who's been abducted and murdered, from what I can make out. And he says he saw the same girl in the dream he had last week. Then he went on to say that she's dead, but there's another girl who's still alive. It's unbelievable. But I do believe him. This has to have something to do with the nightmares. I've been lying awake thinking about it."

Helen repeated the whole conversation to Jim word for word, hoping she'd missed nothing out. Finally, she finished, and sat, shakily, on the edge of the bed.

"Why didn't you come get me earlier? I could maybe have regressed him at the time. The news finished ages ago."

"Jake was terrified, he begged me not to leave him. And I was scared it may have been a portent for a nightmare. But he's sleeping fine. Do you think we should call the police?"

"First things first, I have something to tell you too. Especially in view of this latest turn of events. I was contemplating whether or not to come knock your door, when you turned up at mine."

"Why? What is it?"

"I finally got an email from my colleague with the Welsh translation. It makes pretty harrowing reading. I didn't know what it meant. But I think I do now."

"Why? What was the translation? Was it definitely Welsh?"

"Yeah, we got that part right. Look ..."

He handed Helen a piece of paper, with English translations printed alongside the Welsh in Jim's neat hand writing.

"Oh my God," Helen said, as her eyes followed the list down the page. "This is awful. Just terrible. But how and why is this happening, Jim?"

"It's new to me, Helen. I've been trying to work it through. It seems to me that it must be Jacob, relaying this information through Jake. But what I don't understand is how Jacob would know?"

"And if it is Jacob, why didn't he tell us during the past-life regression interview, and why doesn't he speak English, because we know he can?"

"I don't have any answers yet, Helen. But an educated guess would be that Jacob is channeling this information only at certain times, possibly when his presence is so badly shocked that he reacts in a certain way. He may not be responsible for his actions, or he may be going through the spiritual equivalent of a panic attack."

"And talking in Welsh …?"

"Well, we know it was his native tongue. It would be his first choice language. So it would be natural that's what he'd speak when he was upset, scared or angry. And he wouldn't know that Jake didn't speak that language. How could he? He would probably have no perception that not everyone speaks Welsh. He spoke to me in my own language during hypnosis which is usual."

Jim stood and crossed the room. Helen watched as he pushed open the window and took deep breaths of sea air.

"Jesus, Helen. What are we into here?"

Helen shook her head. "I've no idea. This is getting way more serious than I ever imagined."

"I knew there was something more, something worse if you like, that had to be triggering the nightmares. But how could you ever dream up something like this? Don't they say that truth is stranger than fiction?"

"So … should we go to the police?" Helen repeated.

"And say what?"

Helen opened her mouth to speak, and after a while, closed it again.

"Exactly," said Jim. "I had the same problem. When I tried to run the conversation through in my head, it sounded ridiculous."

"But I believe Jake. Implicitly."

"Yeah, so do I. But we're not Officer McCabe, or whatever you said his name was."

"McRae," Helen corrected. "Detective Chief Inspector."

"McRae, then. Can you imagine the look on his face when we walk into his police station and announce that we have come to solve this crime? Well, no, let's get the facts straight. We aren't solving the crime ourselves. It's been solved by a six-year- old boy, with the help of an eleven-year-old boy who's been dead just a shade over a hundred and eighty years."

Despite herself, Helen felt a smile tugging at her lips.

"Well, when you say it like that ..."

"When you say it absolutely any goddamn way at all ... it sounds absurd. They would throw us out of the station, and probably out of Wales for that matter."

"But you believe it," said Helen. "And you're a professional man. They would respect the opinion of a psychiatrist. You know, international acclaim and all that."

"Maybe. Under normal circumstances, I'd agree. But if I marched in there with this tall story, they'd think I was a flake and laugh me out the joint. Either that or arrest me and carry me out in a straitjacket."

"Okay," said Helen, "so we have an alternative, right?"

Jim remained silent.

"Oh, so we don't. I see. The alternative is to just ignore everything we know, everything we've learned, and most importantly everything we totally believe in. We just pack up the car tomorrow, drive home like nothing has happened, and not switch the news on for a month in case some other poor young girl's body has been found."

Jim moved back to the open window and stood breathing in the night air. Helen could hear the distant tinkling of boat's rigging in the harbour as the wind gusted. The humidity outside matched the tension inside the room.

"So?" prompted Helen, the fire in her belly aglow.

"I don't know," Jim mumbled.

"I'm sorry, but I do. I could not live with myself for one minute if I went home thinking I'd not done everything I could to try save a young girl's life. Jake says this guy's killed before. The news bulletin says this is the fourth student to die this year. It adds up, Jim. We have to do something. We can't let there be a fifth."

"So, what do you suggest?" asked Jim.

Helen took a deep breath. She couldn't believe the role reversal. She was the strong one, the one making all the decisions, ready to face whatever lay ahead.

"I suggest we get a few hours' sleep. And first thing in the morning, we find out which station this McRae is based at, and we drive over there and talk to him. If he dismisses us as flakes, then at least we can say we tried. But we can't simply do nothing, can we?"

Jim shook his head. "I think all this has happened for a reason. And if that reason is to save an innocent life, then you're right, we absolutely have to try."

Chapter Twenty Six

The boat bobbed gently as he manoeuvred it into position. Luckily, the tide was on the ebb and the wind had dropped. Today, in the lee of the old Menai Bridge, the currents were relatively mild. Several locals chose to moor their boats, knowing the huge concrete supports offered some shelter from the vicious riptides that affected this part of the Straits. The Swellies – the stretch of water between the two bridges – was notorious for its dangerous currents and underwater whirlpools.

He anchored the small fishing boat next to a larger wooden hulled vessel, pleased to see it blended in with the surroundings. Crouching low inside the small cabin, he rubbed the grimy glass and peered through the porthole, training his binoculars on the steps that led through the woods, down to the Belgian promenade and across the causeway to Church Island.

He checked his watch. 5:45 am. Sighing, he lit another cigarette, and lay back on the bunk that served as his bed. He blew out a long stream of smoke, closed his eyes and allowed himself a few moments of relaxation. It had been a busy few days getting his affairs in order. Disposing of his car had been the biggest headache. In the end, he'd driven to Chester, left the car in a multi-story car park and caught the train home. If the connection was ever made, he'd be out of the country and untraceable.

He had it planned down to the last detail. He wanted to slip away quietly, disappear one day and never return. Like, who would miss him anyway?

Maybe his boss would get annoyed when, after a week or so, he noticed he'd not been attending his rounds. Maybe he'd realise when the next field trip failed to turn up. But there would be little he could do about it. The company mobile phone was disconnected as of midnight last night. He'd removed the SIM card, smashing both it and the handset, and throwing them into the Irish Sea.

Other than that, no one would miss him. Certainly not his family.

Since the age of thirteen, this day had been his sole focus. His ultimate dream. The one thing that drove him every morning and kept him warm in his empty bed each night. The overwhelming, burning hatred for the man who had stolen the only happiness he'd ever known.

The whistle of the kettle boiling on the small gas ring brought him back to the present. He shook his head to clear the grogginess. Leaning across to switch off the gas, he poured boiling water onto a teabag in a chipped yellow mug. He stirred the tea, strong and black, threw the teabag into the sea, and watched as it disappeared below the surface, leaving a golden smear in its wake.

He blew on the tea and picked up his binoculars, focusing on the steps again. 5:58 am. Ah, this time there was movement. He made out the figure of a man between the trees, dressed in a green-waxed Barbour jacket and jeans. He turned the wheel to adjust the focus. Yes, he could make out two blue sports bags – one in each hand.

A strong surge of emotion – a white-hot hatred – left him weak. He hadn't expected to feel such intense bitterness after so many years. *Charlie Morton*. The man he'd spent over half a lifetime hating with a never-decreasing passion. Morton didn't look anything like he remembered. In his mind, the shiny black hair and tanned, muscular body hadn't changed over the past thirty years. In reality, his nemesis was now a silver- haired, overweight middle-aged man, with a paunch and slight limp.

He followed the progress of the figure as it strode across the causeway and up through the graveyard on Church Island. It disappeared briefly as Morton made his way along the twisting path between the gravestones. He couldn't see the door of the small church, but guessed Morton had entered from the far side.

A movement in the woods across the water made him jump. Immediately alert and suspicious, he focused the binoculars. He glimpsed a flash of red between the trees, just in front the steps. *Bastard!* Despite all the warnings, Morton had tried to outplay him. His heart hammered in his chest; he could hear it reverberating through his ears. He realised he was holding his breath and forced himself to breathe out. Morton would pay a heavy price for double-crossing him.

Abruptly, he swung the binoculars back across the island. Morton hadn't re-emerged from the church. What was he doing in there? Waiting for an accomplice to turn up? Or waiting for the police to find the kidnapper? Well, Morton would have a long wait. There was no one else on the water. No strange boats in the vicinity. He knew he was safe, they hadn't considered he might come from the sea. He'd always known he was smarter than the police; this just proved the point. He'd sit it out here until the fuss died down.

He trained the glasses back on the steps. Whoever was in the woods was hiding, taking their time to appear. Another glimmer of red flickered through the dense foliage and a little silver Yorkshire terrier darted from the undergrowth, sniffing the ground as it jumped down each step. A white-haired lady in a bright crimson fleece appeared. She took the steps slowly, one at a time, leaning heavily on her walking stick for balance.

He laughed out loud. An early-morning dog walker. How ridiculous. Who on earth would want to walk their dog at this god-forsaken time?

He turned his attention back to the island. Morton reappeared, walking briskly along the causeway that led back onto the mainland. He swung the binoculars round in every direction. No sign of movement. He checked the road and the bridge and followed the Straits in both directions. Nothing. That was the beauty of the spot – so remote any disturbance was immediately distinguishable. He'd leave it half an hour then take the boat round to the far side of the small island. There was an old Victorian fish trap there, with a mooring point and some worn stone steps. He could be in and out in less than a minute.

One million pounds. It was more money than he could imagine. What would he do with that kind of money? He felt no guilt. He'd studied Charles Morton's business empire religiously over the years, and knew that a lot of his money came from some very undesirable contacts. Middle-Eastern businessmen, looking for a way into the British market, had crossed Mr. Morton's palm with many a piece of silver. An infamous East End gangster, renowned for his drug-running empire, was allegedly in the MP's back pocket. Yes, the squeaky clean Charlie Morton had much to fear from adverse publicity. A simple blackmail attempt would no doubt have been enough to send the MP rushing to hand over the money.

But that wasn't good enough. He wanted Morton to feel pain as he had felt it, to grieve as he had grieved, and to lose the one thing most precious in the whole world. He had lost his mother, his sister. His whole life. Charlie Morton was about to lose his only daughter. The thought of Morton waiting for a telephone call he'd never receive caused a bubble of laughter to erupt from him like trapped air from a bottle. He'd never find his daughter's body and he'd have to live with that pain until the day he died.

Nia. His thoughts went back to her. She spent more time inside his head than he would have liked. He had to walk away now, it really wasn't his choice. It hadn't been an issue with any of the others. He'd just stayed away until it was over and then got rid of the evidence.

Nia. What could he do? He couldn't go back to the island - it was too risky. There was probably enough food and water for three or four days. Why the hell should he care? Now when he should be glad it would soon be all over and he would emerge the victor. He had to get away, stay focused and stick to his plan.

And forget all about Nia Morton.

* * *

The cold, damp blackness was beginning to play on Nia's mind. She started to believe she could see and hear things that weren't there. The scurrying tread of rats, the hissing of snakes and the gentle rush of wind through trees kept her awake half the night. She fought against this alternative reality. She wouldn't surrender to the thoughts that kept pushing their way into her conscious.

He said he was leaving her here. That he had no option but to grab the money and run. He made it sound as if he was trying to pass the blame onto someone else, probably her father. A kind of 'he made me do it' excuse you'd expect to hear in a school playground.

But it was more than that and Nia knew it. He wanted revenge and he wanted her father to suffer. The loss of a million pounds was never going to be enough, for him it was just the icing on the cake. What he really wanted was to hurt her father. To really make him suffer just as he had. And unfortunately for her, she was the punishment.

Despite the circumstances, she had begun to find herself moved by the kidnapper's story. She could tell he was irrational – probably psychotic – not to mention a cruel, clinical murderer. But something in his story touched a nerve. She could understand his bitterness and anger, his intense loneliness. And in a way, she understood his feelings towards her father. She couldn't condone, or begin to understand, what they'd led him to do. But she knew enough about her father to know that he'd probably done the same thing hundreds of times throughout his life. He was more than likely still doing it today without an ounce of remorse. Women to him were an expendable commodity, to be tossed aside when they'd served their purpose.

The thought of her mother caused her heart to swell and a lump lodged in her throat. Thinking of home and family – what must they be going through? She couldn't just sit here, shivering in the dark. She had to keep searching. There had to be something she could use, maybe something she'd missed, that would help her escape. How could she just sit in this dungeon and wait to die?

She sat up and took several tiny sips from one of the water bottles. Just enough to wet her lips and keep her mouth moist. She stood and made her way forward, holding one arm out in front of her until she touched the nearest wall. Again, she rubbed the lump next to her eye and nursed her throbbing hands. Her t-shirt was dry, but stiff with blood and it crackled as she walked. Her hands reached the brickwork; it felt cool and damp. Dropping to her knees, she ran her finger tips along the bottom of the wall where it met with the floor. No gap. Nothing. The wall definitely did curve in on this side of the room. It was almost semi-circular.

Nia reached the stone steps that led up to the door. If there was any chance of escape, it looked as if the door was her only option. She gripped the handle and tugged and kicked at the solid timber. It barely moved on its latch. She ran her fingers over the keyhole. Even if the lock was easy to pick, he'd left her nothing she could use as a tool.

"Shit." She jumped at the sound of her voice. It echoed around the small room. She kicked the door. "Shit, shit, shit, shit, shit!"

It was pointless. There was absolutely nothing she could do to escape. The bed wobbled and creaked loudly as she threw herself back down. She beat her fists against the stained mattress and kicked out against the metal frame, screaming to block the noises. They came to her again, louder and more intense now. Inside her head, crawling, jostling, scuttling, pressing against the inside of her skull to find release. She sat up and groped around the bed for the water bottle. Her fingertips touched plastic, and she unscrewed the cap, relishing the last of the stale warm liquid as it moistened the burning dryness in her throat.

Nia threw the empty bottle as hard as she could into the darkness, listening as it clattered against the far wall. She slammed her palms against the bottom of the bed; the framework moved and groaned against her weight. With a rasping noise, she pulled it back into an upright position, then pushed against it again. There was definite movement in the legs on the bottom of the bed. She gripped the frame tightly and shook harder. The bed creaked, metal scraped against metal.

She dropped to her knees on the dusty floor and ran her hands along the bottom of the bed. The metal felt cold and heavy. Her fingers traced the nuts and bolts holding the leg to the frame. The top bolt turned in her fingers and she unscrewed it. It dropped to the floor with a metallic clink. She tugged on the leg. It felt a lot freer now, and sturdier than she'd imagined.

Besides, she had nothing else to do. Having something to focus on was better than having no hope at all. The bottom bolt refused to budge. She twisted and turned the bolt and nut in sequence, using her thumb nail to scrape the rust from around its head, but still the nut remained solid. Beads of perspiration ran down her face; she felt blood drip from under a torn fingernail as she brushed her hair from her face. She scowled and grunted in determination, flinching in pain at the same time.

But she couldn't stop. She worked as if her life depended on it. It was an obsession now. She had to get this bolt undone. She had to.

* * *

His eyes were glued to the small white and red oblongs of paper. He literally could not drag his eyes away from the vision. He lifted a bundle and held it under his nose, savouring the musty smell, rifling through the pile, handling it as gently as a deck of the world's most expensive playing cards. If he'd ever seen a fifty pound note in his life before, he had no recollection of it. And now, here he sat, surrounded by them. A million pounds of them to be exact. Exactly as he'd instructed.

He could hardly believe how easy it'd been. Five minutes to moor the boat, walk to the church, recover the bags, return to the boat and away. His knees had shaken as he hurried across the island. Expecting any minute, some shaven-headed heavy to wrestle him to the ground, or feel the snap of handcuffs behind his back.

Despite everything, he hadn't trusted Morton to keep to his word. Morton was a man who had no understanding of the word. His sister, his Grace, had trusted him and look what had become of her.

But Morton had gone along with the instructions. A testament to just how much his precious daughter meant to him, how much he worshipped her.

Nia. He looked out of the cabin window at the fading sunlight glinting off the calm green water. From his position in the small harbour at Caernarfon, he could just make out the outline of Llanddwyn Island, dominated by the lighthouse on its highest tip. He imagined her there, in that dark, dank cellar. He could still see her pale, porcelain-like face in his mind's eye; her blue eyes shining up at him from her bruised and bloodied face. He remembered the touch of her young, soft skin, and drew in a long breath.

He shook his head to clear the memory as he stuffed the bundles of bank notes back into the blue bags. Lifting the grubby brown padding of the small bench seat, he squeezed the bulky bags into the enclosure beneath it. He folded Grace's belt with a gentle reverence, placing it on top of the money, her name glinting like treasure.

As he dropped the cover back into place, his gaze once again followed the surface of the ocean until his eyes found the outline of the rocky outcrop.

If he filled up the boat with provisions first thing in the morning, ready for his trip across to his new home in Cork, would it take more than half an hour to stop off at Llanddwyn and free her? By the time she'd walked to Newborough, he would be half way across the Irish Sea. Besides, she didn't know his name, and even if she did, he had a new identity planned out when he reached Eire. Geraint Jones, his new pseudonym, had a job waiting on a fishing fleet out of Cork. He would be at sea for the next month or so. Well out of the way of any police investigation. Where was the risk?

He slammed his palm to his forehead. What was he thinking? Why take the chance? He'd already let himself get carried away by provoking that copper. Besides, she was the seed of Morton, why did she deserve to live when Grace was dead? And more importantly, why break his vow to follow his plan down to the smallest detail? Why gamble with a life's work?

He grabbed his tools, and a can of oil, and lifted the flap that covered the boat's engine. Dependent on the weather, he had an arduous journey ahead, and he wanted to make sure the boat was in top condition. He couldn't hazard getting stranded in the middle of the Irish Sea.

As he worked, his thoughts returned yet again to Nia. He remembered the stolid unblinking gaze of her blue eyes. Grace's eyes. How was she coping in that dungeon, waiting to die?

Stop. Goddamn it.

The wooden hatch slammed down with a clattering jolt that rocked the small boat on its moorings. Wiping his hands on an oily cloth, he clambered onto the deck and mounted the rusting metal ladder that led up to the dock. Spotting a new moon, he flipped the coins in his pocket. That was a good omen. A sign. With a jaunty gait and a whistle, he headed off for his meeting, hoping to enjoy one last pint of Welsh ale. With the morning tide, he could make sail. His new life beckoned. Cork was less than six hours away.

Nia Morton had served her purpose well. She was already part of his past. Geraint Jones was his future.

Chapter Twenty Seven

"Parry, it's McRae. Where are you?"

Gareth held the phone close to his ear, pushed the button to close the electric window and hunkered down in the driver's seat of his car. Better for now McRae thought him still in his bed.

He feigned a yawn. "Just about to make a start on following a lead, sir. Why?"

"Developments. Major ones. I'm on my way to Abbeyfield Hotel to interview Charles Morton –"

"The MP?"

"The same. Seems there *was* an abduction on Friday night. His daughter. Nia Morton."

"What?"

"Yes, she's a student at the university. But there's a massive change of M.O this time – a ransom demand."

Gareth's head spun; all the previous evidence pointed to this being a psychotic, probably sexually deviant, killer. Now, suddenly a blackmailer? It didn't make sense.

"But that's not his style, sir. Are you certain it's the same guy?"

"Not totally. But the more you think on it, the more it begins to add up. Perhaps this is why he contacted you – delaying tactics as we guessed. And maybe this is why he delayed us finding the last body."

"But ransom demands have never figured before. Why now?"

"Off the top of my head, I have no idea. Perhaps I'll be wiser once I've spoken to Charles Morton." There was a pause as the signal crackled. "... contact Coleman, but his phone is off. Again. Will you try to find him, get the team together, and I'll meet you all back at the station in a couple of hours."

"Of course, sir. We're up against it now if the kidnapper is going to contact the father again. I'll make a start, get onto the lab, get some traces set up –"

"Too late. Morton has already handed over the cash."

"You are joking?"

"I don't make a habit of joking about such things, especially when it's to the tune of a million pounds."

Gareth swapped the phone to his other hand; sure the signal or his hearing must have failed him. "One mill?"

"Yes, he made the drop as requested at 6am yesterday. According to his private secretary, he was trying to avoid publicity. I've not spoken to Mr Morton in person as yet, but I shall be demanding some answers from him, for sure."

"Where was the drop?"

"Place called Church Island. It's on –"

"The Straits. I know it, just next to the Menai Bridge."

McRae cleared his throat. "Seems your idea might have legs after all. So, your next job is to go and check out the location. Morton left the bags inside a cupboard in the church. I can't imagine you'll find much, but if you pick up anything, anything at all, I want it secured as a crime scene until SOCO get there. But something tells me the clever sod chose a Sunday as there's now been a day's worth of activity to cover his tracks."

Gareth thumped the steering wheel, eyes trained on the building opposite. He wanted to scream down the phone at McRae, berate him for dismissing Connolly's findings. Now wasn't the time for pointing the finger, but he hoped that time would come.

"I'm on my way. But any idea why Mr Morton didn't come to us sooner? Why now? Talk about bolting the stable door after the horse has caught a ferry out of here."

"No idea, Parry. The secretary was tight-lipped and I have a feeling they've turned to us as a last resort. But I'm on my way to find out. I'll fill you in later."

"And no news on the girl? No clues where to start?"

McRae gave a deep sigh. "Nothing. Morton stayed in his hotel room all day yesterday waiting for a phone call as promised. He gave it twenty-four hours, went back to the island and checked the money had indeed gone – surprise, surprise – and then called the head of Scotland Yard, who called me. When I tried to telephone Morton, I got no further than his private secretary. I'll withhold judgment until I've met him. But he's either a naïve father or a pompous idiot."

"He's an MP, probably both."

"Like I say, judgment withheld. Find Coleman and then get yourself over to Church Island, rule out that line of enquiry. If Nia Morton is alive, we don't have time to waste."

"Yes, sir."

Gareth ended the call and laid his head back against the car seat, taking deep breaths. Shit, he needed a fag, but he'd smoked his last in the middle of the night as he tried to battle fatigue. Now, his mind spun with a multitude of questions, but other than a deep-seated belief that the killer was on a boat somewhere in the vicinity of the Menai Straits, he had no answers.

Why hadn't he taken it on himself to search the Straits? Hired his own boat or something. Because he was a good copper, obeying orders, being ruled by the chain of command. And perhaps because of that another young girl would lose her life.

A movement caught his eye, a figure crossing the road, disappearing into the shadowy doorway opposite.

He would be a good copper again, follow orders. But firstly, he needed to bend a few rules. A bit of unfinished business he had to get out of his system.

He jumped out of the car, sprinted across the road, and pushed open the door the figure had entered seconds earlier. With a click, he secured the dead bolt behind him and leant back, heart thumping.

"Sorry, we're not open for another half hour," the voice called from the gloom of the back room. "Can you call back later? I've a delivery that needs sorting."

Glyn Rogers appeared at the curtained alcove; the smile slid from his face.

"Good morning, sir," said Gareth. "Why didn't you tell me you had a brother?"

Gareth studied Rogers' face, noted the nervous tic in his left eye, the lip curl revealing small white teeth. A smile which more resembled the snarl of a trapped beast.

"And good morning to you," Rogers replied, forcing his face into a blank expression as he crossed his arms and propped himself against the stool. "It's barely daybreak. Have you never heard of police harassment?"

"And have you never heard of assisting the police with their enquiries? Or the maximum punishment for obstructing the police in a murder investigation?"

"I'm sorry, Detective *Sergeant*, but you may need to make yourself a little clearer. I'm not sure what crime it is I'm supposed to have committed by having a brother. Or even worse, God forbid, not admitting to this sibling when questioned by the police over a matter that has absolutely nothing at all to do with said relation."

"But that's not entirely true is it, sir? And I think you know that. Or have a very strong suspicion. You see, I've spent all night going through my notes, combing through records, replaying interviews. And I can see I've been an idiot. I will admit to it. But the stupidity stops right here, right now. And you start to tell me the truth."

"Or what?" replied Rogers, heavy derision in his voice. "You arrest me? Because I'd be very interested to hear the explanation you'd come up with when my solicitor arrived …"

Rogers paused as Gareth shook his head, a pitying expression on his face. "You don't get it do you, sir. I'm not here in my *official* capacity. See, no fancy suit and tie. And look," he raised a leg, showing a scuffed trainer, "no dancing shoes either. So the verbal tango ends now. The bullshit stops now." Gareth took four strides across the shop, and levelled his face right up to the other man's. "Because I've had enough of you and your smart-arse answers. I am sick of you meddling in my investigation. So, from now on in, we're going to cross to the other side if you like, cross the line of the law that you have decided to play me with. We're going to do things my way. And if you lie to me just one more time I will make sure you spend a good long stretch in jail."

Rogers threw back his head with a snort of laughter. "This is no Hollywood movie, detective. You sound like Bruce Willis, but alas you are about as threatening as Bruce Forsyth. Do you think I would let someone like *you* intimidate *me*? Are you for real? Whatever side of the line of the law you care to tread, how the hell do you think you will scare me? Some threat about jumped up charges for obstructing a police enquiry?" Rogers turned his back with a wave of his hand.

Gareth spoke quietly, hoping to keep the tremor from his voice. "No, I shall expose the ring of perverts that congregate under your roof. And I can't wait to see your mother's face when I do it. Then, I shall expose you as the head of an escort agency that supplies male students to said perverts in exchange for cash. I shall dig and dig until I prove what I suspect – that there is also paedophilia involved in this group. And if I find nothing, I will fabricate the evidence I need. Finally, I shall provide evidence of mortgages for houses that you have bought in the town as student accommodation, and prove that no money in rent ever changes hands. And I shall call on at least two witnesses who will testify against you."

Gareth bit down hard on his lip; the last part was a lie. But he'd seen fear in Liam Cooke's face from the first day they'd met at Ty Mawr, and the previous night in a sobbing telephone conversation, Liam revealed the truth. Liam had put Gareth onto The Muse, because he was still trying to extricate himself from Rogers' clutches having moved out of one of his shared houses the previous term. As far as Liam knew, Edwina had been unaware what had gone on in the upstairs flat after hours. For that at least, Gareth could be grateful. But unknowingly, Edwina had been put in mortal danger. But not with Glyn. No, she wasn't his type.

Rogers turned slowly and his eyes widened, darting to the door.

"It's locked, don't think about it," said Gareth. "You should be more careful where you leave your keys too." He held the bunch of shop keys aloft. "And just to show what a thorough type of guy I am." Gareth shoved the curtain aside, took one step into the back room, pressed eject on the CCTV recorder, and was back in the shop with the tape in his hand before Rogers had chance to move from the counter.

"Now do you understand?" Gareth hissed. "This is a new game. My rules. So are you going to start telling me the truth?"

Rogers gulped, eyes still darting back and forth.

Gareth took a step closer. "And as I said, I've spent the past few hours going over old ground, retracing my steps, realising just what a fool you've taken me for. And I'm not a happy bunny."

Gareth concentrated on the rush-hour traffic, throwing the odd glance at Rogers as he drove. The handcuffs jingled as Rogers tugged in vain against the door handle.

"Quit struggling," Gareth snarled.

"I hardly think I need to be trussed up like an animal. You have me by the balls, detective. I'm not likely to do a runner."

"A chance I can't afford to take. A young woman's life could be at stake, and as far as I can see you're the only chance I have to save her."

"You do know you could lose your job for this?" asked Rogers, unable to mask the fear in his tone.

Gareth laughed. "Think I care?"

Rogers swallowed, looked down. "Where are you taking me?"

"I told you. You're going to take me to your brother."

"Why?"

"You tell me."

Gareth risked a sideways glance and saw the flush in Rogers' cheeks. But the other man remained silent; his lips a pale pink scar across his face. Gareth wasn't sure yet, and he needed to be; he had to push harder.

"Tell me the truth."

"How'd you know about Geraint?"

And now he had a name.

Gareth shrugged. "I'm a detective. It's all in the title."

In fact, he owed his revelation to the tarty-looking woman with the obnoxious laugh outside The Freemasons last night. Her prominent teeth took him back to Vanessa Hughes's description. His rotten teeth, she'd said. His awful breath. When the first thing he'd noticed about the man next to him was his artificially whitened smile and his attention to personal grooming. Why had it taken him so long to realise they were discussing different men?

"You have suspected your brother's involvement in these abductions, haven't you?" said Gareth. "From day one. From the day Edwina disappeared. Tell me the truth."

His hand trembled as he changed gear.

Rogers shrugged. "I've no proof. I doubt I can be much help to you. The only time I see my brother is when he wants something. Usually money." He looked out at the passing landscape. "But he came to the shop a few times. Times when he knew Mother wouldn't be there – and so met Edwina." He paused, swallowed. "They don't get on, my brother and my mother. No contact at all.

She goes so far as to say she doesn't have another son anymore.

"Anyway, I got there one day and he was there, talking to Edwina. She looked a little uncomfortable, but assured me afterwards he'd done nothing. I think like most people, she just found him quite creepy. After that I found him hanging round the shop more and more. Saw him loitering outside a few times around closing-up time. I confronted him about it, but he insisted Edwina was his friend, that he'd put her in touch with his bosses at CADW and she'd started doing weekend voluntary work for them."

Gareth nodded. "So you knew there was something going on?"

"No, I asked Edwina. She was fine about Geraint. I think she pitied him, thought she could help him. He had his demons, you know."

"But for your brother it was more than that?"

Rogers licked his lips. "I think he got a bit obsessed with Edwina. I think it was his way. He wasn't confident with women. We had a difficult childhood and I think most women scare him. But for some reason, something about Edwina made him feel safe. Sometimes I think he could get a little confused. He was the same with a woman who served him breakfast at his local café. He convinced himself they were a couple, but I knew, like Edwina, it was all in his head."

Gareth had a sudden flashback, a vision of the board in the investigation room. The name of victim one – Kerry O'Grady, age twenty-two. Not a student, lived with her boyfriend near the station, worked as a waitress at a café.

Shit. Did Rogers know? Or was his innocence to be believed? Right now, Gareth feared his judgment was too screwed up to make that decision, but it didn't matter. His instinct was right, it had to be. Whether Rogers knew the extent of his brother's involvement or not, he was the only link to the killer, and this was the only way he was ever going to assist the police. Fight evil with evil. Push harder …

"So, when you say your brother visited you mainly for money, I'm guessing this wasn't a voluntary arrangement?"

Rogers remained tight-lipped, but shook his head.

"So, he is a blackmailer." Gareth nodded, another good sign. "And let me guess. He found out some – if not all – about your sordid personal habits, and he decided to extort money from you. What was he going to do? Tell the police? Your mother?"

Rogers shrugged. "I never gave him opportunity to enlighten me. I'm sure torturing my mother would have been pretty high on his list though. I was her golden boy, you see. As much as she adored me, she despised Geraint. It's a long and boring story, but I think he finally found a way to get back at me. And he revelled in it. I had to pay for his silence, simple as that."

"So, you say he keeps this boat in Port Dinorwic. Are you certain he'll be there now?"

Rogers shook his head. "Not at all. He's a loner. He works as a forest ranger in Newborough, and arranges field trips for CADW all around that coast. He lives on his boat but travels all around the island. I've no idea where he's likely to be."

"It's imperative we get to him as soon as possible. Do you have a phone number or anything?"

"No. We didn't have that kind of relationship. And I hope you realise this could all be a wild goose-chase. I have no proof of his involvement –"

"But you have gut instinct. I can tell. Or he has said something, probably boasting, and you know. Even if you will never admit it. You've only kept silent because you fear your own sordid secrets might be exposed. In my eyes, that makes you as guilty as him. How could you ..."

Gareth's mobile flashed and beeped. He lifted it from the dash to his ear.

"Chris, mate. Have you spoken to McRae?"

"No, not yet. I'm about to go into an interview. Might have some news."

"Forget it. There's been another abduction. High profile.

Daughter of Charles Morton, the Conservative MP. McRae is interviewing the father now, and he wants a meeting in about an hour. Get it sorted."

"Where are you?"

"Bang in the middle of something. I can't talk now. I'll update you later. Try and contact McRae. Okay? For your own good."

He disconnected the call, and slid the phone into his pocket.

Rogers cleared his throat. "Erm, did you say the latest victim was something to do with Charles Morton?"

"Yeah, why?"

"Shit."

"I asked why?"

Rogers sighed. "I think I need to fill you in on our childhood."

Chapter Twenty Eight

The heavy door swung open, hinges creaking. Light flooded the room.

"Nia?"

Silence.

"Nia?" The voice wavered with uncertainty this time. Torch light flashed. He took two steps down the stairs, peering into the gloom. "You there? I got the money. Your daddy paid up. But I couldn't just walk away and ..."

Nia screamed. A wild, guttural sound. In one fluid move, she kicked the door shut and swung the heavy metal bar downwards. It smashed into the back of his skull with a sickening crunch. She stepped forward, bed leg raised in both hands above her head, panting, ready to strike again.

As if in slow motion, the man dropped to his knees and collapsed head-first down the remaining steps. The torch clattered to the floor and rolled, causing shafts of light to bounce around the walls as if she'd stepped into some macabre disco. He crashed forward, his weight on his face as he fell, too shocked – or too paralysed – to attempt to break the fall. He hit the ground with a dull thud. Nia heard the snap of bone as his nose shattered.

Ignore it. Ignore him. Get out. Get out. Move!

Panting, she gripped the handle and pulled.

Locked.

"No!"

It was solid. How could it be locked? She rattled the handle and beat against the wood with her fists. Somehow the door had locked as it slammed shut.

"No, no, no," she whispered as she twisted the handle, tugging at the door harder and harder. She turned back to face the room and shone the torch on her captor's face. His eyes were closed; his face sunken and corpse-like. "Where are they? The keys! Where are they?"

Expecting and getting no reply, she jumped down the steps and leaned over the prone figure. She held her breath as she slipped her hands into the pockets of the grey jacket and grubby jeans. Nia grimaced as she felt the warmth of his body through the clothes.

"Nia … dead bolt … keys outside …" He opened his eyes, rasped air into his lungs. "Help me, Nia …"

"No!" Nia kicked out at his body.

"Help …" His voice faltered and he fell silent.

"Shut up!" Nia screamed. "Shut up. Shut up. Shut up."

Nia stumbled back to the door and dropped to her knees. She slumped down against the door, put her head in her hands and sobbed as she rocked back and forth, keeping her eyes on him, expecting at any moment he'd roll over and leap to his feet. Her senses buzzed and her breathing came in heavy, ragged gulps. Eyes fixed on him, she gripped the bed leg, ready to use it if he made the slightest move towards her.

The figure remained motionless, the moaning stopped, replaced by a thick gurgling noise. Was it really a dead bolt? Or did he have the keys? She couldn't give up; she had to get out. Had to. Legs trembling, she trod carefully around his body. Using her right foot, she rolled him onto his back. Grasping the torch, she aimed the beam of light across his features. Grimacing, she averted her eyes from the mass of congealing blood in his hair, slowly seeping across the floor to pool around his shoulder. His eyes were closed, his lips drawn back to reveal blackened teeth.

His nose a mess of crimson. She studied his chest, looking for the telltale rise and fall. Nothing.

The iron bar slipped from her hand and clanged noisily onto the stone floor. He looked dead. Very dead. But she had no experience. She had to be sure. Dropping to her knees, she leaned forward and held her face close to his. Hovering barely centimetres above him, she searched for any sign of movement or breathing.

There was none.

Her heart hammered. Terror slipped through her bloodstream like ice cold alcohol in her veins. She'd watched too many horror films. This was the moment he would open his eyes, stare up at her and smile an evil smile.

But he didn't. Gingerly, she placed two fingers on his neck, searching for a pulse among the dark stubble. His skin felt slimy and clammy, but she could find no sign of a heartbeat. She shone the torch directly onto his closed lids; he showed no reaction to the light. Fear prevented her pulling back his eyelids. Nothing could force her to touch him that way.

Nia rocked back onto her heels and studied the body. How could it be so easy to kill someone? All she'd intended was to knock him unconscious so she could escape. But the blood, the mess … she was a killer. My God, a murderer …

She struggled to her feet. She needed to toughen up and get the hell out of there. If she could get out, she could get help. Medical help, someone might still save him. Move girl. Find a way to get that door open! She turned towards it, stepped around the body and headed towards the stairs.

A hand grabbed her ankle.

"No!"

She kicked out instinctively as she struggled to keep her balance. The pressure on the hand increased, the grip tightened.

"Nia –"

The voice was barely a croak.

She looked down into yellow-tinged eyes; his gaze desperate and pleading.

"Nia, I … I …" again the voice broke. "I came back for you …"

"Don't," said Nia, putting her hands over her ears. "I don't want to hear it. Let me go. Just let me go."

She tugged her foot away.

"Nia –" he repeated. "I came back. Why …?"

"Shut up."

"Why … did you do this?"

He coughed weakly and spat. Nia swallowed back a wave of nausea and clenched her fists.

"I said shut up! You think I owe you an apology or something? Why the hell should I explain anything to you? Why should I pity you?" She gulped air and her voice shook. "You were going to kill me! Just like those other girls. I hate you! You left me, you bastard, you left me to die here – just like you left them!"

Nia's voice rose until she was screaming the words down at him. "I am doing this for my father – for me – and for all of the other girls!"

"Not … my fault. You don't understand –"

He tried to lift himself onto his elbows. Nia kicked him hard in the chest. He collapsed with a groan, and rolled onto his side, clutching his ribs.

"I understand totally," she hissed. "You are a sick, evil, perverted, murdering piece of scum. And this is my – our – revenge. I hope you rot in hell where you belong."

"But Grace," he whispered, his voice breaking as he looked up. "My Grace …"

"Your Grace would never have wanted this. This is all you. You are evil and sick. You don't deserve to live. My father may be no angel, but neither he nor I deserved this. How dare you? Who do you think you are? God!?"

Nia knew she was hysterical. She couldn't stop shouting. Tears poured down her face. Her mouth was dry, her throat on fire, and her body shook with rage.

He coughed again, blood oozed from the corner of his mouth, pooling around his right ear.

"Nia … help me … help me please …"

He struggled for breath – gurgling, rasping noises shuddered from his lungs as he fought for air. She felt no compassion, no pity, and no remorse – just an overwhelming wave of anger that refused to release its grip on her. Impatiently, she wiped the tears from her face.

She bent and picked up the iron bar. Standing behind him she raised the bar above her head. Her eyes met his for the last time. She closed her eyes and bought the heavy rod down onto his skull. A hot spray of blood hit her ankles. As she opened her eyes, his head lolled to one side, touching her bare foot. Gagging, she jumped away, dropping the bar onto his stomach, leaping over the body as she rushed towards the door. Working on auto pilot, she leapt up the steps.

"Nia –"

She heard ragged breathing. My God, he was still alive. How could he be?

"Why?" she moaned. "Dear God. Why?"

She wrapped her arms around her knees, rested her forehead on them, and sobbed. The voices were back, whispering and scrabbling inside her skull. She screamed to silence them until her throat burned in agony and she was unable to scream anymore.

Chapter Twenty Nine

Coleman leaned forward and flexed his fingers. It had taken Jim and Helen almost an hour to complete their story from beginning to end. As promised, the police officer hadn't interrupted, except to clarify an occasional point. Now, he ran a hand over his brow, slumped back into his seat and let out a long intake of breath. He tapped the end of a blue biro against his teeth.

"Well, Doc, that is one hell of a tale," he said eventually.

"I know," said Jim. "And I know what you must be thinking. As an expert in the field, this is the most fascinating case I've come into contact with. So, I fully understand how unbelievable it must seem to you."

"I think you'd be surprised," the detective muttered.

"Sorry?" asked Jim.

"Nothing, I was just thinking aloud how I could use this information to help me solve the case. I mean the obvious thing to do would be to interview Jake. But I'm led to believe it's Jacob who has all the answers. So, how exactly do I interview a boy who's been dead a few hundred years?"

"I know ..."

"And secondly, how do I convince my bosses that this is a reasonable line of enquiry? Who's going to get behind me on this one if I pursue it?"

"Perhaps ..."

"And thirdly, if I go along with the Jacob-Jake thing, how the hell do either of them know anything about these abductions in the first place?"

"Look," interrupted Jim. "I don't have many answers, admittedly. But I suggest the best way of moving this forward is to put Jake under regression again. Contact Jacob and find out what, if anything, he knows."

"This is just too bizarre …" began Coleman.

"Is it?" asked Jim. "Because I know for definite in the States, and I'm sure I've read the same applies over here, that mediums and psychics have been used to help solve missing person and murder investigations."

"Trust us, Detective," said Helen. "We didn't come here to waste police time. We came here to help. I couldn't live with myself if we did nothing. I know you probably don't believe a word we say, but our intentions truly are genuine."

"Oh, I know that, Mrs West, I assure you. And it's not a question of me believing you. There are procedures. I have to think of the rest of North Wales police force."

"So don't tell them," said Jim, leaning forward so that his elbows rested on the edge of the table. "You don't strike me as a policy and procedures kind of guy. Let's talk to Jake first and take it from there. Look, I get the feeling this is a difficult case. Surely a lead, any lead … however tenuous, is better than nothing?"

"Well, you got me there." The detective slipped more papers from a manila folder and studied them for a second. "No clues, no evidence, no mistakes. Nothing." He let out a deep sigh and rubbed his palms together.

"Well, it's up to you, of course. But I think we should try regressing Jake again. What's to lose? Except your credibility as a police officer, I guess." Jim smiled.

"Believe me that wouldn't take a lot in some quarters. It seems fate that I've interviewed you. Had you met anyone else in CID, you'd have probably been laughed out the station. In fact, we're probably the topic of huge amusement as we speak. But I have past experience with this kind of thing, so I am willing to listen."

"We kind of expected a negative reaction to be honest. Well, Jim did," added Helen.

"You mention experience, what do you know about past-life memories, detective?" asked Jim.

Chris shook his head as he got to his feet. "It's a long story, maybe I'll get to tell you one day. Right now, time is crucial – let's go speak to Jake."

Coleman and Jim sat facing Jake across the hotel room's writing desk; shafts of sunlight mottling the mahogany surface. Jim had talked Jake through the regression process again and he'd shown no sign of distress. His head slumped forward now, so that his chin rested on his chest. His eyes were closed but flickering beneath the lids.

Helen gnawed at her thumb nail. She knew this wouldn't harm Jake, but she still hated seeing him in this state. Jim took him through the three stages of regression slowly, so he didn't become upset or confused. By the time Jim reached twenty, Jake was completely under and fully compliant.

"Jacob, are you there? Can we speak to you? It's Dr Crawford and Jake's mom, Helen. We spoke last week."

A short pause. Jake's eyes continued to flutter beneath his lids.

"Hello, Dr Crawford."

Jake spoke in the deep, monotone voice Helen remembered from the previous regression. It was so perturbing to hear this stranger's voice coming from Jake.

"Is that Jacob?" Jim asked.

"Yes, sir."

"Jacob, I need to ask you some more questions. Is that all right?"

"Yes, sir."

"Right, I need you to tell me what you know about bad dreams that have been affecting Jake recently. Do you know anything about them, Jacob?"

"I … I don't know. I think so, sir. But I don't remember now. It's all confusing."

"I need you to think very carefully for me. I need you to try to remember. It's very important, Jacob. I need you to tell me everything you can."

The pause lengthened into a silence.

"Jacob …" prompted Jim.

"Please sir, I'm trying to remember. I have seen things. Bad things."

"You came through in Jake's nightmares. You shouted in Welsh. Can you remember anything?"

Jake shook his head, a slight movement. "No, sir."

Jim took a sheet of paper from a plastic folder. He scanned his notes, before reading in a halting voice.

"Rhiwch gymorth imi. Mae'r mached wedi marw."

Jake turned his head to one side; like a small bird listening for worms underground.

"Dwi dargedig. Rwyf yn clywed llefain. Rwyf yn clywed screchian."

Again his head tilted, as if attempting to translate the sounds.

"Mi Foddodd. Mi Foddodd."

Silence.

"Do you recognise any of the words, Jacob?"

After a pause, Jake nodded.

"I can hear crying. I can hear screaming. The girls are dead."

"Do you remember saying any of these words? You screamed them during some of Jake's nightmares."

"I remember having bad thoughts. But I forget them straight away. I wanted to warn Jake. I wanted to tell him about the bad man."

"Yes, we understand that. We know you were trying to help

Jake. What we need to know is how you knew about this bad man in the first place?"

"I saw him."

There was no hesitation in his reply; it was the most positive answer he had given. Jim shot a look at Helen and Coleman. It seemed Jim had managed to penetrate, not only Jake's, but Jacob's subconscious mind.

"You saw the bad man?" asked Jim.

"Yes, sir."

"What did you see him do?"

"I saw him hurting the girls. I heard the girls screaming and crying. He is a bad man, a very evil man."

"Were you upset by it?"

"Yes. I was frightened. I wanted to stop him, but I couldn't. I wanted to protect Jake. Stop the bad man hurting him too."

"Why did you think this might happen?"

"Because I knew you were taking him back there."

"Back where?" asked Jim.

He glanced at Helen with a puzzled frown. She shrugged.

"The island."

"Llanddwyn?"

He nodded. "Yes, sir."

The three adults all exchanged shocked glances.

"You mean to say the bad man is on the island?"

Jake nodded.

Chapter Thirty

"Can you remember the last time you saw Geraint Rogers?" Gareth attempted to keep his tone polite; little point taking out his frustration on the harbourmaster. He glanced across to his car, satisfying himself Glyn Rogers was still there.

"Ah, got me there now, you has. Can't rightly say. As long as I get the harbour fees on time, I don't tend to keep a tight check on the comings and goings. But I don't recall him being around the past week or so, maybe more. Mind, he was always an odd one, you know?" The elderly man stopped chewing, wrinkled his nose, and spat into the dust.

"Anyone else you can think of who may have information?"

"No, I can't say I do." He leaned over the railing, and with a loud cough spat into the water. "Hey, Roddy. Have you seen that Rogers fella 'round recent?"

A bespectacled red-headed youth appeared on the deck of one of the elegant yachts moored along the quay. He shook his head. "Not for a while. Sorry."

The harbourmaster turned back with a shrug. "Roddy spends his life here. If he ain't seen him around then no one can help you. Sorry an' all. If he does turn up, you want I should get in touch?"

Gareth sighed and handed over his card, thanking him for his troubles, and headed back towards his car, shoulders hunched.

Another dead end. Why did it always feel like this guy was one step ahead of them? Was it anything to do with his brother? Or was that his persistent paranoia? Besides, he'd put distance between himself and the area now he'd pulled off a successful blackmail scam to the tune of a million pounds?

According to Glyn, if his brother was behind these crimes it was all in the name of revenge. Revenge for their sister's death, for which he held Morton responsible.

And while all of this historical stuff may well be true, a million pound was still a million pound. Four innocent dead girls was yet another matter – although he'd yet to make the connection between them and Morton. Revenge or not, the guy was still insane and dangerous.

"Dead end?" Rogers asked as Gareth climbed into the driver's seat. Was there a trace of a smug smile on his lips?

"Seems like it. Not been here for some time."

"I did warn you."

"So, any other suggestions, Mr Smart Arse?"

"I have actually. Let's take a boat out – cover the Straits and the island. We've got a far better chance of finding my brother if we search from the sea, rather than land. I know a few places round Newborough where he spends a fair bit of time, and they're only accessible by boat. I could even give them a call at the station, see if they'd send the lifeboat out for us. Or I'm sure we could hire something nippy from here."

Gareth swallowed and rubbed his palms down his jeans. The thought of getting on any type of fast boat, let alone with Glyn Rogers, made his insides spasm with fear. But he could see the logic in it. Plus they were running out of options – and time.

"How far is Newborough from here?" he asked, trying to visualise a map of the island.

Rogers raised an arm, pointed away to the left. "Along the Straits on a decent vessel, fifteen minutes tops. By car at least an hour." He took a deep breath. "Look … as hard as you may find it to believe, I don't want this girl to die any more than you do. I don't carry whatever psychopathic gene motivates my brother. I may have my own failings – but murder isn't one of them. I don't want Charlie Morton's daughter's death on my conscience any more than you do."

Gareth turned, studied Rogers' expression. He looked genuine enough. But the thought of speeding across the water with him …

He swallowed the dryness in his mouth, coming to a decision.

"Okay, let's go and talk to the harbourmaster."

Rogers rattled the handcuffs.

"If I release you, doesn't mean you're a free man." Gareth reached under his seat, pulled out his small Colt pistol, making sure Rogers saw what it was, before tucking it into his jacket pocket. "Understand?"

Rogers nodded as Gareth leaned across and unlocked the handcuffs.

"Shall I do the talking?" asked Rogers as he rubbed his wrist. "Flash my RNLI identification and see if it helps in the bargaining stakes? If they trust I can handle a boat they're more likely to let us hire a vessel alone."

"Sure. But no funny business. You've had your last warning."

Fifteen minutes later, Gareth stood on the quayside, the smell of seaweed heavy in the air. He took a deep breath, mouthed a silent prayer, and climbed down the rusty metal ladder, stepping with care onto the deck of a shining speedboat. He was still annoyed that he'd been forced to hand over his car keys as security, despite all Rogers' attempt at negotiation. But knowing they didn't have time to argue, Gareth threw his keys on the desk and within minutes a boat had appeared.

Rogers looked in his element, stood next to the steering wheel – or whatever the nautical version was called.

"Better find your sea legs, detective. I adore these old Sea

Rays. I intend making this baby fly!"

Gareth kept hold of the chrome rail and slid along the cream leather seat. "Great."

No way was he going to let on how terrified he felt. His mouth dried up and his lungs tightened with the memory of cold water engulfing him, pulling him deeper …

"… towards Llanddwyn Island."

"What's that?" asked Gareth as the noise of the engine drowned out his words.

Rogers negotiated the boat through the narrow channel, keeping to the required five knots. "I said I'm going to head along the Straits, out as far as Llanddwyn. Then turn inland and follow the estuary, along Newborough forest towards Maltreath. That's where he works. I'll keep my eyes open for his boat. Hold on tight!"

As they exited the harbour and reached the choppy water that swirled through the Menai Straits, Rogers pushed down on a lever and the boat reared up out of the water, like a wild stallion straining for freedom.

Gareth stifled a yell and clung to the seat frame. He planted his feet against a step to stop himself shooting backwards across the deck, and struggled to keep his expression blank as Rogers shot a glance in his direction.

"You might want to grab a lifejacket from under the seat." Rogers nodded to a side locker. "Health and Safety and all that. I wouldn't be doing my job as a servant of the RNLI if I didn't insist on passenger safety." Rogers smiled, tossing his head back as the boat increased speed. "Besides, you don't exactly look comfortable."

"I'm fine," muttered Gareth as he inched along the seat and pulled out a lifejacket from the space beneath.

The boat bounced along the water, each rise followed by a resounding splash and a wave of fine spray. Gareth wedged his feet and tugged off his bulky jacket. He slipped the Colt into his jeans, and slid his coat under the nearest seat, hoping to keep it dry.

"Here, let me," said Rogers, leaning away from the controls as Gareth struggled with the complicated straps and buckles. "It's like removing a woman's bra, so I'm told. Once you know your way around it, you can do it one handed, with your eyes closed. Not that I'd know, of course."

Gareth flinched as the other man pulled the material tight with his free hand. "That's fine. I can manage, thank you." He patted his pocket, ensuring the Colt was still secure. "How long?"

"Twenty minutes tops. I'll slow down at Foel, just check the moorings there, then head out round Llanddwyn."

"I think he may be keeping the victims on his boat, so if you do see it, let me take over. I don't want him startled."

"Sure, detective. You're in charge."

"I am. And don't forget it."

"Aye, aye, Captain," said Rogers with a mock salute. "Take it you're a land lubber then? You don't know what you're missing, living near the coast and not enjoying the ocean. I love it." He leaned back, eyes closed as the wind ruffled his hair.

"I can admire the view from the safety of terra-firma. I've been involved in enough sea-related accidents and investigations to put me off for life."

Not to mention a near-death experience as a child, and a paralysing fear that stopped him even daring to learn to swim.

"Right, this is Foel. I can't see his boat anywhere here. I won't pull right into shore, the tide is fierce today, and it's on the turn. Let's carry on, okay?"

Gareth nodded, turning in his seat to study the old wooden jetty and a scattering of boats bobbing on their moorings.

"Foel Ferry used to be the main crossing point before they built the bridges," said Gareth, raising his voice over the wind. "You can see Caernarfon clear now, see?"

Gareth could make out the Castle and the harbour entrance.

"Another few minutes we'll be at Llanddwyn."

Chapter Thirty One

Coleman hurried out of the room, reaching into his pocket for his mobile. Helen and Jim continued to study each other. It made her skin crawl to think they'd visited the place and unintentionally put themselves and Jake at risk.

Jim struggled to keep his voice under control. "So, can you tell us exactly what you saw and where, Jacob?"

Jake's brow furrowed. "I can't remember everything – just bits." He paused and began to rock back and forth. When he spoke next, his voice was barely a whisper. "I saw him dragging one girl and carrying another through the woods onto the island. They weren't moving, I think they were hurt. And then last time, I saw him walking through the woods with another girl. I saw her face – she looked so scared. Me too, I was scared –" His voice trailed off and he rocked harder.

Jim whispered to Helen. "He must have passed this image onto Jake. That's how he recognised the face on TV."

She nodded.

"Did you see where he took the girls?"

Jake nodded. "He took them to a cellar. He kept them there. I heard them screaming and crying. They kept trying to escape. To start with, he came back. But then he stopped coming. He just left them."

The boy's voice broke off.

"And then what?" Jim urged. "You're being very brave, Jacob.

But we need to know all the details. Please tell us everything you know."

Voice shaking, Jake continued. "I saw him take the girls away. One was wrapped in a blanket. He dragged another down onto the beach at night. They weren't screaming anymore."

Tears streamed down his face.

"Did he carry them back through the woods?"

"No." Jake shook his head, sniffing loudly and wiping his eyes with both hands. "He had a boat. He took them away in a boat. I watched him as far as I could see. He went over the bar and out to sea."

"Okay," said Jim. "But the last girl, the one whose face you saw …"

"She's still here, sir, on the island. She's still alive."

"No, Jacob. That girl isn't there anymore –"

"Yes, she is. She is! I wanted Jake to tell you, to let you know. Please, I remember now. I want someone to stop the bad man and keep him away from my island!"

Jim shot a look at Helen. She shrugged.

The voice that wasn't Jake's rose until it verged on a scream. Jim calmed him, keeping up a steady stream of soothing talk until the rocking stopped, and Jake's breathing returned to normal.

After a few minutes, Jim added. "Is there anything else you can tell us? Have you seen where he keeps the girls?"

"In the cellar."

"Which cellar?"

"The cellar."

"Can't you give us more details, Jacob?"

Silence.

"Jacob?"

Despite a number of attempts to urge Jacob to respond, Jake remained silent.

"Bring Jake back, Jim," Helen whispered. "I'm scared."

"I know. Don't worry. I'll bring him out now."

Using the usual instructions and counting technique, Jim brought Jake slowly out of his trance. Helen stood at Jake's side and hugged him tightly as his eyes opened and he focused on her face.

"Did Jacob tell you the bad man scared him, Mummy?"

"Yes, sweetie, he did. Do you feel okay?"

"Yes, but ..." His small shoulders trembled as he tried to act grown up and not cry, but his eyes were brimming. Helen could see the fear in them. "Jacob's scared. So, it makes me feel funny too. Sometimes I can see what he sees and hear what he hears. And it's scary. Can't you make it stop? Please, Mummy, make it stop."

"We're going to try, baby." Helen folded Jake into her arms, resting her chin on top of his head. "I promise you, we're all going to do everything we can to make it stop."

Jim pressed 'End' on the tape machine.

"For all our sakes," Helen added in a whisper.

Jim left the room and returned with DI Coleman moments later. Both men were conversing in hurried, hushed tones. Helen settled Jake on the bed with a packet of crisps. His eyes were glued to the cartoon on the TV.

Jim was the first to speak. "Jacob seems desperate to get across to us there's another victim, still on the island. He's convinced she's still alive."

Coleman glanced across at Jake as he spoke. "Jesus. This is amazing. Until an hour ago, we weren't even aware of another victim." He shook his head. "Why's he so convinced?"

"It's all on tape." Jim tapped the machine. "He's actually seen him take bodies off the island by boat. But he hasn't seen him move the last one."

"I've just been onto the nearest station. We need a patrol car out there as soon as possible. If this is all true, time is of the essence."

"Yes, it is." Jim nodded. "And I believe it's true."

"But, why?" asked Helen. "Why has Jacob come through to Jake in this way? Surely it's not normal behaviour?"

"Helen, I stopped wondering what normal was a long time ago," said Jim. "I've studied so many cases; I can't begin to tell you the variables of every one. From my studies, I've learned that many psychics claim to be able to access past-life information simply by asking their spirit guides for it. There are a couple of pretty famous cases where both paranormal forces have linked. And putting my scientific brain aside, I believe Jacob is Jake's spirit guide – but also his incarnate.

"It's my personal opinion that in this case, Jacob has built up such a bond with Jake that their subconscious minds have begun to overlap. When Jacob is scared or distressed, Jake has begun to pick up on it. And Jacob has passed on information to Jake in this way. Also, as he said, when he became aware Jake was returning to their island home, he wanted to warn him. But it's only under regression that he can vocalise this. In normal circumstances, he can only transmit himself through invoking these nightmares."

"But Jacob's a ghost …" muttered Helen.

Jim nodded. "Yes, Jake's spirit guide. Jacob's soul remains on Llanddwyn. Like many children whose death came too soon, too suddenly. Basically, they refuse to let go. What complicates this scenario is Jake being his incarnate."

The words hovered in the air as the room fell silent.

"It's powerful stuff," said Coleman. "And I might be in the minority in my profession, but I believe every last word of it. And if we believe all the other stuff – that has already been proved – why should we stop believing now?"

"Exactly," agreed Jim. "And in the same way that Jacob and Jake have developed a bond, I think the boys have developed strong links with Llanddwyn. We've all felt it – the island is a special place. Jacob's soul remains there. You heard him say 'my island'. I think he does truly see it as his home still. And now he has Jake to care for, he wants to protect him too. And although I admit I've never come across such integrated behaviour between the past and present before, like I say, every case is different. Jake's case is certainly unique. But I think it's very real, Helen. Your son is a remarkable young man."

Coleman nodded. "He'll be even more remarkable if he ends up saving the latest victim, Nia Morton's, life –"

The detective's mobile buzzed. "Yes? … Yes. I want Evans and Lewis to meet me at Newborough Warren – the forestry commission park. I've already asked for a patrol car to meet us there. I think there's a car park almost on Llanddwyn Island, but according to Evans we need a key for access. She's already checked up on it, so can you get another patrol to call at the local post office, on the crossroads in the centre of the village. They have a key for emergency vehicles, apparently. Don't let anyone else through, and detain any cars that try to enter or leave until I get there. Okay? Oh, and try to contact Parry for me, will you? Yes, fine. Bye."

He ended the call and turned to face Helen and Jim.

"I'm taking this seriously. We have nothing to lose and everything to gain if the information is accurate. However, if it proves to be a false lead, then I want you to know I won't hold any of you responsible."

"I don't think it will," said Helen. "Unfortunately, I think it's accurate. Like everything Jacob's told us so far."

The detective nodded. "So do I." He paused. "Helen, I don't know how you feel about this, but I'd like you and Jake to come with us. I'm hoping maybe when we get to the island, he may be able to put the last pieces of the jigsaw puzzle together."

Helen looked at Jim.

"Your choice, Helen," he said simply.

Coleman touched her sleeve. "I know you probably want to protect Jake from any more distress. But we need to find this cellar as quickly as possible. He may recognise something, some detail we haven't been able to get from Jacob."

Helen glanced at her son. "Will it cause Jake any distress, Jim?"

"I don't believe so, Helen, but I can't say for sure. But I think we have to take the risk. If we do nothing and the girl dies, how will that affect Jake? Besides, it may be this young girl's only hope."

Helen nodded. She turned to look at Jake. A child again. He pushed handfuls of crisps into his mouth, giggling at the scene playing out on TV, oblivious to the drama unfolding around him. She wanted to protect him, to guard him. To keep his childhood intact and shield him from evil. But she couldn't, she knew she couldn't.

"It's just … you know … I don't want him having to face a dead body or …"

"Of course not," interrupted Coleman. "We wouldn't allow that to happen. You need to make a decision though, I'm going to have to leave right away."

Helen walked to the wardrobe, removed her fleece and Jake's parka, then crossed the room and turned off the TV. She held out her hand. Jake grumbled as he allowed her to pull him up off the bed and fasten the zip on his jacket.

Eventually she turned to face the men, taking a deep breath.

"Okay," she said. "Let's go. Before I change my mind."

Chapter Thirty Two

"So tell me about your mother," said Gareth, raising his voice above the combined noise of the engine and the wind. "You mentioned her disowning your brother?"

Rogers turned, one hand raised to shield his eyes from the bright sunshine. He pulled back on the lever and the boat slowed a little. "It all started because of Grace. Mother had a complete mental breakdown. There's probably more technical terms for it nowadays, but she was a different person. She didn't recognise anyone, even my father, for months. And when she came home after nearly a year in hospital, she refused to believe I wasn't Grace."

Rogers paused. A dark expression crossed his face.

"How'd you mean?"

"She dressed me in girls' clothes, tried to make me grow my hair long – or as Geraint referred to it 'turned me gay'. Perhaps he was right." He paused. "For a good five or six years, my father had a hell of a life. I can't help thinking that's why he died young. It was about the same time she began to ostracise Geraint. Who knows what was going on in her head?"

"And how is she nowadays? She didn't seem ill when I met her."

Gareth kept his tone light, unconfrontational, sensing he might get more out of Rogers by getting him to confide. The role Gareth often employed in interviews when Chris preferred to play 'bad cop'.

"She has good and bad days. Some days she doesn't recognise anyone, others she seems perfectly normal. Thirty years of drugs and therapy have helped, but she's not in touch with reality most of the time. Keeping her in a strict routine works better than anything; she can't cope with anything out of the ordinary. All this would ..."

His face creased and for a moment Gareth thought he was on the edge of tears.

Gareth sat up straight, wincing at a bubbling sensation in his gut. "Tell me about Grace."

Rogers shrugged. "I can't tell you much. There was a massive age difference. I was a menopause baby, a complete shock. Grace was sixteen when I was born. I don't remember much. Her beautiful hair, and sometimes maybe the smell of her. But that could be my imagination."

"And after she committed suicide, why did your mother turn against Geraint? Breakdown or not, why single him out? He was little more than a child himself."

"Because in her eyes, it was his fault Grace died. She loathed him. As much as Geraint hated Charles Morton. I think it's called projection tactics. The need to remove any trace of blame from herself, pass it onto Geraint. She'd treated Grace badly. After the miscarriage, she threatened to disown her. Most probably what pushed her to overdose. The fact that Geraint lay beside her as she died and did nothing to help, was enough of a reason for my mother to cling to. It probably helped her recovery, but I can see now it ruined Geraint's life. She refuses to acknowledge she has another son."

Gareth ducked as a particularly large wave crashed over the bow. As he bent, a stomach cramp ripped through him; his hand went to his midriff. He grimaced and exhaled. "That's not strictly true," he said. "I went through my notes. When I interviewed her, she made some reference to 'both her boys' spending their lives at sea. I didn't take it in at the time, or I thought she meant your father, but now I'm certain she was talking about her sons."

"Really? That's interesting. She certainly never discusses him with me."

Gareth swallowed, his mouth filled with saliva. "When did you last see him?"

"God, I'm not sure. Last Monday or Tuesday? He made some veiled comment about a big event coming up, and when he won the Lottery he was leaving the country. I gave him his money and told him to have a nice time. He was always talking crap like that. Besides the new assistant was in the shop, and I saw his eyes, so I tried to get rid of him …"

"It might not have been crap this time –"

Gareth broke off as a wave of sickness washed through him from nowhere. He swallowed the urge to vomit, feeling tears spring to his eyes.

"No?" Rogers turned. "Say, are you okay? You look like shit."

Gareth nodded, stared down at his feet, not willing to risk speaking until his stomach stopped performing somersaults. Fucking sea sickness. On top of everything else.

Rogers stared out to sea as he upped the speed. "There, see that peninsula – the lighthouse – that's Llanddwyn. Hold on tight!"

Gareth's stomach rolled as Rogers opened the throttle – or at least the nautical equivalent. The boat seemed to lift off the surface of the water and fly through the air, bouncing every few seconds over the tip of a wave. Spray misted the boat and Gareth grabbed for the deck rail, gripping it with white knuckles. Bastard. Rogers was doing this on purpose, sensing his sickness and unease. He wanted to shout at him to slow down but his rattling teeth made talking impossible.

The passing scenery blurred into a great rush of blue and grey. The mist turned to splashes of water. Gareth fought back panic; the fear of drowning gripped him and shook him like a dog with a toy. His stomach rolled, and a gush of vomit shot into his mouth.

He spun round, just in time, retching as his face levelled with the side of the boat. A fountain of fluid sprayed out, hitting the wind, and thankfully for the most part disappearing into the churning foam beneath him. Vomit filled his mouth again; the wind whipped it away before it hit the water, splashing it back into his face. He groaned as his mouth filled again with bitter bile, this time hitting the rail of the boat and dribbling down the glossy paintwork.

"Oh, deary me." He heard Rogers' voice from a million miles away. "Chin up. Not long now."

"Slow down! Jesus, slow …"

Sickness took hold again before he could complete the sentence. Wave after wave of pain shook his body, his knees buckled and he slid down onto the seat. Noting the pool of brown liquid staining the cream leather, he tried to lean further out, opening his mouth as another rush shot up from his stomach.

The boat lurched beneath him; the engine changed tone, then fell silent as it stopped. At the same time he sensed movement behind him. A shadow crossed the cream leather, and he turned just as Rogers landed on him with all his weight, hands either side of his neck, squeezing. Taking the impact, Gareth grabbed hold of Rogers's jacket. A blow landed on his right temple and for a moment he was giddy and spinning.

"What the hell are you doing?" yelled Gareth.

Rogers' face loomed, a sneer on his lips. "I told you, didn't I? You'd never beat me, never scare me. I told you!"

With a grunt, Gareth pushed upwards, trying to rid himself of the other man's weight. Another wave of nausea settled just below his throat and his arms shook under the pressure of holding Rogers. Another punch landed next to his right eye. He could feel his strength draining from him as the boat continued to rise and fall on the choppy sea.

"You should have listened," hissed Rogers. "Did you really think I'd trot along behind you like a lap dog? Let you ruin my life? My mother's? Expose me and my friends? No way. Better to arrange a *tragic* boating accident, with the good detective being such a bad sailor an' all. Like you say, it happens every day!"

"Let me go!" Gareth grunted, twisting and turning, feeling his head spin as Rogers' fingers dug into his windpipe. "It's your brother I want –"

Rogers threw back his head, peals of manic laughter whipped away by the wind. "My brother? Really? Do you honestly think he has the intelligence and aptitude involved to successfully carry out a million pound blackmail scam … on his own?" More laughter. "Then you really don't know my brother! I allowed him to indulge in his perversions, encouraged his little games with various girls as he honed his craft. I wound him into such a fury about Morton, he really went for it. Oh, yes, I let him believe he was the main man. He was good for the dirty work, and giving me a watertight alibi, that's about all. But hey, I was happy for you to go jumping to *all* the wrong conclusions …"

Blood roared in Gareth's ears, and the words seem to come from a great distance. "What do you mean?" he gasped.

"Work it out, detective." Rogers sneered. "That's your job!"

Gareth took advantage of the other man's lapse in concentration and with every last ounce of strength, lunged forward. Rogers' eyes widened as he staggered, arms flailing. Gareth sucked in deep breaths and concentrated on holding onto his attacker. As the boat rolled, Gareth stumbled, pulling the other man down with him. Limbs entwined, they slid around on the deck covered in sea water and sick. Rogers scrambled backwards, and Gareth hung on, knowing the least distance between them the better.

He remembered his Colt and released one hand, groping for his jeans. His waistband had been yanked up under the padding of the lifejacket, and as he twisted and pulled at his clothing to try and find the pocket, Rogers dragged himself to his feet. Gareth pulled himself upright, clinging on desperately with one hand.

The boat caught in a strong current and began to turn in a circle, one way then the other. A huge wave hit the boat side on, picking it up and rolling it over, almost forty-five degrees. Rogers slid across the cockpit, from one side to the other, Gareth followed.

Rogers screamed as they hit the starboard rail, his back taking the full impact and combined weight. There was a loud crack. He screamed again, louder. A wild sound. His eyes widened in shock, then glazed over, and his mouth slackened. As if in a slow-motion replay both men toppled over into the grey water.

For a fraction of a second, Gareth was weightless, suspended in mid-air. He scrambled his feet, trying to get a grip on the slippery deck, pulling Rogers' weight back towards him, hoping to tip the balance, alter the centre of gravity enough to get them both back on deck.

He failed.

They hit the water with a splash. Air was sucked from Gareth's lungs and replaced by mouthfuls of cold, salty water. Something dragged him down, lower and lower, trapped in a swirling whirlpool. His eyes, ears, nose, mouth, were filled with salt water. His head was ready to explode. He knew he mustn't try to breathe. He bit down on his lip and rotated his arms like a windmill, mimicking swimming actions.

Images swirled through his head. The weight of the canoe pushing him lower, he had to try and free himself. He kicked out with his feet, finding his target and pushing against it with all his might. He opened his eyes, saw a shimmering light above him, and punched his feet through the water.

One. Two. One. Two . Head for the light, push for the light.

He looked down. Rogers' face hovered beside him; his curls spread out as he sank lower, arms wide as if awaiting an embrace. Gareth held out a hand, waving frantically, grunting for the other man to take hold. But Rogers' eyes were closed. A single bubble escaped through the thin lips, and with a sudden jerk, the body was pulled away, swirling out of reach like a ballet dancer performing a graceful routine.

Gareth watched the body sink. His lungs screamed for air,

and at the same time he felt himself sucked upwards. At the exact second he could no longer control the urge to breathe, he exploded through the surface of the water. He took greedy breaths and screamed, long and loud.

Above surface, all was calm and peaceful. Heaven in comparison to the hell beneath the waves. The roaring in his ears receded as he dragged in greedy mouthfuls of air. The sun warmed his face, the sky was crystal clear; the only noise a flock of squawking seagulls passing overhead.

Gareth bobbed along for several moments, content to fill and refill his lungs, breathe until the panic began to subside and the cold began to seep into his bones. He had to get moving. He knew the risks of hypothermia. He spat in the water as he rose and fell on the tide. What the hell happened? How did he survive? He laid his head back and closed his eyes. His ears brushed against a waxy fabric. The lifejacket! It had saved his life. Thank God.

He used his hands to turn himself, a full rotation, searching the ocean for any sign of Rogers. Sign of land. Sign of help. Nothing. Just a wall of water on every side; a watery gaol.

Rogers. He'd heard the snap of bone as they'd hit the deck rail. He felt sure Rogers' spine had broken. Once they hit the water, the fight had gone from him, and Gareth was sure he was dead before the current dragged him away. At least, that was what he would tell himself.

A wave lifted him and a flash of white caught his eye. The boat. He pushed himself forward onto his belly, and kicked with his feet, slapping the water with his hands. Fear still gripped him, but motivated him to get to the boat, get onto dry land, not to give in now. He began to move forward, aided by the tide, and within minutes he'd reached the boat. He manoeuvred himself along the side, hand over hand. Reaching the back end, he paused, teeth chattering, summoning inner strength. After four unsuccessful attempts, he heaved himself far enough out of the water, propping one knee on the recess, before dragging the rest of his weight upwards.

He flopped back onto the deck, lying on his back, arms crossed, he took gasping breaths. He was sick and exhausted. But alive.

The boat continued to bob in a leisurely fashion, turning slowing, one way, then the other. At least he was safe, he wouldn't drown. He might not be able to move, but at least he could wait here. Someone would see him eventually, someone would save him.

A persistent trilling noise woke him. What? His mobile. He crawled to his knees, slid along the deck, and pulled his jacket from beneath the seat, fumbling till he found his phone.

"H-hello. Who is this?"

"Hey, buddy, it's Chris. Are you okay?"

"N-no. Wh-where are you?"

"I'm on the way to a crime scene … Look, I need your help, right now. Where are you?"

"Gareth swallowed. "On a b-boat?"

"You? On a boat? What the fuck's going on?"

"Rogers is d-dead. His brother is the killer." Gareth paused, remembering the man's final words. "Involved. We were trying to find him."

"Rogers' brother? Rogers dead? Buddy, you sound out of it. What are you going on about?"

Gareth slumped backwards, too weak to hold his weight. "I don't know, s-so much has happened. I need to t-talk to you."

"Buddy, we don't have time for talking right now. Where are you?"

"I told you, I d-don't know." Gareth sat up, pushing himself above the edge of the boat.

He saw the lighthouse; its white tower gleaming in the sunshine. "Yeah, I do. I'm at Caernarfon end of the Straits. Just off Llanddwyn island."

There was a pause.

"Llanddwyn?" Chris repeated.

"Yeah. Why?"

"Bud, I don't have time to explain right now. But you have to trust me. You have to drive that boat, or whatever the fuck you do, and get onto that island. Now. Nia Morton is there. Somewhere in a cellar. Don't ask me anymore questions, because I seriously don't have the answers right now."

"I c-can't drive the boat. I don't have a fucking c-clue." Gareth's teeth chattered as water dripped down his body, pooling round his trainers.

"Then you better learn, and quick. I'm just leaving the station. I'm best part of an hour away. I'll be there as soon as I can."

The line went dead.

"Chris?"

Silence.

"Chris? Oh, shit."

He pocketed the phone and pulled himself to his feet, stumbled his way round to the bow, and gripped hold of the steering wheel, looking down at the complicated buttons and gauges.

Where the hell to start?

Chapter Thirty Three

Nia woke with a jolt. She opened her eyes to complete blackness. She squeezed them shut and opened them again. Black. She'd prayed so hard it was all a dream. It clearly wasn't. She could smell him. She flicked on the torch, the dwindling beam confirming her reality.

Choking back a sob, she turned off the light, better not to see, better not to know. She wrapped her arms round her head to keep out the cold. It was intense. A damp, creeping chill that penetrated every inch of her body. She laid her forehead on her knees, smelling the dirty, coppery, sulphur-like stench that clung to every inch of her. His blood, mixing with her own.

She could cope with this, all of it, if she could just get some silence from the voices. Whispering, murmuring and buzzing around her brain. Like a swarm of bees around a hive. Was this what happened to murderers? Was this purgatory?

She started as she heard another noise. Lifting her head slightly, she could hear a rasping, gurgling sound. It was the sound of a man dying. Unsure how she knew, but she did. There must be a technical term but she didn't know it. The last breaths leaving the lungs. He may not have been dead, but he soon would be.

It had no effect now on Nia one way or the other. She was far beyond caring whether he lived or died. She'd passed the point of caring whether she lived or died herself. What she couldn't face was a long, drawn out agonising death.

Immediately, her mother's face filled her mind, and she imagined the depth of her family's pain and grief.

Then … never seeing her friends, her family, her home ever again. Never waking up to the smell of frying bacon on a Sunday morning. Never seeing her kitten, Taboo, getting his fat little belly stuck in the cat flap …

No, no, no. *How can I?*

But, alternatively. An end to the tears and pain. An end to the darkness.

An end to everything?

She closed her eyes, picturing the scene. Another irony. Now she understood the motive, she was without the means. Crawling forwards, she held her breath and forced herself to search the dying man's pockets. Empty. Apart from a few loose coins, and a faded photograph. She flicked on the torch. A beautiful blonde-haired teenage girl, with a plump toddler on her hip.

With a snarl she threw the photo to the floor and ground it into the dust.

"Help me!"

She paused, ears straining for a reply.

Silence.

She wanted this to end.

She heard a rattling sigh. It sounded like the air escaping from a balloon. She shone the torch across the body of the kidnapper. His face was turned towards her. One cheek against the dirt, the other caked in dried blood. She was sure he was dead now. His eyes were wide, staring straight at her. She shone the beam of light directly towards his retina, no sign of reaction.

Dead. She turned off the light and pulled herself to her feet. Broken pottery crunched under her feet. The smashed chamber pot. She searched for a large piece, fingering the edges. It was sharp, but not sharp enough. Not sharp enough to slice through her wrists. But now she had a new plan. She slid down into a squatting position against the far wall, and with the same tenacity she had shown removing the leg from the bed frame, began to file the edge of the china against the brickwork.

Chapter Thirty Four

It was easier than it looked. Just push the lever forward and point the pointy end. Within minutes, Llanddwyn loomed as tall as a mountain, and Gareth saw there were two lighthouses, not one. Plus a row of small white cottages, what looked like a pile of rubble, or perhaps stone ruins, and a huge stone cross.

Shiny black rocks appeared all around the boat, and he realised that although he knew how to go forward at speed – he had no idea how to stop or go backwards. As panic began to bubble in his chest, he spotted a sandy alcove, just below the row of cottages. He yanked the small wheel to the right, flinching as the bottom of the boat grated against a rock. He headed straight for the middle of the beach, noting the incline of the sand and hoping it would stop the speeding boat. With a silent prayer, he pulled backwards hard on the chrome lever.

It appeared to be the right choice. The engine changed tone, and the boat began to slow down just as it left the water. About ten feet further, it came to a halt, engine running but at least stationary. The boat shook like a panting dog.

He shielded his eyes from the glare of the sun and looked up. Nia Morton was being held in a cellar, Chris said. And if only half what Rogers told him was true, it made a lot of sense. A remote place, accessible only by boat, would be the ideal place to imprison the victims. But how had Chris found out? Gareth had been with Rogers until he died, so it must be either through her father, the MP, or the missing brother. So, whether Rogers ever had any intention or not of bringing him to the island, he had to be careful, it was likely the killer was here somewhere.

He jumped down from the boat and headed across the beach; his sodden clothing and aching muscles made the going tough. He swallowed and spat, trying to ease the burn in his throat. He could still feel Rogers' fingers digging into his flesh.

He came to a path leading from the beach, through thickets of heather and gorse. He paused awhile, leaning against a rock, staring up at the dark windows of the cottages above. He shivered. A feeling came over him. Someone was watching him, someone hiding in the shadows. Was it the brother? Was it Geraint?

Gareth's fingers closed over the Colt and he slid it from his pocket. Six bullets, that was all. He gripped the handle tightly, keeping his arm vertical at his side. Once on the pathway, he would be in the open, no cover until he reached the cottages. And he was certain there was someone else here, perhaps it would be better not to take the chance. He cleared his throat and took one step forward; the hand with the gun resting on a rock to his right, out of sight.

"Hello?"

Silence.

"I know you're in there. This is the police. I am armed. I'm going to count to ten. Give yourself up and come out quietly."

Silence.

"One ..."

Gareth kept his eyes trained on the cottages and outbuilding, looking for the smallest movement. Ears pricked, searching for the slightest sound.

"Two ..."

Silence.

Still the heavy feeling of being watched. But he was the law, had to abide by the law, and he'd now made his intentions clear. If anyone else got hurt today, he didn't want it on his conscience.

Rogers' death was more than enough for one shift.

He continued the count. He jolted as a fish jumped; a flash of silver, and a splash just off the beach. Other than that, nothing.

"Ten. Okay. I'm coming in, and I warn you again, I have a gun."

Gripping the gun in both hands in front of him, he followed the path up the incline. He ran across the grass, kicked open the small gate, and propped himself against the front wall of the end cottage, panting.

He inched along to the door, swung round and kicked it open. The door crashed inwards. Feet apart, he stood on the threshold, gun raised.

The room had been converted into an information centre for the nature reserve. Pictures of birds and fish covered the walls. A huge map of the Anglesey coastline was spread out on a glass covered table in the centre of the room. A rack of leaflets and a visitor book on a small table nearest the door. A quick tour of the other rooms revealed nothing of interest.

Once back out into the sunlight, Gareth felt it again. The hairs on his neck stood erect and he swung round, certain he would see the shadow of someone slip behind the dry stone wall, or catch the tread of a footstep on gravel.

Nothing.

He kept his back to the cottage wall, scissor jumped over the small hedge, and kicked open the next door.

The room was decked out in old-fashioned furniture, obviously in an attempt to recreate the living arrangements of the period the cottage were in use. He slid back a dusty curtain to reveal some rickety stairs. Each tread gave an alarming creak, and he knew that anyone hiding upstairs would be well aware of his arrival.

"If you're up there, show yourself. I know there's someone here. I have a gun. No sudden movements or you could regret it."

The final tread squeaked as he pushed open the door, ducked

his head and entered the small room, taking in the surroundings. An iron-framed single bed, a couple of cheap bits of furniture, and a wash stand with a bowl and jug.

Gareth rubbed his arms, surprised to find the skin goose-fleshed. So odd. He was certain he'd seen someone in the shadows of this room. He'd certainly sensed a presence. If they'd escaped, they must have the powers of Houdini.

He checked both upper rooms, even thumping the ceiling to check for any movement in the attic space. Other than the flutter of a trapped bird, the house was empty.

With a sigh, he headed back outside, glad to be free of the dusty cool interior.

Gareth carried out a full circuit of the cottages, searching for any outside cellar access. When the search was fruitless, he entered each cottage again in turn, checked each room for a trap door. Finally, he pushed open the rusted door on the tumble down barn, and went through it inch by inch.

No loft, no cellar. Nothing.

He followed a track that led to the highest point, up on the headland, next to the lookout tower. From there he would have a better view. The sun beat down on his back, drying his hair and clothes, and, as he negotiated the worn cliff path, he noticed a chasm, leading to a small inlet. There, wedged between two shelves of rock, its bow resting on a shingle beach was a blue wooden boat. To his untrained eye, it looked like some kind of fishing boat.

Gareth almost thumped the air. He'd been right. There was someone else here. A handy little natural harbour, well hidden between rocky outcrops, probably not even visible from the open sea.

He slipped the gun into his back pocket, and used both hands to help him slide down the springy grass, coming to a halt on the beach. He edged round the grassy dune, trying to muffle his footsteps, and climbed up onto the rocky ledge. He stepped over a thick rope, secured from the bow of the boat to a rusty metal hook. His heart pounded as he jumped onto the deck. He spread his feet, grabbed his gun, and kicked the cabin door. The door creaked, but held. He kicked again, harder. This time the lock disintegrated with a loud crack.

"Police! Freeze!"

Gareth tensed, gun aimed. The small space was cluttered with furniture and rubbish, discarded food and utensils, but not a person in sight. It smelled disgusting; a mixture of sour milk, rotten fish and sweaty socks.

He pushed his way into the cabin, checking there were no trapdoors leading to a lower level. He swept a pile of newspapers to one side, opened a small chiller box, grimaced and dropped the lid. He pulled out a dirty duvet and tatty cushion from beneath a bunk bed, and kicked a pile of clothes to one side. A long vinyl seat ran along one side, lifting the lid, it exposed a large open space, almost a coffin sized box.

Nerves crept through Gareth's body. Wedged in the furthest corner of the hollow space was a blue sports bag. He yanked it out, and with a metallic jingle, a thick leather belt fell to the floor. He picked it up, turned it over, and recoiled as he fingered a large brass buckle.

A name. Grace.

Aware of fingerprints, he dropped the belt. A sudden flashback of the picture of Edwina's neck struck him like a lightning bolt. The irregular markings on every victim. Connolly's stolid determination it was made by a belt, the same belt. Even going so far to guess at a name. A letter. 'C'.

She'd been wrong. It was a G. G for Grace.

Shit.

He tugged on the zipper of the sports bag, already fairly sure what he would find. The blue material fell back to expose bundle upon bundle of bank notes. Fifties. More money than he'd own in a lifetime.

Gareth dropped the belt into the bag, and lowered the lid.

So, they had the evidence. They just needed the criminal.

One was dead. They had to find the brother in order to bring closure to the case.

He ducked his head, stepping back out onto the deck, searching the surrounding cliffs. He was here. Somewhere close he had to be.

But where?

Chapter Thirty Five

The sound of a vehicle approaching behind them startled Helen. Turning, she tightened her grip on Jake's hand and pulled him to her side. A blue Land Rover bounced along the rutted track from the car park towards them.

"Sir!"

A thin blonde woman, wearing police body armour, jumped down from the passenger seat as the vehicle stopped.

"This is Simon Ford." She gestured to a heavy set, bearded man climbing out of the driver's seat. "He's the Area Manager in this region for CADW. They manage properties on behalf of Trinity House. He has keys for the cottages and knows the island."

The two men shook hands.

"Good work, Evans. Bloody good work." Coleman turned to the latest arrival. "So, do you work on Llanddwyn on a regular basis?"

Simon Ford spoke with a thick Welsh accent. "No, see, one of my local men, Geraint Rogers, covers this area."

Coleman slipped a notebook from his pocket, his eyes alert. "Can you tell me more about Mr. Rogers, sir?"

"Well, see, he's in charge of maintaining the buildings and looking after the wildlife on Llanddwyn and Newborough Forest. He supervises field trips from local schools and Bangor University. Knows Anglesey like the back of his hand, he does."

Helen didn't miss the glance that passed between the two police officers.

"Would it be possible to contact Mr Rogers and ask him if he could join us on the island?" asked Coleman.

"Well, see, I've tried a couple of times already, but his phone's switched off, so I've left him a voicemail. I'm sure he'll be in touch as soon as he picks up his messages. I don't have his diary with me, so I'm not sure where he is today."

Coleman nodded.

"Anyway," continued the ranger, "see, if you want to climb in the back, I'll give you a lift over to the island."

"Thank you." Coleman turned and spoke to the female detective. "Make sure this whole area is sealed off. Keep all public off the beach and out of the woods. Close off the car park at the first entrance. We could be in the middle of a crime scene, and I want a forensic team over here as soon as possible on standby. Although our main focus is obviously Nia Morton right now, we have four other murders to consider. I don't want any more mistakes. I've had enough drama for one day."

"Yes, sir."

Helen heard Coleman mutter as the rattle of the diesel engine blurred his words. "And make some discreet enquiries about this Geraint Rogers. See what you can find on him, okay? I spoke to Parry earlier, I think he may be the brother of Glyn, you know, the book shop fella."

Evans nodded and headed back along the path.

Jake giggled as the Land Rover bumped along the wooded track towards the beach. Helen leaned out the window, and breathed in the salty air, blinking as the trees came to a sudden end. Sunlight glistened off deep blue water. It was clearly high tide, the water much higher up the beach than on their previous visit. There was only a thin shelf of sand that joined Llanddwyn Island to the mainland now. Noisy seagulls circled overhead, their cries echoing across the ocean.

A distant voice came to them, carried on the wind, and

Helen spotted a man on the cliff path, waving his arms above his head.

"Great, he's here," said Coleman, offering no further explanation.

* * *

Gareth spotted the blue Land Rover bouncing along the track up onto the island. He raised a hand, recognising Chris in the passenger seat. The vehicle parked on the grassy bank in front of the cottages. Gareth sprinted down the track and greeted Coleman.

"Shit, buddy, what the hell happened to you?" Coleman asked.

"I got into a fight with Rogers."

"Take it he lost?" Coleman raised his eyebrows. "The guy in the Land Rover works for CADW. Geraint Rogers is the ranger round here. Not been able to contact him though."

"No sign of him here either." Gareth dropped his voice, suddenly aware of a man, woman and child climbing from the back seat of the Land Rover. "Found the boat though … and the money."

"Shit, really? Where?"

"Inlet on the far side of the island. I think it's secure enough. But I've searched every inch of the place. No sign of Rogers." Gareth nodded to the family. "Who are they?"

Coleman exhaled. "You aren't going to believe it, buddy. And I'm not sure I want to go into specifics right now. The young kid gave us info that Nia Morton is on Llanddwyn. Can we leave it at that for the moment, trust me, okay?"

Gareth held Chris's gaze, and saw the nervous energy in the other man's expression.

"Okay. For now." Gareth paused, looking round. "So, has this

CADW guy got any ideas?"

"Let's find out shall we?"

Chris headed back to the small group. Gareth followed, noting a small blond boy with a serious face, gripping the woman's hand. He caught up with Chris in time to see the bearded man shake his head.

"A cellar, you say? No, sorry. I can't help you, I'm afraid. I'm quite new in the area, moved up from the Rhondda a few months back. Geraint was the expert round here. If only I could get hold of him ..."

Gareth turned as the child mumbled. The woman, he assumed the mother, bent to hear.

"What, sweetie?" she asked. "What did you say?"

The tall muscular guy – the father? – knelt on the ground in front of the boy, while the mother gently eased his thumb from between his lips

"Are you okay, little guy?" the man asked in a strong US accent, placing a hand on either side of the boy's temple.

"They're not in there," said the boy, pointing towards the cottages.

"Not in there?" the man repeated. "How do you know?"

"There's no rooms under the floor. No rooms without windows that are really black. Even the room in the roof had a little window. I know 'cos that was my house. They're not in there. You're looking for where the girls are, aren't you?"

The boy lifted his head, turning his expectant face towards Coleman. Something in the blueness of the child's eyes chilled Gareth.

Chris nodded. "Yes, Jake. What do you know, little buddy?"

"They're not in there," Jake repeated.

Gareth cleared his throat. "He's right. The cottages are empty. I've already searched them from top to bottom."

"So can you tell us where they are then, Jake?" Chris asked.

The boy frowned; his eyes squeezed closed as his mother stroked his hair. He shook his head. "I can't see where. It's all blurry again. But it's very dark and scary."

The tall man, with the American accent, nodded. "I know, Jake. This girl, her name is Nia – she must be real scared. But I bet she's so grateful for your help, little guy. Can you try to think about the room? Can you close your eyes real tight, and imagine walking out the room …"

"They can't get out!" yelled Jake. Gareth jumped. "None of them. They tried. I heard them crying!"

"I know, Jake. It's okay, shush now," soothed the American. "Don't think about that. Think about helping Nia escape, okay?"

Jake nodded.

"If you were there and you could help, where would you take her? Can you tell me what you can see? Can you tell me what Jacob showed you? It was Jacob who showed you in the dreams, wasn't it?"

Gareth looked from Coleman to the boy. Chris' attention was totally focused, while Gareth hadn't a clue what was going on. The boy, Jake, nodded again; his eyes still tightly closed; his face pinched in concentration.

"Can you try to picture you and Jacob rescuing these girls? Talk me through it, Jake. Me and the policeman want to help you. Tell me what you can see, each step of the way. First step …"

"Steps," said Jake.

"Excellent!"

"No … no … first is a big door that the bad man keeps locked."

"Hey, that's cool," said the American, glancing up at Chris. "So … a big door and then steps. What kind of steps, Jake? What do they look like?"

"Like stone. Brown stone."

"Okay, and these steps … are they going up or down from the room where the girls are?"

"Up," replied Jake. "They go up and up, and then they go

round and round."

Jim frowned. "Round and round?"

Jake's eyes opened. Gareth's stomach contracted at the empty blue pools. Something flickered in the child's face, and his lips twitched into a small smile.

"There," said Jake.

All heads turned, followed the direction of the boy's finger, which came to rest at the tall, white imposing building that was Llanddwyn Lighthouse.

Chapter Thirty Six

"Do you have keys?" yelled Coleman over his shoulder as the small group hurried up the slope to the lighthouse.

Helen gripped Jake's hand and made sure she walked on the side nearest the cliff edge, keeping her eyes averted from the crashing surf below. She trod carefully over springy grass and boulders worn smooth in places.

"I'm not sure," replied Simon Ford. "I'll try all the keys on here, but to be honest, I doubt it. The lighthouse is privately owned, you see. We maintain the property on behalf of a private firm. If anyone had keys it would most likely be Geraint."

"Great," muttered the detective under his breath.

Helen looked up as the white building loomed suddenly nearer. It looked much bigger now they were virtually underneath the tower itself. At the end of the path, a solid black metal door with huge bolted hinges faced them.

"Jim, remember Jake's reaction when we came here last?" said Helen.

Jim nodded. "Sure, he freaked, didn't he? Held his hand to the door and said it was a bad place."

Helen nodded, rubbing her arms as the wind whipped across the headland. Heavy grey clouds had appeared across the Irish Sea, and the drop in temperature added to the atmosphere. Helen bent and pulled the zipper up to Jake's chin.

The other detective, who Coleman had introduced as Parry, jumped up the steps and rattled the handle. The door was locked. He gave the door a solid shove, then gestured for the estate manager to take his place on the narrow step. Helen watched as Simon Ford tried each key. Only one fitted the lock, but that failed to turn. She gripped Jake's shoulders harder as fear rippled through her with the turn of each key. Jake on the other hand appeared calm. He sucked his thumb as he watched the proceedings with a reflective look on his face.

Eventually, Ford turned away from the door, his shoulders slumped. He rubbed his hand through his beard.

"No good. See, I've tried every key," he said with a shake of his head. "Let me try Geraint again. I don't understand why his mobile's switched off."

"I wouldn't bother," said Parry. "I'm certain you won't get him. What are the chances of breaking the door down, do you think?"

"Remote, I'd say. Probably made of wrought iron and solid as a rock. Trinity House buildings are designed to cope with premature rusting from the salty sea air. But I couldn't possibly authorise that anyway. Not without the owner's permission."

"If it becomes unavoidable, I won't wait for authorisation, I assure you," said the detective curtly. "Not with a young girl's life potentially in the balance."

Ford gave a helpless shrug

Coleman asked, "Do you know if there's a cellar in this lighthouse?"

"Not for sure, I'm afraid. I've only been in once, see. Went up to the top though, don't remember no cellar. But like I say, Geraint …"

"I know, I know. He's the expert," snapped Parry. The detective looked visibly frustrated and Helen noted that it crept into his voice. "Okay, so an educated guess then. Is it normal for lighthouses to have cellars?"

"I would imagine this being a remote island, there would be

a cellar or a cold store underground."

Coleman approached the door and examined the lock. "This looks as if it's had regular and recent use."

"Shit, this is so bloody frustrating," said Parry, his cheeks flushing as he glanced at Jake. "Let's get onto the fire service. Get some cutting gear over here. I can't walk away now. We're so near – I can feel it."

Coleman nodded. "It feels right. I think Nia's there. Or at the very least, has been," he continued to Helen. "Nothing I've seen or heard has persuaded me that Jake's story is fictional. He's been spot on up to now, so why should we suddenly doubt him? I suggest Helen you head home; it could be a long night –"

"I'm not going home."

All heads turned to Jake. Almost forgotten in the intensity of the moment, he spoke now in a loud, firm voice.

Helen picked him up and balanced him on her hip, brushing his hair from his face. "Sweetie, we have to get back to the hotel and let the policeman do his job."

Jake shook his head. "I have to stay, Mummy. I have to –"

"Jake …"

"Put me down, Mummy. I have to stay!"

The first tendrils of a grey dusk slid across the sky. As shadows lengthened and the last rays of sunlight slid below the pine forest behind them, the moon rose above the mountains opposite. It covered the island in a translucent veil and turned the sea into an expanse of shimmering mercury.

Winding up the window to keep out the chill, Helen leaned forward and stared through the windscreen. Millions of stars twinkled. From nowhere, images of Mark flooded her mind. In her darkest days, when grief consumed her totally, she'd clung to the belief that Mark was up there watching over her. Her own bright star – protecting her and Jake. Many nights she'd talked to Mark, imagining him listening and smiling from his seat in the heavens. It helped her cope. It made her strong. And she needed his strength right now.

She turned in her seat, glancing into the back of the Land Rover. Jake was curled into a ball, sucking his thumb and covered by a blanket. She smiled as her heart did its familiar flip flop whenever she watched him sleeping. He looked so perfect. So innocent. He'd tried hard to stay awake, but exhaustion had finally got the better of him. Thinking of sleep triggered a huge yawn. Helen covered her mouth, and turned to the front.

"Are you okay?" asked Jim from the driver's seat.

She jumped. Her thoughts of Mark had pushed Jim to the back of her mind.

Helen nodded. "Mmm, just tired. It's been a long day."

"Wonder how long it will take now?"

"I'd hope not too long now most of the firemen have arrived. Coleman said it was a 'logistical issue.' I think he meant they couldn't get the fire engine onto the island and were having to carry the cutting gear and generator over manually."

"It's sure turned into a major procedure."

Helen nodded. The last couple of hours had flown by in a blur of activity. An army of forensics arrived, like a colony of white ants scuttling all across the headland. Teams of police moved in, setting up huge arc lights around the lighthouse. She watched as three fireman, carrying huge cables and what looked like a chainsaw, climbed the slope up to the tower. A few minutes later there was a flash of silver, followed by a deafening grinding noise. A burst of blue sparks exploded as two metals collided.

Helen shivered.

"Cold?" asked Jim. "Do you want my coat?"

"No, no, I'm fine thanks."

"What's wrong?"

"I was just thinking …" Helen trailed off and bit her lip.

"About?" prompted Jim.

"What if we've got it wrong, Jim? What if Jake's wrong and Nia isn't in there? Or anywhere on Llanddwyn, for that matter."

"I don't think we should worry too much on that score. Coleman said right at the beginning of all this, he wouldn't hold any of us responsible if it turned out to be a false lead."

"I know he did. But that was then. Before any of this." Helen gestured around them. "How guilty will we feel if this turns out to be a waste of everyone's time?"

"We're not responsible, Helen. Not you, not me, and certainly not Jake. We're trying to save a young girls' life here; we're all working on the same side. Besides," he paused for a moment and glanced outside. "I don't think it will be an issue. I think she's in there. My biggest worry is, where's the guy?"

"I still can't get my head around how Jake knew about it so accurately."

"I don't think we'll ever know for certain. I doubt even Jake knows. But I don't think now is the time to analyse it either. Let's focus on our priorities for now, and thank our lucky stars when, and if, it all works out. Okay?"

"How come you always know what to say?"

"It's my job," Jim said with a smile. "Looks like that's one hinge off … one to go," commented Jim. "Won't be long now with any luck."

Helen wrapped her fleece round her and settled her head back against the headrest. It was chilly now, even inside the car. She'd done her utmost to persuade Jake to let her take him back to the hotel earlier, but he was adamant he wanted to stay. Despite her exhaustion, Helen had to admit she would have found it hard to walk away. She closed her eyes for a moment.

"Mummy!" Jake's voice woke her with a start.

"What, Jake? What's the matter?"

She and Jim turned in unison. Jake was sitting bolt upright.

"They need to hurry. Tell them to hurry."

"Why, Jake? What's the matter, little guy?" asked Jim.

"The girl is hurt. She's hurting, Mummy. Tell them. Tell them to hurry!"

Helen opened the car door, jumped out and climbed into the

rear seat. She took Jake in her arms and rocked him. He didn't pull back this time. He continued to mutter into her hair.

"Please … go tell them. She's hurting. I can hear her screaming."

"Jim, he was asleep," said Helen. "It's another dream. I think it's real."

Jim nodded. "I'll speak to Coleman."

"Yes!" Jake's eyes opened wide. "Tell them they have to hurry. Before it's too late."

Helen felt a chill creep across her body that had nothing to do with the temperature. She continued to rock him, waiting for the memories of the dream to fade. She knew the routine now. It no longer gripped her with the paralysing fear she once felt, but it still tore at her heart.

"It's okay, baby," she whispered into his hair. "Jim's gone to tell the policemen to be quick. Don't get upset."

"But if they don't hurry, I think she's going to die, Mummy."

Helen bit her lip. "Shush, Jakey. Shh."

"But she's hurting really bad. I could hear screaming."

"Okay, shush now. Don't think about it anymore. Jim is talking to the policeman. It will all be fine."

"I don't want her to die like the other girls."

"She won't, sweetie. Everyone is doing their best to get to her."

Jake began to sob. "But they have to hurry!"

"I know, Jakey. Now don't cry. Everyone's working as fast as they can."

"I don't want her to die."

"None of us do."

"If she dies, it will be my fault."

"What?"

Helen pulled away and looked down at Jake. His face wet with tears, hair stuck to his forehead.

"I should've helped save the others. If this girl dies it will be my fault because I didn't stop the bad man in time."

Helen took hold of Jake's shoulders. "No, Jake. No. You mustn't think like that. None of this is your fault. Without you, the police wouldn't even know where to look. If Nia is saved, it will be because of you."

"But if she dies that will be because of me too."

"No!"

"I don't want her to die. Please tell them to hurry."

He turned his head away and stared through the side window. She followed his gaze, squinting her eyes against the glare of the arc light. Jim stood with Coleman and Parry a little way in front of their vehicle. Beyond, clouds of blue sparks and smoke were continuing to billow from the door.

"Is that why you wanted to stay, Jake?"

He nodded. "I want to help."

"Oh, sweetie, you are helping, more than you can know. But you mustn't for one second blame yourself. The bad man is to blame, not you. Okay?"

He didn't reply; his gaze still drawn to the lighthouse. Helen could see twinkling flashes of blue reflected in his eyes.

"Jake? Do you understand?"

He nodded and turned slowly towards her.

"Yes. But I think it's too late. I think she's dead, Mummy."

Chapter Thirty Seven

Nia opened her eyes, and immediately closed them again. Such pain, deep burning pain. She swallowed, lifting her head as a noise echoed around the dungeon. Her prison. Her hell.

Something had woken her. Cut through the pain and the blackness. What was it? A band … a marching band, somewhere in the distance. Yes, yes, it was!

She could make out the boom-boom-boom of the bass drum and the buzz-buzz-buzz of the bazooka. Oh, such memories, such wonderful times with her mother – village fetes and street parties, carnivals where she'd marched proud as punch, swinging her baton high into the blue sky, listening to the cheering crowds.

Then she'd taken up the bazooka, played until she was thirteen, and could still feel the sting on her lips. The Chelsea Champions, the band were called. She'd joined because she'd fallen in love with the lilac uniforms and the bouncing white tassels, not because she had any serious musical ability. Probably why she'd never progressed further than the bazooka.

She remembered the heat of the summer sun beating down on her as they marched, beads of sweat trickling from beneath her peaked cap. How she'd wanted to wipe the sweat off her face, but was too terrified to take her hand off her instrument, too worried about missing a beat and losing her step. Quick glances sideways to see if her family was among the crowds lining the pavements. Her mother always there to support her. Her father rarely.

She could hear crackling noises now. Sparklers! A firework display too …

Nia tried to stand and yelled as she collapsed to the ground; her hands covered in warm sticky fluid. She lay still, panting from the exertion. Her hands were cold and aching, her wrists burning hot. A wave of sickness overwhelmed her. She was so weak; the need to sleep was a physical ache. She longed for darkness to engulf her, and something told her that the end wasn't far away.

She guessed she'd never get a chance to see that carnival again. Feel the sunshine on her face, watch the baton flying high. A sob escaped her. She lay back down and closed her eyes.

Boom-boom-boom. Buzz-buzz-buzz.

The gentle monotony almost sent her to sleep.

Boom-boom-crash! Boom-boom-crash!

The cymbals. That was it. Graham Cox on cymbals. A spotty guy, with ginger hair and glasses. Always out of time with the rest of the band. She smiled.

Crash!

"Nia …Nia …"

Hello? Who's there …

Too tired, so very tired.

Her chin dropped. The carnival was over.

Chapter Thirty Eight

Gareth turned as a voice broke through the noise of the electric cutter. It was the boy's mother. Gareth still hadn't a clear idea what was going on, but he trusted his partner.

"Jim!" Helen waved her arms above her head. "Jake says Nia's dead."

"What?" said Jim.

Gareth met Chris's eye; the tough detective looked visibly shaken.

"Go back. Stay with him, Helen," Chris muttered.

She nodded; her shoulders slumped. "He says we're too late."

Before they had a chance to respond, a resounding crash echoed around the island, reverberating off the surface of the ocean. Cheers, hollers and a round of applause sounded as the massive steel door finally gave up its hold and crashed to the ground in a curtain of dust and sand.

"Shit!" Chris grabbed Gareth's arm. "Come on!"

Gareth raced towards the lighthouse, making it in half the time. Chris followed, shouting orders for everyone else to stay back. Inside the ground floor, a circular room with a few boxes covered with dustsheets.

"Here!" Gareth yelled, spotting an open door. He raced across the sandy floor, through the door and found himself at the top of a spiral staircase. Just as the boy had predicted. He jumped down, three at a time, slipping on the damp surface.

"Nia!"

Coleman was yards behind him. "Nia?"

Gareth groaned as the stairs ended at another door, as sturdy-looking as the last. He felt Chris' breath, coming in short gasps, on the back of his neck. "Is she there?"

"Another door. Fuck!"

"Buddy, the lock. Look! The keys are in the lock!"

Gareth turned the key, fingers shaking as the lock grated. The door creaked as he eased it open with his foot and peered into the pitch blackness.

"Hello? Police!"

* * *

As Helen approached the Land Rover, Jake thumped on the window, motioning for her to hurry. His face, white and pale in the moonlight, pushed against the window, breath misting the glass. Helen opened the rear door and Jake jumped out.

They stood together, Helen's hands clasped on Jake's shoulders, watching and waiting for what seemed like forever. Jake pulled against her, wanting to get away, but Helen held him back, fingers gripping the hood of his coat.

A distant voice shouted from inside the lighthouse.

"Paramedic!"

Two figures dressed in green rushed forward from the crowd. One carried equipment, the other a stretcher.

"Is she dead, Mummy?"

Helen shook her head, unable to speak.

Nothing happened for what seemed like an eternity. Then suddenly, she saw the detective, Parry, appear at the doorway, coughing, but brusquely shaking off offers of assistance. Helen's stomach somersaulted. Under the bright lights, she could see his face was wet with tears. Her own eyes filled up. No, please, no …

Coleman appeared, arms aloft, a wide grin. "We've got her! She's alive … just!"

Helen felt her knees tremble as she bent to cuddle Jake.

"Did you hear that, sweetie? She's alive!"

Jake nodded and smiled, clapping his hands, jigging on the spot. "I said a prayer," he said. "Thank you, God."

"Yes," said Helen, looking to the stars … to Mark. "Thank you, God!"

Epilogue

Helen pulled up the collar of her coat against the biting autumn wind; the gusts whipped fallen leaves around the exposed island in the middle of the Menai Straits. Low clouds obscured the usually breathtaking view of Snowdonia across on the mainland. The grey September sky, and fine drizzling rain, draped Church Island in an eerie veil that, to Helen, perfectly matched the solemnity of the occasion.

She hated graveyards, found the atmosphere difficult to cope with – memories of Mark's funeral rushed to the surface. But when she'd received an email from Ivor Williams, the genealogist they visited on Anglesey, she knew she had to make this final step in the journey.

Ivor had traced a surviving relative of the Lloyd family, who still lived in the area, and who confirmed the Lloyd family connection with Llanddwyn and the heroic deaths of Jacob and his father. Ivor also discovered there was a memorial to the victims of The Rothsay Castle, in the graveyard on Church Island – ironically the same location where Charles Morton left the ransom demand.

Helen shuddered; a firm hand on her shoulder reminded her of Jim's reassuring presence. She turned and smiled up at him, trying hard not to think of his upcoming departure. Tears were coming easy enough today. That was the future. Unspoken and yet keenly aware it was a subject they needed discuss. And they would … but not yet. She wasn't ready yet and Jim understood that.

She gave Jake's hand a comforting squeeze as he fidgeted beside her, as a slim, blonde-haired girl stepped forward from the group of people assembled in front of a grey stone obelisk. Carefully, she placed a bouquet of white lilies against the memorial stone.

Helen bent forward to read the worn lettering on the tombstone. The Welsh words meant nothing to her, but as she followed the list of individual names, her eyes came to rest on one.

Jacob Lloyd (11)

Nia Morton stood and smoothed down her long cream-coloured coat as she took a step backwards away from the grave. She beckoned Helen. Jake tugged impatiently on Helen's grip, urging her forward. He reached out and took Nia's left hand in his right. All three of them stood in front of the grave, heads bowed, arms linked.

Nia spoke to Jake, her voice quaking, but her eyes fixed on the memorial.

"Jake, this is really hard for me. But I owe you –" Nia touched her fingers to the memorial, "– along with this young man here – my life. I'll never be able to thank you enough for helping me … for saving me. I won't pretend to understand everything that has happened, but it seems fitting that we come and speak to Jacob as well. So thank you, Jacob Lloyd. I hope you can hear me."

Nia squatted on her haunches to make eye contact with Jake, then bent forward to kiss his nose. "Thank you too, Jake West."

Jake pulled his hand out of Helen's grasp and held out his arms to Nia as she enclosed him in a tight embrace, wrapping her arms around his blue anorak and pulling him close. Helen turned away, her own eyes flooded with tears.

After several minutes, they broke apart and as Nia wiped her eyes, Jake said, "Don't cry, Nia. I think Jacob is happy now. I said a prayer for him and I told him you thanked him. He's happy now the bad man has gone. I don't get scary dreams anymore. Mummy says he can rest in peace on his island."

"Will you take me back to Llanddwyn one day, Jake?" asked Nia. "I don't think I'm strong enough yet, but one day I want to go and visit. I want to see Jacob's home and the lighthouse, the ruins and the crosses you describe. I want to imagine it exactly as Jacob knew it in his day. I need to get rid of the bad memories. I know it's a special place to you, I want it to be special for me too."

"Yes, I'll take you." Jake nodded enthusiastically; a beaming smile spread across his face. "Mummy says we will be here on the island a lot more."

Helen watched as they hugged again, before Nia stood and reached out a hand to grasp her own. As Nia's coat sleeves inched up her arm, Helen caught sight of the deep purple scars on each wrist. The wounds were still healing for Nia – inside as well as out.

"And thank you too, Helen … you and Dr Crawford ... from the bottom of my heart. If you hadn't had faith in your son, and made people listen to you – then I wouldn't be here today. It can't have been easy to put Jake through all that, and I'll be eternally grateful."

She turned to face the two police officers, Coleman and Parry, who stood looking nervous and awkward on the path.

"And you, too." Nia closed her eyes and sniffed. "God, I really must stop crying. Thank you both, for everything. For saving me."

It was Gareth Parry who spoke; his face grey and solemn. "I only wish we'd been able to stop these men before they got to you, saved you the hell you went through. I'll never forget what we found in that lighthouse, what you suffered. You are a remarkable young woman." He paused, swallowed. "My only regret is with both of them dead, we'll never know the whole truth. Who was truly responsible. But perhaps they got the justice they deserve."

Nia nodded. "She was your cousin …?"

Parry nodded, looked to the ground.

Helen watched the small group as they mingled, each awkward in their own way, then made her way across to a wooden bench overlooking the Britannia Bridge in the distance, needing a few moments contemplation

"Mrs West?"

Helen turned. "Detective Parry. And Helen, please."

"Gareth." He dropped down on the bench beside her. "I wanted to grab a moment before I left. I'll admit I hadn't a clue what was going on, that day at Llanddwyn. In truth, I probably acted like a bit of an ass. But Chris has explained it to me now, and I'm blown away by what you did –"

"It was Jake. Not me."

Parry turned, to where Jake stood, hand in hand with Nia. "It's remarkable." He paused. "You know, I always considered myself a skeptic. But that day, on that island, I felt a presence. Like someone was watching me, you know?" Helen nodded. "I mean, I'm a copper, right. I don't do *spirit guides* and all that nonsense Chris has been going on about. But I felt something. That's enough for me. That's why I'm here today."

"Nia …" Helen dropped her voice. "Will she be okay?"

"She's strong, given time I'm sure she'll make a full recovery –"

"No, I mean … well, she killed him, didn't she?"

Gareth nodded, flashing a glance in Nia's direction. "Self defence. There will be no case to answer."

"Good. That's a relief. I'd hate to think she went through all that and then, you know …"

"I know. As far as I'm concerned the guilty parties have all been punished. Maybe we'll never know the specifics, although my guess is Glyn fuelled his brother's anger and hatred of Morton, and used it for financial gain. Glyn was clever, very much so, making sure his brother would be the scapegoat, letting him think it was all his idea. But the important thing for everyone is it's over. Thank God."

"Yes, we can all try and get back to a normal life. Thanks for coming today, you and DS Coleman, we appreciate it."

Helen held out her hand, surprised when the policemen leaned forward and embraced her.

"Thank you," he whispered. "For believing in your child, and for giving my family closure."

Translation of the memorial inscription:

In Silence here we lye Cut down as at noon day
For our God saw best We shou'd no longer stay
So Friends don't grieve Nor yet Repine
For 'tis to God you live & must to God resign.

Here lyeth the Bodies of thee poor unfortunate Souls
theyr Lives loste fore
the wreck of the clipper Rothsay Castle
on Lavan Sands, Anglesea
August 15
In the year Our Lord 1831.

May God protect.

THE END

"It is not more surprising to be born twice than once;
everything in nature is resurrection."
—Voltaire

Also from Triskele Books

THE OPEN ARMS OF THE SEA

England in 1965 is enjoying a cultural revolution, while far away in the British-occupied territory of Aden it is revolution of quite a different and dangerous kind.

Fleeing the guilts of his youth, Lieutenant Leslie Deacon has escaped to hide in the army and the vast rock deserts of a scorched and war-ravaged Aden . Adoo rebels hurl grenades from the shadows and a hard-pressed British Army is struggling to keep order and control. When the Adoo bring the war inside the city, a new guerrilla warfare is needed to keep the rebels at bay and the garrison and its civilians safe.

Into this fearful, threatened city comes the adventurer Clemmie Ross and the charismatic Captain Villiers. Deacon's world of duty, honour, courage and love begins to explode and fragment about him.

In Aden's scorched deserts and bombed streets, duty only brings death, and honour offers no reward. Only through love will Deacon find peace. All he has to do is find it.

Also from Triskele Books

RAW MATERIAL

Bank Holiday weekend. Beatrice Stubbs takes some holiday snaps on a secluded Welsh beach. Those innocent pictures reveal rather more than cliffs and seagulls, and someone wants them destroyed. But Beatrice has other things on her mind.

Assigned to the London Transport Police, she's pursuing the Finsbury Park Flasher, trying to pre-empt a serious sexual offence. Meanwhile, neighbour Adrian and companion Matthew decide to play Poirot, and investigate the mystery of the disappearing photographs. Amateur detectives and professional criminals are a dangerous mix.

From deserted Pembrokeshire beaches, through the shadowy underpasses of North London, to the remote Irish countryside, Beatrice discovers the darker side of human nature.

"The characters leap off the page, the prose is witty and intelligent, and the twist of plots keeps you hooked to the last. What more could you ask? –"

Barbara Scott-Emmett,
author of European thriller, Don't Look Down

Lightning Source UK Ltd.
Milton Keynes UK
UKOW02f0611011016

284239UK00002B/21/P